The
Enlightened

CEM BILICI

CONTENTS

ONE

"You know I think we've met before, you and I, in our travels. Yes. I'm certain our paths have crossed."

"Really? And what was our connection? Were we friends? Lovers?"

"I think I may have killed you."

"Not friends then." The man in the white coat chuckled.

From the angle and lighting, his face was mostly hidden, but it was the same doctor giving the TV nervous glances. His demeanour was completely different from his mirror image on the video. Whereas the man on the tape sat as if lounging at a bar, openly arrogant and acting as if he owned the place, his flesh and blood counterpart was limp and shrunken, colour bleached. Like a party balloon after weeks in the elements.

It could've been a trick of the light or O'Donnell's mind. O'Donnell narrowed his eyes on the reflection of the man behind him. The grain, washed-out colour and static on the overused VHS tape made it near impossible to tell, but whatever the case, the man seemed a different person.

"And how did you kill me, Nathan?" the doctor on the video said.

The man behind O'Donnell jerked his hand to his mouth and began chewing a cuticle.

O'Donnell concentrated on the video tape.

The young man across from the doctor pouted his bottom lip in thought. He eased into the uncomfortable-looking seat. While the doctor was plain, the only way to describe Nathan's clothing was drab. An inoffensive grey sweat suit with a white T-shirt peeking from beneath the partially unzipped top.

Nathan pursed his lips. "You... You were a woman. A prostitute. I paid you, then killed you after we had sex. Then I had sex with you again."

"Is it called sex, Nathan, when it's with a cadaver?"

With an almost imperceptible movement of his shoulder, Nathan shrugged.

The doctor's demeanour shifted, becoming more casual as he nodded. "And when was this?"

"Oh, I couldn't say really." Nathan motioned at a pack of cigarettes across the table from him, then took up the packet and lighter when they were slid across. Slipping one out, he lit up and nodded his thanks before pushing the items back. "It was a while ago though. Carriages. Big flowing dresses and whatnot."

The doctor took his cigarettes back and lit one up himself. "Don't tell me you know the identity of Jack the Ripper?" His crooked smile held open sarcasm.

Nathan's expression mirrored the man's as he sent smoke billowing at him.

The doctor sat up straighter, mirth faded and eyes narrowing. "And did you recall this... this *memory* just now?" His shoulders slipped down as amusement tugged the corner of his mouth once more. "Or did it come to you in another dream?"

"Came to me. Just now." Nathan waved his hand, inscribing the air with a trail of smoke that was already dispersing. His other hand lay limp across his stomach as he slouched, legs apart.

The doctor looked him over, taking him in before scribbling in his notebook with a tic of a smug grin. "So tell me your theory, Nathan."

"I've already told the others." Nathan turned the cigarette so it was held between thumb and fingers. With its glowing tip, he pointed at the notebook in the doctor's hands. "I'm sure it's all in there."

"I'd like to hear it for myself."

"From the horse's mouth?"

"Yes."

"Very well. However, for a start, it's not a theory. It's reality."

"Then tell me your *reality*."

"It's all of our reality, Doctor, whether you believe it or not. We all, each and every one of us, are reborn when we die."

"Reincarnation?"

"Yes. Reincarnation. We go through the humdrum cycles of our lives. Born, live out our days long or short, and then..." He took a long drag of the smoke and, shaping his mouth, blew a smoke ring that floated above them. With a casual wave of his hand, he dragged his fingers through it, destroying the circle. "But we're not gone." He pointed at the single incandescent bulb in a grey enamel lampshade above them. A cone of golden light stood out in the smoke. "We simply lose coherency to join with the aether. Then our soul is drawn back." He took another pull on the cigarette. Speaking as he exhaled, he said, "From the wellspring of the aether and given new form. Uncontrollably. Inescapably. Even though we're no longer physical. Like light into a black hole, and just as powerless."

Silence stretched between them, counted off by the crackle of the cassette, which had probably seen hundreds of interviews such as this. Though none had ever ended as this one did, James O'Donnell wagered.

"Go on," the doctor said.

"We each go through this cycle many times. It's not chronological. At least not in a linear fashion those without vision might imagine."

"Those like myself?"

Nathan lifted his chin. "If there's anything you take away from this, Doctor, is that the hands of our clocks do not follow a circular course. One minute it might be six-thirty. Next, ten-past-three, two hundred years before. Do you follow me?"

"Oh, I *follow* you." The doctor scribbled furiously, glancing quickly at the camera recording it all, giving his unseen audience a smug grin.

"There is no true cycle," Nathan said. "Even the word is nonsensical in relation to reality when you consider the implications. *Cycle*," Nathan said, snorting in disgust as he sat up, leaning across the table to speak in hushed tones. "Time means nothing in the aether—in limbo. We can be reborn the next day, yesterday, the same day, or in a hundred thousand years from our last death."

"Is that so?"

Nathan nodded and hummed.

"So you can tell me what shares to invest in then? Because, I can tell you, my portfolio is a little threadbare."

"Ah, but it doesn't work like that."

"Right. Of course it doesn't. And why is that exactly, Nathan?"

Nathan shook his head, the shoulder-length mane of brown hair shimmering. "The future is... diaphanous. We sometimes get glimpses, but that is all."

"So then, what's the point of it all?" the doctor sad, pen scratching at speed.

"Point. Yes." Nathan's expression was now beatific. More than his expression, his whole presence, his face almost glowing as he exuded an air of benevolence. "What if you could stab your pen the scribble of pages that is and was your lives and know everything you knew wherever the tip stopped? That point in the lifeline of your soul, Doctor? If you knew everything that incarnation of your soul had known? And then, to go even further, what if you could know the entire contents of every line of ink, right now, in this instant? Remember the yesterday, today and tomorrow of *you*?"

"Except, didn't you say I can't see the future?"

Nathan chuckled.

"Okay. I'll bite. What then, Nathan? What if I did know what all my past lives had known?" The doctor's grin widened. "Would I be an Einstein?"

"No. You would be a super-man."

"Superman? Well, I have always wanted x-ray vision." The doctor licked his lips, eyes shining.

Lip curling in distaste, Nathan crushed the still unfinished cigarette on the corner of the table, turning from the man to watch the ashes. "What they say is true. Knowledge is power. More than you can know." He brushed the ash and butt to the floor and glanced up. "The more knowledge a man has in his head, the more power he gains."

"Power? Like... ESP?"

"No. Like magic. That's what it is to be Enlightened, Doctor. To be magic. To be a god."

O'Donnell had watched the video in a bemused state. The doctor had been nervous from the start but insistent that he watch the recording. O'Donnell suspected he knew more than he was letting on but had humoured him. He had not, however, expected Nathan Mortimer's supernatural delusions.

He had a friend in high-school that ended up in mental institutions much like this one. Jason. Whenever O'Donnell saw a hospital, Jason always came to mind. Never more so than today.

Jason's mother had blamed all the pot that he had smoked as a teenager and continued to smoke into his adult years. That had been the doctors only diagnosis for his schizophrenia, she had told O'Donnell at the funeral. One of the pitfalls of starting out of the academy in the small town they grew up in, everyone knew you. And you knew everyone.

Jason's mother had done her best to support him, picking him up from the station when O'Donnell or one of the others would receive the call and put him in lockup. But they were not equipped to handle the mentally ill. Even the local hospital struggled and referred Jason on to an institution in Melbourne when he became violent.

That was when they received the call.

O'Donnell swallowed and cleared his throat. He caught his own reflection in the curved glass of the darkening TV as it switched off. He smoothed out his face as he turned to the doctor slipping the VHS cassette in its sleeve.

O'Donnell hated hospitals.

"What's Nathan Mortimer on?" O'Donnell said.

The doctor shook his head and attempted to put on the same persona on the tape, flashing his teeth. "As far as we could tell? Nothing."

O'Donnell frowned at that and pulled out a cigarette on reflex.

"If you don't mind, Mr O'Donnell..." The doctor indicated the cigarette packet.

O'Donnell re-packeted the offending cigarette and shoved them back into his pocket. Good enough for the loony but not the PI? Typical. He had been doing that all too often of late anyway. Pulling the little suckers out like his lungs were invincible. He smirked at the idea of his organs having a greater longevity than his own.

The doctor frowned, obviously mistaking O'Donnell's smile as some sort of private joke at his expense.

"That's the same night he vanished?" O'Donnell said, quickly straightening his face. It would not do to upset the natives now, would it? Especially when they were his only lead.

The doctor nodded curtly, pulling off his glasses and rubbing his eyes as he shook his head. "You can imagine the kind of uproar this has created with our heads of staff. Luckily the general public don't know of this escape." Pushing his glasses back on, the doctor let his hands fall and he glanced at O'Donnell. "Which, I might add, we would like to keep that way?"

"My discretion is assured, Doctor. It wouldn't serve me or my client to have this go public. But... is he dangerous?"

O'Donnell shuddered to think what a true psycho from one of these prison-like hospitals could get up to on the loose. If that were the case, he could not, and would not, keep his mouth shut. Not in good conscience anyway. Once a cop, always a cop, as some would say.

"Not as far as we know," the doctor said, words spilling from his mouth, his body tensing. "Yes, he has some wild notions and delusions. But otherwise he was always calm and collected. Never once violent. Despite what the name of our facility would have you believe, not all our patients are evil axe murderers, Mr O'Donnell." The doctor gave a brief smirk. "He seemed contemplative, in fact. Almost as if... he was planning this." The doctor lifted his head sharply. "I say that only in retrospect, of course. Had we any inkling of his plans—"

O'Donnell nodded. "Of course."

Bloody quacks. Here they were, a handful of years away from the magical two thousand, the Millennium, and they still had no idea. O'Donnell doubted they could fix a decent cup of coffee let alone someone's head. They flooded the patients with chemicals and droned on, hoping to cover the voices in those heads with their own and convincing them they were sick. It was practically brainwashing as far as O'Donnell was concerned. They had certainly not done any favours for Jason.

"He hadn't been taking his medication for some time we discovered later," the doctor said. "He had been secreting them in his mattress."

O'Donnell nearly laughed out loud. Not so crazy after all this Nathan. Or maybe he had watched one too many movie.

Why had he taken this job?

Because you need the money, you dumb fuck.

Talking to myself?

Perhaps he should ask the doctor if they had any vacant beds.

As he walked down the weather stained stairs to the hospital carpark, O'Donnell was met with a grating, tinny sound.

Music blared in the ears of a girl in school uniform. Her hair was a mess, sticking out in all directions, a dull sheen from who knew how much hairspray coating it. It had probably taken her hours to get it that way in an effort to match the faded, over-sized flannel shirt tied around her waist. Along with her torn stockings and untied, scuffed boots, she could have come straight off a teen grunge magazine cover. She nodded her head with her eyes closed, the tether plugged into the Walkman swinging wildly. The music was so loud it was no longer personal but a public affair.

What happened to Cyndi Lauper and Madonna? O'Donnell shook his head and took out his cigarettes to finally light up as he passed the girl.

She jumped as he blocked the light. Seeing him, she tore the foam padded headphones from her head by a thin metal band and let them hang around her neck, the music immediately becoming louder.

"Hey… Sir?" the girl said, lowering the foot she had up on brick wall to stand straighter. "You got a spare?"

"A wha—?" O'Donnell frowned before he realised what she was after.

"A smoke?" She shot her eyes upwards as his frown turned to a scowl.

"Yeah, I do." Her aloofness turned to triumph. "You got ID?" Suddenly it was O'Donnell who was beaming.

"Fuck you. Arsehole." The girl put the headphones, still grinding out grunge music, back over her ears and returned to leaning on the wall like she owned it, though her expression was far more dour.

O'Donnell pulled out his wallet and flashed a badge at her quickly and pocketed it before she could see it. He made a show of pulling a notebook and pen from an inner pocket. Just like the old days, except now he was technically breaking the law too.

"Shit," she muttered, her head falling back to stare at the sky. She pulled the headphones down by the cord so they fell back around her neck.

"Got your attention, have I? How about you don't use that kind of language with your elders. Especially when you don't know who they work for."

"Sorry," she said, rolling her eyes. Her expression suddenly became one of fear. "Are… Are you going to book me?"

His hand hovered over the notepad, pen in hand. He hoped his expression was more concerned and kindly than it `. "Who are you here with?"

"My mum. Please don't tell her! I'm already in a shit-load— I mean—"

"Yeah. I know what you mean."

"She caught me smokin' twice already. But ever since Dad..." She cast her eyes over her shoulder to the building, forlorn.

O'Donnell sighed. He pulled the cigarette packet out and popped the lid. Glancing into the depths of the carton, he shook the few that were in there, then glanced up at her. Fishing one out, he handed it over.

"Oh, sweet! Thanks." She took the smoke, turned around with a nervous glance at the hospital. The coast clear, she deposited it in her mouth to fish for a lighter from a beige knapsack that had been defaced with permanent marker and liquid paper.

"What the hell, huh?" he murmured to himself as he walked away. "She's only going to come back through the aether anyway."

Smirking, he walked around his hatchback to the passenger door to deposit the manila case file and closed the door with too much force, the thud of the door shaking the small car. He still wasn't used to the lightweight construction of the thing, too used to his old Ford Falcon. But first impressions made a hell of a difference, and he needed something newer and nondescript. Something that was in abundance on the roads, harder to keep an eye on and did not stand out when tailing targets.

He got in the car and started it up, cranking the window with the push of a button. He definitely did not miss the hand-crank window from his old car.

O'Donnell glanced up at the girl. Her legs partially obscured metal lettering declaring it as the Rowville Psychiatric Hospital. They'd tactfully decided to leave off the fact it was a high security hospital with a ward for those deemed criminally insane.

What had the girl's father done to earn a spot in this place? And, for that matter, what had calm and collected Nathan done to join him?

"How the fuck did you escape this place?" O'Donnell asked aloud, shaking his head.

Maybe he should have given the girl two smokes.

The client had called up to make the appointment after vetting O'Donnell with the usual questions about his background, experience with missing persons cases and the like. Then, she had dropped off an envelope of money to get him started. At least enough to warrant a drive out to Rowville to check it out.

He'd taken the call himself. No sexy or quirky receptionist for O'Donnell like the PI's on TV. No Hawaiian shirts and Ferraris. The budget was always tight and he was on his own. His office also didn't have an impressive frosted-glass door with his name on it, nor a big antique wooden desk, or photos and newspaper clippings on the wall of ongoing or solved cases. The place was an old accountant's office on a highway stuck between a fish and chip shop and an Indian store selling clothing, small goods and bootleg video tapes.

But he made ends meet. Of course, it helped that the office he rented was dirt cheap and was also his place of residence. And the chipped laminate desk, several tall filing cabinets, an old computer, fridge and fold-out sofa bed had all come with it.

O'Donnell had asked the real estate agent what had happened to the accountant to leave all his stuff behind. The question had been answered with a smile that was either meant to be awkward or enigmatic. No doubt the agent thought it made for an exciting tale at the pub when he was trying to get laid. No ring, or ring marks, on his finger.

He had that in common with the TV investigators. Being attentive and sharp-eyed got him results. His old police contacts, those that still talked to him, filled in the gaps where he needed, as they had with the accountant. He had made sure the guy had not offed himself in the office or gone on a murder-suicide spree. That made for an altogether different sort of tall tale, the kind of bad publicity O'Donnell didn't need.

From what O'Donnell had worked out, the old coot had taken to bringing prostitutes to his office and had gone out with a bang. If any of his customers since renting the place knew the story, they never mentioned it. And everything but the fold-out sofa bed had stayed. O'Donnell had tried not to think about the desk too much but had given it a thorough wipe down in any case.

The day after the call his appointment arrived on the dot. He half thought she was crazy herself, dressed up in a 50s rockabilly outfit, like something out of *Grease*. She was oddly stunning, though, in her black-and-white polka-dot halter dress, especially with the splashes of red painted by her accessories, nails and lipstick. O'Donnell didn't remember anyone in that film having any ink, however, let alone the number of tattoos on his client. The pale skin of her left arm was a three-quarter length sleeve that flowed over her shoulder. She was petite. Cute was the word that immediately came to mind—he thought she would be more so without the strange getup.

She had to be half his age. It was hard to tell in her outfit and with the amount of makeup, but he thought she couldn't have been more than twenty-two, possibly even younger.

She didn't talk like a woman of her age, however.

"Coffee, Miss Lawler?" O'Donnell said, lifting the glass pot from his machine to pour himself a cup.

She eyed the carafe kin his hands suspiciously. "No. Thank you."

"Hell, if it wasn't my own coffee, I wouldn't either," he said, smirking as he finished and pushed the pot back into the machine.

She gave him a thin-lipped smile that made her appear his grand-mother's age.

"So... now's when you tell me why you're trying to find Nathan Mortimer." He took his seat at the desk opposite. The case file sat open next to the computer that he would two-finger type his notes in after he had scrawled them in his notebook, which he far preferred. "Relative? Boyfriend?"

"Nathan's a friend. I'm sure you know by now he's been missing for several weeks. The police aren't any help because he has a record. They said they're looking, but we seriously doubt it. And neither are they too interested in apprehending him because his prior offences were misdemeanours at best."

O'Donnell paused from sipping his coffee to stare her in the eyes. They were a piercing blue, assessing him as much as he was her, if not more. "We?"

She gave him another tight-lipped grin, though this time it seemed more to indicate she would not be disclosing who the others in her concerned group were.

He nodded and returned the facial gesture. "So, tell me about these priors." He took the long overdue sip of coffee and replaced the mug in his hand with a pen.

"Drugs mainly. Possession. A few break and enters."

O'Donnell's brows rose, his pen stopping as he lifted his eyes from it.

"I know what you're thinking. He's probably dead in a gutter or park somewhere, but he'd been clean for years. Those convictions were in his teens."

"People turn back to drugs for all sorts of reasons, Miss Lawler. Stress, relationship troubles..." He glanced up at her from his notebook, but she was a blank page. "Especially if they have a history of mental illness, I've found."

"Well, he may have done. He's been under a lot of pressure lately. But his body certainly hasn't turned up anywhere. As I'm sure you already know. And I know he's alive." Sitting straighter, she let out a sharp sigh. "Will you take the job or not, Mr O'Donnell?"

Letting out his own, longer sigh, he threw down the pen, the blue plastic facets tapping as it rolled to a stop. "How will you be funding this search, Miss Lawler?" He took up the steaming mug again. "I don't know if you've spoken with other agencies—" her eyes darted about his office, her lips holding the hint of a smirk "—but it's not cheap."

She was silent a moment before her lips pulled wider, her eyes narrowing. "I was hoping I could pay you in sexual favours."

O'Donnell would have choked on the coffee if he hadn't been fast enough to stop mid sip, but the girl barely flinched, her eyes boring into his. She was good.

"I only take cash or credit, Miss Lawler," he said, meeting her frank, amused stare. Opening a drawer, he hefted a credit card imprinter he called the click-clack-machine from a desk drawer and slapped it on the tabletop. "Unless you have some pretty numbers hidden amongst those tattoos and can somehow fit your arm in there…" Picking up his mug, he smiled with affected cordiality, steam wafting across his face and filling his nostrils with the bitter-sweet smell it carried.

"Never mix business with pleasure, is that it?"

"Something like that. Let's call it professional integrity."

Her expression flattened in a moment, facade and games well and truly over. The appearance she was older than her skin increased, her true age written in the flecks of blue in her eyes rather than the lines of her face. It left him unnerved.

"Let's cut the bullshit and the Miss Lawler bit then."

"Fine, *Cassie*. You got the money or not? I don't give credit, and I charge by the day plus expenses. I have overheads."

She looked around at his overheads with a distasteful smirk and then reached for her handbag to pull out what was unmistakably an envelope stuffed with cash. "I believe that's enough to get you started for a week."

The envelope landed in the middle of the table with a satisfying thud. Reaching across, he slid it to himself and lifted the unsealed flap. A wad of yellow and white bills. Fifties and hundreds. The aroma of the paper within was heady. He stopped his eyebrows mid-rise to frown as if it was no big deal.

From her bag, she pulled out her own manila envelope and slid it across to him. "Everything you need is in there, including my contact details should you need them."

He flipped open the envelope and pulled out the first page, which appeared printed by an expensive inkjet. O'Donnell hadn't even bought a new ink ribbon for the old dot matrix the accountant left behind that was now stashed away in a corner.

"Do you have email?" Cassie turned to the aged, bulky and beige PC and monitor by the large touch tone Bakelite phone that was nowhere near it. "Of course not."

O'Donnell matched her smile as he shot a business card across to her. "I have a fax service." He pulled out a handful of the bills and fanned them. "I have to ask, where does a girl like you get so much money?"

"And what sort of a girl do you think I am, Mr O'Donnell?"

"Well… to be honest, I don't know much about your type."

Cassie's eyes twitched, her nose wrinkling.

A reaction from her, finally. He shouldn't have been so amused at rankling a customer, but he smiled all the same. "But I find it hard to believe that you, and whoever this mysterious *we* are, would pay so much money to find a simple friend."

"Does it matter?"

"Does to me. If you're, say, working for an assassin, or drug dealers, organised crime… Well, see, that kind of rubs against my moral fibre, so to speak. So where'd you get it?"

"Flipping burgers at McDonalds."

He chuckled. "Touché. But we both know you're not quite that young."

"Maybe I flip other sorts of buns." She smiled sweetly now.

"Can I get fries with that?" he said, not breaking eye contact. He stood with her as she rose from the chair. "I still haven't agreed to take the job."

Her smile stayed on her lips as she turned and walked out the door, the bell that had also come with the office clanking as it closed.

"Jesus, O'Donnell," he said, shaking his head and letting the cash fall to the table. "Beaten by a bloody Betty Page wannabe. What's happening to you?"

With a sigh, he pulled his worn leather wallet from his back pocket and scooped up several of the notes to slide them in. He stuck the rest back in the envelope and stashed it in an old safe hidden beneath the desk. The lock to the safe no longer worked, having been drilled out well before he had come along, but he figured the power of persuasion the massive thing had would be more than enough. It helped that he had filled the hole in the mottled green door with a piece of spearmint gum that would, without closer inspection, fool most.

He returned to his coffee as he chided himself for both arguing with and exchanging sexual innuendo with a client and spilled the contents of the manila envelope.

Each sip of coffee was colder by the mouthful as he flipped through the papers and made notes, until it was no longer drinkable.

He opened his notebook to the page from Rowville and positioned it by the stained beige keyboard. He jumped as the loud bells of the old phone rang, spilling the whiskey he was adding to his coffee mug over several papers and photos.

"Shit! Hello?" he said, angrier than he meant to as he snatched up the receiver.

"Mr O'Donnell?"

The ear-piece was crackly. Either the phone itself or the line was faulty. He never had the inclination to find out which. O'Donnell sighed and rubbed his eyes. "Yeah, speaking."

"It's Cassie Lawler. I know I only left you a little while ago, but I've some new information that might be of some use to you."

TWO

O'Donnell decided to take his old Falcon instead of the newer Civic, as he did if he thought there was any chance something might go wrong. Back in the day, the sharp angled lines and boxy body was common. Now it was his fall-back vehicle, one he wouldn't mind if it got scratched, bashed or stolen. People did unpredictable things when confronted by an investigator. So far both he and the Falcon had sustained only a few dents and scratches and always come out on top. The Honda, however, had to be inconspicuous and it, unlike the Ford and himself, had insurance premiums he had to worry about.

The Ford could also, as they used to say in the town he grew up in, thrash the shit out of the hatchback. He had made sure of that. It looked old and slow but was far from it.

It was dusk when Cassie had called to tell him she'd heard of a squat that Mortimer had been sighted at. Squats usually meant the homeless and drugs—the other reason he'd taken the Falcon. Put a shiny modern car in a bad neighbourhood and anything left in sight would be grabbed. Of course they had to smash through the windows to do so. They wouldn't be industrious enough to actually steal the car itself, but the pain of replacing the window and any tools of his trade? Not worth it. The old Falcon on the other hand? It could belong to any number of people that frequented the area. He even left some clean take away bags and wrappers screwed up in the back seat for authenticity. Free of any actual food stains, they made great emergency note paper too.

Outside the address he was given—more a rough location than address proper, but the dilapidated house across the road gave it away—he exited to cooling night air and moved to the boot of the car. Easing the key into the lock, he opened it with his office keys grasped firm in his fingers. He removed an old coat, and then from its pocket a revolver he'd acquired from a friend of a friend off the back of a truck. Checking the pistol, he put it back in the coat, its large pocket hiding the thing with ease.

He retrieved his large Maglite, shining it into the confined space to ensure it was working. The light was bright and strong. Its metal body made for a good club too. From another large pocket of the coat, he removed a disposable camera with a flash and checked the counter. Still a handful of shots left on it. He had a big expensive camera but bringing that would have stuck out as much as the Civic and made him more of a target. The Civic also held a similar large, nondescript coat though much newer.

The well-oiled hinge barely made a noise as he brought the lid down and used his body weight to engage the latch. He wasn't worried so much about his own safety as much as he was spooking his target, if Mortimer was here. The heavy torch would be more than enough to deal with most, but these days it wasn't only the down-and-outs that inhabited these abandoned buildings. Frequently there would be teenagers—high, drunk or both. While an old toothless man would be no trouble, some punk who was too young, dumb and full of cum to know better? Mister Maglite was ready and waiting.

Then there were the crims. That's when the pocket would come into play. Then and *only* then. The safety was on and it would never leave his pocket except in the direst of circumstances. And it had never once left the pocket let alone been fired after its initial testing.

The thigh-length weeds and grass swished as he trod through the front yard, yellow stalks glinting in torchlight, tendrils pulling at his feet. As a child, he'd played in such jungles. What he wouldn't give for a stick sword now to blaze this trail through bright summer sunlight.

He made his way to the back of the lot. That would be where squatters came and went, the most hidden route. It both served his purpose and proved a risk.

"Think of the money," he said as he turned the corner.

He'd been reluctant to come here when Cassie had mentioned the place. Until, that was, she had said whether he found Mortimer or not he could keep the money, and if the search stretched on there was more where it came from. It hadn't eased his trepidation at where the money had come from, but it was a great motivator for venturing deeper.

If anything the back of the property was worse than the front, littered with trees that had been choked by vines of some sort he couldn't identify even if it were daylight. The block was expansive, stretching back farther than he'd first assumed. It was more jungle-like and frightening than anything from his childhood. Someday someone would probably build a very big house or a block of flats here. But now, it was a dangerous wasteland of dead grass and discarded trash.

O'Donnell turned to the back porch after noting the darkest spots that could be hiding potential danger or, if it came to it, a hiding place.

With slow steps, he climbed the concrete stairs and stopped at the fourth and topmost. The decking of the porch—probably hardwood judging by the age of the place—was missing. He kept the torch aimed straight down, his hand cupped around the front of the lens to curb any stray light. A wooden beam left of the centre of the steps was clean of dust and dirt for the most part, clearly a well-used walkway. The rest of the beams were in various states of squalor, as was the cavity below, full of bottles, food wrappers, syringes and other detritus that put to bed any doubt this was a squatter haven.

Detecting a faint light and crackling noise from within, O'Donnell turned off the torch. Keeping a tight grip on its handle, he let his eyes adjust before walking across the beam and into the husk. With a wary eye, he checked every corner, his police training serving him well and coming back to him even after all the years since the academy. When he'd first been put on the streets, every encounter had been a flashback to training before that had faded to become background noise. Now, he was thankful he remembered it.

The first room through the doorway was a laundry, or had been when it still had running water and fittings with which to run it through. Now there wasn't even a trough. Whatever had once lined the floor, it was just filthy concrete now.

A quick glance through the door showed a hallway that led off in either direction. To the left was the glow. He ignored that path to explore the darker areas first, but there was nothing but more rubbish and discarded items. There was a mattress propped against a wall in a bedroom that he checked behind cautiously with the torch, this time covering its lens fully, the light making his fingers glow an angry red as it played through them, uncovering enough to light the space.

Nothing but empty beer cans, crushed newspapers and rat droppings.

The other rooms revealed much the same. No one was there. At least he wouldn't have to worry about being attacked from behind.

He approached the glowing light. It came out of a solitary room that would have been a living room once upon a time. It was a decent size and L-shaped. Around the corner was an open doorway, a fire beyond it in a forty-gallon drum, rusted and burnt through in spots. An old man stood over it, eyeing him furtively.

O'Donnell put up his hands and waited.

The old man snorted and spat a thick gob into the fire, throwing his gaze back to it in disdain. "Fuckin' cops," he grumbled, but didn't move.

"You mind?" O'Donnell said after a moment, approaching when the man made no reply.

He inspected the shell of a kitchen. No one else was in there with the old man. It was still early, the sun only recently setting. They'd probably be out at soup kitchens, drug deals, or wherever they went when the lights went out. O'Donnell noticed there was another doorway that had been blocked off by a large board or something.

From the dank hallway he hadn't even been able to tell it was there. There was another door that led to the side of the house, closed to the night air. He pulled something from the back pocket of his jeans and held it up for the man.

"I'm not a cop. I'm an investigator looking for a missing person." He waited as the man glanced quickly at the photo.

"Same shit to me, cop or investigator."

"Maybe. But there are some people that care about this guy and want to know he's safe, that's all. If you could please…"

The man tore his eyes from the flames, a glint in his eye that had nothing to do with firelight.

O'Donnell nodded, tilting his head. He pocketed the photo, replaced it with his wallet. He cursed inwardly as he saw the fresh notes. He lifted a yellow bill.

The man tensed as he saw the fifty and licked his lips, possibly at the thought of whatever food or liquor he was imagining buying with it.

O'Donnell waved the fifty. "So. You seen him or—"

"Mighta. Dunno."

The man tried in vain to play the hard-to-remember game. People who saw it on TV and movies always thought it was a good idea.

O'Donnell pursed his lips and nodded. "That's a damn shame," he said, tearing a corner off the bill and dropping it in the fire.

The man balked, almost breaking from his freeze. He shrugged. "Your money, copper. What do I—"

O'Donnell tore the bill in two and moved his hand over the flame. He didn't pause or take his time. That was a fool's game. He intended to drop it and leave if the man didn't react.

But he did. Gasping, his hand shot out and caught O'Donnell's wrist. He ripped the half note from his fingers as O'Donnell opened his hand. He kept the other half screwed tightly in the other, wedged between his palm and the heavy-duty flashlight.

"Yeah, I seen him, okay? But not for a week. Maybe more."

"What's his name?"

His bushy grey-and-white brows pushed together. "Wha—?"

"If he hung here, you know him. So what's his name?" He could see the man thinking in a panic, trying to recall. "You want the rest, I need proof."

The man's soiled fingers trembled across his equally dirty brow. O'Donnell sighed and pulled the scrap of paper out with his free hand to screw it up in a ball and aim it at the circle of fire below him.

"Nate!" the man shouted. "His fuckin' name is Nate, okay?" he said with more certainty. His hand flicked out and his fingers danced.

O'Donnell nodded. "Any ideas where else he squatted? Known associates?"

"Yeah! I know a few places. But I ain't tellin' ya until—"

O'Donnell slapped the balled-up paper in the man's hand. The old man told him what he knew, which wasn't much but better than what O'Donnell had started with.

"Thanks," O'Donnell said and turned to leave. He stopped.

He hadn't noticed earlier, possibly because all the walls were marked with layers of graffiti, but between two small, grime-encrusted windows on the wall behind him there was a large, ragged circle. Someone had gone over it in spray paint repeatedly in what appeared to be every colour they could get their hands on. He lifted the Maglite to inspect it. Multicoloured stains dribbled from its perimeter.

"The gateway."

O'Donnell turned back to the man who had secreted his booty and was warming his hands once more. "'Scuse me?"

"Nate. He called it the gateway."

O'Donnell nodded, took a disposable camera with a flash from where he left it in the other pocket of the jacket and took a snap of the thing. That was the only shooting investigators really did, and the only shooting that really mattered.

And the only shooting O'Donnell ever wanted to be involved in again.

The morning country air cleared his head of a whiskey fog as O'Donnell pulled the hatchback into the small roadhouse service station. He hadn't needed to travel incognito, even though he would appear like any weekday tourist who may have hired or borrowed a car. The old Ford was simply more expensive to run. Especially with the extortionate prices out here being a full four to five cents a litre dearer at sixty-six odd cents. Every bit mattered when you were your own boss. And the Falcon drank almost as much as he did.

Once inside, he ordered a greasy breakfast with the lot. The eggs, bacon, sausages, fried mushroom and tomato all dripped grease on toast already soaked in butter when it came out. The mug of filtered coffee that came with it was marginally better than his own, but it helped to wash it all down. Just the way he liked it.

As he sat and ate, he went through notes of the few other cases he had on the books but kept coming back to the Mortimer case. The information was all fresh in his mind, but in short supply, so he didn't need to actually review it. But something about it stuck in his head.

"You some sort of artist?"

O'Donnell glanced over his shoulder at the woman with the coffee pot, who leaned in and poured him a top up. She was eyeing the scribbling he'd made of the graffiti art from the squat. It was rendered in green, blue, red and black from a four-coloured pen.

"No chance," he said, looking at the mess.

"Good," she said. "Because I was goin' to tell you not to quit your day job." The corners of her mouth and eyes wrinkled. Her name tag said Judy.

She was perhaps a little older than him, not unattractive, and he watched her ample hips sway as she walked away—again, not unattractive.

"Say, Judy," he said as an afterthought. She stopped and turned to him. "Do you happen to know anything about a property out here? Goes by the name of Gateway House?"

She studied him, eyes narrowing.

"Thought you said you weren't an artist."

He smiled as he pulled his ID. "Private investigator."

Judy seemed intrigued, shifting from her sideways stance to turn back to him and lowering her free arm from across her ribs, head lifting. Body language, while no exact science, was usually very telling. She didn't fully trust him but was curious and believed him at least.

"Who are you investigatin'?"

"It's a missing person case. Maybe you've seen him?" He took out the photo and held it out to her.

She approached, her curiosity growing. He had snagged her with the bait. If she knew anything, she would tell him now. Judy set the coffee jug down on the chipped melamine and gently took a dog-eared corner of the picture. Her brow creased, lips puckering as she chewed the inside of her mouth. She shook her head more to remember, he suspected, than a negative response.

"He does look familiar," she said, still unsure. "But he has one of those faces, you know?"

He nodded and made to take the picture back, but she stopped shaking her head and her eyebrows dipped further.

"Actually... come to think of it, I think I saw him in here not too long ago. Came in a Kombi van with a few hippie, artsy types. The only reason I remember is because they weren't all like that. There was a guy in a suit, and a woman who looked like an uptight librarian with them. And a pregnant woman. Out to her nose, she was."

She handed the photo back as she stared out the window in deep thought. He didn't need to prompt her on whether she remembered anything else and instead wrote down what she'd already imparted.

"The pregnant woman. She was like... What do you call them religious types? Long dresses to the ankle, tops to the wrists? Scarf on the head?" She clicked her fingers several times, trying to recall.

"Quakers? Mormons?" he offered.

"Mor... No. Moslem. Yeah. Her face wasn't covered or nothin' but the head scarf was coverin' her hair. I could only see her face. I thought that was weird. The suit guy and librarian were out of place enough, but she really didn't fit in."

"Okay. Interesting. What about the suit? Anything stand out about him? The type of suit maybe?" She had been fixated on the outfit.

Judy turned from the window. "It was expensive looking. Tie, shoes and watch too. He looked like some high up hot-shot executive or somethin'. Maybe a lawyer? I dunno."

O'Donnell frowned. A heavily pregnant Moslem woman and a sharply-dressed man in a Kombi out in the rural hills of Melbourne with Mortimer and a bunch of hippie types? It didn't make sense.

"What about the librarian?" he said, still writing in his notebook. He glanced up at the woman when she didn't answer.

She was shaking her head. "That's all I remember. That she looked kind of like a librarian. Not old. Just… dressed older than what she was, if you get me. Hair tied up all tight, dressed all stuffy, big glasses. Just the one guy came in, paid for the petrol. Then they all got back in and drove off."

He opened his mouth to ask but she answered before he could.

They'd driven in the direction of Gateway House.

He had a lot more to chew on now than the sausages and bacon Judy had served up.

O'Donnell slowed the hatchback outside the property, pulling it to the side so it sat out of the way. The car leaned to the left on the uneven path. The gravel track had been overtaken by dirt, replete with potholes, and the car sat in a shallow ditch that served as a wash-off channel.

He got out and blinked at the sight that confronted him. He lifted his disposable camera, took a picture with a plastic click. He stared ahead as his hand fell to his side, winding the film forward with his thumb, the bright yellow cardboard box in his hand ratcheting.

"Gateway House," he said to himself as he slipped the disposable in his coat pocket. O'Donnell opened the farm gate before driving through and shutting it behind as the sign on the front asked all visitors to do.

As he drove up the fruit-tree laden track, he eyed the rear-view and saw the back end of an archway made up of loosely interwoven rusted wires, each painted a different colour. A gateway.

He stared into his coffee and didn't know what to make of things. The wild-haired man before him had an easy air, loping casually when he moved. Even seated as he was now, his tall frame draped like cloth in the old armchair, peering over his own steaming mug with rapt attention.

"So, what do you make of our property, Detective?" he asked.

"Please, Gunther, I'm not a police officer. Call me James. And it's very nice here. Peaceful."

The man nodded, smiling as he lifted the drink to his lips. O'Donnell imagined he would smile while he drank if he could avoid the lapful of hot liquid.

O'Donnell scanned the paintings hung on every wall, some perched on easels of various age and size. Each was marked with a single large G in the top left corner.

"These yours?"

Gunther nodded.

"Aren't you supposed to sign on the bottom right?"

Gunther smirked. "It is an artist's calling and duty to buck against preconceptions and challenge all notions."

O'Donnell nodded, humming. "That sounds rather anti-authoritarian." It actually sounded like a bunch of wanky bullshit to him. The man's answer would determine which it was.

Gunther kept smiling. Anti-authoritarian it was.

"What can you tell me about Nathan Mortimer?" O'Donnell had already established the man knew Mortimer when Gunther had asked about the nature of his visit.

"Oh," Gunther said, putting down his mug and steepling his fingers. "Nathan is a brilliant mind. Quite singular. He opened the eyes of many here with his words and art both."

"Is the gate his?" He studied Gunther's face for any sign of change but the man was as immobile as one of his paintings.

"No. It's been there for quite some time. What makes you ask?"

"Oh, I found some graffiti in a squat, his last known location. Looked like that gate is all."

"And that drew you here? Of course." Gunther nodded slowly, still showing his teeth. Far too straight and white for a poor, coffee-swilling artist. "Well, Gateway House is known to many in… our circles."

"How long was Nathan here?"

"He came on and off for maybe six… eight months. I'm not entirely certain. We have an open-door policy for members of our community."

"And who did he associate with while he was here?"

"There was a young lady, if that's what you're asking." Gunther paused, waiting for O'Donnell to give something away, he suspected. When O'Donnell didn't elaborate, Gunther went on. "Leila." He pronounced the name oddly. "I can fetch her for you?"

"If you don't mind. That would be great," O'Donnell said, framing it less than a request.

Gunther didn't react apart from to continue his Cheshire Cat impression. "Won't be long. Do make yourself at home."

O'Donnell noted the name Leila down as the man left the building, right below where he had written Gunther. He resisted the urge to add 'curiouser and curiouser' beside the scribble.

When the quiet got to him, O'Donnell went from room to room. The wooden flooring of the old farm house creaked and bent as he walked. There were varying huts and shacks he'd seen on the drive through the expansive property, and he could see the closest of them from the windows of the main house. There were probably many more he hadn't seen. Judging by the various trails of smoke he had seen floating to the clouds, there could be any number more out among the trees, not accounting for any without fires.

None of the paintings lining the walls of the rooms had titles or dates, but all appeared relatively new, though he was by no means a connoisseur. The styles also varied. More odd, though, were the signatures. He glanced at several that held actual signatures where he expected. Others that did not, the squiggles of paint occupying spaces about the edge of their canvases or hidden in the subject. All of those used a simple, solitary letter. G. It was if he was travelling through time as he inspected them. The style of painting and even the letter-signatures themselves changed. Maybe a change in style over time. Or perhaps, he mused, the artists were all different.

Could charming Gunther have artists from his commune paint for him? While unscrupulous, that was not why O'Donnell was here.

One painting, though, caught his interest. Covered with a cloth, it sat upon an easel in a small room. He approached it slowly, unease building within him. Pushing through the fear, he carefully lifted the cloth by a corner. He froze as he saw the familiar, swirling, central circle. He took the camera from his pocket and stood back, ready to take the shot and stopped. There was no signature.

Clicking off a shot and winding the camera, he stepped back to it and lifted the draping sheet where it hid the top left corner. Nothing. He flicked it up over the top bars of the easel to reveal it fully and took another closer shot. Covering it up, he returned to his seat and waited.

Gunther arrived with an attractive, short, of Middle-Eastern appearance, her curly hair flowing freely about her shoulders.

"Leyla," Gunther said, pronouncing the name with a Y rather than an I as O'Donnell had originally assumed. He made a mental note to correct his scribble. "This is the Detec— I mean, the private investigator I was telling you about. The one searching for Nathan."

"Is he all right? Is he in trouble?" Her thick eyebrows knotted as her hands opened and closed.

"As far as I know, miss, he's fine. Some friends of his just miss him and want to find him." Leyla nodded as if she understood. "Forgive me for asking," O'Donnell said, affecting slight embarrassment. "I don't suppose you were recently pregnant?"

O'Donnell was used to being asked to leave places. He could no more compel anyone to give him information than the police, and even they would be required to vacate private property without a court order.

Leyla had been pregnant, she said, but a long time ago and lost the child. Gunther asked him to leave as O'Donnell was upsetting her and they had no more information to give.

He decided to swing past the roadhouse again and see if the waitress—Judy her name tag had said—could fill him in on Gunther at all. Maybe grab another coffee. And she'd appeared to be O'Donnell's type.

He quickly changed his mind about hitting on the waitress when he found a dead older woman out the back of the empty roadhouse diner. The midday sun beat down on the body, accelerating the already cloying smell. She'd been dead a long time. Near her body he found the woman's handbag. Obtaining some disposable gloves from the kitchen, he called the police and identified the dead woman.

"What the hell is going on, Judy?" he said to the dead woman.

THREE

"Fucking Christ, Jimmy."

O'Donnell sat on the hood of the hatchback, feet nestled on its black plastic bumper, and rubbed at the pain above his right eye with the ball of his hand, lowering it to inhale the smoke down to the filter before throwing it aside.

"How long was she—"

Robbie held up his hands and shook his head. No info then. None that he would divulge here in any case. It officially had nothing to do with O'Donnell. And if it was in any way connected to his missing person case, O'Donnell was now obligated to share any and all information and files. That made his job difficult. And that was an understatement.

"You know what they're going to say, don't you?" Robbie said.

O'Donnell nodded solemnly in response.

"Fucking cults!"

O'Donnell hadn't been there for the raids in 1987 on the cult property in the Dandenong Mountains. He'd been off the force for nearly a year by that time. The group was still talked about to this day and he suspected it would continue to be for decades. It was the type of thing that happened in the rest of the world, not Australia. The kind of thing that stayed in people's memories.

"At least there are no kids here," Robbie said, hands on hips and taking a deep breath. He snapped his fingers repeatedly at O'Donnell, holding his fingers out to indicate what he wanted. O'Donnell handed over his cigarettes and watched Robbie light up before tossing the packet back. "Fuckin' cults. Fuck."

"You sure it's a cult?" O'Donnell said after lighting another of his own.

His nerves were shaken after the discovery of the old woman. It had been a while since he had seen a body, and that always brought back memories of Jason. Memories he didn't ever want to revisit.

He concentrated on the case and the revelation the real Judy's death brought. The killer was one of them. She must have called ahead to warn Gunther and the others. That also left only one possibility. The vagrant in the squat had been one of them too, sending him on this goose chase to begin with. But to what end? And who were *they*?

Robbie shook his head. "You know what the head crackers are saying already?" Robbie pressed the fingers holding the smoke to his temple as he spoke of the forensic psychologists. "The paintings and other shit in this Gunther's house alone are enough to make them jizz their pants and thinking about trying to get into his head. Forget about all the sheds, caravans and other shit. It's like a fucking orgy for them, and they brought their own pills."

O'Donnell glanced at Robbie, hand still pressed to his head. Robbie lowered it when he saw O'Donnell watching him, visibly attempting to calm himself.

"What does this place have to do with your case anyway?" Robbie said.

"Fucked if I know, some bum pointed me here. Who I gave a fifty to for the info, by the way."

Robbie snorted a derisive laugh. "You always were a soft touch." O'Donnell gave Robbie the finger with a laugh. "I could book you for that, son," he said, mood improving. "You gave your statement, yeah?

Why don't you fuck off out of here then so we can sort this shit out and I'll see you later."

O'Donnell nodded. It was almost evening. His morning jaunt and fresh air had been thoroughly ruined. "I'd appreciate any crumbs, mate."

Robbie laughed "What's wrong, Hansel? Some bird ate your trail?"

"Yeah, and made off with my worm. I was looking to go fishing, too." He slid off the car, shook Robbie's hand and fished his keys from his pocket. The door clicked and he pulled it open, stopping. "Hey, Robbie?"

Robbie turned on his heels with a grunt.

"If I'm Hansel, does that make you Gretel?"

"Fuck off, wanker." Robbie flicked his cigarette butt at O'Donnell.

After sobering enough to awaken, O'Donnell sat on the pull-out bed and fought to recall his dream. Flashes of the dead Judy came to him, though she was not where he'd found her. Instead her body had been in the holding cell where Jason had been until they had moved him all those years ago.

He did his best to wipe both memories from his mind. Getting up, he made to refill the coffee machine on the small kitchenette bench across from him with water and ground, stopping with a frown. He couldn't recall when he'd last changed the filter. Usually the cigarette that went with the drink as his breakfast would make up for the taste. Today though a takeout coffee was in order as he didn't have any smokes left.

Freshening up in the small bathroom in the back, he dressed and walked to the nearby shopping centre and dropped off the disposable camera at K-Mart to be processed. He always made sure to flirt enough with the photo centre manager so she would ensure his prints came out before any others. She would ask him in hushed tones, leaning in, about what juicy case he was on. He'd sworn her to secrecy, but he knew she was peeking. There was nothing salacious, and he would never bring anything important to be processed, but he was sure the woman made up all manner of stories. She gave him a good discount, too.

He'd yet to work a case where the partner actually asked for photos in the act. Usually information and dates of meetings was enough with a few photos thrown in of people going into and leaving apartments or hotels together, embracing and kissing as they parted. And he hadn't taken a photo of Judy's body. Not his case and not respectful to the dead. He'd seen all he had to of the poor woman's demise.

He walked to Safeway and went past all the groceries and straight for the aisles he knew he wanted. The most important items were coffee and filters, which he dropped into the basket before hunting and gathering the rest.

"Morning, love," the cheery middle-aged woman at the register said to him when the elderly woman before him had finally finished paying with all coins and shuffled on.

"Morning, Jo. How's that husband of yours treating you?"

"Minute I suspect the bastard is straying I'll give you a call to find out, don't you worry." She winked as she scanned his items.

O'Donnell gave a chuckle. "Well, he would be a fool if he did. Then you'd be free for me to whisk you away."

She gave a throaty laugh, a flush welling up from her chest to her neck and cheeks. "As pleasant as that sounds, I seen your office a few times. Not exactly the lap of luxury, is it?" She bagged the last of the items and without asking turned to the cigarette counter around from her and fetched a large blue-and-white carton.

"Investigating the investigator, Jo?" He clucked his tongue and handed over several notes.

She went a few shades brighter. "No!" she said and slapped his upper arm. "Girl's gotta keep fit. Been walking in me breaks."

"I thought there was something different about you, other than your new hairdo that is." He leant forward and checked out her behind.

She handed back his change. "Oi! You'll keep, sunshine."

O'Donnell laughed and picked up the two bags. "You have a good one, Jo."

"You too, love."

As he walked to the food court to get his usual McDonald's breakfast on these trips, he nodded and exchanged greetings with several other store keepers as they went about their business. Wherever he went he made an effort to keep on good terms with people, nowhere more so than in the immediate vicinity of his office. It wasn't hard to do with his small country town upbringing. Everyone knew everyone and their business. You couldn't fart sideways without it getting back to you somewhere. But word of mouth was also his best advertisement next to the Yellow Pages. And more than once he had managed some business and discounts through bartering alone.

He ate his bacon and egg McMuffin washed down with the brewed coffee and a smoke and planned his day as he waited for the photos.

O'Donnell returned to his office in the late afternoon after having followed a suspected cheating husband to and from a restaurant where the man met a woman. That in itself was no indicator of infidelity. The both of them leaving after eating with his arm about her waist and driving to a small beach-side apartment nearby certainly was. For those tasks he had his trusty Minolta with auto-focus and zoom lens. He was definitely no photographer, so the added expense of the camera had been well worth it. He'd met others who insisted manual focus was better and developed their own film, but he didn't have the patience to learn the skills let alone put them to use. He had enough contacts to turn to when he needed pictures done discretely.

He checked the camera and decided the last few exposures left on the film weren't worth keeping it. He had enough to take to the wife who had been waiting impatiently on any news over several weeks. He set the camera to wind itself and went through the office partitions he'd arranged to form something of a living space as it whirred in his hand. Sliding across a cheap Asian-style privacy screen that acted as his bedroom door, he put the camera down and went for coffee—always on and always warm.

The phone jangled and he ran to it, coffee jug in hand. He would have to buy a modern phone with an answering machine one of these days. Maybe even a cordless.

"O'Donnell Investigations," he said, somewhat out of breath.

"Mr O'Donnell? It's Cassie Lawler."

"Oh. Yes. Miss Lawler. What can I do for you?" He put the jug down and leaned against the desk, pulled out the already crumpled cigarette packet from a front pocket and thumbed it open.

"I know you hit a road block a few days ago with your investigation and the new police involvement—"

"Yes," O'Donnell said, bitterly. "Murders have a habit of doing that during investigations."

The line was silent for several breaths. "I can assure you Nathan had nothing to do with that," Cassie finally said.

"And you know that how?"

"I don't. But it's what we choose to believe. What *I* choose to believe. In any case, I may have a new lead for you."

He frowned. It had been several days since the incident, and though it had been on the news there had been no mention in any reports of Mortimer's involvement. What was she playing at? He didn't have the patience to mince words.

"Listen, I don't know what Gunther and Nathan were up to at Gateway, but you mess me around I'll—"

"I don't know anything about Gateway House."

"But you have a magic new lead right after the shit goes down?" He let out a snort, smoke billowing from his nostrils.

"As I said when we met, Mr O'Donnell, it's not simply myself that is concerned about Nathan. We have mutual friends and they keep their ears to the ground."

"Let's get something out of the way, Miss Lawler. I find out that you or your so-called friends are mixed up in what happened up there at the roadhouse, not only do I walk away with the money, but I will hand your arses in to the cops myself. We clear?"

"What makes you think we're involved, Mr O'Donnell?"

"You know too much. Which makes me ask, if you've got such connected friends, like you say, then why haven't they found your boyfriend?"

He listened intently to the buzzing of the line for several seconds before he heard the intake of breath and a sigh.

"Firstly, he's not my boyfriend. We were intimately involved once, Nathan and I, but that was some time ago. We were different people. As to why my friends can't find him? Well, they may know and hear things but unfortunately their skills fall short when it comes to tracking people down. Especially when it comes to Nathan."

"Why? What's so special about him? Apart from the fact he can ninja himself out of secure lockups?"

"He is... Let's just say very resourceful. Which is why we need you." She was silent again a moment before there was another sharp intake of breath and she continued. "Gateway House was something that only recently fell into their scope as events unfolded. We had no idea of his involvement with them or indeed who *they* might be. Does that sufficiently answer your questions?"

"Nope, not even a little," he said, pinching the bridge of his nose. The beginnings of a headache loomed. "But enough that I believe you. For now.

"So you'll remain on the job?"

"Yeah, why not. I'll keep looking into it. So tell me this new info before I change my mind."

"I've already sent it to you," Cassie said, her tone lighter. "You'll find it with your fax service. *Bon appétit*, Mr O'Donnell."

The line clicked as she hung up, a tone chirruping in his ear. With a snort he put down the receiver and grabbed his jacket from across the corner of his bed. The bell on the front door clanked as he opened it. The thing sometimes got stuck and sounded like it belonged around the neck of an old cow. He'd fix it when he returned from his fax service. He didn't bother to lock up. He was only going two doors down.

The smells of cooking hit him in the face as O'Donnell entered the Chinese take-away. He slapped the bell on the counter beside a small folded sign that instructed to do so for service. He stared at the sign, a piece of bent, black Perspex with chipped gold lettering on it.

A young Asian man walked through red beaded curtains leading to the kitchen. He grinned wide as he saw who was summoning him. He rounded the tall desk, painted garishly in red, black and gold, with his hand open at chest height, clasping it to O'Donnell's similarly held hand. The younger man pulled O'Donnell to himself and patted him violently on the back.

"Bro'Donnell! How you been, brother?"

"Yeah good, Benji. You?" O'Donnell cast a suspicious glance at Benji, the smile not leaving his lips. "Keeping out of trouble?"

Benji scoffed. "You know me, dude."

"That's why I asked, Benji."

They shared a laugh before the younger man held up both forefingers, shaking them, and ran back to the kitchen. "Got your fax and your order ready," he said, exploding back through the noisy plastic beads.

"My order?"

Benjamin Tran had gotten himself into trouble some years back and O'Donnell had managed to get him on the mostly straight and narrow after his parents had hired him to find their son. Drugs again, as he suspected was the case with Nathan Mortimer. Though then there had been no murder or possible cult link. O'Donnell had even gotten him the job here, though he was Vietnamese and not Chinese, as O'Donnell had been vehemently told by Benji's parents at the time, and whenever he came across them, which as the young man had grown became more infrequent.

Benji returned with a plastic bag laden with several take-away containers in it, and a roll of thermal paper he pulled from under his shirt.

"Sorry, bro. Have to keep it on the DL. Boss gets crazy pissed when too much of the paper roll goes." O'Donnell accepted the curled thermal paper sheet, eyeing a wet patch dubiously. "It's oil, man," Benji said as O'Donnell sniffed at it. "I tried to hide it in the bag first but—"

"Benji. I'm messing with you. And I'll get you a new roll next time I go shopping, okay?"

"No sweat, man. I know you're good for it." Benji stared at O'Donnell, waiting expectantly.

"Oh, yeah." O'Donnell patted his pockets for his wallet, realising he hadn't brought it.

Benji waved a hand. "Nah man, the woman paid."

"She did?"

"Yeah, so don't keep me hanging, bro! Who is she?"

"She's a client, Benji."

"Yeah? Why's she ordering you dinner then? With extras? And paying over the phone with Amex."

"Must be my good looks and charm."

"I dunno about that. But if she's swinging by, let me know because she sounded hot."

"Good night, Benji."

He left the restaurant and meandered toward his office, trying to unfurl the fax one-handed as he walked, which proved futile as the flimsy sheet curled inward with the slightest breeze. Resigned to wait the short distance, he entered his office and again didn't lock the door. Late night clientele was unseen but he would remember to lock it before he retired, not that there was much to steal. Although the loss of his coffee pot would more than likely cripple him.

Sitting at his desk, he ate with a plastic fork and played solitaire, eying the fax he was ignoring. Though curiosity gnawed at his mind, the call from his stomach was stronger. Midway through the meal and on his second unsuccessful hand, he shoved the soiled mouse away and pulled paper serviettes from the plastic bag the food had come in to wipe his mouth. A pair of break apart chopsticks fell to the floor.

Benji put them in to mess with O'Donnell as he could never use them. O'Donnell snorted and leaned to pick up the chopsticks, opened the bottom drawer of his desk to drop the paper-wrapped packet amongst the pile of others. They came in useful sometimes. He had a handful in the glove compartment of both his cars now. And he was still trying to amass enough that he could prank Benji with them and get him back.

O'Donnell reached across the desk where the fax had rolled. The shiny paper was out of reach, rocking back and forth as his fingertips brushed it. Opening the desk drawer, he pulled out a pair of chopsticks and flicked the paper toward himself.

"Who says I can't use chopsticks."

Smoothing out the fax, O'Donnell frowned. A psychiatric patient admission form. The patient's name was all too familiar, but the hospital was not. That was no mystery in itself. People who suffered mental illness tended to get bounced around in the system unless they had money or major issues that required constant care.

The date on the form was a week prior to Mortimer's admission to Rowville. Again, nothing suspicious there. He still had more of the roll to unfurl, though. Continuing, the lines in his brow deepened. Two other admissions, both from regular hospitals, though for psychiatric monitoring.

The phone rang and he picked up the receiver still frowning. "O'Donnell Investigations."

"Jesus fuck, Jimmy, you're a hard bastard to get a hold of."

"I told you years ago, Robbie," O'Donnell said, the lines on his face softening. "I don't swing that way, mate, so stop trying."

"Yeah, well if we both did, I would be the one batting and you'd be walking with a limp the rest of your life."

O'Donnell released the fax as he laughed. The thing curled up and rolled away again and off the tabletop. "Don't suppose you called me to say you found my missing person?"

"Actually, no. I was calling to ask you the same."

O'Donnell frowned again. Robbie coming to him was odd. Were they getting desperate? What had they found at the commune? Leading with those questions wouldn't help him.

"No. Nothing new on my end," O'Donnell said. "Nothing we don't know anyway. That our boy was a few cans short. Admitted a few times at different hospitals and facilities. Nothing on whatever crazy shit he might've been doing with Gunther and the rest."

"Christ, ain't that the truth. You should see the shit they've been pulling out of that place. The Gateway Cult they're calling it."

No wonder Robbie was calling him. If they'd named the thing, O'Donnell knew from experience it had to be serious. "Shit, Robbie." He swivelled in his chair and transferred the receiver to his other ear. "If I come across something, you'll be the first to know."

There was a pause on the noisy line. O'Donnell could hear Robbie's hesitation despite the buzz.

"Even before your client?"

Now O'Donnell paused. "Of course, mate." Robbie gave an uncertain hum, O'Donnell thought. The line was bad enough that he wasn't sure, but he sensed his friend's trepidation. "I won't risk her or her mates tipping these pricks off, Robbie. You can bet on that."

Robbie seemed to accept that. He gave a long sigh. "Yeah, all right, mate. Cheers. I didn't mean— Things are just tense, you know?"

O'Donnell knew. "Anything I can do, let me know."

"Thanks, Jimmy."

The speaker clacked in his ear as Robbie hung up. O'Donnell reached over and casually dropped the receiver with a clatter and soft ringing of the bells within. He picked at the Chinese but decided it was best left for tomorrow. He placed it in the small fridge he'd bought second-hand years ago. That thing had followed him around from place to place. It made strange noises sometimes but those were now familiar to him. He had once turned it off to defrost and the silence had almost driven him mad. He'd have put the TV on but with no antenna in the office and no reception with rabbit ears, he hadn't needed that any longer and sold it.

A beer in hand, he closed the fridge with his foot. On the freezer door was a wooden board with a bottle opener attached, held fast by magnets. He popped the beer, caught the lid and tossed it at the bin nearby, noting it was starting to get a little ripe. By the time he was on his third beer he'd ceased caring about both bottle caps and the smell.

He raised the beer to the rolled paper on his desk. "Cheers, big ears."

Both the smell and the case could wait till tomorrow.

With a snort in the back of his throat, O'Donnell started, waking himself. He was draped at an odd angle across the sofa bed and his neck was stiff. At least, he told himself, he'd remembered to take his shoes off this time, if not his clothes. Sitting up and stretching, he rose to walk to his desk and proceeded to light up.

Cigarette dangling from his lips, he rolled his head in a circle to work out the knot that had built in his drunken stupor. The woman's body and the memories it had dredged from the murk of his mind had been too much for him last night. He'd even forgotten to switch off the old PC. It came alive as he bumped the desk and moved the mouse.

The curved glass of the monitor lit up and he barked a laugh and shook his head at the jagged edges of the low-colour dot rendered breasts of Elle McPherson on the screen. That and the other images on the floppy disk had also been courtesy of the office's previous occupant. He'd pulled it out with the thought of releasing some of his tension but hadn't been able to unzip his pants let alone start plying at his flesh in the hope that it responded.

Not that he'd been in such a state that he was physically unable to undo his fly, but because he'd been unwilling. Like the food he'd not finished, he'd lost the stomach for it.

Reaching out, O'Donnell depressed the power button for the screen and inhaled deeply on the cigarette, rubbing his eyes to reduce the effects of the glow from the phosphor tube. He blinked at the screen as the tip of the cigarette moved across it. It left a bright reflection behind, but it was all the wrong colour and moved out of time with him.

Moving aside as quick as his sleep and alcohol fogged brain

allowed, the large knife reflecting on the monitor sunk into the flimsy back of the faux leather chair.

O'Donnell swung around with the empty beer bottle he'd snatched from his desk, and was greeted by the satisfying hollow thunk of bottle hitting skull. His assailant fell to the floor with a cry and the clatter of metal, the knife gleaming near O'Donnell's foot. Grabbing the knife, he flicked on the desk lamp and pulled it forward.

"What the fuck?"

An elderly woman in a once white nightgown lay on the floor, rocking her head drunkenly from side to side, eyelids fluttering.

FOUR

Two uniformed officers begrudgingly watched the haggard woman as others canvassed the area. Not that O'Donnell expected them to turn anything up. The woman had no belongings. She didn't even have any underwear on under her stained nightgown. Her pissing herself as he'd knocked her out hadn't helped her appearance or smell.

Sitting on his desk smoking, he felt a presence at his side and offered Robbie a smoke without looking to confirm it was him. He knew it would be. All the other cops gave him a wide berth. Being a pariah had hurt him, but tonight it was a perk. He didn't want to speak to them, or anyone really.

"Were you really that hard up, Jimmy boy?" Robbie said as he accepted the smoke after blinking at it. He'd been trying to quit for over a year.

"Well, your mum was at the international porn star awards, so..." O'Donnell sparked his lighter and Robbie leant into it, giving him the finger as he did.

"She sends her love to your mum, by the way."

O'Donnell nodded. "Thanks. I'll let her know when I talk to her next."

Growing up in the same country town, their parents had naturally known each other and socialised. It was hard not to in rural areas. And when both O'Donnell and Robbie had expressed interest in the police force, they had gone on together. They'd played football together. Done most things together.

"You want in on the questioning?" Robbie said, idly playing with his wedding band that was too loose.

O'Donnell raised his eyebrows and stood. Robbie knew damn well he wanted in. It was too much of a coincidence this woman attacked him after everything with Gateway.

"Go for a smoko, guys," Robbie said to the men inside.

One of them turned away with a sneer.

The other stared at Robbie in defiance. The uniform waved a hand at the old woman. "You really wanna be left alone inside with—"

"I think I can handle a bat-shit crazy old lady by myself. Don't you, Travis?"

Travis turned to O'Donnell, eyes narrowing. He snorted in disgust, then walked out followed by the other man.

"That's what I thought," Robbie called after them.

O'Donnell had only been partially listening, though he'd registered the contempt aimed at him. He was used to it.

He watched the old woman carefully as she muttered to herself. Her eyes roamed about with no fixed point of interest and she'd ignored all questioning so far. He stood and smoked as Robbie rolled the slashed chair to her and sat.

"You mind if I smoke?" Robbie said to the woman.

She ignored him.

"I'll take that as a no. Do you maybe want one?"

She didn't so much as look at him, her eyes following something else entirely.

"I'm Detective Robbie Thomas. Can you tell me anything about Gateway House? Or Gunther Franklin?"

After several long moments of silence, O'Donnell ground his cigarette in a thick ceramic ashtray and turned to face Robbie, clenching his teeth. "She's not going to talk, Robbie. She doesn't know her own name let alone jack-shit about what's going on."

"Why'd she try and kill you then, numb-nuts?" Robbie said without taking his eyes off the woman. "Someone must have put her up to this. Probably told her you're the antichrist or some shit. My money's on Gunther. Or your boy. If I catch who it was, though, I swear I'll be questioning him alone in a cell. And he might just have an accident, if you know what I mean."

The woman's eyes snapped on Robbie. Her lips stopped partly open. Saliva gleamed on the thin, blue-tinged lines of flesh. The red cracks running the lengths of her mouth brightened, like they would start gushing blood at any moment as she drew her lips tight against her teeth. Her eyes almost bulged and O'Donnell thought Robbie might burst into flame soon if she continued.

Robbie grinned down at the old woman. "So. Which one were you sucking off, Granny Psycho? Gunther?"

The woman's heavy breathing continued, the thin, white material that clung to her sagging breasts with sweat and God knew what else rising and falling at a good clip.

"Mortimer?" Robbie said.

The woman's breath faltered, her nostrils flaring and eyelids fluttering.

"Yeah," Robbie said, drawing the word out as his grin grew wide and lewd, nodding like he was in on it. "I bet he liked it when you played with his balls. You did too."

The woman grew more crazed if that were at all possible. It was the most colour she had since O'Donnell had clashed with her, her pale skin reddening, turning almost purple.

"Nah," Robbie added. "I bet he liked you to wriggle your bony fingers up his arse. Am I right?"

The woman lunged at Robbie with surprising speed and ferocity. Her hand was at his throat in a flash and they both sped back as the wheels of the old chair scraped on the painted concrete below. With a crash, the chair hit the desk. The metal lamp fell off with a clang. The monitor jumped back, teetering wildly. The old woman leapt, her bare feet leaving the floor and planting between Robbie's thighs, perched on her toes like a carrion bird.

O'Donnell halted as Robbie held up a hand. He stared at the woman's back, her arms scrawny, hair like straw. The bottom of her feet almost black with dirt, grime and blood. Both her hands were clutched around Robbie's throat.

"You would do well to heed my words." Her voice was a rasping hush but it carried to O'Donnell's ears as though she were facing him directly. "You are a dead man. You will die in agony. Slaughtered like the pig you are." She spoke softly, but now became animated, shaking him by his neck. "I place the mark upon you!" She spat on Robbie's forehead and tore her right hand from where it was doing its best to squeeze the life from him. The hand slammed palm down upon the gob of saliva. "You will never be one of The Enlightened!"

"Jimmy," Robbie croaked as the crone's body shuddered atop him. "A little fucking help here!"

O'Donnell jumped to action and grabbed the frail looking woman's right forearm. He pulled, trying to pry her hand from Robbie's head. The arm vibrated in his hands but wouldn't budge.

"Never!" she half yelled. More spit foamed at her mouth as she spat the word.

O'Donnell pulled as Robbie pushed. Her nails tore at Robbie's temples as both men struggled. Before he knew what was happening, the uniformed officers pushed O'Donnell out of their way and pulled the woman off. Robbie grunted loudly as they literally tore her from his throat, her hands raking his flesh as she went. The lines on Robbie's forehead and neck were red and swollen, crimson welling within the channels.

"Fucking crazy bitch," Robbie yelled as the men made a makeshift shackle of handcuffs to hogtie the struggling woman.

As they carried her out in that same position, she turned to Robbie.

"Within a decade, your soul will cease to be. Never to be Enlightened. Never to be Enlightened. Never to be…" She repeated the same phrase as the bell on the door gave a dull rattle and she was carried away.

O'Donnell jumped as the office chair toppled sideways violently, eyes leaping from the woman to Robbie. Robbie's foot lowered to the floor where the chair had been, and he touched his fingers to his neck with a hiss.

"Those bastards are never going to let me live this down you know," Robbie said, the bulging of his neck muscles and throbbing in his temples making the wounds appear worse. "You got any antiseptic or something?" He didn't wait for a response, clicked his fingers impatiently at O'Donnell, outstretched fingers shaking.

Lighting one up, he passed it to Robbie then lit his own. "Christ, Robbie. What the fuck was that?"

Robbie snorted a laugh. "That's nothing, Jimmy boy. The amount of fucked up shit I've seen working homicide? I tell you, you were smart to get out. Nothing but garbage out there." Robbie hitched his thumb at the window. "She was a pussycat by comparison."

"Yeah? Well if she's the fucking pussycat, I'm not sure I want to meet the lions."

Robbie laughed, hands shaking less as he sucked on the cigarette. "Hey, remember when we watched *Smokey and the Bandit*? And we decided we wanted to buy a Trans Am and a semi-trailer and smuggle shit across Australia?"

"Yeah," O'Donnell said, chuckling. "And we'd ride our bikes around by the river near the police station pretending Smokey was hot on our tails."

Robbie's face split as he cackled. "Man, we should have been crooks instead of cops." The smile faded from both his lips and eyes.

O'Donnell had seen a similar look in the mirror whenever he remembered Jason's body. Robbie's went much further though. His eyes were a much deeper, darker well of blackness. He must have seen a lot more. Apart from Judy, Jason, his grandmother and a few other funerals, O'Donnell hadn't seen many dead people.

"How're Kelly and the kids?" O'Donnell asked, trying to change the mood.

"Two kids and as hot as ever." Robbie's sly grin didn't reach his eyes. "Bet you're sorry you let that one get away, huh?"

O'Donnell laughed. He hoped his eyes were not a mirror of Robbie's darkness.

"Yeah. They're good, Jimmy. Kids are growing. Never fucking stop, littler bastards. You still haven't come 'round for that roast dinner after all these years of me inviting you."

"You know me, Robbie. I don't like to mix my business and personal life."

Robbie's eye did not leave O'Donnell's as he smirked. "That's not what Elaine down at the old precinct said." O'Donnell shook his head. Robbie glanced around the office and nodded. "You should come. When all this shit dies down. You should come."

"Yeah. I might do that." O'Donnell stamped out his butt and lowered himself off the desk. "So what do you make of our crazy lady?"

Snorting in through his nose and pulling on it as if to clean it, Robbie walked to O'Donnell's side and put out his own smoke. "Oh, she's a right fucking loony-toon. At least you and I have still got it in the good cop, bad cop department though. She fell hook, line and sinker."

"Not that she gave us anything useful." O'Donnell rubbed at his face and head, ending at the back of his neck where he gave the stiff muscles there a squeeze. He turned to Robbie, jutting his chin. "On top of all that, she put a death curse on you."

Robbie gave him the finger. Wincing, he gingerly touched his throat and forehead again. "You think I'm going to need a tetanus shot? I feel like I'm getting lockjaw."

"I should be so lucky."

Sucking air through his teeth as he poked at his wounds and inspecting his reflection in the dark monitor on the desk, Robbie spoke over his shoulder. "She gave us plenty, anyway."

"How do you reckon?"

"Well, she skipped over mention of the Gateway nut job Gunther, and didn't go all psycho—" Robbie turned around, eyes wide and crazed as he stabbed at the air, "until we mentioned your client's boyfriend."

"And you think that means what?"

"She was protecting him. What the fuck do you think that means, Sherlock?"

O'Donnell chewed on that a moment. It didn't make sense. The Gateway people were after Nathan as well. What did that mean for Cassie Lawler and her so-called friends? For all he knew she was one of the Gateway Cult.

"No. I don't buy it," O'Donnell said. "The old bird started babbling about The Enlightened, whoever the fuck they are. Nothing to do with Gateway."

"Christ, Jimmy. Don't tell me you've gone and got your nuts twisted up about another girl." Robbie smirked. "At least you finally forgot about Rochelle." Laughing, he picked up O'Donnell's smokes. Opening the blue-and-white packet, he stared at the contents. With a resigned shrug, he pulled out a cigarette and lit up again. "Kelly will kill me when she smells it on my breath." He laughed again as he dropped the packet. "Remember when you, me, Kelly and Rochelle went down by the river on the dirt-bikes and had our first cigarettes that you'd nicked from your old man?"

O'Donnell laughed despite the pain the memories of lost love and what might have been. Was Robbie right? Was he the type to get hung up on a girl? Even if he were, Cassie Lawler wasn't anything to him. It was true he was strangely attracted to her. She was not his usual type with her odd style and tattoos. Although he'd not been in a relation-ship in several years and couldn't recall when he'd last actually had any physical contact with a woman. At least not in a sexual context. Was he losing his sex-drive? Was he getting old? He had tried to go back to the roadside cafe to hit on a probable murderer. What did that say about him and his state of mind? Or even his client?

"Shit, I thought we were going to cough up a lung," Robbie said, laughing. "Lucky we still had enough breath in us though, eh?"

O'Donnell's smile was half-hearted. Out in the scrubland by the river was the popular spot to lose one's virginity in their little country town. Probably had been for generations. There was a derelict car for those too shy to do it out in the open. Or if you were lucky enough you had a tinny and could take the small metal boat out on the calm water in the shallows, hidden by the hanging willow trees. Or there was even a small island that they used to call Pussy Willow Island, named creatively for the trees about it among other reasons. For all O'Donnell knew, they still did. If you had been able to convince a girl to go with you to Pussy Willow Island, that made you pretty much the king of the town until the next guy came along. He heard there was a tree in the middle of the island the boys would carve their names and the name of the girl they had taken to the island, though he'd never seen it to corroborate the story.

O'Donnell and Rochelle had made out in the smelly derelict and he had even managed to cop a feel, but they had not gone the whole way, though each had made a deal to say they had as they both knew Robbie would be spreading the story. At that age, the news of it was more important than the actual deed itself. And somehow, he couldn't bring himself to tell Robbie any different. It hadn't been that Rochelle wasn't an attractive girl, and she said the same of O'Donnell. She had said it was because she liked Robbie. And O'Donnell…

Thinking about Robbie with Kelly under the Willow brought the same pang of regret and anger to O'Donnell's mouth. He stoppered it with a cigarette of his own and did his best to suffocate those pangs.

"I still don't buy it," he said.

"Well obviously, Jimmy, the bastards aren't going around calling themselves the Gateway Cult. We named the fuckers that. It would be no fun if they handed us an embossed business card with 'Nathan Mortimer, Cult Leader, Murderer, and Funny Farm Escape Artist' written on it, now would it?"

"Jesus. A woman died, Robbie."

"People die every day, Jimmy. I'm the one that has to clean up the shit, or have you forgotten that? And I don't walk away from it." Robbie dropped his half cigarette to the floor and ground it roughly with his heel. "Your boy is going to be on Australia's Most Wanted. Congratulations. Did you want to pick the actor who plays you on the show for the re-enactment, or are you happy for the TV station to do it?"

Not waiting for an answer, Robbie grabbed his jacket and walked to the door, his shoulders squared. O'Donnell wanted to say something, but what could he? Maybe this was Robbie's way of dealing with it all.

Robbie stopped at the door. "Do me a favour? Stay clear of that chick, Jimmy. And my investigation. All right?"

O'Donnell gave a nod and with that Robbie left. Following after him, O'Donnell watched Robbie drive away then locked the door, rattling it by the handle for good measure.

After a fitful night's sleep, O'Donnell walked to the nearby shopping centre and treated himself to a cafe breakfast. He couldn't stand to be in his office. He'd actually milled about in the all but empty building as stores opened and people had filed in, more to ensure he was not alone. He listened to two middle-aged women talking about their husbands. Filled with euphemisms and double entendres, the discussion filled him with a sense of normalcy.

Throughout the meal though, he couldn't shake the impression of being followed. A niggling sensation itched at the base of his skull, prickling the skin of his neck. More than once he caught himself turning about, trying to catch a reflection in shop windows. After finishing his second coffee—espresso this time, the cafe apparently too trendy for filtered—he walked until he found an exit and lit up. Leaning on the stained beige walls, he closed his eyes and enjoyed the light breeze and sunlight on his skin.

Apart from his office, he preferred to never smoke indoors. Never in anyone else's home, at least not without their insistence. Even when he'd been on the force he'd step out to smoke, joking that he was going out for fresh air. He'd grown up outdoors, and his mother had always spoken out about smoking in homes. She'd say that if people wanted to choke their lungs, they could bloody well do it outside and away from her and her kids. In businesses, he didn't mind so much. And everyone in the shopping centres smoked. But not this morning. He wondered why.

Moving on, he contemplated what he could do with his day. And the following days to come until a new client came in. The worst thing about the job was the sporadic nature of work at times. And now he wasn't entirely sure Robbie and his other contacts wouldn't freeze him out entirely. The way his friend had spoken, he could well be on the blacklist completely.

With a groan, O'Donnell rubbed at his hair and stretched his neck, hearing it groan and crack. Making similar sounds from his throat, he straightened and finished his cigarette and turned to walk back into the drowning noise of the shoppers. By now there would be the usual crowds of mothers with young children too small for school, more old people, and the unemployed, some of them teenagers. Then there were other teenagers, like the one he saw walking towards the slowly opening double glass doors, who were in uniforms and skipping school.

The girl stopped as she saw him and did a quick about face, hurrying away and around the corner.

O'Donnell's forehead wrinkled, his brain tingling. The girl was oddly familiar, and the way she had run from him—

The furrows and tingling deepened as recognition dawned.

O'Donnell ran for the full glass wall and nearly knocked himself and a laden trolley over. Apologising, he sprinted from the woman who hurled invectives at him, swearing despite the child in the carry seat of the rickety cart.

Scanning the thin crowd as he powered along the brightly lit way, O'Donnell caught sight of the girl as she ducked down a side path, a sign indicating that it led to public toilets. It wouldn't be the first time he'd had to break the sanctity of restroom segregation, but he still didn't relish the thought.

As he reached the narrow corridor, he was almost pleased to see that he wouldn't have to venture into the women's bathroom. A heavy fire exit door clicked into place softly as a pneumatic closer did its job.

He groaned to himself as he skipped into a jog. He also did not want to have to run, but there was little option.

Hitting the door, he leaned into it as he pushed the horizontal bar that ran the width of the opening. His footfalls echoed in an empty loading bay that reeked of rotting food and diesel, ringing off the tall, hollow metal bins that ran along it. As he passed them, he quickly scanned the spaces in between for a hidden figure. O'Donnell contemplated going back to search the large bins more thoroughly when he reached the end and cast his eye around a mostly empty car park.

Then he spotted a flash of pale leg as he saw the girl leap down from a chain-link fence, her school skirt catching atop it momentarily on her way over. She was off like a shot as soon as she landed.

As O'Donnell mantled the obstacle at the same spot, a commuter train rushed past, its horn surprising him more than the thing itself. It was too far for it to endanger him, though close enough its tearing through the air tugged at his hair and clothing as he pelted down the gravel and grass. The girl was nowhere to be seen.

Winded and holding the stitch in his side, O'Donnell stood from where he was doubled over as the bells and lights of the rail crossing switched off, the booms raising in slow, bouncing jerks. As the few cars on the road resumed their transit, O'Donnell spotted the girl across the rails.

He ducked down and watched as she entered a car and spoke with someone before the car pulled a U-turn and thundered past him. Through the passenger window, he saw Cassie Lawler berate the girl from Rowville Psychiatric that had taken the cigarette from him.

Easing himself to full height, he tapped the top pole of guard rail of the crossing several times with the side of his clenched fist before giving it a final wallop, his fingers white from the strain.

FIVE

THE SQUAT WAS EMPTY. No one at Rowville Psychiatric recalled seeing the girl out the front that had spun the story of a sick father, or at least they couldn't remember. They saw a lot of kids and people waiting. The Gateway community was still swarming with cops, as was the diner, not that anything there would be of use to O'Donnell. No avenue of investigation that merited following bore fruit.

Then, after days of futile search, O'Donnell finally struck it lucky.

As well as attempting to chase down any leads on Gateway, these Enlightened, or any of the people surrounding it all, he had also been trying to find Cassie Lawler. Her distinctive car was what he had been using to track her down. An interest in cars was one of the things his father had passed on to him, so he could ask around for the red Valiant with surety when describing it.

Given the young girl had been local to the shopping centre—or at least that was the assumption he was going on, she could well have been further afield but he had to start somewhere—O'Donnell started in and around his locale, then spread out. He was used to leg work and the time such things took, and it wasn't like he had anything better to do.

He'd chanced upon her while he was in a fish and chip shop, seated at a chipped laminate bench ingrained with years of greasy food, eating a steak, egg and onion toasted sandwich. The car drove right past the shop. He made no rush. Rushing was how you got caught in this business.

After slowly finishing the sandwich and cola, he made his way back to his car and threw on a jacket that was too big for him and not his usual style, then a baseball cap that matched. The trick was to hide yourself while not sticking out, to act like you belonged. If he'd worn a ten-gallon cowboy hat the stares alone would have caused a target to turn and glance. As it was, Cassie was nowhere in sight.

Over the next few days he became a VIP at the fish and chip shop. He chatted it up with the old Greek couple that owned and ran the place, gave them a few business cards. Though they had no information, O'Donnell learned from the husband that he'd seen the car around. It was hard not to notice. They, or someone they knew, could be potential clients one day, though. So he chose this as his base of operations. He'd also often found that the best food, while not the best for you, was in places like this and the roadside cafe near Gateway.

Thinking of the cafe and its victim, O'Donnell glanced at the shop's proprietors. Paranoia gnawed at the edges of his internal organs. How could he even be sure after recent events? These unassuming elderly Greeks could be in the cult for all he knew.

When he turned back to the window, the highly polished back end of a car flashed red and chrome, gliding away down the road with the purr of a tiger. The Valiant.

Without a word, O'Donnell stood and walked out, slow and calm. He slid the helmet in his hands on his head, not bothering to fasten it, and kicked his leg over the small red scooter. It started on the first try, as he had ensured it would do with both its postman owner and his several tests since borrowing it. He pulled the bike onto the road in a calm manner and followed the classic car from a distance.

While the scooter he rode stuck out, the profession it came with did not. If he'd been following her on a sports bike or some huge noisy Harley, then Cassie might have sensed that she were being tailed. Posing as a postman, as he had done many times since making acquaintances with the scooter's owner, people rarely looked once let alone twice. As it was, she didn't look at all as he puttered past her when she pulled the car into the drive of a sumptuous, gated town-house both large and luxurious enough most would call it a mansion.

Lapping the neighbourhood several times, he swung past the property again, stopping at equally large houses and fussing with the saddle bags while he inspected the mansion with side-long stares. Electric gates with a security PIN panel. No cameras he could see but then again, he wasn't casing the place to break in. Noting the polished brass number on a gate pillar, he made his way back to drop off the postal scooter and drove back to his office.

Pulling into his parking spot in the alleyway behind the row of stores, he paused before unlocking the car door and making his way out. He had been jumpy since the attack from the old woman, but not without reason. Only a fool would ignore instinct at a time like this. He was just as wary when he entered the office, checking the bathroom at the rear and around each corner once entering the main space, then on the other side of the partition separating office and living space.

Glancing out the large dirty windows to ensure nothing was amiss outside, he added a mental note to clean the windows and get some blinds. That list contained those particular items many times over, he knew. Though now he had incentive.

With a sigh of resignation, O'Donnell eased into the chair at his desk, doing his best to ignore the knife wound on its rear, and lifting the phone receiver dialled before he held it to his ear.

"Benji? Yeah. Wanna make a quick buck? Uhuh. Yep, like last time. ASAP. Great. Thanks, mate. Ready for the address?"

***

After receiving a call from a prospective client whose hand had been hovering over the go button a while, O'Donnell had gone to meet her.

She was late and he suspected she would be a no show. She had been more than reluctant, she said, to both hire someone of "that sort" and to confirm her suspicions that her well-to-do husband was keeping a mistress.

It was understandable. He came across it a lot. Most people didn't want to know, to not shatter their idyllic picture-perfect lives. It wouldn't be the first or last time someone piked after calling him.

It was like, he would say to them with a knowing nod and a comforting smile, they were encased in a beautiful crystal glass dome that held their lives within. That dome was set carefully on a hall table. Positioned perfectly. They didn't want to reach out and push it off.

Most would agree, smiling back as if let off the hook.

Then he would frown in concern and shake his head. "But is it better if someone else knocks it off for you? Leaves a mess in your home for you to find and clean up?"

It usually worked. Not always. This woman was one of the ones it had not hooked. He hated playing salesman, but he had to sometimes. If they hadn't wanted to hire a detective in the first place, he would also say—and definitely prescribed to this line of reasoning outside of simple sales—they would not have reached out to one.

Then there were people that simply didn't like him for whatever reason. It happened. You couldn't like everyone. The ones he disliked the most were the ones that had the "oh you don't look like the PI's on TV" mentality. He would usually joke that his Ferrari was still in Hawaii, depending on how serious the situation and potential client was.

A woman clutching her handbag to her breast sidled up to the table and sized him up after glancing around. People did that too, acted as if meeting a criminal or male prostitute. He wished he earned that much an hour.

"Mrs Inglewood?" he said, keeping his voice low and soft.

"James O'Donnell?" she said, softer still.

He nodded and indicated the chair opposite. She sat. Didn't take off her large sunglasses or hat. If only she knew, he thought.

She was what his mother would call "a timid bird of a thing". Frail and flighty. Her age was hard to determine but he pegged her at mid to late forties, estimating down as she had that younger-than-she-looks vibe about her. To look at her casually he might have thought she was a decade older.

The exact opposite of Cassie Lawler.

"I took the liberty of ordering a pot of tea for us," he said when a waitress approached.

The woman shrank into herself. O'Donnell couldn't figure out why she was so nervous. She'd chosen the meeting place herself. She lifted her head and he caught a glimpse of her face under the wide, black brim of her hat. He gripped the white, wrought-iron chair.

The crone-like woman with her butcher's knife, face moulded in rage, flashed out from under it momentarily. Ready to rise and fend her off, he stopped as he confirmed it was the frightened Mrs Inglewood.

That was it, O'Donnell thought as he calmed his nerves and released his fingers, wishing he was drinking something far stronger than tea. Inglewood was terrified. He lifted the teapot to pour for them.

"Are you ok, Mr O'Donnell?" the woman said. "You looked a little pale there for a moment."

Her voice wavered as much as O'Donnell discovered his hand was as the china spout of the teapot rattled against her cup. He gave the woman a polite wave, then used the hand to steady the pot. He declined the bowl of sugar and milk from her. He hoped the sharp taste of the tea would distract his senses.

He gave a dismissive shake of his head. "Must be all this fresh air. Maybe, though, you should tell me what has you so scared, Mrs Inglewood? If that is your real name." Best to come out of the gates running.

The woman gave a bitter, thin-lipped smile before taking a sip. The expression appeared to be a permanent one for her, O'Donnell decided as the wrinkles around her mouther eased into place. It certainly accounted for her older appearance, or part of it.

"Well, at least I know I would get my money's worth. *If* I hire you," she said. She took another sip before abandoning the drink and explaining her story and what she wanted. His own tea was stone cold when O'Donnell finally picked it up again, long after her departure.

He slipped the thick envelope she had given him into his pocket.

Four days later, when O'Donnell had all but forgotten about tasking Benji with watching the mansion and stalking Cassie Lawler, Benji turned up with an envelope of his own, this one almost as thick but much wider and taller than Mrs Inglewood's. He dropped the package with a thud on the desk and placed two beer cans dripping with condensation beside it, stowing the rest of the six pack in O'Donnell's fridge.

"Man-oh-man, bro! That chick is some piece of work," Benji said, indicating the envelope then shaking his hand and blowing air through his pursed lips. He placed a receipt for the photo processing on top of the yellow manila package.

"I told you not to get the eight by tens, Benji," O'Donnell said, further annoyed when he saw that the kid had paid more for matte finish and white borders also. Taking out his wallet, he handed over the money for both the pictures and the promised fee. "I expect extra dumplings as change."

"Yeah, fine. But trust me when I tell you, dude." Benji tapped the envelope. "You will lose your shit when you see these snaps."

The corner of his mouth twitched. "You better not have kept any, Benji."

Benji shook his head, his beer sloshing as he crossed his heart with the can. The grin on his face said otherwise. Whether he kept any or not made no real difference once the pictures were slowly spread on the work surface.

O'Donnell's wide eyes were fixed on the pictures. "I hope to hell you documented all of this."

Benji's hand reached forward and flipped one of the photos over. Scrawled on its back was a time and date stamp, address, and where the shot was taken from roughly.

"I could kiss you." O'Donnell beamed.

"Only if you look like her."

Benji held out his beer and O'Donnell tapped his can against it, then stared at the photos once more. What was her game?

Without having meant to, O'Donnell had found himself drawn to the most prevalent location in all of Benji's photographs. As it happened, it was the right day for it.

He'd been out canvassing for the Inglewood job, and had been reminded of the images when he'd driven past another such location. A mass of people milled about outside the building, waiting to get their regular fix. They smoked, talked, laughed.

Parked outside the address on the back of the picture, he'd chewed on the inside of his lip wondering if he should be brazen in his approach. He had still been wondering as he walked through the establishment's doors.

Filing out with the rest in a semi-daze, O'Donnell ruminated on when he'd last received communion. His mum would have been proud, though not of his reasons for being within the church. He'd scarcely paid attention to the preacher's words, more intent on examining the building and its occupants in as casual a manner as he could. He had not seen Cassie, nor any of the people in the images taken by Benji, within the walls of the church, who he kept watching as they filed out of the building well after he had dropped into the driver's seat of his car.

"Did you find your god, Mr O'Donnell?"

He jumped and twisted his head sharply to the passenger seat, heart leaping with him as if it were bouncing around his ribcage.

"I don't know, Miss Lawler." He snarled the words, straightening in his seat and turned bodily in his seat, hand falling on the steering wheel. "Did you?"

Cassie's dark red lips curved, her eyes shining. She knew exactly what O'Donnell meant, he thought. The idea annoyed him more. He wasn't going to give her the satisfaction of asking how she had gotten into his locked car and his not noticing her there. Clearly, he had been far too intent on the church, he told himself.

"Why are you stalking me, Mr O'Donnell? Shouldn't you be out finding Nathan?"

"You know full well there's heightened police involvement in all this now with the murder and activities at Gateway. Don't even try to deny it, Cassie." He stared her in the face, as still as cast steel. O'Donnell nodded, his lips and face pulling in frustration. "You know, I've worked cases with gang involvement before. Other dodgy shit. But never once have I had any shit fall on my doorstep. What the fuck have you dragged me into?"

This entire time, Cassie had been staring dead ahead. Now her face eased around to his. She lifted a hand, a lit cigarette held between her fingers that he hadn't smelt prior to seeing it, but now its aroma filled the interior.

"There's one address that your sidekick failed to collect," she said, neither her face nor voice revealing her thoughts on the matter. Her free hand, which had been resting in the crook of her right arm, lifted. With a slow flourish, she revealed a business card held between her first two fingers. "Meet me here tonight if you want to see, Mr O'Donnell. But be warned. Once you've seen, your eyes will be forever wide open."

Her hand seemed to float toward him, her movements lithe and graceful. He took the card and held it with both hands in front of him, resting on the steering wheel. "What is it? A magic show?" O'Donnell coughed a laugh.

"Ensure you want to truly see before coming, Mr O'Donnell. Not simply look, but truly see. Do you understand?" Her face was a mask.

Licking his lips, O'Donnell nodded, though he had no idea what she truly meant.

With a flicker of her lashes and tug of her ruby lips, the mask shattered. "Oh. And wear lots of black."

He heard the door open then close, but when he turned to it, she was already lost in the crowd of churchgoers. Tapping the business card on the steering wheel as he read it, he wondered if the faithful outside would approve?

Parking well away from the club, O'Donnell had arrived before any such establishment had a respectable right to open. Walking to the building, he found a good vantage point to eye it from. As staff arrived one by one, he took pictures. Through the viewfinder, a few of them appeared to be from Benji's photos, but he could only be sure once they'd been developed and compared.

After waiting a while to ensure no others would arrive, O'Donnell returned to his car and stowed his camera, removing the film from it first and secreting it away in a compartment under his seat. He'd made it a force of habit after hearing a story about a PI who had lost a whole host of evidence after his camera bag had been stolen, laden with the camera, and his current case-load worth of film.

He also made it a habit to label the developed film and file them well away from the prints in his personal Fort Knox, the spare room of his mother's house. He went at least every six months, if not more often. And until he could go, he stored the negatives in the broken safe. O'Donnell also took her his taxes as she was an accomplished accountant and bookkeeper. After seeing some of the things left behind on the computer, he thanked his luck he didn't have to deal with someone he didn't know.

Thinking about how he had to update his ledger so he could take it to his mother for his taxes, O'Donnell walked back to the club under darkness. He'd already eaten, so if he had to drink, he'd be fine. Though what he might find to drink inside, he wondered as he walked up to the doors of the Goth club, he wasn't sure.

As it happened, he needn't have worried. There was beer and he was glad for it, though he would have been as happy with a bourbon and coke or whiskey. He leaned against the bar and watched as the crowd thickened. There was a surprising—to him at least—amount of colour and diversity in the people, but the majority wore black, as Cassie had promised.

"I see you dressed to fit in," Cassie said close to his ear.

He turned sharply toward her. Her lips were close to his shoulder, but her voice had sounded louder to him, almost in his head. She was not much different than when he had last seen her, her clothes a slight variation in colour and style.

He, by contrast, had dressed up and worn a long coat, some boots and a polished belt buckle, much as many others wore, but the styling differed greatly.

"How do you like the club?" Cassie said.

"I'm disappointed really. I was hoping the cowboy look would cause more of a stir." O'Donnell cast his gaze around the club with a slanted grin as most of the patrons ignored him.

"Well, see, you forgot the hat, so—"

O'Donnell lifted his hat from the seat beside him and adjusted it on his head, tipping it back with a practiced tap of his knuckle.

"Yippee ki-yay," Cassie said before pointing at the bartender.

The young man with the black died asymmetrical hair-do prepared her a drink and passed it to her, without word or payment O'Donnell noted. She held her drink. O'Donnell picked up his own and raised it before she took a liberal mouthful, he mirroring her. The beer was of a boutique variety he hadn't ever tasted, and probably wouldn't again, but it was refreshing. And beer.

"So. What's a nice girl like you doing in a place like this?"

"If you're trying to pick me up, Mr O'Donnell, you're going to have to do better than that."

"Usually I let my cowboy boots do all the talking."

"Maybe that works for you at rodeos," she said, the smirk on her lips a sarcastic slash across her face, "but here, you'll have to do a lot better."

"Actually, that's the belt buckle."

"Excuse me?"

He patted the engraved rodeo trophy at his waist, and she leaned forward, moving close to inspect it. From the same position, her eyes rose to his, peering through her long, darkened lashes.

"Am I supposed to be impressed?" she said.

As she eased herself back to standing, he was taken but her strange litheness. He found himself intoxicated, his breath catching. He'd seen women move similarly before. While he was no regular patron of strip clubs, he had certainly gone. More so when he was in the force, he realised. And once for an actual client who herself had been a dancer.

Cassie, though... Whatever her story, he did not think it was in any way related to pole dancing. It may have been to whatever skill she employed to sneak into his car with him in it, though.

"Junior regional roping champion," O'Donnell said.

"That so?"

He gave her a curt nod. "Yes, ma'am. Pure silver," he said, rapping it with his knuckles.

Cassie's eyes widened in mock surprise, not leaving his for a moment. "Better be careful not to touch me with it then. I may be a vampire and burst into flames."

"I thought silver was for werewolves," he said, matching the intensity of her stare.

"Silver works on many things."

"Does it now?"

There was activity in the back of the club. Cassie turned her head to the barman as he motioned for her attention. He indicated the gathering that was building with a flick of his head.

Downing the rest of her drink, she placed the glass on the bar top. Stepping forward, she ran her finger across O'Donnell's belt, her manicured fingernail grating on the etchings.

"Am I smoking?" she said, leaning close enough to press her lips to his ear. She walked toward the doorway that had opened, only certain people being allowed through. She glanced back at him once before heading through that portal.

For some reason, O'Donnell thought of the Gateway graffiti at the squat house as he saw the open passage.

"Just a little," he muttered to himself before downing the majority of the beer and following.

SIX

Stumbling back into the office, O'Donnell dumped his keys, wallet and other belongings on the floor and fell into his chair. His hand fell to the bottom draw and withdrew a half-finished litre bottle of bourbon and worked on ensuring the job was finished. Spinning the cap off with a slap of his hand, the thing fell to the desk and skittered to the floor somewhere in the dark. Lifting it, he drank straight from the bottle and tried to make sense of what he had witnessed at the Goth club.

The gathering of people at the end of the dark staircase behind the black door were not at all what he expected. He stepped onto the second floor and his feet faltered. As he'd climbed the old wooden steps, his mind painted a picture of darkly-clad youths, possibly wearing robes and other accoutrements, the walls and area decorated with things such as ram skulls and lit black candles. All of that was missing and couldn't have been further from the truth.

Instead of a Hollywood induced witches coven, the space and group both were... mundane.

"You're all normal," he said, taking in the faces around him.

"Don't sound so disappointed, Mr O'Donnell," Cassie said over her shoulder as she walked through the crowd.

They were so ordinary that it was O'Donnell who stuck out like the proverbial sore thumb. He was the most oddly dressed of them all, apart from the young barman with his half-shorn locks—the other half looking like freshly ruled, wet ink, his hair so dark and straight.

There were roughly twenty people surrounding him all told. A middle-aged balding businessman in a worn suit. An older man and woman with silvered hair and designer clothing and jewellery—O'Donnell thought he spotted a thick Masonic ring on the man's finger—who appeared to be a couple, though emotionally distant from one another. A biker. A stunning Indian woman in her thirties, dressed conservatively. A young blonde woman with dreadlocks, a thick, ornate nose ring jutting from one nostril, and loose clothing that did nothing to hide the fact that she obviously went braless and didn't care a bit. She did not however, O'Donnell noticed, have hairy armpits. That was a stereotype, but not one that he certainly hadn't witnessed.

He moved on to the few others about, who didn't stick out and would be lost in a crowd.

Then there was the girl from Rowville and the shopping centre.

She gave him an awkward smile. "Don't suppose I can bum a smoke?"

He continued to scowl at her in response.

"What's *he* doing here?" the biker said to Cassie, his crooked nose wrinkling, thick beard and moustache undulating as he sneered and flexed his facial muscles.

"Things have taken a turn and we need him to up his game," Cassie said, voice as even as every other time O'Donnell had heard it, despite the bigger man's confrontational demeanour toward her.

"I don't understand why we can't just find Nathan ourselves," the Indian woman said.

"Because, Rani... if Nathan doesn't want to be found, he can't!"

Dreadlocks argued, her voice straining to contain frustration. Clearly, they'd had this same argument before.

"How can we trust him?" the barman said to Cassie.

"How can we trust *anyone?*" one of the lurkers in the background shot out.

"I trust him," Cassie said. "And Nathan trusted me."

"And you expect that to be enough for us?" the businessman said, inciting the greater majority to agree with him, and those that didn't to rebuke those that did.

O'Donnell had been acutely aware, as he'd turned and took in the people about him, that he was surrounded. Though he'd convinced himself if they had meant him harm they could have easily overpowered him and done whatever it was his dark, paranoiac thoughts had conjured when he first stepped through the door.

"Who are you people?" he ventured after watching them argue amongst themselves and established the cliques.

As a group, they stopped and all took on the same expression, turning to Cassie, their spokesperson it seemed. He turned to her.

Her expression shifted from frustration to amusement.

O'Donnell pulled the hat from his head and with his free hand squeezed the instant headache from his sinus, palm wiping down over his nose and mouth.

"Shit," O'Donnell said. His lips pulled down and he blinked rapidly as he glanced around. "You're the Enlightened." He shook his head, a bitter laugh coughing out of his mouth as he took in the group again. "Nathan was your leader. And I'm right in the fucking middle of another cult."

If they took offence at his use of the word, they didn't show it.

"We really do need your help, James," Cassie said.

O'Donnell gave her a wry grin. He knew what she was doing. Speaking in a more familiar tone, using his given name. Trying to show that she was his friend. She would have made a good interrogator.

"Let's cut the bullshit, shall we?" he said. Her expression shifted from beatific to her usual ironic slant. "If your great leader has pissed off and doesn't want to be found, why are you so determined to get him back? And if these Gateway arseholes aren't part of this, who are they? And why are they after Mortimer too?"

Cassie stared at him as if contemplating what approach to take, her eyes shifting around in thought. It gave O'Donnell the impression more and more that he was being assessed as a potential mark. If she was somehow hoping to convert him to their cause, she had another thing coming. Even as a boy O'Donnell had bucked trends and ideas, though not always successfully or openly.

Her decision made, Cassie glanced around at the congregation. "Make preparations while I speak to James alone."

The group did as told, though most of them made their displeasure at their interim leader's choice more than clear, moving about gruffly and openly staring him down.

Without a word, Cassie moved to a bar in the corner of the room. It was probably only used on busier nights or for functions. Lit up brightly the way it was, the space appeared less like a club and one could be forgiven for mistaking it as a dance studio with its scuffed polished wood floor. If it weren't for the alcohol lining the space behind the counter and the bass thump through the soles of his boots, that was.

O'Donnell waved his wide-brimmed hat at her. "Whatever you think you're going to tell me to get me to turn, you'd better—"

"How did you get into rodeos?"

His head jerked back. She had caught him off guard. Dropping the hat on the counter, he leaned against the bar. Without a throng of sweat and perfume-soaked bodies, he could smell the alcohol permeating it and the floor. Thankfully there was no carpet to stick to.

"There wasn't much else to do in my town and—"

"That's crap. *How* did *you*, James O'Donnell, get into rodeos?"

His eyes narrowed and the headache return from the pressure his frown forced on it. "My father," he said. "He used to ride back in the day and started me on it too."

"Did you enjoy it?"

He cocked a shoulder. "I enjoyed the time I got to spend with him."

She made a face, rolling her eyes.

"A little," he said, pre-empting her interruption. "At the start I enjoyed it more. When I was a kid the barrel races were fun. Me and my horse, racing together. Working as one."

She walked around to the bar flap. Raising it she stepped through and pulled down a bottle of whiskey. "But?" she said, collecting two shot glasses from a glass shelf with a rolling motion of her fingers, setting them right way up in the same manner.

"But... he insisted that I move on to more 'manly' events. And I didn't want to. But I did anyway to make him happy."

She nodded as she poured. "Your dad's passed?"

O'Donnell took the shot from her hand but didn't answer.

She downed the liquor in a swift motion, then moved the bottle to refill the small, heavy glasses as he set his own beside hers.

"As fascinating as I'm sure my old rodeo days are, what do they have to do with all this?" He motioned around them.

Her eyes lit up, mouth widening as her teeth flashed. As she handed him his recharged shot, she pointed at him. "Old rodeo days? You saying you wore this same outfit as a kid?"

He didn't answer again as he downed the whiskey. It was smooth stuff, just as he liked but never bought.

"You saw the video of Nathan at the hospital. You know what we're all about. But you're too afraid to say it out loud."

"Reincarnation? Yeah. I saw it. You can't seriously tell me—" He downed the third shot and placed the glass down heavily, upside down. "Your little cult is based on reincarnation? I mean, it's not like it's a new concept. Couldn't you have at least chosen aliens or something more original?" The alcohol worked to loosen his lips, as tight as they were drawn in his sarcasm.

"Do you believe in God, James? Do you believe in Satan? Angels? Do you even believe in aliens?"

"I liked the movie." He gave a nervous chuckle.

He had been trying to incite a response from her. Or at least, he told himself, that he had been. But she kept going in good humour, as if they were having an everyday conversation, and he found it utterly charming. And disarming. He cursed inwardly. She was getting to him instead of the other way around.

"What do you think happens when you die?" she said.

His shoulder hitched. "Not a lot."

"We simply vanish, is that it?"

"Pretty much. You use up the energy in a battery, then chuck it in the landfill. Unless your lot are rechargeable."

Her teeth flashed. "Well, batteries is not quite what I had in mind, no. Let's imagine instead that the electricity you used in that battery was not depleted. That there is no battery. And we're all little toy robots running around."

"Okay. So are these toy robots solar powered?"

"For arguments sake, let's say the battery they work on is non-corporeal. Not physical. The energy is an infinite source in the shape of a battery."

"What? A ghost battery?"

"If you like. So you slip this ghost battery into the compartment, and the robot goes off and does its roboty thing. Still with me?"

"So far."

"Okay. So the robot powers around and eventually breaks. It's broken before, but the warranty covered it and it was repaired. Never as good as new, but it kept running until the end. So you take that robot and send that to the landfill."

O'Donnell shrugged. "Okay, I get it. The ghost battery – the soul – moves on into another robot. Again. Nothing new."

"Does that crap-heap of a computer you have use the little floppy disks or the big ones?"

He laughed at the sudden change in her line of questioning. "It's got hard disks."

She smirked. "Three-and-a-half inch floppies then."

"If you say so."

"Do you use those disks for anything but getting porn from your mates?"

"Sure. I save some case information on them sometimes. But I usually prefer pen and paper. Call me old fashioned."

The strong tang of whiskey hit his nostrils. He scowled at a line of four shot glasses beside his overturned glass, only the first of them filled. They hadn't been there moments ago. Her fingers slipped between the other glasses to pick up the charged glass.

"So you live—" She downed the shot. "You die. You're born again."

The glass knocked on wood as she hit it down hard. The one next to it was now full, he saw. The pressure from his confusion built on his forehead as it added another layer onto the building headache. She picked up that next shot, repeated the process. The third glass, empty moments ago was now full.

He had no idea how she was doing it but saw the simile. Each shot represented a new life, the contents the soul, emptied from one vessel and moved to the next somehow.

Vowing not to entertain her with asking how she was doing it, he moved back to the only logical question that mattered.

"What does that have to do with any of this, Cassie?"

Raising that last glass, she answered him. "What if you wanted more than one drink? What if you could have all the whiskey from all the glasses you've ever had before or will ever have?"

She moved the shot glass over his. Reaching out, Cassie flipped O'Donnell's shot glass and started to pour into it. She stared into his eyes and he had to tear his gaze from hers to watch.

The glass filled to its brim. But the whiskey kept coming. His mouth crept open as the liquid cascaded onto the bar, the pool spreading further from the base of the tiny cup as he watched. When the liquid finally stopped, she placed her now empty one beside the others and picked up his, the liquid doming above the lip trembling as she did.

"And what if you didn't have to let all that good whiskey go to waste?" She downed it one gulp.

O'Donnell nodded, remembering the conversation from the video tape at Rowville. "Supermen," he whispered.

"We're ready," the barman said from behind O'Donnell, making him turn in surprise. He watched the young man join the others as they spread out.

Cassie made her way to his side and started easing his stockman's coat from his shoulders.

"I don't know how you did that," O'Donnell said, shaking his head. "But if David Copperfield can make the Statue of Liberty disappear on TV, then you can sure as shit muck around with a few shot glasses. It doesn't mean anything."

"Well then, if they don't mean anything, there's no harm in letting us show you one more parlour trick."

Folding his coat, she placed it beside his hat and guided him toward the others.

"Are we going to hold a seance?" he said, eyeing the large circle on the dance floor the Enlightened had formed.

"Something like that." She narrowed her eyes, smirking. "You're not afraid, are you?"

He returned her smile. "I don't believe in ghosts."

"Good," she said, grin widening. "This will make you piss your tight jeans even more then."

O'Donnell lay on the floor, eyes darting to the faces around him, fingers of one hand pressed within the other, both pulled tight against his diaphragm. He swallowed and shifted his shoulders.

"Close your eyes and lay still until you're ready," Cassie said.

"How will I know I'm ready?"

She gave him a knowing, enigmatic nod.

With a sigh, O'Donnell relaxed, as much as he could with a mind full of cynical thoughts, wondering when the chanting would begin. But they sat around him in silence.

Absolute silence.

He could no longer feel the beat of the speakers through the floor, the sound and vibration gone. He could no longer smell what he had assumed was wood polish mixed with hundreds of dirty, alcohol impregnated footprints. He started to panic when his backside, shoulders and head went numb against the floor. The cotton of his shirt beneath his fingers became insubstantial.

Then there was a sudden sound and a smell...

His phone rang and he jumped up from his desk, face hurting from being pressed into it. When had he come home?

Snatching up the receiver, he tried to place the smell that was permeating the air.

"Hello?" he said, voice slurred.

"Are you all right, James?" Cassie asked down the buzzing, clicking line. "You were rather freaked out when you left the club."

"I— Yeah. Yeah, I'm fine," he lied. He couldn't remember coming home, his face and body was numb, and his stomach churned.

"I think you had far too much to drink after we showed you what we did," Cassie said, almost amused.

The hum and click of the line grew, as did the smell, the two almost linked.

"Yeah, I think I must have," he said, trying to sound as nonchalant as her.

"I really don't think you should have driven home. But you insisted."

"Sounds like me," he said, laughing.

"I'm rather worried about you though, after everything. Would you be okay if I... If I stopped in to see you? Tonight?"

He looked around the office, saw the now empty bottle of bourbon on his desk—empty but for a thin film-like layer of amber he'd missed —and checked the time. A little after two AM.

"Now?" he asked, stupefied.

"I'd really like to."

Her voice had taken on a new tone he'd not yet heard from her. Seductive. Suggestive. Absolutely sultry.

"Yeah. Yes, I'd like that too."

"I'll be there soon." Her soft whisper buzzed with the line, which started to chirrup in his ear, telling him she'd hung up.

In a daze, he placed the receiver in its cradle and rubbed at his eyes, shutting them tight. The removal of that sense amplified the others, the unidentified smell doubling.

He flinched back as something brushed his thighs, the chair rolling back unevenly a short distance, its dodgy wheels lazy in their abuse over the years.

Cassie was between his legs, dressed in lingerie. Black and lacy and fitting her to perfection. Her hair was coiffed in her rockabilly style, and in the suspender belt and stockings and red high heels, she was every bit the fifties pinup he had compared her to when they'd first met.

"Cassie? How did you—"

"Shhh."

Her lips, painted to match the shoes, glistened as they puckered to make the sound. Her hands moved inward from his thighs and planted on his crotch, fingers slowly massaging through the cloth, her eyes boring into his with desire.

His own desire surged as she undid his belt and pants, urging him with her hands to lift so she could pull them down past his knees. Then, focused intently on his eyes still, her lips moved to engulf him. He gasped at the heat and softness of her mouth, eyes momentarily closing from the sensation.

When he opened them, they again met her stare and he watched in captivation as she deepened her strokes, exploring him with her tongue at the same time. Without missing a beat, she reached behind her back to unfasten her bra and let it fall away as she freed her arms from it.

O'Donnell's eyes widened as he took in the sight of her breasts, milky white in the street lit dark, their dark tips tight and erect in her own excitement. The pleasure was almost too much for him after his prolonged abstinence as she continued, and with a grunt he guided her to stand. Standing himself, he picked her up by her buttocks and sat her on the edge of the desk. Slowly, he slid his hands down her thighs as he lowered to his own knees.

As he fell to kneel, Cassie pulled aside her panties to reveal herself. Before allowing his face to fall forward, he took in the sight of her.

The dark patch of trimmed but full hair against her pale skin and the enticing folds beneath that he set first his sights then mouth on.

She writhed against his face as he worked at her flesh with lips and tongue, sounding out her own pleasure as her fingers brushed and clasped in his hair. His hands kneaded her thighs and, feeling only nylon, he slowly moved them higher until he grasped her flesh. By then she'd seemingly had all she could handle herself and, clasping his head, she eased him up to kiss her.

Lips and tongues meshed and he didn't think he could wait any longer when she pushed him back to the chair, ripped the clasps of her suspenders off and pulled the underwear down to fall to her ankles. Stepping to him and out of the cloth at her feet at the same time, she put one foot by his thigh before repeating the motion on the opposite side and lifted herself from the floor, the chair giddily spinning. Then, ever so slowly, she eased herself onto him, maintaining the same speed until there was no more of him.

Even then she pushed down until there was an absolute lack of doubt that she had all of him. Then her eyes, which had been closed throughout, flew open and, for a moment, they simply stared at one another.

He searched her eyes, his gaze darting back and forth between their dark centres, hers held straight and true, as if seeing into him rather than looking at him. She was so close he could taste her hot breath as her bosom rose and fell against him ever faster, their breath mingling and fuelling each other's lust.

Behind it all, the same acrid taste and stench.

Fingers grasping the back of his head, Cassie yanked his face to hers as she bucked wildly atop him before he knew what was happening. He rose to meet her as they clashed. Their motions were sharp and deep, their mouths not leaving one another's, their tongues as wild. Breath and sound became as one. His hands clawed at her naked back as she ripped open his shirt and the blazing, sweaty tips of her breasts slid across his chest.

Letting out an almost animal groan, Cassie leant back, her long nails biting into his shoulders before they raked across his chest as she pulled herself back to him, hair springing. Her nails clawed down his arms to his hands. Pulling them up, she pressed his fingers to her breasts, prompting him to firmly knead them.

His eyes screwed closed of their own volition as pain and pleasure mingled and sensation took over as he neared climax.

"Look at me," she gasped against his face.

As if at her command, his eyelids flew open.

O'Donnell yelled at the wrinkled face that confronted him. With that same recognition came the source of the bitter reek that had been there the whole time, ignored when Cassie had been before him.

The old crone was astride him, scrawny legs holding onto him no matter how he bucked and pushed. She was bereft of her stained night-gown, but the smell of urine and other filth was worse than ever.

His hands fell from the sacs of flesh drooping from her bone-lined ribs.

Her eyes were missing and the orifices poured blood down her face.

"Once you see, you cannot unsee. You cannot unsee! Cannot unsee!"

He flailed his balled fists at that corpse-like face, but still he could not escape. Her spindly fingers slapped his punches aside before falling to the sides of his head and capturing him in a vice grip, thumbs pressing on his eyes with such intensity he though they would burst.

"Your friend will never see. But I will help you to see, O'Donnell! You… You shall become Enlightened!"

Hands slipping over his skull, she turned her thumbs to slip the clawed nails on her thumbs between his eyelids and pushed.

O'Donnell screamed.

SEVEN

WAKING with a deep gasp of air as if he'd been drowning, O'Donnell sprung into a seated position. His lungs gulped hungrily for the stale oxygen of his office. In complete confusion, he searched his face with his hands, then his surrounds with his eyes upon finding them intact.

He was still in the Goth club. Alone and on the floor.

Walking down the stairway with heavy feet and a light head, his body stiff from laying on the cold floor for what was apparently an extended time, he found he was completely alone. The club was empty. No patrons. No staff. No Enlightened.

Stumbling out the front door, he was assaulted by bright, migraine-inducing daylight.

The door slammed shut behind him, pulled closed by a heavy-handed closing mechanism that left him cringing in pain from the noise.

After finding his bearings, O'Donnell managed to limp to his car, working the kinks out of his limbs and the blood back in them. He attempted glancing around for any sighting of the people who had obviously drugged him last night. He both hoped and feared he would see Cassie among the faces around him, but there was not a single familiar face among the pedestrians that gave him a wide berth, eying his strange and dishevelled attire.

The sun and his brain conspiring against him, he quickly gave that idea up and lamented the fact he had chosen to park so far away. When surveilling, it was ideal. With a drugged hangover however... Well, until this day he had yet to experience such a thing, but it was proving to be the worst morning after of his life.

As the hatchback came into view, light glinting from its polished windows, he raised his hand to shield his eyes and his stride broke. He'd been wishing for a hat and remembered the discarded coat and hat on the stool. If they hadn't held emotional value, he would have contemplated leaving them behind, such was his discomfort.

Digging in his pocket for the keys, he planned to drive to the club's doorstep and see if there was some other means of entry. He knew without a doubt he'd heard the heavy door lock behind him after he'd left, but perhaps there was a back way. They had left him there alone after all. He had no idea what that, or the stage show they had put on, meant. If they had meant him harm, though, they'd had ample opportunity.

Settling into the driver's seat, O'Donnell leant for the glove compartment to retrieve his sunglasses and froze. The sunglasses were sitting on the passenger seat in their cloth bag. Neatly arranged atop his hat and oiled stockman's coat.

Forcing what little saliva he had around his mouth, he swallowed, hand poised over the sunglasses.

They had taken his keys from his pocket, nothing more. Given that Cassie could get in and out of his car, that was no big mystery. It was a simple but effective strategy. Or would have been if he was not aware of it.

Cassie wanted him to think they cared for him.

Hand falling on the sunglasses, the plastic within creaked as he squeezed. Just as the Crone had squeezed his face and eyeballs before—

O'Donnell sent the hat, coat and glasses tumbling to the passenger footwell. He'd had enough. Slamming the car into gear, he made his way home. Not to his office, but home.

It was a three-hour drive normally, but he took his time, stopping to fuel both the car and himself, though stopping at the service station roadhouse dredged up images of Judy and sapped him mentally. The car had had about to run dry. He could have gone without, he'd told himself, but once he'd smelled the food and started eating found he was much the same.

While his energy levels crept up, his mood remained mired in the depths of Gateway and the dead woman until the familiar landmarks signalling his return into home territory began to crop up. Coming home always eased his mind, and no matter how long he'd lived in the suburbs, this was undoubtedly home.

Using his key, he let himself into the house after taking off his boots. He grinned as a familiar warmth swelled in his chest. Everything was exactly where it always had been.

In his old room, stripping down to his boxers, he slid into his old bed. Every muscle in his body was tense as he eased into it, but as he pulled the covers up and his body fell into place in the old indentations, it all fell away.

As he was about to fall sleep, the vision of the Crone came back to him. He threw his eyes open, breathing sharply until he could drive the invading image away and finally nod off once more.

The sound of the curtains being thrown open and streaming sunlight woke him. Like the bed, the light and warmth through the window was a familiar and comforting sight.

"Morning, sunshine," his mother said, smiling.

"Morning, Mum," he said, giving her a half smile.

Perching on the edge of the double bed, she frowned. "You all right, love?" She always knew when he was off.

With a nod, he rubbed the sleep from his eyes to hide them from her as he sat up.

She nodded back in her knowing way, not buying his story for a second, but knowing also that he'd be out with it on his own time. She'd always been good that way.

She indicated the folded clothing at the foot of the bed. "You know the next rodeo's not for another couple of months."

He nodded in response, silent. "Needed it for a fancy dress." Neither he, nor his mother from her expression, felt the humour he had intended.

"I'll fix us some breakfast, shall I," she said, and left him be.

Putting on his usual home visit clothes, he joined his mother in the kitchen, sitting opposite her at the breakfast bar on the same stools he used to as a teenager, many times as sullen as he was now.

The ritual had been the same. His mother would make them something to eat, they would eat in silence and he would soak in the well-worn comfort of his old clothes, his mother and the house. Then he would unburden himself as they smoked together outside. The irony was never lost on him that his mother would have issues with other's smoking and smoked herself. She kept her smoking to a minimum though. Always had. Three a day. Never more. Never fewer.

His father had practically been the Marlboro Man. Despite Cassie's inference that he was dead – though O'Donnell had often wished it on the man in his youth – he was alive and well, if a little worse for wear.

Taking his own and his mother's coffee mugs outside, O'Donnell wiped the remnants of the toast and eggs from the corners of his mouth with the pad of his thumb before lighting up. His mother joined him, giving him a look as smoke wafted in through the sliding door before she could close it.

He offered to light her cigarette with his Zippo, but she waved him off as usual. She didn't like the taste, she said. He always claimed to forget, his manners dictating that he offer anyway. Manners had been drummed into him.

Taking in a deep breath—again as he always did, no matter if the subject had been a girl, issues with his father, applying for the police force—he held it as he decided how best to approach his latest predicament requiring the guidance of his mother's steady, analytical mind. Despite that his father had been the stricter of the two, he had also been the passionate one. Which was how he had ended off in The States with some young cowgirl, the latest in a long procession.

"I'm seeing someone," his mother said before he could speak.

O'Donnell's lips closed before opening again.

"Did you have anything to say, or were you going to make fish faces all morning?"

"That's... That's great, Mum."

"Is it?" She seemed genuinely curious at her own question, her confusion on the matter written on her face.

He couldn't unburden himself on her now. Not with something so heavy. This was not like when Kelly went with Robbie when they were teenagers and broken his heart. Not that they had ever been an item. Or even like when he had caught his father making out with a young woman in pigtails and a red gingham shirt at a rodeo, like they were teenagers. His father had urged him not to disclose what he'd seen.

"It is," he said. "Of course it is."

And he meant it. His mother had been alone long before his father had left, which had been not long after the incident with the pigtailed woman. They hadn't spoken since, his father blaming O'Donnell for ratting him out. The truth was his mother had found out herself. O'Donnell never had been able to reconcile whether that had been better or worse than if he'd told her, and he never did ask how she had come about the discovery.

"It really is, Mum," O'Donnell said in answer to her screwed up face. "I've been telling you for years you should date. I worry about you all alone here."

Her expression ironed out to a dead stare, her best "don't you dare" look that he would often get.

"I didn't mean—"

"I'll have you know I was a better shot than your father ever was with a rifle, so I can take care of myself."

"That's not what I—"

"And I was always the one that took care of all the rodents and creepy crawlies. Not to mention that snake!"

The creature had slithered into the house one summer night, giving them all a fright, though least of all his mother. She had softly, yet firmly, told the two men of the house to stay still as she had crept off for the shotgun.

O'Donnell now mirrored her earlier look, drawing it out. "Finished?"

She sipped her coffee by way of answer.

"You're evading. You forget, I get my detective skills from you. And I'm very patient."

"You get that from me as—"

"So, who is this gentleman caller? And do I need to wait up late with the snake killer on the porch?"

O'Donnell was fairly certain the weapon had become legendary in and around town.

Peering over her mug, she answered him. "Vincent."

"Vincent Azzini? The butcher?"

"Please do not make any crass remarks based on his profession."

"Oh, Mum!" O'Donnell's face screwed up. "Is that what you and the ladies talk about over bridge?"

She slapped his arm. "I do *not* play bridge!"

They chuckled together.

"I'm happy for you, Mum. Really. If I remember correctly, he was a nice bloke."

"Still is." Her smile was open and reached every corner of her face. It had been a while since he had seen her like that. "But you didn't come down here to talk about my love life. What's got your knickers in a twist?"

Seeing his mother like that he definitely couldn't ruin the moment. Not that he had intended to reveal all of the details to her, gaining her wisdom and comfort as indirectly as he could.

"Nothing," he said. "I just wanted to see you."

"Oh, pull the other one. Come on. Out with it." He shook his head. "James Douglas O'Donnell, I was never fooled by you when you were a boy, and I'm not fooled by you now that you're a grown arse man."

"It's nothing, Mum. Woman troubles, that's all." A half lie, he told himself.

"Don't tell me you've gotten some poor girl up the duff?" She joked. "I suppose it's the only way I would expect to see a grandchild."

"Very funny. And no. It's not important. A case that's got me wound up, and dating troubles at the same time. I don't want to spoil your good mood."

She bought it. Or wanted to. He was a big boy, and he could understand her wanting to not have any drama in her life. She'd had plenty enough of that already.

"Are you staying the night?" she asked, glancing at her watch.

It was a new watch. Not the tarnished old thing she'd worn for years saying "it was only a watch". He did his best to conceal his smile.

"If it's okay. I mean I can go if you—"

"Don't be daft. We were going to meet at the pub for dinner and a drink. Takes him a while to freshen up after work. I was thinking... I was thinking you might want to come?"

"I'd love to."

With her smile returning and a nod, his mother left him outside to go and call her beau.

O'Donnell lit up another cigarette and tried to take his mind of cults and murderous geriatrics. A few beers would definitely help, he decided.

———

Refreshed if not unburdened as he'd wanted, O'Donnell pulled up out the front of the office. Normally of a weekday morning there was hardly any traffic. Today was no exception. There was a renewed spring in his step, which was the exact reason he had and always went home, for a recharge.

Images of batteries and toy robots, Cassie Lawler, and the Crone flashed through his mind.

His foot slipped as he attempted to hop up the step of the gutter around his car. Seeing his mother laugh and share stories with Vincent had been oddly more therapeutic than he'd thought it could have been, but the oddity of this case, the murder... the Crone... Everything about it was too much to dispel.

Cupping a hand over his eyes, he glanced through the dirty glass into his office. Nothing untoward. Twisting his key in the deadlock, he gave the door a push only for it to skid and shudder to a halt. Something was jammed beneath it.

After battling with the door and offending mail, tearing the topmost letter half to shreds, O'Donnell was in a worse mood. He was adamant that he would not lose the entire calming effect of his visit, even as he flipped through the pile of bills. Talking himself out of making another useless call to the postal service to tell them not to put his mail under the door, he noticed the torn telephone bill envelope. Something was scrawled across the crumpled paper.

Smoothing it out, he forgot all about home, his mother and Vincent, and happy times. He slammed the door closed and got back into his car and drove to meet Robbie after he had given him a terse call. The note on the torn shred of envelope had been simple and with no signature, but he had known immediately who it was from. The note said:

The old bird has flown the coop.

When he arrived at Rowville, Robbie was already there, sitting on the wall where the girl had been in almost the exact same spot. O'Donnell wondered for a moment if the bricks were polished from all the rumps over the years, inviting others to sit because of the difference in shade, or merely a coincidence. He was starting to think there was no such thing any more.

The look on Robbie's face meant only one thing and the cigarette was already hanging out of the packet as O'Donnell held it out. Robbie snatched it and the Zippo and lit up.

"De ja *fucking* vu?" Robbie said as he exhaled a cloud, nodding at O'Donnell as he stared up at the dark, drab building. "I know I have it. And it's fucking me in the head. Right fucking here!" He stabbed the side of his temple several times. Hard enough that it would have caused a person to have a headache from the pain. "They're going to chuck me off as lead investigator if I don't get answers on how the bitch escaped. Can you fucking believe it?"

"Going that good then, is it?" O'Donnell's voice was flat. This didn't bode well.

"Understatement of the fucking century, mate. You have no idea. So far all we got are Jack and shit. Jack had already left town, now fucking Jill went after him. And I'm the stupid prick left tumbling down the hill."

O'Donnell gave Robbie a look.

"Sorry. Kids. Nursery rhymes. You'll get it. One day."

O'Donnell laughed. "You sound like my mum."

There was no way he was going to tell Robbie about his mum and Vincenzo The Butcher, as they'd called him back in the day. They'd made up countless stories about his mafia connections and the nefarious uses of his shop.

"Fuck." O'Donnell sighed out smoke from his nostrils. "Did you find out who she was?"

Robbie shook his head. "If I don't get some answers though, Jimmy boy, my arse is right royally fucked. And I'm talking Johnny Holmes fucked!"

"What? Along with your head?"

Robbie gave a blank stare.

Searching his friends face, O'Donnell saw it was true. Whatever pressures were on him it was showing. Robbie looked tired. Drained. Was his colour off? The Crone's warning echoed from his memory.

Never to be enlightened. He shook the morbid thoughts and the old woman's babbling off.

"Whatever I can do, Robbie, let me know."

Robbie sucked on his lower lip. "First I need you to be fucking straight with me. Have you got any new information on this cocksucker at all? Anything from his girlfriend?"

O'Donnell shook his head, lifting his shoulders slightly before letting them drop. Robbie already thought Mortimer was the leader of Gateway and the Enlightened. In terms of actual information, it wasn't a lie.

He wondered if he was trying to convince himself.

Robbie wrenched his head to the side before swinging it back toward O'Donnell, the heel of his palm pressed above his eye, cigarette raised between his clawed fingers. "All right. Two crazy cult fuckers from the same hospital is too much of a coincidence for me. We go in hard and fast. Get these head crackers to crack. Show them how it's really done. You ready?"

He was.

Or at least he thought he was.

O'Donnell's money had been on the doctor who had shown him the tape, a suspicion that appeared confirmed when they were told the doctor was now AWOL. The hospital had not heard from him in nearly a week. So Robbie started busting down doors, figuratively, calling out as many senior administrators and staff as he could in an attempt to find the man.

When that failed, he started blasting them about how they could have let a senile old woman escape them.

"Believe me," an older woman from administration said, her face as gruff as her voice as she looked around the room, glaring accusation down her nose at her colleagues. "We're trying to figure that out ourselves."

"You do understand that this woman is dangerous, don't you?" A few of the staff laughed. Robbie slammed his palm on the table. "You think I'm fucking joking? She broke into his office," he stabbed his thumb at O'Donnell, "and tried to stab him with a butcher's knife as big as your arm. She got the jump on me and it took several trained men to get her off again. She's associated with a cult who has already murdered one woman. That we know of."

No one laughed after that.

"Do you have any ideas how she escaped?" O'Donnell added in a calm voice after Robbie gave him the signal with a glance. Time for good cop.

"None of us can figure it out," one of the orderlies said.

"Pull the other one, mate. What about your security?" Robbie glanced around the room. "Did they find any clues or have any theories as to how both Nathan Mortimer and this Jane Doe both escaped your facility? Is there no fucking tape from cameras?"

Every man and woman shook their head.

O'Donnell squinted. "Could someone have... helped them? From the inside?"

Now the gathered staff looked about furtively, suspicious with the implanted idea that one of their colleague's was a secret cult member. It would either provide Robbie a result by flushing the perpetrator out or send the hospital into complete lockdown. It was a risk, but with little to go on, it was one they had to take.

"Someone had to have helped the old woman, for sure," a young woman said.

Robbie turned on her like a shark smelling blood. He moved closer, but would let O'Donnell keep talking. O'Donnell was the smooth talker, he'd always said.

The bullish older administrator glared at the younger woman, but now she'd opened the floodgates she wasn't able to stop. She either feared the law more than her bosses, or she was terrified of the cult and wanted whoever might be around her found and arrested. Luckily, she had not thought that last fear through. If that were the case, she may have feared reprisal and clammed up instead.

"Why do you say that?" O'Donnell said, keeping his voice low.

She looked from O'Donnell, to Robbie, and quickly back, licking her lips in a quick motion. "Well, she would have had to, wouldn't she? How else could she get down out of that hole?"

Robbie and O'Donnell glanced at each other with the same look. Someone wasn't telling them the whole story.

"What hole?" O'Donnell said

"Show me. Now," Robbie said, turning to the now red-faced senior woman.

As much as she protested, Robbie fought back, threatening to bring all manner of hell down on her and the hospital along with slipping to the media that they'd lost not one but two dangerous criminals tied to a cult.

She eventually led them to a common area for patients. Robbie and O'Donnell looked about but could see no obvious means of escape. All the windows were covered with both bars and mesh. They didn't even look like they opened.

"Show them," the woman grunted.

Two of the orderlies moved to a whiteboard at the far wall. One proceeded to roll it aside, the other moving to a low book case behind it and sliding it aside with squealing scratches on the floor.

Mouth hanging open, O'Donnell stepped toward a hole in the double brick wall big enough to walk through. Unable to believe it, he poked his head out, clutching at the surprisingly intact and firmly held edge. A breeze whipped at his hair and clothes as he inspected the edges of the cut-out. They were on the third floor and it was a long way down. He pulled his head back in and stepped back to inspect the damage.

Near the clean plaster on the interior, the hole was neat. As it moved outward, the first line of brick was likewise clean, as if some precision instrument had been used to cut to that precise depth. Looking outside again and down, O'Donnell saw a mess of plaster, mortar and brick on the ground.

Backing away from the dizzying sight, he was led outside by Robbie and one of the orderlies, grabbing his good camera from the car before heading to where the pile of rubble sat. Robbie hunched down and looked the mess over.

"Jesus. Someone cut a circle in the wall and pushed it out."

O'Donnell lifted his camera and zoomed on the hole above. The bricks on the outer wall were a jagged mess, some still half hanging, pushed outward like snaggled teeth. He fired off a few shots, then of the pile behind him.

He stared at the broken, painted plasterboard glued to bricks in large broken pieces. Not a single drop of blood on or around the bricks and plaster. No signs of any tooling either. No cuts. No gouges. Definitely no explosion. There had been no chemical smell inside apart from antiseptic cleaner. No burnt smell, and no charring on the paper or paint over the plasterboard.

The only thing that stuck out was the multi-hued lines on the edges of the plaster.

"What is that?" O'Donnell said, rubbing his finger on the line work. It was waxy, smelt familiar.

"Crayon," Robbie said, naming the stuff from sight alone.

"We don't allow the patients to have pens or pencils," the orderly said, more as a distraction to himself, O'Donnell thought. The man stood with hands on hips, shaking his head as he looked from the bricks to the hole in the wall and back. "Too dangerous for themselves and others."

O'Donnell stood to look at the pile at his feet once more, though it didn't help make any more sense of what he was confronted with. He grabbed a piece of plasterboard with a clean, curved edge and pulled it free of the brick.

Exactly where there was now a hole in the wall, the old woman, or someone, had drawn a multi-coloured Gateway.

EIGHT

"HOW THE FUCK does an old woman manage to do something like that?" Robbie shook his head, massaging his temples in deep concentration as they sat in O'Donnell's car. "I mean, I know she was bloody strong. But this hole in the wall and Spider Man shit?" He had the passenger seat pushed all the way back so he could slouch his lanky figure in it, though his knees still touched the dash.

There had to be someone helping them. Multiple someone's as far as O'Donnell was concerned. As a group, all the staff that had been on shift that night said they'd heard nothing the night of Jane Doe's disappearance. Not even the crash of debris. Neither had any of the patients, they said.

Robbie had railed again and again. How was such a thing possible, he'd argued, accusing them all of colluding with the cults. Not getting anywhere, he had called for backup and forensics along with a warrant. If they wanted to play it that way, he was willing to take them all in as suspects.

Backup had arrived to relieve Robbie, where the gathered staff were now holed up in the meeting room. Another man guarded the pile of detritus in the yard. He had been none too pleased with that task, but Robbie had given him a direct order.

"I see these little cheap shit-boxes everywhere," Robbie said, peering around the interior of the hatchback.

"That's the point."

"You're really into this investigator stuff, huh?"

O'Donnell shrugged. Then, thinking about it, answered. "Yeah. I am actually."

"Don't you miss this?"

It took him but a brief moment of thought to answer. "No."

Robbie snorted a laugh. "Don't fucking blame you."

"What about you?"

He seemed taken aback at the question. "Me? I still love it. No matter what shit it throws at me, I'm doing good." He gave a nod after several moments, though appeared far from good.

Was he trying to convince himself, or was Robbie genuinely satisfied? They'd both gone into the job with lofty goals. Only one of them had stuck it out, and O'Donnell had learned there was a stigma around those that left early. You were either a quitter or a lifer, many would say. Robbie, O'Donnell thought, was a lifer. He would live and die on the job.

O'Donnell glanced sidelong at Robbie's clammy, off-colour skin.

Whatever their individual stances, there was no question in O'Donnell's mind whether he'd done the right thing or was still doing good. He suspected that, at least on Robbie's part, his questions were more to do with their camaraderie of old.

Or maybe it was O'Donnell that was fooling himself. He took on jobs no cop would to pay the bills. The police didn't have to capture salacious images to break up marriages and make their living. They didn't have to spy on people whose only wrongdoing was to love or desire someone other than their partner, for whatever reason. He helped people and families, like Benji's, that was true enough, but that was few and far between.

With a backhand to his arm, Robbie broke O'Donnell's introspective spiral. The forensics van was finally here. Asking him to stay clear —"You know, for official purposes," Robbie said—O'Donnell stayed with the car while the lab guys did their thing.

There weren't any cases O'Donnell had been part of that had required this level of investigation before he'd left the force. And the deepest he'd ever been was also the cause of his leaving, and then he'd been on the outside looking in. Robbie and those up the chain of command were clearly getting desperate. And with good reason. The last thing they, or anyone, needed was some cult digging in somewhere and doing who knew what. And somehow, O'Donnell didn't think Gunther was the cyanide-in-the-punch type of guy.

After an interminable wait, Robbie returned, exhausted but his expression hopeful.

"The lab guys pull up anything interesting?" O'Donnell asked as Robbie leant in the driver's window.

"Nah. Nothing stuck out. They were left scratching their heads and balls as much as we are. But I got a good feeling."

"How's that?"

Robbie gripped the top edge of the open window tight and gave the car a solid nudge. "Well if nothing sticks out then that means these bastards used something that isn't common. That could be just the lead we need to nail their arses to the wall. Anyway. You've done your fair share for the day. I can't get you a consult on this one, sorry mate, but it will go a long way. Next time. Promise."

"Cross your heart and hope to die?" O'Donnell said.

Robbie lazily motioned over his heart. "Stick a needle in my eye. Now go on." Robbie gave the roof of the small car several slaps. "Fuck off out of here."

"You don't need to tell me twice," he said, through a stifled yawn.

"You need to get off the street corners late at night," Robbie said, pointing out O'Donnell's outfit when he gave a bemused look. "You're obviously selling your arse on the streets in your old cowboy gear. Mate, if you needed money you could have said. I can get you a gig as supermarket security."

Hitting the button to raise the window, O'Donnell drove away, pulling a U-turn and flipping Robbie the finger as the car eased down the asphalt drive of the hospital.

An acrid taste built in the back of his throat as he remembered what he had said to Robbie and the Crone's words.

Cross your heart and hope to die.

Starting on the 'Inglewood' file was one of those cases that left him in a state of confusion as to what he was doing and why. There was no way he was going to use the woman's real name anywhere, despite the fact she had disclosed it during their meeting.

"You do know that I used to be a cop, right?" he'd said to her.

"I know all about your past, James," she'd said with a smirk. Unlike Cassie's, Inglewood's grin held a threat. Not even thinly veiled. "That's precisely why I chose you."

O'Donnell didn't particularly relish the idea of spying on a mobster for his wife, but it was more to do with the danger surrounding the job than the act itself. She said that her husband had been cheating on her with multiple women throughout the years but she could never prove it. And only now had she found the courage to do something about it.

"No offence, Mrs Inglewood," he'd said, still using her pseudonym. "But what makes you think he's going to let you go?"

"Because, you're going to collect more than just pictures of him with his young whores for me. Those are personal so I can hit him in the balls with it. The rest is business."

"And what are you going to do with those?"

"I'm going to blow his brains out." Her lips parted as she smiled. "Figuratively speaking, of course."

Hands gripping the steering wheel, he steeled himself for the task ahead.

"Taking on cults and now the Mob?" he muttered, shaking his head. "You must be nuts, O'Donnell."

Mrs Inglewood's story of ongoing mistreatment starting from when she was a young woman and falling in with her criminal husband without knowing, along with the thick wad of cash she had given him, were compelling reasons enough. This was not going to be like any other job, though. Which was amusing in itself given the oddities of the Mortimer case and everything that came with it. But your usual cheating spouse, while careful, did not generally expect to be followed or photographed. Nor did they retaliate with severe beatings and executions. At least usually. There were always exceptions. Either way, O'Donnell had no desire to dig his own grave.

What he had to do now was something more akin to stalking. Or true spying. He was no Double-O agent, though, and did not have the resources of one. But with the right know how, anyone could pull this off with the right motivation and careful planning.

He didn't need to capture any audio evidence and wouldn't have agreed to even attempt it if Inglewood had asked. That would require something far too invasive and bring him well within the radar of Mr Inglewood, but more importantly his guards and enforcers.

And O'Donnell did not need that.

After Mrs Inglewood had gotten O'Donnell some info, he was now set to start the preliminary scout work. His plan of attack was simple enough. Stalk Mr Inglewood and his lieutenants and plot their movements. Find intersecting points of convergence and gather as much intel as he could, both himself and a few paid colleagues in the industry so none of them could be easily spotted. All of this from a distance. He wouldn't risk using someone like Benji. He only employed the young man for simple things to throw some extra money at him when possible.

Then, once he had enough information, he would get incriminating shots for Mrs Inglewood to use in her dead man's switch of a plan and keep her husband away for good.

Or so the theory went.

"What if he kills you anyway?" he'd asked Inglewood.

"Then, one way or another, at least I'll still be free of the bastard."

The softly, softly approach worked well for cases such as this—not that he had ever had such a case to compare it to—but it made for a more tedious time. The thing the TV shows never went into was how dull real investigative work was. Most of it was sitting around watching people for hours while doing your best not to be seen and not falling asleep from sheer boredom. He wouldn't have that particular problem to worry himself with here, he mused as he glanced around.

Once he had sussed out the level of awareness of his targets, the initial adrenaline wore off and it became far more routine. Not that one could ever truly settle on such a job. Relaxing meant that you did not stick out. Being nervous around a regular mark could get one noticed, but most people did not expect to be spied on. Not so with Mr Inglewood and his people.

It had helped that O'Donnell had a lot on his mind to distract him.

Things had not progressed on what the police were now calling the Enlightened Gateway cult, merging the two together. The labs had presented nothing of note on the section of wall at Rowville. No chemical residue. No signs of cutting. There was no external sign that the wall had been drilled and then pulled free. Every possible method would have drawn attention.

And the way in which the wall pieces—of which one piece of plaster had mysteriously vanished into O'Donnell's pocket—was reconstructed in their lab suggested that the cut-out had been to almost laser precision on the outer edge of the drawing. The only sense that could be made of it all was that this was some elaborate scheme to give the cults claims of powers validity, which again pointed to inside involvement at the hospital.

It was far too elaborate for O'Donnell.

"Well that's because you want to see the good in people," Robbie had said. "We've done a lot of training on cults since you left and a lot of them are just scams for making money. Pseudo-religions are popping up all the time. I mean, Christ, that mob all those Hollywood stars belong to have been here since before we were born! But they've been ruled to be a religion by the Australian High Court so we can't even blink at them."

O'Donnell wasn't so sure. Why go to the lengths of murder if all it came down to was essentially a publicity stunt? Robbie had argued that it may have come down to something of a turf war. Maybe there really were two groups, or internal factions, and they were butting heads. They probably even bought their own BS, he said, and thought that Mortimer was some sort of messiah and they were waging a holy war of some kind.

Slipping on the roofing tiles, O'Donnell decided to keep his mind firmly rooted in the present, along with his footing. He stepped on the edges of the waved concrete slabs so as not to crack any. Reaching the peak of the roof, he opened the duffle at his side, thick rubber feet on its base to stop it from sliding away. Taking out a dark canvas sheet with rubber backing, he spread it out then lay down and pulled the camera from the bag.

Not needing the use of a huge zoom lens, O'Donnell had to reach out to a contact in the paparazzi. It was slimy line of work, but the man had proven useful in scoring some jobs, and gladly leant O'Donnell a spare, compatible lens and something called an extender, which basically provided an extra level of zoom.

Carefully fixing the lens onto the extender after first locking that to the camera, he eased the massive barrel down and peered out over the expanse of similar pyramid-like structures interspersed with greenery, and focused on his target.

The house he had chosen after scoping out the hill-top street was empty during the day, and the pitch of the roof and its angle afforded him an excellent vantage of the Inglewood house. With the help of the lens, he was well and truly out of sight, unless they were searching the rooftops with binoculars. The other danger was of the rooftop itself. While it was no phobia, O'Donnell was not a fan of heights.

Especially when that height was above two storeys.

As time and the hard roof wore on his knees and elbows, he dug in and waited.

Inglewood had told him there would be a significant meeting

happening today. She was being shipped off on a day retreat, an insistent gift from her husband. Whatever was going down was going to be big and all the players would be converging on their house. To say the dwelling was modest would not be an outright lie. It appeared very much like the other homes around it, only bigger and more fortified. Each window was fitted with roller shutters. There was a tall brick and metal fence across the frontage and the side and back fences had been extended taller. There also appeared to be security cameras dotted around the structure.

Cars dribbled in one by one, their arrivals spaced out. O'Donnell held down the trigger, the camera doing the work for him as men climbed out.

There were several thuggish types walking the perimeter of the house with two stationed at the gate, probably more out back, making him doubly glad he had chosen the safest approach. He had arrived much earlier than the meeting's appointed time, had watched a man drive Mrs Inglewood away. To her credit, she had not searched the area for him and was inconspicuous. Years of living the life, no doubt. The only people who behaved like that were people who were always paranoid.

It gave him some comfort by her story being given credibility. He hadn't doubted her so much as the fact he needed the extra conviction rather than the cash to make it worth risking his life and safety, and by extension hers.

Despite that he'd made himself as comfortable as possible, arms and legs nestled in the deep valleys created by the roofing, cramps began creeping in. Once the meeting was under way, he would climb down and stretch his legs, but not before. He hadn't come all this way and gone to these lengths to miss a single detail. Any one of the people involved could lead to a potential—

Ice filled his veins as the latest arrival eased out of a silver Mercedes, wild hair a halo in the sunlight. O'Donnell's gripped the camera tight as he fought to keep the camera steady and the viewfinder fixed. The man ambled to another, shook their hand and chatted casually but did not show their face.

"Come on you bastard," O'Donnell croaked after his long-held silence. "Turn the fuck around, you—"

An amused grin on his face, Gunther turned to glance around before heading into the house.

O'Donnell's finger was still frozen on the shutter button long after he was out of sight, the camera still madly clicking off shot after shot.

———

Arms and legs jittering from the strain of remaining in the same position for a sustained time—he had no idea how long as he hadn't dared check his watch in case he missed anything—O'Donnell did his best to relax his muscles. Trying only made it worse, however. The camera weighed heavily on his arms, despite the fact it was balanced on the ridge cap. His chest felt crushed from the pressing on the peaks of concrete. He was almost certain he would turn out like a toasted sandwich with a pattern of red lines embedded in him.

Gripping the camera tight, he tried to think of all the scenarios that could possibly lead to Gunther being here, but he could think of nothing logical. Drugs? Money laundering? Smuggling? None of it added up in his mind. Was Robbie right? Was Gateway nothing more than a money-making scheme? Had O'Donnell been reading too much into events, with the Crone and Rowville? With Cassie.

Blinking rapidly, he did his best to shift higher against the crest of the roof as the front door of the house opened. He made full use of the camera's functionality, firing off shots in rapid succession, using only two or three for those that didn't interest him. It occurred to O'Donnell that the last to arrive may also be the last to leave, so he changed tack and he switched to using a single exposure to a man until his personal target emerged.

Mr Inglewood's himself ushered Gunther out, smiling genially. O'Donnell's finger jerked to capture images at every movement of the two men, wanting to capture both their faces.

Gunther turned with a smirk after shaking hands with Mr Inglewood and heading for his car and Mr Inglewood returning to the safety of his home as his men watched the procession of vehicles and the surrounds.

Knuckles pressed into the roof tiles, he forced himself to wait long enough to see which way the silver Mercedes was heading, then leapt into action.

Adrenalin fuelling him down the ladder, O'Donnell ignored the complaints of his limbs. His face was resolute when, ladder in hand, he walked to the front of the house and was confronted by the home owner, or at least the husband.

The man glared at O'Donnell as he jumped from his car. "What the bloody hell do you think you're—"

"You think it's fucking funny do you, *mate*?" O'Donnell said, his words clipped, neck already straining from deep, angry concentration. "I come out here to do a roof restoration quote—"

"We don't need a roof restoration!"

"No shit, Sherlock." O'Donnell angrily hoisted the ladder atop the work car and strapped it down. "Next time you want to have a fucking laugh, call for a pizza, arsehole."

Slamming the door, he reversed out of the drive, narrowly missing the confused man's car, and drove off with a strained roar of the old engine.

He had to catch up to Gunther.

If he gunned it, he should be able to intersect Gunther's path and follow him. What he didn't count on, as he turned onto the main road and searched the road in front of him, his eyes and head darting back and forth as his fingers tightened on the wheel, was that his target would be driving slower than he'd expected.

About to lose all hope of catching the vehicle, he glanced into the rear-view mirror and saw that it was directly behind him. He glanced around the cabin of the car and spotted the woollen beanie and sunglasses he'd brought along as a disguise. Indicating to change from the middle to the left-most of the three lanes on the highway, he eased the borrowed work car smoothly in between vehicles with one hand, pulling the beanie on with the other.

As O'Donnell slowed to a less than respectable crawl, Gunther passed him, and O'Donnell turned his head, pretending to rummage for something in the glovebox.

From the corner of his eye, he watched Gunther's older model Mercedes sail past, the man not once glancing his way, though O'Donnell pushed the large sunglasses onto his face regardless.

The blast of a horn from behind O'Donnell had Gunther's gaze fall on him momentarily before moving to the impatient driver in the black V6 thundered past, yelling obscenities and flipping O'Donnell off. Ignoring the man, O'Donnell wondered if he had been made.

Waiting for another vehicle to pull up behind the aggressive black machine and its driver, O'Donnell pulled back into the middle lane and matched speed. The black car sped off into the right lane and pulled away at speed with a growl, leaving a single car between him and Gunther. The V6's windows were tinted, so O'Donnell hadn't been able to make out Gunther through the car to see if he'd been spooked. Now with the Mercedes in clear view through the car in front of him, he saw Gunther shaking his head at the V6, but otherwise appeared to be driving casually, unaware he was being tailed.

NINE

O'DONNELL'S HEAD WAS REELING.

What was Gunther doing at the Inglewood house with all those criminals? Amongst them all, Gunther stuck out like a porcupine in a nudist colony, as O'Donnell's father would say. As a child, he thought it was amusing when his father said it. After his father abandoned them, he resented it.

Now? He didn't think much of it still, he decided, but it described the man he was following—along with his father—all too well. Pricks the both of them. Though he doubted his father could lead a cult let alone be responsible for murder.

He would have to call Robbie and tell him where Gunther ended up. He had no choice. If anything else happened and he didn't report it, O'Donnell wouldn't be able to forgive himself, never mind his oldest friend not talking to him anymore. And he would be an even bigger pariah in the eyes of the police. It would put a dent in his business, no doubt about that, but it would be a bigger bruise on his already battered ego. He had stopped thinking of himself as a cop long ago. That wouldn't make it any easier, though.

Brain tingling with fear as Gunther pulled down a less busy and familiar main road, O'Donnell pulled over into a parking spot and let a few cars in between them.

"Shit," O'Donnell said as he glanced around.

It was the back end of the road leading to mansion Cassie had driven to.

He swerved out in front of a car, its horn blaring as the car came to a shuddering halt. O'Donnell ignored the person and sped up. He could see the roof of the Mercedes up ahead. As it drew closer to the mansion, O'Donnell's pulse quickened.

He let out a sigh as Gunther passed the house. Then swallowed his breath as the Mercedes pulled over in front of the neighbouring home.

Steadying his grip on the wheel, forcing his fingers loose, O'Donnell continued past the man, glancing sidelong as Gunther exited the Mercedes, strode around to the boot and opened it, retrieving what appeared to be a plastic shopping bag. As O'Donnell watched in the wing mirror, Gunther hopped up the gutter and swung the bag casually as he headed for the mansion.

O'Donnell had no choice but to continue forward and double back, park further out or back up the road he had come from.

His fist struck the steering wheel. "Fuck!"

Hiding wasn't the issue. He couldn't call Robbie now. Whatever the connection between Gunther and Cassie, he couldn't believe it was anything other than rivalry. Had he been wrong this whole time? Or was he simply afraid that he might be?

Swinging the car toward the gutter, the tyre hitting it with a squeal, O'Donnell's palms slapped at the wheel as he spun it and waited to execute his U-turn.

Gritting his teeth, he chastised himself for acting like a teenage fool. He had always done it. Always. His mother said he wore his big heart on his sleeve, wrapped in cheese cloth. It was hanging there, hidden, but slowly bleeding out. But she also said he had cheese for brains when it came to girls, either picking the wrong ones or making the wrong moves, saying the wrong things.

"I guess I'm not like Dad when it comes to that, huh?" he had said once when lamenting the breakup of his then girlfriend.

"And for that," his mother had said, waving a cigarette between her fingers, "I am eternally grateful!"

Pushing concern for the borrowed vehicle out of his mind, O'Donnell pushed the engine of the ute, feeling it tilt as it turned. Tools crashed and the large ladder he had hastily secured slid with a metallic grind, but stayed put. The last thing he needed now was for the thing to go flying free and under another car. If he hadn't already by driving around like a maniac, that would definitely draw Gunther's attention.

As he fought the steering to straighten the ute, there was no sign of Gunther. He must have gone inside. Slowing, O'Donnell passed the house, staring out the driver's window, and continued up the road before pulling up. Using the ladder as an excuse, he jumped out and took his time in straightening up both it and the tools that had flown about. It would give him a good chance to spy out the mansion and also to calm himself. He was letting this get personal, and getting emotional would risk everything, especially if Gunther was tied to Mr Inglewood.

With a sigh, he climbed back into the car. Cranking the driver's window down, he angled the mirror toward the house and waited.

He didn't like it. He didn't like what it implied. Was Robbie right and the Enlightened and Gateway were one and the same? Or, as O'Donnell's suspected, perhaps tangentially linked? Whatever the case, it didn't bode well for Cassie or the investigation as a whole. It all left a bad taste in his mouth.

Turning to his bag on the passenger seat, he reached to pull out his cigarettes. A flash of stained white cloth and oily grey hair framing a papery face in the passenger side mirror stopped his hand and breath.

Throwing open the door, O'Donnell leapt from the car and ran around the front, breath ragged.

Nothing.

But moments ago, the Crone had been standing there on the grassy nature strip by the ute, smiling at him.

Hands shaking, O'Donnell strode to the back of the vehicle and looked up and down the road. There was no sign of her. No sign of anyone. Grass rustling under his shoes, he pulled open the passenger door and rummaged through his bag and ripped out the cigarettes. He dropped it and the lighter in the rough direction of the bag and slammed the door shut.

Pinching the bridge of his nose, O'Donnell leant against the cabin with his forearms and hung his head, cigarette hanging from his lips and streaming smoke back up at him. Slowly lifting and shaking his head, he stared at the house and finished his cigarette before climbing back into the car and dropped into the seat.

Hanging his head back, he forced his muscles to ease.

———

Gunther loped out of the gate with a casual stride. Whatever he had taken in with him, he was empty handed now.

O'Donnell eased up from his slouch and dropped his third cigarette, half finished, from the window. Gunther whistled and pulled his keys from his pocket, his shaggy hair waving as he nodded to his tune.

Starting the ute's engine, O'Donnell waited for Gunther to pull away and ducked down as Gunther turned his car around and passed by.

He pulled out slowly behind another car and flexed his hands around the wheel, willing his pulse to slow. He needed to stay calm. If he continued the way he had earlier, Gunther would definitely make him.

His slowing heart leapt into his throat as the car in front of him jerked to a stop, horn blaring, O'Donnell's arms ramrod straight against the wheel as he slammed on his own brakes.

Gunther's Mercedes screeched as it arced across the road in a fast U-turn, burning rubber in the opposite direction. As it passed, Gunther smirked as he waved casually at O'Donnell, as if they were old friends.

"Fuck!"

Cursing, O'Donnell grappled with the steering of the old ute to bring it into a three-point turn, blocking the road and earning him several angry blasts of horns as he gave chase.

Gunther was toying with him. He had known he was there the whole time, there was no way that he hadn't with the rookie mistakes O'Donnell had made. He should have called Robbie.

"Fucking fuck!" O'Donnell yelled, slapping the steering wheel with a hand.

There were no cars ahead of him, but the Mercedes was a distant shimmer of metallic silver. A car pulled out of a driveway, and O'Donnell grit his teeth, pummelling at the wheel with both fists. If Gunther was smart, he would make a left somewhere and lose O'Donnell, who would be none the wiser. Until he either caught up to the car ahead or it diverted, he would have no way to know until it was too late.

The old engine spluttered as O'Donnell pressed down on the gas and pushed it. It wasn't well maintained, and he had no idea if it would cope.

O'Donnell yanked the sunglasses from his face as a shimmer, like heat haze off the road, swam across the asphalt between the ute and the car in front of it, moving with them. O'Donnell rubbed his eyes and eyed the distortion.

"What the fuck?"

O'Donnell screamed, jumping as the shimmer raced with dizzying speed toward him, melting through the front of the car and windshield and coalescing into a gossamer figure in the passenger seat that quickly solidified.

Gunther grinned wide. "Nice to see you again, Mr O'Donnell."

O'Donnell lashed out with his fist, acting on instinct, but too late to realise that the man wasn't fully corporeal. His fist passed through the man, connecting with nothing but air.

Gunther's wide smile grew, his face and body distorting as the skin on his body festered, his clothing mouldering until he was naked. Gunther's mouth widened into something unnatural, his teeth yellowing, elongating and sharpening. Horns the same off-white shade of those fangs sprang from the decaying forehead, spraying blood and pus as the creature lunged, twisting its head to aim at O'Donnell's throat.

Lifting his arms in self-defence, he slammed on the breaks, waiting to be torn apart.

Nothing.

He pried his arms from his face, an echo of laughter fading. The cabin was empty. O'Donnell slammed the ute into park, yanked the hand brake and spilled from the door, fighting the seatbelt that snagged at his arm. Backing away, he stared into the dark interior, hands shaking.

Light flashed as an explosion rent the air, throwing up billowing flames and debris from the direction of the mansion.

O'Donnell shot a glance back up the road, but the Mercedes was gone. The only cars were those stopping and, like him, staring at the black smoke rising from the remains of the mansion.

"Fucking Christ, Jimmy!"

O'Donnell slumped against the ute and hung his head. "I know, Robbie. I—"

"No! I don't think you *do* fucking know!" Robbie looked back to the mansion, still smoking as the fire crews worked at putting it out, and shook his head. He pulled out a packet of cigarettes and lit up, not offering one to O'Donnell.

He was back on them again. Or, If O'Donnell knew Robbie, he had been smoking all this time but had hidden it, from himself as much as Kelly. Robbie was the type of person who believed out of sight was out of mind and could fool himself as much as anyone else. O'Donnell also knew that it also meant if he was no longer hiding it, things were bad. Real bad.

"I didn't have time to call you or I would have," O'Donnell said. "If I had any fucking idea what Gunther was planning, don't you think I would have?"

"I dunno, mate," Robbie said, smoke streaming from his nostrils as the shake of his head continued. "Would you? I used to think so... but now?" He threw his hand up at the mansion and turned around to start pacing. He stopped as he stepped on some unnameable piece of the house and angrily kicked it away. "Fucking Jesus! Look at this mess!"

"I know you're angry—"

"Mate, I'm *way* past angry. Angry is where my balls are. I'm fucking here!" He lifted his hand to the extent of his reach and chopped the air. "So, when they come for my balls, *James*, my hands will be up here so I can't stop them. I mean... what do you want me to do? Tell them that my old mate Jimmy O'Donnell did his best?"

"We've been friends a long time, *Robert*, so I'm going to let you have that one." He straightened to stand off the side of the car and stared Robbie in the eyes, doing his best to loosen his jaw. "But if you call my integrity and ethics into question again in front of other people, we are going to have fucking problems."

Unblinking, Robbie stared right back. "Is that a fact?"

"Too fucking right it is."

Robbie held his ground, but so did O'Donnell. With a sigh, O'Donnell relaxed. Someone had to be the bigger man, he just wasn't sure that was him anymore. That Robbie wasn't at least partly right.

"I *am* doing my best. That's all any of us can do. But you tell me with a straight face that you would have suspected that prick Gunther would have pulled something like this and hell... I'll cup your balls for you and take the heat coming your way."

Robbie searched his face. Then scoffed. "You always did have a thing for my balls."

O'Donnell smirked. "Well you keep them so nicely shaved."

"Fuck off." Robbie laughed. "Fine!" He threw up his hands, then tossed his cigarette, still a third left on it. He pulled out the pack and lit another. He shook his head, fresh smoke whipping around his head. "I would have had no fucking idea the bastard would do something like this. Okay? Happy?"

O'Donnell looked to the house and shook his head. "Nowhere near happy." He glanced back to Robbie. "Any word if anyone was..."

"Not yet. Still too hot for the firies to go in and check for crispy critters." Robbie threw a hand toward the firemen in their suits. "They've got it under control so hopefully they'll get some kind of idea soon." Taking a puff, he pursed his lips as he sucked on his teeth, then spat out on the asphalt. "If what the neighbours say is true, though, the chances are high."

Glancing nervously, O'Donnell licked his lips. "What did the neighbours say?"

"Not much, but enough to know there's people here all the time, coming and going. At least a dozen at any given time."

"You think this is... what? Their headquarters?"

Robbie gave a noncommittal shrug. "It's not exactly Waco. But sure, why not? If the fuckers have money, why not have a swanky clubhouse."

"Do you still think that Gateway and the Enlightened are together after this?"

Corners of his eyes wrinkling as he narrowed them, Robbie's cheeks rose as he grimaced. "Who the fuck knows anymore. All I know is, we're putting that arsehole's name on Australia's most wanted list. Hell, we might even get the fucker on the TV show."

O'Donnell nodded absently.

"So you know, Jimmy..." O'Donnell's eyes lifted. "We've also put out a KLO4 on Cassie Lawler and her boyfriend."

Opening his mouth, O'Donnell shut it before nodding once more. KLO4, or KALOF—keep a look out for—was the Australian equivalent of an APB or BOLO.

"Guess that means I'm out of a job," he said with resignation.

"Didn't you say she paid you in advance?"

"Yeah, but—"

Robbie slapped him backhand on the chest. "Then take a breather. Go home for a bit. Come to dinner at ours like I said."

"Maybe. But I still have a few other cases, you know."

"I'm sure you can find those cats and dogs later, Ace Ventura."

"Yeah, very fucking funny. Dickhead."

"You seen that yet though? Fucking hilarious."

"Yeah, you would think so. And no, I haven't."

"There's meant to be a sequel coming out later this year. We should go. My shout."

"You taking me on a date?"

"Sure, why not." Robbie's waggled his eyebrows. "I'll even let you rummage in the popcorn bucket on my dick then suck the butter off later."

Shaking his head, he turned as someone approached. The Fire Officer in Charge. The corners of O'Donnell's mouth turned down at the grim expression on the man's sooty face.

***

One after another, five stretchers in total were wheeled out of the mansion. Each laden with a body bag. O'Donnell had remained at the scene the whole time but had to stay back from necessity.

He wondered on the condition of the bodies and if any were identifiable. The place was huge, though he had no idea the extent of the fire following the blast.

Doing his best to remain nonchalant, he waited as the FOC spoke to Robbie and another officer in hushed tones. There was nodding and shaking of heads, but he could glean no meaning behind any of it. Then, when the trio broke apart, Robbie shook his head as he walked toward O'Donnell.

"She's not in one of the bags. I know that's what you were wondering."

O'Donnell made to deny it but stopping himself, shrugged instead.

"What's it with this chick, mate, that's got you so whipped?"

"I have no idea."

"I mean, I know she's young and hot but—"

"It's got nothing to do with that."

"Certainly doesn't hurt." Robbie smirked, relaxing his face when it wasn't mirrored.

"There's something about her."

"Yeah. It's called being a fucking crook."

"Seems that way."

He said it, but he didn't feel it. His head told him he was being foolish, but his gut that it was otherwise. That was the only way he could explain it. He knew what love was, or at least thought he did. This definitely wasn't it. It was some sort of… instinct.

An extra sensory one?

He would have scoffed at the idea only weeks ago. But after today? The last few weeks? Could any of what Cassie and the others told him be true? Did they do something to him? Open his third eye, or whatever it was they did? What had they done? More to the point, had they done to him?

"Too many questions and not enough answers," O'Donnell muttered.

"You got that fucking right."

"Anything useful inside for your investigation?"

"Fucked if I know. The FOC said the fire was isolated to one section, likely where the bomb went off, but we have to wait for their lab guys to do their shit. Then ours. *Then* we lowly coppers can get inside and dig through the leftovers. And you know how much I hate sloppy thirds. Seconds I can handle."

"Just when you thought you got a break, huh?"

Robbie's stare became steely. "Oh, don't you worry about that." Placing his hands on his hips, he nodded at the house. "We're going to get him. When we find all the ends of threads, it'll all come unravelling like one of my grandma's bad jumpers."

Smirking, O'Donnell frowned. "That's very descriptive of you."

Shrugging, Robbie pulled out his smokes and lit up. "I like to read in my spare time, and granny loves to knit in hers."

"Get out of here! You learnt to read?"

"Yeah. Who knew. One of Kelly's many bad influences on me."

O'Donnell's chest tightened at the mention of the name. "Well… if you lose your job maybe you'll have it made as an author."

"Yeah. I'll write about all these crazy fuckers. Be the next fucking Stephen King."

"Speaking of bad habits…" O'Donnell pointed at the smokes.

"What? You want to bum another fag?"

"I'm good. But how does Kelly feel about it?"

Robbie shrugged, avoiding eye contact.

"You haven't told her."

"You know what they say. Sometimes less is more. One day you'll see. You know, when you meet the right man."

"Uhuh. I'll keep that in mind. Don't forget what the old woman said though."

"Oh, fucking Jesus, don't remind me! I made the mistake of telling Kelly, thinking it was a laugh, you know? Taking the piss. She started on me about transferring. Imagine!"

"Hey, why not? Better yet, you could quit altogether and become a PI like me, writing your novels on the side."

"Yeah, ha-fucking-ha."

"They could make a film of it!"

"Yeah? And who would play you?"

"Mel Gibson," he said without pause.

Robbie chuckled. "And me?"

O'Donnell snapped his fingers and pointed at Robbie. "Jerry Lewis."

Robbie swiped at his head, O'Donnell ducking and weaving away.

"Get the fuck outta here, private dick head."

* * *

Returning to his office after dropping off the ute, O'Donnell collapsed into his chair and must have fallen asleep. It had been a long day, and waking up with a sore back and neck did nothing to improve his mood.

Cracking his neck and massaging it with one hand, he rose and pulled his cigarettes out with his free hand. Lighting up, he shuffled to the front door and kicked mail aside then exited, locking it behind him. A short time later, he peered through the glass door of the Chinese restaurant, holding a hand over his eyes.

Tapping on the glass with his knuckles, he got Benji's attention and signalled him with two fingers held high, then swapped them for his thumb which he tipped back toward his mouth.

Benji nodded and gave him a thumbs up his teeth flashing.

Nodding, O'Donnell turned from the door and went for a walk to the bottle shop up the road. It would take him a good ten to fifteen minutes to get there and back, but he knew Benji was on shift and finishing up around that time anyway.

Selecting Benji's usual six pack, he paid the attendant and walked back to his office, holding the cans by the plastic rings that connected them. He took his time. Benji would need to finish up, balance his till, and help clean up the dining area if it had been a particularly busy and messy night.

Leaving the door unlocked as he entered, O'Donnell placed the beer in the small fridge and headed for the shower, taking his clothes with him and locking the bathroom door. He doubted an old woman, no matter how psychotically strong, could break it down… if she came back.

Letting the water sluice the smoke smell ingrained in his nervous sweat away, he played the events of the day through his head. But every time he started, one image overwrote everything else.

The vision of the demonic Gunther slipped into his mind as easily as it had the ute, haunting him like a ghost. He hadn't been able to touch the spectre, and Gunther hadn't harmed him. But that didn't mean the demonic thing couldn't have hurt him if it had wanted to.

The opaque plastic shower curtain pattering with raindrops shifted and swayed suddenly.

Wiping water from his face, feeling a chill creep over his body despite the steaming water, he scrutinised the wavering sheet and the shadows created by the folds.

Whipping out his hand, he yanked the curtain back.

Water flicked the smoky surface of the mirror, the shape of the steam and dripping lines much like the Crone's face with her lank hair.

Grunting in satisfaction, O'Donnell scooped water into his mouth, then obliterated the image with a quick jet spurted from his lips.

"Go fuck yourself, ghosts."

"I'll drink to that!" Benji held out his second beer, obviously a little tipsy. It didn't take much.

O'Donnell raised his own and tapped the younger man's, the cans letting out a dull thunk.

"Been a while since we had some Chinese, a few tinnies and shot the shit, hey Bro'Donnell."

"Yeah. Sorry, Benji. Been a little caught up in this whole case. Actually, it's been busier than I would have expected lately all around."

"No sweat, man." Benji gave him a huge grin. "And by case do you mean that hottie from the photos?"

"Not specifically. But she has been—"

Benji threw out his hand, rising from his seat, and snapped his fingers. "Knew it!" His body relaxed and he lowered himself, smile fading. "Hey, is it true about that bombing? That her, too?"

"You heard about that, huh?" O'Donnell nodded. "Yeah. Well, the cult."

"Fuck, man! Did they really blow it sky high?"

"Not quite. But there was a fire."

Benji's eyes widened. "Shit... you were *there*." O'Donnell nodded slowly. "Was... she..."

"No, Benji. The object of your desires is fine. As far as I know."

"You don't know?"

With a shrug, O'Donnell took several gulps from the beer. "Not a clue, but since there's been a bombing, I'm officially off the case."

"Officially? So you're unofficially still looking into it."

O'Donnell frowned. He hadn't actually thought of that. Hadn't had *time* to think of it. Was he going to continue? Benji hadn't posed it as a question, it had been a statement.

"I guess I am," O'Donnell said.

"Yeah, no shit you are."

"Oh? You know me that well, do you?" Benji laughed. "So tell me, oh wise one… seeing as you know everything, are ghosts and psychic powers real?"

Benji's eyes narrowed as he smirked. "Fuck yeah they are."

O'Donnell gave Benji a bemused look. "I wouldn't have pegged you for a…"

"What? Tree hugger?"

"No, just… I don't know."

Benji shrugged. "What about you?"

Swirling the beer in his can, O'Donnell took a swig before answering. "A few weeks ago, I would have categorically said no. But now? I'm not sure what the fuck to believe anymore."

"Do you believe in God, bro?"

He was sure the expression he gave Benji was idiotic. "Where did *that* come from?"

Benji shrugged. "I didn't use to. I didn't even really think about it. Not any of it. Ghosts, ESP, God, reincarnation… But when I OD'd that time…"

"Shit, Benji." The tension at the awkward question left O'Donnell's shoulders. "I didn't know."

Benji gave another shrug, one that reached his face. "My parents don't talk about that. As far as they're concerned, I was 'on the edge' of drug addiction. But if you OD? Well, then you're another junkie. So they edit the story when they do have to talk about it. Which is fucking never! And it always somehow involves Jesus." Benji snorted a laugh. "Funny thing is, they have no idea how close I actually came to dying." He shifted in his seat. "You know that stuff they talk about? White light, the voice, tunnel…" He tapped his chest, raising his brows. Benji took a sip of his beer, smiling as he lowered it. "The voice told me an angel would save me and that it wasn't my time. That I had things to do." He gave a small smile. "Then you came along."

O'Donnell returned the smile, but shrugged. "I'm glad I did. But I'm definitely no angel, Benji."

"Dude… angels come in different shapes. I don't have to be enlightened to know that."

The beer in O'Donnell's hand stopped swirling. Leaning forward, he almost dropped it on the desk. "What did you say?"

"What?"

"Why did you use *that* word? Enlightened."

Benji shrugged. "After my 'near death experience', I did a lot of reading on reincarnation. Everything I could get my hands on. Christian, Hindu, Buddhist. Enlightenment is pretty big there."

Benji's expression was casual, his eyes reflective, a darkness there that couldn't be read.

Was his suggestion that O'Donnell continue the investigation encouragement, or manipulation? Was the glint in his eyes the memory of his drug habit and near demise, or the same expression in the eyes of the people at the Goth club? At Gateway house? On Gunther?

On Cassie?

Or was O'Donnell being paranoid.

With a nod, he eased back into his chair, picking up his can as he went to drink deeply. He nodded and gave Benji a small smile.

TEN

BENJI HAD BEEN RIGHT. There was no way O'Donnell would have been able to drop the investigation, whether he was somehow part of it or not. Not after everything that had happened. Somehow it all tied together. And in the process of the knots being tightened, O'Donnell had become entangled in the middle of it all.

It all circled back to Nathan Mortimer. O'Donnell was sure of that. He just didn't know how. What O'Donnell did know, though, was his job. He couldn't find Mortimer in the present, but there was no way he could outrun his past. He somehow linked it all together, Enlightened, Gateway and all. And the most recent point of convergence was the mansion.

Gunther could have attempted burning the place down completely. But instead, he opted to blow it up. Why? And why that particular area?

A full-blown blaze to raze a house that big would take time. Time and enough accelerant to do the job. An explosion, though...

He knew what Robbie would say. Rivalry. Cult psychosis. To get rid of as many of the Enlightened as Gateway could.

But that wasn't it. O'Donnell simply knew. It scratched at the back of his brain like a painful hangnail catching on clothing, unbidden and surprising. He scoffed a laugh. Was he starting to believe that the Enlightened had actually awoken something in him?

"That would be the day."

But the feeling persisted. He *knew* there was more to it. Something Gunther wanted to get rid of, perhaps. He had no doubt that any loss of life would be an added bonus, but no. That was not his main objective.

O'Donnell didn't think too hard on why he was so sure of that fact, tucking it away in the darkness of his mind as he would his dirty clothes under his fold-up bed until washing day.

Either way, now was the perfect time to find out.

He made no effort to quiet his car door as he exited, or to sneak across the road to the mansion. The less you tried, the less you stuck out. A lesson quickly learned on the job that he had been forgetting of late. Time to go back to basics. He didn't even try to hide that he was attempting to get in through the gate, though, unlike he had hoped, the electronic gate was still active and firmly in place. Along with the blue-and-white chequered police tape.

As he had done with the girl form the hospital, he planned to flash his investigator license if anyone came snooping. And if someone called the cops, well he was hoping he would be good enough to hide. Experienced police learned the spots to check. But on a call like this, someone poking around a burned down house... well it could go two ways. Being an affluent area, they could investigate it seriously. Or they could send some tired guys on shift who would take their time getting there, thinking it was some kids or a reporter.

He was hoping it was the latter.

Turning his back to the wall, giving it a quick glance to size it up, he leaned against it and lit up a cigarette. He smoked half of it, casually examining the road, and the houses opposite any sign of conscientious neighbourhood watch types. Not a single tell-tale crack of a curtain or porch light coming on.

Turning on his heel and dropping the smoke, he leaped for the top of the wall and pulled himself up. His toes scraped the textured rendering, but he didn't slow or stop. In a few moments, he dropped to the other side and casually strolled to the side of the house. He cursed as he saw a floodlight with a motion sensor but thanked his luck as it stayed inactive. Most people had them wired on a switch and forgot to turn them on or failed to set the timers and sensors correctly. Even when they went off, if you hid properly and sat still, most people thought it was triggered by a cat or a possum and ignore it.

His luck grew as the side of the building came into view. A large window had been blown out. The wiring could have been damaged in the explosion and power more than likely switched off. A blue plastic tarp was nailed over the window, the loose bottom flapping in the gentle breeze, crinkling softly. No light, and noise to cover his entry. Things were looking up.

Slipping on leather gloves as he strolled to the window, he waited for the tarp to billow away from the wall before slipping his hand beneath to gently pull it back and easing beneath it. Glass shards cracked under his shoes, but the window was over a flower garden and the soft soil muffled the sound, mixing with the crumpling tarp.

O'Donnell waited for his eyesight to adjust. Going in blind would get him hurt. He caught the toothy glint of the jagged remains of the window on the bottom of the frame, several above it.

In primary school, Robbie and he had a teacher who always used idioms. Putting your head in the lion's mouth was one he used repeatedly. After that, they had used it every chance they could, much to the teacher's delight. He had even used it once during assembly and O'Donnell and Robbie had burst out laughing.

The broken window was a dark maw, and he couldn't shake the sensation he was stepping into jaws of some beast beyond him.

The detention they'd received from their outburst in assembly had been worth it. O'Donnell had no intention of getting into any sort of trouble here and now though. Especially not the sort that would end up in his bleeding everywhere and leaving evidence.

Taking the first large piece firmly in both hands, spreading his fingers evenly, he waited for the tarp to move and yanked sharply. He stood still a moment, then dropped the glass in the dirt and grabbed the next piece. He worked his way around the frame until there was enough space for him to climb through.

Reaching into his pocket once in, he pulled out a diminutive flash-light and turned it on. It was low powered with a shield and red light, perfect for sneaking around and not ruining his night vision. He'd learned the trick from an amateur astronomer client. O'Donnell had given him a dubious smirk when he had explained, especially given his many telescopes and love for them, but the man explained he used it to view star charts when out in the bush. Plus, he'd said, it was far easier to get porn from the local newsagent than to try and find someone attractive to spy on.

Luckily, he had only hired O'Donnell to trace down a person who owed him money. And not a woman.

The smell of the fire was strong. Damp ash and burnt plastic permeated the place. It would take a lot of work to get rid of it. A lot of stripping out and renovation.

Some people had a morbid fascination with crime scenes, espe-cially where people had died, though he never understood it. Like rubbernecking drivers at the scene of a horrific accident, it angered him when he came across those dark tourists. Death and destruction at the cost of life, it only made O'Donnell sad. A life had been lost, or in the case of the explosion, multiple lives. Whatever they had done, they had been a person once, and all that was gone, whether they deserved it or not.

Few people who truly deserved it met that end. O'Donnell wasn't usually an eye for an eye person, but some...

He played the light around, searching for the centre of the destruc-tion. It wasn't too difficult. He only had to follow the charred mess and stench. O'Donnell came to a stop at the centre of the blast.

Contrary to what most thought, unless there was an incendiary of some sort used, bombings didn't result in huge fires. The force is what caused the destruction, and whether there was any shrapnel on the bomb. After the bombing of the police station on Russell Street in '86, there had been a lot of education and information. He never thought he would have to put any of it to use, though. Especially not after leaving the force. He'd seen photos of the bombing and recalled news reports on TV and the papers.

Even with that training, having been right outside the mansion when it happened, having heard and felt the destruction, O'Donnell could scarcely imagine what it would have been like being inside when it went off.

Where the floor used to be was a drop to bare dirt, pale concrete posts sticking out of it like finger bones, their tips charred and chipped. There was scraps of what had remained of the flooring littered around the posts, hardwood splinters and chunks with blackened edges. Scraps of other things reduced to coal black hunks, some colour poking through. He couldn't help but wonder if any of it was human. Cast in the red light, it was hard to tell what was what, but the shade did nothing to improve his morbid thoughts.

There was nothing here to find. Not in this room anyway.

He went searching the rest of the house, red circle of light dancing in front of his feet. A powder room beneath the stairs. Access to a large double... maybe triple garage, no cars within, only shelves lining the walls stacked with camping gear, and lots of it. For a quick escape, perhaps.

Then a study.

The earlier tug at his gut returned. This was it.

There was nothing outwardly apparent. A large desk with drawers and filing cabinets, bookshelves, some coastal photography prints.

Chiding himself, he stepped to the desk and pulled the top left drawer, but his eyes were locked on one of two tall, black file drawers. Rifling through the desks confirmed his... What? Intuition? Newly gifted psychic ability?

"Christ," O'Donnell muttered at the thought, closing the last drawer and heading to book shelves instead of the filing cabinets. He was starting to sound like *them*.

The shelves, of real wood and antique at first glance, were lined with books old and new. There were tomes of all sizes on occultism, past lives, past life regression, near death experiences. Shelves of texts in many languages on Buddhism, Christianity, Islam, Judaism, and other religions O'Donnell hadn't ever heard of. He stifled a laugh as he saw one on something called Zoroastrianism and imagined a religion of people worshipping a masked figure with a sword carving Zs everywhere he went.

All the things Benji had mentioned reading up on. He pushed that to one side.

Nothing useful on the bookshelf either.

Stepping past the filing cabinet he had been staring at but ignoring, he opened the bottom drawer of its twin defiantly. File after file. Tax documents, land deeds, employment records. Nothing naming Mortimer or any other name he knew. After searching the three other drawers above it, he defied the urge to slam the last one closed, sliding it to click into place softly instead.

"You should have listened to your first instincts, James."

O'Donnell let his hand fall from the drawer. "Cassie," he said before turning toward her grinning face. Even in the darkness, she shone. "Passing through, were you?"

"If that's what you want to call it."

"Well, as long as you're not carrying a massive knife in your purse."

Cassie nodded. "Lucky for you, because I got the drop on you. And she's truly disturbed."

O'Donnell snorted. "Understatement of the century. Question is…" He wagged his finger at Cassie. "Is she Enlightened, or Gateway? I can't figure that out. Or if there's even a difference."

Her smile faltered, lips pursing as her face wrinkled. "Not so intuitive, then."

"You know what, *Cassie*? How about you and all your crazy people stop fucking with my head and tell me what the hell is going on. For starters, why did Gunther bomb this place? Why that room out there."

Her eyes narrowed, interest sparking in them once more, her head tilting slightly as she regarded the doorway.

Letting out a long sigh, O'Donnell palmed the flashlight into his left hand and massaged his temples and forehead, squeezing his scalp between thumb and fingers. "I *know* it wasn't only about killing your people."

"How?" She turned back to him. "How do you *know*?"

He let his hand drop. "Don't try to pull me into your batshit crazy psychic cyclone! And don't cold read me. I just know, okay?"

"Really, James? Cold read?"

"I can see it. The wheels turning and ticking over in your head. What to say. How to play me."

"You still think of us that way. That we're charlatans."

"Talking like you're older than you are doesn't mean anything. Anyone can do that."

"And what we showed you at the club?"

"Showed me? You left me drug-fucked on the floor."

She cocked a single brow by way of answer.

"What are you doing here?" he said.

"I should be asking you that. Though I know the answer. As do you."

He didn't, but he didn't say. "Well as long as you're here, why don't you tell me what I'm looking for. Save me the trouble."

With a shrug, Cassie moved to the desk and perched on its edge. She took a textured black cigarette case from a small purse of matching colour and pattern. Carefully extracting a cigarette, she held it aloft, elbow of the raised arm resting on the case in her other hand.

"Aren't you going to be a gentleman and offer me a light?"

O'Donnell gave her a black stare. "Can't you use your 'powers'?"

The corner of her lips crept higher. Dropping the cigarette case back in her purse and snapping it shut, she lifted her hands and turned them back and forth like a stage magician. She let her left hand fall to the edge of the desk, then put her cupped right hand to the tip of the cigarette and held it there, eyes still on O'Donnell. She puffed several times as a glow lit smoke wafting between her shuttered fingers.

"What happened to no parlour tricks?"

Cassie smiled around the cigarette. "That's nothing compared to what we can actually do."

O'Donnell must have given something away—his eyes flinching, or mouth turning down.

She frowned. "You've seen something?"

He shook his head. "I don't even know how to begin."

She stared back at him.

With a sigh, he pulled out his own smokes. At least the cigarette smell might overpower the burnt house. For a moment.

"I was following Gunther when he did this." He waved his hand around. "And he..." With a bitter laugh, O'Donnell grabbed his forehead, cigarette held in his fingers. He peeled his hand away and took a deep pull on the cigarette. "He became a fucking ghost and... *fell*—floated, whatever—into mine."

Inhaling on her own cigarette, Cassie frowned, and waited.

"Then he turned into a demon, or something. Attacked me."

"Did he hurt you?" Her voice held no concern, only curiosity.

He shook his head. "No. I don't think he was ever really there. It was like a projection or... something."

She nodded. "A projection of his mind. To distract and stop you, no doubt."

Puffing and exhaling, he nodded. "Well it worked, I can tell you that much. Scared the absolute shit out of me. And I'm not sure but I'm pretty sure the Crone has been doing the same thing to me."

"The old woman?"

"I keep seeing flashes of her face. At first I thought I was being paranoid, but now..."

Cassie chewed the inside of her lip, brow creasing. "This isn't good news."

He waited for her to elaborate, but she stayed in silent thought. "Because...?"

Cassie's eyes shot to O'Donnell. "Ask me your questions. If that one's not answered, I'll elaborate."

Snorting, he shook his head. "More games?" She only smiled back. "Fine. Whatever. Let's start with Gunther. Who is he and how is he connected?"

"To tell you that, first you need to know about Nathan."

"That's why I'm fucking here, Cassie!" O'Donnell threw up his hand and shook his head. "You know what? Sure. Why not? Tell be about your boyfriend."

Easing up on the desk further, Cassie crossed her legs. She lifted the cigarette to her lips and O'Donnell thought it was no more burnt down than when it had been first lit. He'd ashed his own twice already but had not seen her once do so.

"Nathan was from a middle-class family. Not well to-do, neither were they poor. Parents both worked and he was at university, studying marketing and economics. From out of nowhere, as the story he told us went, he inherited a property. A run down old Victorian house on a large parcel of land in a well-to-do suburb."

"Let me guess—" O'Donnell swung his hand in an arc to encompass the imagined boundary of the land the mansion stood on.

Cassie gave a single nod. "When he was taking possession of the property, something happened."

"Something?"

"There was a woman. A social worker. Claimed that she was executing the instructions of a 'long lost relative' of Nathan's. An old great-aunt."

The scratching feeling at the back of his brain returned, and it had a familiar... scent was the only description he could think of. A smell that triggered a memory of a place, thing... or person.

"The Crone," O'Donnell said.

"Yes. And the so-called social worker was one of hers."

"Hers?" Deep in thought, O'Donnell drew on his cigarette. "She did the same thing to that social worker and Nathan that you and the Enlightened did to me, didn't she?"

Cassie nodded. "Her and the woman Enlightened Nathan, yes. There was a gateway symbol drawn on the wall in excrement and blood, bones of birds and cats and other small animals embedded in it."

O'Donnell grimaced. "Jesus." He tried to imagine what once stood here and the vile Gateway she described. "How did Mortimer afford to build this?" he said, glancing around at the modern construction. "I'm assuming it's his."

"After his experience with the Crone, he started to tap into his lives and experiences. Future lives are problematic, but being one of the first, he had glimpses. He used that to hit the stock market, hard."

"And he made a shit-tonne of money. Right?"

She gave a small shrug.

"Isn't that cheating?" he said, smirking.

She laughed. He wasn't sure if he'd truly seen her laugh before. It suited her face, almost giving her the features of someone else. Someone he didn't know. A part of him yearned to meet that person.

"I guess it could be considered insider trading, of a sort," she said. "Your future self, or a possible future you, providing information on what to trade."

Swallowing hard, he pushed the yearning aside. "So, was this before or after the Enlightened formed?"

Her smile was sad, her eyes faraway, caught in some memory. "I know what you think and how it sounds. That Nathan started to amass money and people and a religious following. But it wasn't like that."

"Uhuh." He crumpled the cigarette butt between his thumb and fingers, rolling it to separate the still hot embers from the filter. "Why do I get the feeling there should be a 'but', or 'at first' at the end of that sentence?" He pocketed the butt.

Cassie gave a slow, single nod. "It was all happening before Nathan realised it."

He searched Cassie's face. "Gunther."

"He was one of the first."

"Who is he, Cassie?"

Shrugging, Cassie turned and stubbed her cigarette out in a large brown glass ashtray. There were several more butts in there, some probably hers. "He used to be a stock trader. That's how Nathan met him."

O'Donnell frowned in thought. "He used Gunther to do his trading. Gunther gets curious, asks him how he's doing it, so Nathan tells him. Gunther wants in."

"Exactly. After a while, Gunther became like Nathan's right hand. Then Nathan learnt of his betrayal."

"Betrayal?"

"Gateway."

O'Donnell began pacing. "So, behind his back, Gunther had set up his own little cult, maybe not agreeing with the way things are being done. He wants more. Using Nathan as some kind of figurehead, he brings in his own disciples and converts them. Then Nathan finds out, has his falling from grace moment, and disappears. Ashamed or on the run."

"Only in his own eyes. We never blamed Nathan. We only wanted to make sure he was safe."

"And not in Gateway's hands."

She stared into his eyes without any emotion in her own for several moments, then closed them. "Yes. But not—"

"Save it. Whatever your reasons, real or imagined, I agree with you. If Gateway get their hands on Nathan, they'll be even more dangerous. Gunther will think he's got control of him. Whatever he thinks Nathan is and can do for him, his people believe it."

"You think he'll do *more* than he already has?" She glanced around. "My friends died in here, James. He killed them."

"And if he gets Nathan, you and the Enlightened won't stop, will you?" She stared back at him. "If I know it, then Gunther definitely does too. And he'll kill all of you. Right now, he needs at least some of you alive, because you're his only leads to Nathan. He probably has you all watched. No telling how many people he has."

And O'Donnell was right in the middle of them all. It dawned on him, that's why Gunther hadn't killed him too.

"What about your lot, Cassie? The Enlightened?"

"What about us?"

"How do you and Gateway differ? How do you work?"

"Work?" She scoffed. "We're not a criminal organisation, James."

"But you do organise. Like at the Goth club. You have to own that too, right?"

"We do. We've many properties and investments set up to support our lives as they continue on."

O'Donnell let out a chuckle that was louder than he had intended. "See, that sure sounds like crazy cult talk to me. Setting up a portfolio to fund your future lives. And this place—" He stabbed a finger at the bookshelves. "Sure as shit looks like cult HQ."

"This is merely a halfway house. One of many."

"Funny, I thought halfway homes treated the ill."

"Stop!" she said loudly. She dropped off the desk and fixed him in her gaze. And he froze like a rabbit. "Stop trying to make us out to be more than what we are. Just because you refuse to believe in something, stop shitting all over anyone and anything that does."

He let his amusement out in a single coughed laugh, catching himself by surprise as much as it did Cassie.

"What?" she said sharply.

"That's the first time I've heard you talk like an actual young woman."

Snorting, she hung her head, shaking it. "Cassie Lawler is still in here." She tapped her chest gently with her fingertips. "The girl before all this. Enlightened. Gateway." She looked up, eyes sad. "Sometimes I wonder if it's all worth it. If I had been better off as little bogan Cassie, working at *The Reject Shop*."

"How did you get into all this shit?"

Hitching one of her shoulders, she all but fell back on the desk, legs ramrod straight and jiggling as she snatched up her purse and pulled out a cigarette. She didn't bother with any tricks, lighting it with a slim, gold lighter with a jet flame. She blew out a stream of smoke and played with the lighter.

"I was in a bad place. My stepdad was a real prick and my mum... Well, let's say when he didn't have her wrapped around it, or high to her eyeballs, he punched her into shape around his little finger. But I got older, and more defiant. So he started on me."

O'Donnell's eyes flinched. "Did he—"

"No." She shook her head. "Though I'm pretty sure my mother wasn't spared any indignity or pain." She shrugged and drew on the cigarette. "And when she wouldn't leave him, take us both out of danger, I left."

"How old were you?"

"Fourteen. Barely."

"Jesus."

She shrugged again, but her lips twisted bitterly. "Anyway. I didn't know anyone or have anyone, so I was out on the streets. And I stayed on and off the streets for a good three, four years. Then I met Nathan."

"He... brought you in?"

Cassie's smile was light and genuine. "He was so nice. So unlike anyone I had ever met. When he told me that I was special, that he could see it inside me, I didn't once think that he was saying it in a creepy way. It was weird, you know? Even now knowing what I do, it felt so bizarre."

O'Donnell knew what she meant, but said nothing. Cassie had given off that same strange air and magnetism. If he had been young and troubled, at an impressionable age and in need of help and approached by Cassie like that, he would have gone with her too. Probably still would.

"He took me in. *They* took me in. Fed me. Housed me. Taught me. Cared for me when no one else would and helped me to become the woman I am now."

"And turned you into a believer."

"If you only knew, James."

"What? I thought you *had* enlightened me. Given my initiation."

"No. That would have been irresponsible. To do that to you and leave you on your own."

"So, what then?"

"Let's say we nudged you in the right direction. Opened a curtain instead of a door, so you can peek inside."

The sensations, the intuitions. Was that it?

"Why though? Why not go with me?"

She shook her head. "Because Gateway knows us all. We needed you to be impartial and not get drawn in. But you were losing the trail and turned far better at your job than the recommendation we got gave you credit for."

"Word of mouth, cheaper and more efficient than the Yellow Pages."

"A pity they undersold you. In any case, you were getting closer to the truth than we anticipated. So I decided you needed a push toward the truth and give you some assistance on your search."

He didn't really understand, but he nodded. "What about Gunther? You said you would explain. Why was what I told you about him, what he did to me, not good news?"

"He's far stronger than we ever imagined."

"And that means, what exactly?"

Her eyes darted around as she bit her lip in thought before turning back to him. "What you experienced after we took you to the club was essentially us... Not opening your third eye, if you want to use that expression, but making you aware of its existence."

"Right..." O'Donnell said, trying to wrap his head around the concept. "And that's what Nathan does? He opens people's third eyes for them?"

"Something like that. Imagine if you've got your eyes closed lightly and someone comes along and gently opens them. You can then slowly make out what's in front of you and see."

"Okay."

"Now imagine you're in deep sleep. Then someone comes along, forces your eyes wide open and sets of flashing lights and lasers of every colour and loud music of all genres from ten different stereos all at once."

"I thought that's what was happening on the dance floor of the club." Her face was blank. "Fine. I get it. It's a lot different. But again, what does—"

"I'm getting to that." She drew on her cigarette and then dropped it in the ash tray to leave it burn out. "Imagine now, in both scenarios, someone is whispering something to you. A code. You have to transcribe that information."

O'Donnell shrugged. "Yeah, I'd have no chance in the second scenario."

"Exactly. Now, imagine that code is your soul."

Confusion etched his face. A person's soul? What did she mean? He turned to her for answers, but she simply watched him. Sighing, he paced and decided to light up again.

If your soul was you, then obviously having it as clear as possible meant… what? You were right in the head? But from what Cassie had told him, and Nathan on the tape, they were a jumble of souls. Or one soul but spread out, and the Enlightening process stitched it all together. A jigsaw puzzle.

So if the jigsaw—your soul—was scrambled, with the wrong pieces in the wrong spots, the finished image would be all over the place. And you'd be crazy and psychotic? Like Gunther? Or dead? Surely the last.

How many more pieces would a soul take compared to a 500-piece jigsaw.

"Shit," he said, turning to Cassie. "That's what happened to Gunther, isn't it? His souls were corrupted."

"Nathan was still young and getting to grips with his gift. And we think, instead of easing Gunther in, he tore open his eye. Into a big gaping hole."

A gaping hole of multiple colours.

"A gateway," O'Donnell said.

Cassie nodded. "And that's exactly what Gunther does to others that follow him. And what he might try to do to Nathan to make him one of them."

ELEVEN

"From now on, we stick together."

He'd told Cassie the same words the previous night. He had no intention of letting her out of his sight. There was too much at risk. And that wasn't even considering what she and the Enlightened believed might happen if Gateway got their hands on Nathan.

If they were to be believed, Gunther and the rest of his nutters were all corrupted souls. And they could do the same to Nathan and anyone else. Force their third eye—or whatever it was—wide open. And with that, they would be tapped into the same turbulent river of soul information, flooding and taking over their original selves. And once that happened, they would be converts. Immediately, and without reservation. If absolute power corrupted absolutely, what would instant absolute power do?

Cassie nodded solemnly from the passenger seat of O'Donnell's hatchback. "I still don't see why we couldn't take my car."

"Apart from the fact that car probably draws attention everywhere it goes, Gunther and the rest of them will recognise it in an instant."

Chuckling, she shook her head. "You're still operating on your normal playbook, James. I told you—"

"Yes, I know. I have to start thinking like an Enlightened." Whatever that meant.

"It means, you have to start assuming your enemy can and will know what you're thinking. Where you are. What your next steps could be."

O'Donnell shot her a look, holding it as long as he dared before turning back to the road. "Because they're psychic?" He wasn't going to open the topic of how she'd known what he was thinking. She was good at her tricks.

"When you're on the job, what do you do?"

He shrugged. "I follow people."

"But how?"

"I hide. I blend in."

"And everywhere you go, where you're blending in, it's full of people. Right?" He conceded with a nod. "And there're your moles."

"The unknown crowds? Are you saying Gateway has *that* many people?"

"No! You still don't get it." She turned in the cramped space to sit almost sideways in the passenger seat. "One day, soon or down the road, they're all going to die. And what happens then?"

He knew what she was getting at. Their souls would be in the stream. "But, if you can't see the future with any control, how is that going to be possible?"

"It's not that we can't see the future. You're still thinking of this as some kind of clairvoyance or being a psychic medium." With a sigh, she lifted off the seat and turned to face front, dropping back down roughly. "When someone becomes Enlightened, they have access to all the knowledge of all their lives! They just *know* it."

"But you can't *know* what hasn't happened yet, can you? Nathan said so to the doctor on the tape as well."

Cassie turned her head and stared out the passenger window. "Like anything it takes time, and there are always outliers. The longer you are Enlightened, the more comes to you."

"And the stronger you get?"

She nodded.

"And by the sounds of it, from everyone in both the Enlightened and Gateway, Nathan and Gunther are the oldest of you. Not including the old woman. The Crone."

"She's something different again."

Of course she was.

At every turn, the more he asked for explanation, the more complicated the questions became. Wasn't that all part of the scam usually, though? The deeper the rabbit hole, the more convoluted it became so by the time you were plumbing those depths, there was no way but to keep going.

"What is she then?" O'Donnell asked, no hope of actually getting the question answered in his voice or mind.

"I honestly don't know. Even Nathan didn't know. She came and went as she pleased, without rhyme or reason. Why she left the property to Nathan? Why she chose him to Enlighten? What she has to do with Gateway?"

"Why she attacked me?"

Turning to him, Cassie nodded. "She's a total unknown."

"Because *that's* what we need in this poker game, a wildcard."

A huge grin split her face. "A word of warning, don't play any of the Enlightened at poker. They'll empty your wallet and your bank account."

"Will they at least leave me my underwear to spare me *some* dignity?"

She looked him up and down and arched her eyebrows. "Probably not."

"Well then, I guess I'd better—"

A strange sensation overcame O'Donnell. Light headedness and a tightness of his chest. His vision blurred. Gripping the wheel tight, he was barely aware of Cassie calling his name, saying something, but he had no idea what.

Slowly, O'Donnell lifted his head. And turned it.

The Crone stood in the middle of a grassed traffic island as wide as two lanes, three lanes of road either side of it. And she smiled at him.

A car blurred past the driver's side window, and when it passed, the Crone was gone. In her place, a shimmer of bright light. The sun reflecting off the back of a car. As it followed the slowly curving road, the rear end of metallic silver car with a chrome three-pronged star flashed in the sunlight.

"James!" Cassie yelled as he turned the wheel sharply, swerving the hatchback through the right-hand lane and into a turning lane. "What are you doing?" she screamed as his head darted left and right and he ran a red light.

He kept his eyes locked ahead of him.

"James?" she said again, voice low but insistent.

He lifted a white-knuckled hand from the wheel and pointed. "Gunther's Mercedes."

Cassie strained, leaning forward. "I can't see anything. Are you sure? It's a common enough car. I—"

"I'm sure."

She peered through the windshield and shook her head. "I'm not getting anything. And even if it is Gunther—"

"It *is*!"

"—we shouldn't be going on a wild goose chase after him! Not the both of us. It's too risky."

O'Donnell realised he had been staring at the road ahead. He blinked, some of the strain relieving.

"You're right. Next red light, you jump out. Call a taxi or one of your mates to come pick you up. Call my office in two hours. If I'm not there, try in another hour. If I'm still not—"

"This is crazy, James."

"If I'm not there, Cassie, call Detective Robbie Thomas. Tell him everything."

"James, I—"

He hit the brakes as a set of lights turned yellow, the car lurching and springing as it stopped. "Go!"

Slapping the seatbelt release, Cassie threw the door open and climbed out. She started to close the door, then stopped. "Make sure you come back, Mr O'Donnell," she said, then slammed the door.

He had every intention, but he knew that if intentions were all it took, the world would be a far different place than it was.

As the light turned green, O'Donnell gunned the engine of the little hatchback and broke the speed limit. As long as he didn't get pulled over, he could catch up to Gunther. But as he glanced at a large green street sign and its reflective white letters, O'Donnell was fairly certain he knew his destination.

Mount Dandenong.

Businesses turned to houses, then the houses grew farther and farther apart as the car wound up the mountain roads and the trees taller and thicker. Soon, the familiar ferns of the Dandenong ranges forests began to dot the landscape and gravelly shoulders of the road, then were a thick curtain of green.

He hadn't come up here in a long time. There had been no need to. It was beautiful, and when he had been dating it had been a good weekend drive for a walk or a picnic. These days, picnics for him consisted of the chocolate bar variety, and exclusively on his own.

He had caught up to Gunther, who was several cars ahead of him. But he knew from both previous expeditions up the mountain there was nothing odd about that. The road wound its way for long stretches with many sharp turns with little to no side branches, and even then no one took them. Most were private or local roads. And most people travelling here were going the same place or further.

But then the left indicator on Gunther's Mercedes started flashing. He was turning into one of those roads. This close, unless others in front of O'Donnell turned down the same road, he had no way of following the man without drawing attention.

The silver car eased into the small side road. The cars between them did not.

As he passed by the road, O'Donnell turned his head and scanned it. He saw a sign at the last moment. Painted green wood and faded, words carved into it that had once been white. He made out the words picnic area.

It was a dead end.

O'Donnell slowed his car, a large white, rust-spotted four-wheel-drive with a massive bull bar drawing in close to the rear of the hatchback. But there, an exit.

Dust billowing behind, O'Donnell pulled into the rest area. It was little more than a spit of dirt with an old concrete table and bin that hadn't been emptied in a long time, a gravel path in an arc leading to them. Somewhere drivers could pull into to rest, possibly to make a U-turn if they'd missed their turn-off.

The car skidded to a halt as he pulled the handbrake and slammed the automatic shift to P, his free hand quickly shutting off the engine and pulling the key. He slammed the door behind him after he jumped out, thumbing the lock button on the key as he ran, not turning to check if he'd managed to do so.

Taking a wild guess, O'Donnell plotted where he thought Gunther would be. These picnic areas weren't usually that far off the main road. If he cut along diagonally, he should make it in good time.

With no thought to life or limb, he ran through the trees and ferns, key clutched in his hand. Where branches were across his way, he either ducked if too thick or lifted an arm to whip them aside. The ferns were flexible, but the frond-laden branches whip-like and he had to adopt a loping gait to keep from faceplanting. Soon his arms began to numb from the branches, and his thighs and calves burned. He would be covered in bruises and feel the ache in his legs the next day. Assuming he was around for it.

Lungs and limbs burning, O'Donnell's feet suddenly found empty air as he fell. For a moment, he thought he would plummet into one of the vertiginous drops that ran alongside the roads. Instead, he dropped a short distance to a gravel road.

He stumbled but stayed on his feet. Looking down the road, he saw settling dust in the distance. Turning, he spotted a thicker cloud of it up the unsealed path. The Mercedes was both out of sight and earshot, but he was practically right behind Gunther.

Climbing down the opposite side of the road rather than back up the small incline, O'Donnell continued jogging beside the road, using the trees as cover. Not too far along, he saw the dull sparkle of the now dusty Mercedes, parked in front of a lush green clearing.

At first, O'Donnell had suspected that Gunther was making off for another Gateway compound, or house. If Nathan had made a lot of money and let Gunther in, odds were the man had done exactly the same. Probably more so given what O'Donnell had seen of him so far.

Now, he was fairly certain Gunther was meeting someone. Or maybe hiding or picking something up. The possibilities buzzed in O'Donnell's head along with the blood of his laboured heartbeat.

The bomb!

What if he was getting another one? Something bigger and far worse? Or more?

Not hearing the car engine, O'Donnell hurried, trying not to disturb the vegetation too much. It already sounded like crashing in his throbbing ears.

Across the grass, a lone figure disappeared into the tree line. He couldn't tell from the distance if it was Gunther, but the Mercedes was the only car in the area.

Chancing it, O'Donnell sprinted onto the road as the figure disappeared, cutting a long diagonal through it and past the silver car. He glanced in it but saw nothing on the seats. Neither was Gunther carrying anything with him. His arms had been swinging free. It had to be a meeting.

Stopping by a tree, O'Donnell scanned the opposing side of the clearing before taking off across it. He could sprint across the grass without making too much sound, especially if Gunther was crashing about through the forest. If anyone else was in there however, his cover was long blown. But no one jumped out. There was no cry of warning, nor attack or bullet coming his way.

Entering the same spot he had seen Gunther disappear, a break in two large trees with a naturally formed archway of ferns, O'Donnell walked on his heels as best he could, scanning the area as he went. His only option was to move forward. It was the logical choice. But soon, he thought he discerned a trail. Maybe the space in the ferns where Gunther had entered had not been so natural after all. But where had he gone?

Gunther had been moving steady but slow, in no rush. O'Donnell was on the chase, so why hadn't he caught up? Seen the sway of branches and their crashing in the man's wake? Could he have left the trail, such as it was?

Ahead of him, O'Donnell saw a large tree. If he couldn't see any sign of Gunther on the other side, he would have to stop and re-assess.

As he rounded the tree, he came to a dead stop and raised his hands.

Gunther's hand was also raised, a pistol in it aimed at O'Donnell's head. The weapon trembled, the black hole at its tip almost a mirage as it jerked about. A sheen of sweat beaded Gunther's forehead and tight lips quivering over his clenched teeth.

"Take it easy, Gunther," O'Donnell said. He gave his head a slow shake.

Gunther's trigger finger twitched and jerked, but otherwise didn't move. Blowing people up where he couldn't see them was one thing but blowing a man's brains out right in front of him was obviously too much.

A branch snapped behind O'Donnell. He whirled around and froze again.

"Hello, James," Nathan Mortimer said, smiling kindly.

Gunther hadn't been pointing the gun at O'Donnell. It was aimed at Nathan. As he slowly moving out of the line of fire, Gunther proved it, his hand not deviating, locked on Nathan. More than locked. He was paralysed.

"What's wrong with him?" O'Donnell said, turning to stare at Gunther.

The man was fighting to pull the trigger but couldn't. He was frozen in place. His body out of his own control.

"He won't scare you or hurt anyone else again," Nathan said.

Gunther's hand jerked, tendons in his arm bulging, the gun rising so the barrel pointed skyward. Just like all those years ago.

"No!" O'Donnell shouted.

The muzzle pressed beneath Gunther's jaw and his finger unlocked.

O'Donnell saw the same scene all those years ago in the cell of his police station. Jason. O'Donnell's own gun. Except then, there was a wall to catch the spray of brain and blood and skull fragments.

Some leaves darkened and Gunther fell, the report of the pistol echoing but quickly fading. Even the disturbed birds settled as if nothing had happened.

O'Donnell stood rooted to the ground, the familiar shock and disbelief sinking in. As he brought his body back under control, he turned to Nathan to find empty air.

"Can you see yet, James?" Nathan's voice echoed around the forest, leaving O'Donnell turning in circles. "My friend assured me you had been given your sight back."

His hand jabbed at the body on the ground. "What about Gunther's sight? He can't see anything anymore."

Something flitted between the trees.

"It's tragic, but it was inevitable," the disembodied voice said, echoing in O'Donnell's skull. "Gunther wouldn't have stopped. Has already wreaked so much destruction."

"So you... what? Lured him here to kill him?"

Several blurs moved at the corner of O'Donnell's eyes, his head whipping to follow but finding only swaying leaves and fronds.

"I didn't lure him, James. I merely showed him myself, and Gunther came of his own free will."

A shadow on the forest floor fell in line next to O'Donnell's.

"Like you did," Mortimer whispered over his shoulder.

O'Donnell spun, but again there was nothing to see apart from Gunther's corpse, weapon still in hand. His eyes darted to the pistol. "Are you going to kill me too?"

"You should be careful, outsider," the hoarse whisper of the Crone filled his head.

A chill clawed its way up O'Donnell's spine, digging claws between each vertebra on its way to his brain.

"Or what?" He crept toward Gunther, willing himself not to see the mess that was now the top of his head. "You'll come to me in my dreams and seduce me? Gouge out my eyes again?" Trying to keep an eye on the whole forest and crouch at the same time, he reached for the pistol. "Try and stab me in the back?"

"Perhaps you would prefer a more direct confrontation?"

The Crone appeared at Gunther's feet, grinning wide, blood smearing her already stained nightgown.

O'Donnell fell back with a cry, pistol forgotten.

She was gone.

"I thought not." Her voice seemed to come from the trees themselves, surrounding O'Donnell, penetrating his body.

"We should be kind to our guest," James said in the same way.

"What do you want from me?" O'Donnell shouted. Lowering his eyes, he saw the broken, bloody chasm in Gunther's head. Something solid dripping within, leaving a trail of blood and fluid in its wake.

"Kind?" the Crone said ignoring him, the trees almost shaking with her anger. "The world is not *kind*, Nathan. Awaken him, leave him be... or kill him. That is the only way forward."

The trees stirred as the voices devolved into chatter, coming fast and thick in argument before descending into a white noise hiss. The leaves stirred and rustled, rushing around O'Donnell in a building whirlwind. And it was growing stronger.

O'Donnell shielded his eyes with his forearm and rose. Something flew past him, stinging his cheek. Hissing in pain, he grabbed his face and pulled his hand away to see a line of smeared blood on his palm.

Something else flew. Then another, then many more. Leaves. Pebbles. Twigs. They lifted of their own accord and joined the wall of air, quickly becoming a wall as the debris of the forest was pulled into it. If he didn't act now, while they fought each other, he'd be trapped, torn to shreds.

Turning, he bolted for the rushing barrier being built around him, curling his arms around his face. Wind whipped his clothing and hair. Projectiles bounced off and tore at him. Something solid cracked the back of his head and he had a momentary flash of pain but kept moving. Above the wind, he thought he heard a scream of frustration, cries of protest. Whoever the Crone truly was—mentor or tormentor—she was not pleased that Mortimer was fighting her. And O'Donnell would be the one to pay the price if she won the argument.

Above the voices was the rush of the wind, like a train in the underground tunnels of the Melbourne City Loop, growing in intensity until it thundered. O'Donnell risked glancing back.

The supernatural wind was following him.

O'Donnell sprinted through the trees, the deadly wind giving chase, voices coming with it. Branches large and small cracked and fell from on high around him, some so close their offshoots and leaves slapped and grabbed at him like fingers. Large gum nuts from eucalypts sailed around him in the process, raining to the earth and sending up small explosions of dirt. He covered the top of his head as several bounced off, leaving scalp and bone bruised.

Something black and shrieking crashed toward his face and exploded in feathers and a sickening impact as he wheeled to the right and it struck a tree. Another and another sailed down. Crows. The birds, caught by invisible hands and terrified, were flung at him, clawing and snapping their beaks at the air. He saw jet-black beak and eyes arrowing toward his face but was too slow to react.

At the last moment, the bird veered as if deflected on glass and tumbled into the whirling chaos behind to be torn to bloody shreds, as if caught in a blender.

"Run James!" Nathan's voice rung out in the forest, setting O'Donnell's faltering feet pumping once more.

As the Crone rained chaos on O'Donnell, Nathan was aiding him. Protecting him.

A shriek or pure rage filled the forest. The entire forest and the air itself trembled as a distortion ripped through the space, weaving in and out of the trees before rushing at him only to be deflected like the birds. The distortion, shimmering as Gunther's spectral form had, whipped as it tore in two, smashing back together ahead of O'Donnell.

Handfuls of crows and other birds and creatures impacted in his path. O'Donnell's chest squeezed with disgust and pity as his foot fell on the mess of fur and feathers, blood and guts that splattered the forest floor. Then slipped.

His foot shoot sideways, ankle wrenching. Fear took hold as he went down. Then was compounded by the figure appearing before him as the shimmering distortion formed.

The Crone lashed out with her hands, lifting them up and bringing them together, fingers clawed. But not to strike him physically.

The deadly wind broke from a circle at her command. Its head rose high like a snake, then streamed in as it struck with a million teeth in its invisible body. O'Donnell rolled away in time and covered his head as the ground where he had been was torn up and turned over. Debris and dirt blasted his body, stinging his skin where it was exposed and biting through his clothing. It collected in his hair, under his shirt, within and behind his ears. Dust clogged his nose and he made the mistake of opening his mouth but quickly shut it as grit and larger particles stuck to his tongue.

The rush of air ceased. O'Donnell chanced a look, eyelids pressed close to keep as much of the debris out of them as he could.

Two figures wrestled in an unnatural way, locked in combat that was anything but physical. The Crone and Mortimer were facing off, their spectral bodies off the ground and still, but strained intently on one another. Shimmers of air roiled around them, lashing at one another, the chasing cyclone surrounding them.

"Quick James!" Nathan said, voice strained, though his lips hadn't moved. "I can't hold her for long!"

O'Donnell didn't wait. Leaping to his feet with a grunt, a shower of particles falling off him, he set off in a sprint, gritting his teeth at the pain from his twisted ankle. Once far enough, he slowed to a hobbling jog and glanced back, but there was no sign of either figure. They'd left as mysteriously as they had appeared, suddenly and without trace.

His foot snagged on something and he went crashing to the forest floor once more with a shout of fresh agony from his ankle before opening his eyes.

Gunther's blank eyes stared back into his.

Rolling off the body in panic, O'Donnell backed away. He had either circled back or backtracked. Or was led here. Perhaps had never left.

Rising to stand awkwardly, O'Donnell eyed Gunther's corpse before setting off at an awkward run, carefully picking his way through vegetation and debris and not daring to look back until he was passing the silver Mercedes once more.

Even though there was nothing following, he didn't slow until he was safely in the hatchback and heading down the mountain and driving past houses and stores. Though with what he had experienced, safety was now a relative term.

TWELVE

THE LIGHT TAP of fingertips on glass made O'Donnell jump from the small table. The bottle in one hand sloshed as the pistol in the other scraped on the desktop. Peering around the room divider, he placed them both down and limped to the door to unlock it.

Cassie looked at him with concern as he all but shoved her inside and slammed the door to lock it again, whatever good that would do.

"Are you okay, James? You look terrible."

He hadn't cleaned himself up. He probably looked a sight. Covered in dirt and leaves and whatever else. Would there be feathers on him somewhere?

He ushered her quickly behind the screen, hand at the small of her back. Once behind the screen, he picked up the bottle and took another swig. Cassie eyed him, eyes flitting to the gun and back.

"What's happened?" she said.

He shook his head, still downing bourbon. Gasping, he lowered the bottle. "He killed Gunther, Cassie!"

"You saw Nathan? Where? Was he—"

"Yeah I fucking saw him. One minute I'm rushing around after Gunther, then the prick has a gun in my face! But he wasn't pointing it at me. It was pointed at Nathan and I walked in on them. Next thing I know, Gunther blows the top of his own fucking head off!"

Cassie blinked, open-mouthed and silent a moment. "How?"

"With a fucking gun, Cassie! Jesus!"

Shaking her head, Cassie fell to sit. "He finally did it."

"Who? Did what? What the fuck did *he* do, Cassie?"

"You said Gunther shot himself."

O'Donnell gulped, nodded. Was his mind playing tricks with him, or had it been *exactly* like Jason? Down to the same movement and everything. The only missing piece had been Jason stealing O'Donnell's own pistol away to do it.

"Willingly?"

"What?"

"Concentrate, James. Did Gunther look like he willingly shot himself, or—" She stopped as O'Donnell's face answered the question.

"His hands were shaking. He— He looked like he was fighting someone, but Nathan was metres away. If he was there at all. Now tell me. What did he finally do?"

"Nathan's enlightened."

"Not this bullshit again."

"It's the only explanation!"

"How? How can that be the only explanation? We're talking about real life here, not some fucking Friday night horror movie. This shit doesn't happen in Melbourne, Cassie. It's not *meant* to happen!"

Cassie shook her head, then narrowed her eyes. "Something else happened, didn't it?"

He shook his head, in denial of what he had seen rather than in answer to her question. It was an urgent and repeated motion, as if to dislodge the memories from his mind. "The Crone."

"Jesus." Eyes widening, she reached out and took the bottle from him and took a healthy sip before handing it back.

"Yeah. No shit, Jesus. That's how I ended up like this."

"She... attacked you?"

He sneered and a scoffing single laugh exploded from his mouth. "Attacked? If you want to call it that." Swigging from the bottle, he slammed it on the table then clutched his head. "They got into some kind of pissing contest and then... It was like the forest was alive, Cassie. The wind. Their voices coming from the trees. Then all hell broke loose. Rocks and branches shit was flying everywhere. Birds were dropping from the trees, smashing into each other. Into me. Nathan seemed to be helping me. I have no idea why, but if it wasn't for him..."

Shaking her head, Cassie dropped into a chair. Even after the bombing, O'Donnell hadn't seen her look so concerned.

"What the hell is going on, Cassie? What have you gotten me in the middle of?"

Lifting her gaze, he could see the answer in her eyes before she even said it. "Honestly? I have no idea anymore."

"Well that's just fucking great!" Pushing a chair out angrily, he dropped into it, slouching. Putting his head in his hands, he leaned his elbows on the table.

Her look was apologetic, but she said nothing. What could she say? By all accounts, Gunther, Mortimer and the Crone were all busy playing their own game.

"Well, as long as you don't try to seduce me, then turn into that wrinkly old psychotic bitch and try and kill me, we'll be fine for the moment."

Her twinkling eyes narrowed. "You've been having visions. Tell me."

He shrugged, corner of his mouth hitching. "You turned up here in... well not much."

"Did I now? Then what?"

He winced at the memory. "Doesn't matter now. It wasn't you. It was her, wasn't it?"

Smile fading, Cassie nodded. "What did she do to you, James?"

"She... stuck her thumbs in my eyes, saying she was going to teach me to see."

"That's..."

"Fucked up? Yeah. Then in the forest, she was telling Nathan to either kill me or force me to see. Awaken me, she said."

"Awaken you?"

He nodded. "Or for him to 'leave me be'. Any idea what she meant by that?"

Cassie slowly shook her head.

"Because, to me it sounded like Nathan had chosen me."

Her head shook more violently. "That's not possible. *We* found you when we couldn't locate Nathan. We got a recommendation from—" Her eyes narrowed. "Unless..."

"What?"

"No." She shook her head again. "It's not possible. Forget I said anything."

"Except you *didn't* say anything. Go on. Say what you were thinking." Cassie glanced up at him. "You think Nathan led you to me somehow. Him or the Crone." She gave him a blank stare. "Jesus. I'm right, aren't I? Why would they want me?"

"I don't know, James. It's only a guess. None of this makes sense to me."

"Well if you're lost, where does that leave me?"

Up the proverbial creek without a paddle was where it left him. The smart thing to would be to get out at the first opportunity. But he had a feeling it would not be that easy. He was as neck deep in it as the rest of them.

"The only thing I can think," she said, fingers tapping on the edge of her chair, "is that they wanted you to join."

He turned on her. "Join? Do I look like the joining type to you?"

"It's not about how you look or feel about it, James. Some people are closer to awakening than others, whatever the reason. Sensitive. And Nathan—the Crone and Gunther too, I'm assuming—can see that."

"You mean, you can't?"

"No. It takes someone far more enlightened than me."

"Then what was all that at the club?"

A long sigh escaped her lips. "As I said before, all we did was give you a little nudge. Even that much took all of us to accomplish. I couldn't have done it on my own. Not even with a couple of us. It was a group effort and it exhausted us."

"So you're saying that all of you together don't compare to one of those three?" They were two now with Gunther dead, he remembered, but that was splitting hairs.

"And now you begin to see the true power of the Enlightened."

"And Gateway."

She shook her head. "Gunther's gone now."

"Gone? He didn't go anywhere, he was murdered, Cassie!"

It sounded strange coming from his own lips after seeing the man shoot himself. But he could no longer deny the things happening around him. Everything else he could put down to tricks, to being drugged. But the experience in the forest... That had been something completely different.

As the truth sank in, he pushed out of his chair and stood. The world around him was closing in, trapping him. And if he didn't find a way out, it would become a coffin. His heart hammered as he leaned on the table and let out a long, shaky breath.

"Easy," Cassie said, on her feet and beside him.

He could feel the warmth of her palm through his shirt as she worked small circles over it. The material soaked up the pinpricks of cold sweat as she did.

"Try to relax," she said, voice as soft and calming as her patting. "I know it's a lot to take in. I was the same when the truth hit me."

Hanging his head further, he let out a nervous laugh that had been building up. "This shouldn't be possible."

"And yet the things you've seen tell you it is." He nodded, head still down. "There's a lot more hidden in the world than you've been exposed. Be strong and you can weather it."

"You know what else has more hidden than you can see? Icebergs. And look what happened to the Titanic."

She laughed.

He looked up at her then, and she back at him.

"Help me," O'Donnell said, his voice barely a whisper.

She smiled again. "How about I prove it to you instead?"

"Prove what?"

Stepping closer, Cassie reached out her hand and stroked his cheek.

O'Donnell was overcome by desire. Not specifically for her, but an overwhelming hunger that had burst up, like a guttering fire fanned by a strong wind, leaping and spitting with heat. Before he knew it, they were both doing the same, bursting forth and tearing at each other until the fuel for the flames had been consumed.

———

They lay naked on the sofa bed, O'Donnell overcome by the dream-like, languorous sensations that had replaced the oppressiveness.

"Proof enough for you?" Cassie said, lying beside him inverted, her hand playing across the skin and hairs on his thigh.

He let out a chuckle. "How was that proof?"

As pleasurable as the sex had been, and as enduring as the euphoria was, O'Donnell didn't feel any clearer on the problems at hand.

Cassie propped her head on her hand. "You obviously had a strong desire to have sex with me. But would you have normally?"

O'Donnell gave a non-committal shrug. "My being horny doesn't prove anything."

"I think that was more than a little bit horny."

He grinned back at her. "Okay, fine. It had been a while. And I'll admit you have an effect on me. That doesn't mean—"

The grin on her lips turned down, as did her brow. "What about the dream?"

"What dream?"

"The dream you had of me coming to you in lingerie before I turned into the Crone and gouged your eyes out?" He shrugged. "Appearing before you? You lifting me onto your desk after I plea-sured you, and lowering to your knees and—"

"What?"

"Then, when I was astride you on the chair, I made you look at me. But it wasn't me. It was *her*."

He sprung up to look her over, eyes straining as if he could pierce whatever illusion might be at play. "How do you know that? Who told you that?"

"You did." She sat up, crossing her legs. "You didn't see it, did you?"

"See what? What are you talking about, Cassie? You still haven't—"

"I saw your dream in my mind as we were having sex."

His mouth opened, but he couldn't think what to counter that with. As implausible as it sounded, was it any less fantastic than what he'd come to believe? Or was it more a case of trust? He had no reason not to. The question was, had she really given him any reason *to* trust her?

"You still don't trust me," she said, nodding.

"I—"

"No. You're right not to. I would think you foolish if you did."

O'Donnell grinned at her.

"What?" she said, almost snapping, lips tightening as she sat back.

"You get all prim and proper when you get angry. And when you were getting all emotional talking about your past your accent was different again."

Cassie glared at him, but there was a flush to her cheeks. "I do *not* have an accent!"

As his grinned widened, he felt his cheek muscles strain. "Oh my god, you're actually blushing!"

Sitting up straighter, she took a deep breath, breasts pushing out as the pink in her cheeks reddened and crept down her neck and chest. "In one of my lives I was a bushido master, James, and could snap your neck where we sit."

A low chuckle built in O'Donnell's chest. "No doubt. But..." He inched forward and pecked her on the nose with a kiss. "I think it's cute."

"Don't get attached to me, James."

He slumped back heavily. Turning, O'Donnell dropped his feet to the floor. He tested his weight on his ankle. It was stiff and bruised but far better.

Leaning, he pulled on his boxers then pants. "I called you cute. That doesn't mean I've fallen head over heels for you, Cassie." He walked to the table and snatched his cigarettes.

"I didn't mean to imply—"

"Save it, please, for both our sakes." Lighting up, he dropped the packet then the lighter on the table.

She turned and dressed. "Sex can be sex without meaning more."

He exhaled sharply, scoffing. "What? You think a poor country bumpkin like me doesn't know that? Can't recognise a fuck for a fuck when he sees one?"

Her hands froze at her back, one of her bra hooks in place. "I didn't—"

"You know, just because you call yourself enlightened, doesn't mean you know everything, Cassie Lawler. Not about the world, and especially not about me."

Her head turned sharply as she looked back over her shoulder. She nodded once, then finished dressing. Teasing her hair neat with her hands, she walked to the table and picked up the cigarettes. She lit one, then carefully placed the pack down, lighter atop it. She aligned the packet to the edge of the table and smoked in silence.

"I'm sorry if I offended you," she said finally. "It was not my intention. And I also did not mean to make assumptions about you."

Grunting, O'Donnell nodded and continued to smoke.

"Contrary to what you may think, I do not think I know everything. None of us do."

"I'm not so sure about Gateway." He turned to her when she didn't say anything. "I'm sorry, too. I shouldn't have lost it with you."

"It's all right. I know many people get offended and hurt at things like that." Looking down, she straightened her dress, then took a drag from the cigarette. "One would think having all that knowledge and history of multiple people would make us more knowledgeable in relationships. But it's actually the opposite."

"Really?"

Her head dipped in a slow single nod. "Quite ironic, isn't it?"

O'Donnell shrugged. "I dunno. Makes sense really. Like how really smart people, geniuses, aren't very good at the basic stuff. Give them huge problems to solve the universe, they're fine. Ask them to make change for a packet of gum, they get stumped. And, in my experience, knowledge doesn't equal wisdom."

Cassie smiled. "Nathan would say much the same thing."

"Do you love him?"

"Yes," she said. "But not like that."

He hummed in thought. "You know, once this is all over…"

"Yes?" she said slowly.

"Maybe we should find an apartment together? Buy a tandem bicycle and a terrier? How does that sound?"

Her wide grin returned. "Terrible. I want a white picket fence in the country and a border collie."

"Ah," O'Donnell said, smiling wide and nodding. "You were a *Famous Five* fan too as a kid, huh?"

They laughed together a moment before Cassie let out a huff. "What are we going to do, James?"

"I wish I knew. I was hoping you and your buddies would have some ideas."

Cassie chewed on her lip a moment. "I've been thinking about that."

"Yeah?"

"I think you're right. What we really need now are friends in the right places to give us some help and any answers we can get."

"Okay. With you so far. So, you *are* going to enlist the rest of the Enlightened?" She nodded in response. "And what about me?"

Her look was telling.

———

"Fuck's sake, Jimmy!" Robbie whipped his arm about and threw away the unfinished cigarette in his hand.

"I—"

Robbie held his hands up, stopping O'Donnell. He turned to watch the men scouring the forest with dogs, crashing through trees and ferns.

His first call had been to Inglewood, or at least he had attempted to reach her. If O'Donnell was right, that was the connection Gunther had used to secure the bomb. But after several attempts, once even from a payphone on his way to speak to Robbie, he had come up against a brick wall. Either Inglewood was laying low, or she didn't want to speak to him. That only left Gunther's body.

He hoped Cassie was having better luck than he was.

O'Donnell was sure he had the right spot. They had passed the large tree he had found Gunther and Mortimer behind. But the police had come up empty. No body. No gun. No blood. There wasn't even any bird carcasses left behind. From what they could see, there were quite a few broken branches and disturbed ground in the immediate vicinity, suggesting someone had been running around in circles. But nothing to the extent of the supernatural wind.

"What the fuck kind of game are you playing, Jimmy?"

O'Donnell threw up his hands in dismay. "I'm telling you, Robbie. I stood in front of the bastard as he pulled the trigger."

"Uhuh. And then you say you got attacked by that crazy old bitch again?"

"I know how it sounds, Robbie."

"No, no, no. Keep going."

Letting his eyes close, O'Donnell hung his head. "She was fighting with Nathan."

"Right! So, not only did you *stumble* upon Gunther, a man not only on Victoria's but on fucking Australia's most wanted list, you decided to fucking follow him! And, as if that wasn't enough of a dumb fuck move, you say you just *happened* to run into a woman who escaped a secure psychiatric facility. Oh, and attempted to stab you in the back, not to mention subduing a grown arse police man—" Robbie tapped himself on the chest. "And she was, what? Up here with Nathan Mortimer?"

"I—"

"Who *also* cracked himself out of a fucking loony bin!" Robbie gave him a wide, sarcastic smile. "And what were they doing here exactly, having a tea party?"

"Robbie…"

"Nah, you know what? I bet they were up here playing *fucking Nintendo!*"

Several men around them snickered.

Robbie threw them glances with eyes full of fire and they locked it down. He threw up his hand, finger raised, and spun it, telling the men to wrap up. He waited until they had all packed up and were walking back to the grass clearing before he would look at O'Donnell again.

"Robbie. Please."

"What? Please what, mate?"

"You've got to listen to me."

Robbie snorted in disgust and shook his head. "You know what? When people said you were incompetent for letting Jason get a hold of your weapon and committing suicide in the station, I told them all to shut the fuck up. Anyone would have shown an old mate who was in trouble some leniency. And who would expect a thing like that?"

Bunching his hands into fists, O'Donnell pressed them into his hips and closed his eyes.

"Then, when you decided to leave the force because you couldn't hack it, and they said you were weak, I told them they didn't know what it was like to watch someone blow their brains out in front of them."

"Robbie, I—"

"*And* then with all this PI shit, I told them you haven't been a copper for years. Didn't know any better. But when you started fucking up my investigation—"

O'Donnell turned his head. "I didn't—"

"And lying to me for a piece of arse?" Robbie leaned in and slapped O'Donnell on the cheek to get his attention. "Hey! You look at me!"

Gritting his teeth, O'Donnell opened his eyes, keeping his anger in check.

"You've lost it, mate." Robbie gave him a sad grin, eyes wide, shaking his head. "You're a fucking lost cause now."

"Gunther was here. Nathan was—"

"Oh, fucking Jesus!"

"They were here, Robbie!"

"Yeah. And the old bird. And Elvis and JFK and his girlfriend Marilyn Monroe, and they all had an orgy then got in their UFO and flew away." He flitted his fingers and raised his hand to the sky. "I get it, mate."

"Somehow I doubt that," O'Donnell muttered.

Robbie's acerbic grin grew. "Tell you what. You see them all again, why don't you reach out and give that doctor at Rowville a call. Or better yet, one of those tabloids. They'll probably put your story on the front cover next to the stories about Bigfoot and Bert Newton's hair." He turned and started storming off after his men for the clearing.

"Robbie! Wait!"

Turning sharply, any humour in his expression was gone. "No, you fucking wait!" he said, and jabbed the air with a finger. "You're supposed to be my fucking mate, Jimmy. What happened to you?"

"I am."

"Yeah? Fucking funny way of showing it, *mate*. There's one thing I can't work out, and I need to hear it from the horse's mouth."

"What?"

Robbie inched forward. "Are you fucking one of them?"

"No! Robbie, I—"

"Because if I fucking find out that you are... Mate or not, I'll fucking string you up myself." Robbie turned on his heel and strode off again. He lifted his hand in the air but didn't turn back. "Oh, and if I catch you anywhere fucking near one of my crime scenes, or someone so much as sees you with someone who looks like Cassie Lawler, I *will* bust your balls for obstruction of justice, aiding and abetting, harbouring a wanted felon... Shit, I might even try for treason if I can get it to stick."

Stopping in his tracks, O'Donnell watched Robbie walk away. That had not gone as he'd hoped. Turning back, he looked the area over, eyes coming to rest where Gunther's body had been.

Had Nathan cleaned up? Or had it been the Crone? Perhaps she was with Gateway after all. The fight between them certainly suggested that. And Gunther was her new hopeful messiah. It would stand to reason she might have taken his body.

But then why allow Nathan to kill him?

O'Donnell had come back up the mountain looking for answers, hoping to get assistance from an ally. Now he had more of the former than he had before coming back, and one less friend.

At least one of those answers—the most pressing of them as far as O'Donnell was concerned—was now answered. He now knew where they needed to go next.

THIRTEEN

THE RED VALIANT thundered down the highway, easily chewing up the kilometres. Cassie had insisted they take it, tired of the little hatch.

"Shitbox little piece of plastic," she said. "Not like this beauty."

"That's not very enlightened, is it?"

Cassie laughed openly. "I told you, James. I used to be a complete bogan."

Turning to her, smirking, he tried to imagine it. "I still don't believe you."

She nodded emphatically. "It's true. I went everywhere in trackie dacks, tight T-shirts and Ugg boots."

He choked down a laugh as he tried to imagine her in tracksuit pants. "Okay, you're going to have to show me photo evidence."

Laughing, she had only responded by shaking her keys, a single key for the car on a rabbit's foot keychain.

That had been some hours before, when their spirits were still high. Now, they had been driving back and forth with nothing to show for it.

Cassie let out a frustrated sigh.

"We'll find something," O'Donnell said.

She nodded, but her eyes were dull and fixed on the road.

They'd started where O'Donnell had, at Rowville Psychiatric Hospital. The staff there were less than willing to let them in now, however.

From there, they had slowly made their way through the list of hospitals Nathan had been admitted to.

When he'd floated the idea to Cassie, she'd been reluctant. "What do you hope to achieve by going to all those hospitals?" She had almost spat out the last word, her thought on the institutions evident as her lips had twitched in a sneer. "You know Nathan turned back to drugs. I as much as told you so. We think he turned back to it after the revelations of Gunther's betrayal. And with that his mental health deteriorated."

"Did you know it was this bad?" He held up the list of the known hospitals Nathan had been admitted to. "I mean, you said you two were close."

She shook her head. "I kept it a secret as long as I could. I only found out after he disappeared myself. But in the end, he began to change, and we drifted apart. He just seemed to... deteriorate."

He nodded. He thought knew what she was getting at, that they had remained physical though emotionally distant. It wasn't like her to mince words. But he decided he wasn't going to read into it. Especially given their own recent intimacy. Not when O'Donnell couldn't be sure that he wasn't up to his own old habits.

"If I had known it was this bad, I would have told the group and we would have intervened and helped him. Instead, he had to be cared for by strangers. And we both know what sort of *care* most of these places give."

O'Donnell mulled it over for a moment. "I'm not so sure." She shot him a frown. "Not of the hospitals. I mean, his reason for being there."

"You think there's more to it?"

From what he had seen of both Nathan and Gunther, they didn't really do anything without reason. Everything was planned. The same may or may not be true of the Crone—or her own reason was so warped it didn't match with any reality O'Donnell knew. The drugs may have been a part of that or a coping mechanism, but he didn't believe it was as simple as Nathan running around blindly and needing help.

"What if Nathan has been going around these hospitals looking for someone?"

He knew he was on to something when she had frowned deeply at that. "Who?"

"Not sure. Maybe someone specific? Or, maybe someone he needs but doesn't know yet? Maybe he's trying to fix his mistakes with Gunther? Or maybe he's not after one person, but a whole bunch."

"That's a lot of maybes." She had narrowed her eyes in concentration after that. "You might be right on that last one though."

"You think he's recruiting? Building the troops for a coming war with Gateway?"

She shook her head. "Not recruiting. Helping."

"Helping?"

"I told you my story. When Nathan started, he was all about helping those who needed it. Setting up the halfway homes. Maybe he's now decided that, after spending some time in one of these places with their archaic practices, the best way to do so was from the inside? That could also explain why both we and Gateway hadn't been able to locate him."

"How'd you mean?"

"Surrounded by all those broken minds, he might have somehow masked himself. Especially if he had awoken a number of them."

If she knew that, Nathan had to as well, and O'Donnell hoped that didn't mean Nathan was hiding from them, but he didn't voice the thought.

One step at a time.

He checked the list of hospitals in his hand. Two left.

He caught Cassie eyeing him sidelong and turned to her. "We'll find him."

Kicking the tire of the Valiant, Cassie cursed and grunted in frustration. "God damn it!"

He couldn't be sure, but O'Donnell thought it someone was deliberately blocking their way into the hospitals. Yet again, someone was one step ahead of them. He wasn't yet sure if that was the very same person they were searching for.

By now, even O'Donnell was losing the steam to keep her positive. He sighed and tapped the list in his hand before shoving it back in his jacket pocket. "We've still got one left."

"No!" She turned to him, her shoulders and face set with determination. "You and I both know that the next place will be exactly the same. It's here or nowhere!"

"Okay, I'm not going to contradict you. But what do you suggest?"

Her face relaxed as she searched the area. The hard line of her thin brows softened then rose. Opening the door and leaning into the car, she pulled out her purse, cranked the driver's window shut, then locked the car. She pulled a dark-red lipstick from the purse and applied it before replacing it with her cigarettes.

"Follow me," she said. "And play along."

She winked at him as he gave her a questioning frown, then Cassie took off at a brisk pace along the path. Soon, they were walking alongside a tall chain-link fence topped with barbed wire, warning notices strung on it at regular intervals. As she walked, she stopped at any junction and peered at her feet, but at each she moved on. Until they came to one not far from the rear of the building.

"Here," she said, coming to a stop.

He peered at the ground and smirked. "Clever."

The stained concrete was littered with cigarette butts, which overflowed through the nearby fence and dotted a nearby garden bed of bare dirt and yellowing bushes.

"Not just a pretty face," she said as she lit up.

They were halfway through their third smoke before three male orderlies strode from the building, chatting and laughing. Two of them looked Cassie up and down with leering interest. The third appeared oblivious, more intent on rolling a cigarette with tobacco from an old shoe polish tin.

The three men talked amongst themselves and smoked, the two who had paid attention to Cassie now more interested in their conversation. But as Cassie put on a show of being upset and talking in a low voice to O'Donnell, now the third was eyeing them.

"I— I want to know what's happened to him, you know?" she said, sniffling and putting on waterworks.

O'Donnell played his part by creasing his brow and consoling her.

"How can someone up and disappear without a trace?"

The man with rollies narrowed his eyes at them.

The two orderlies finished their cigarettes and threw the butts aside without a care, then started walking away. The one with the self-rolled stayed back.

"You comin' or not?" one of the men leaving said.

"In a moment," the man said. He shook his tin at the other two.

The two orderlies laughed then walked away.

"What are you folks doing out here?" the man said.

"I…" Cassie frowned deeply, eyes watering and lip trembling. Her previously straight shoulders and almost perfect posture hung loose, her head craning forward slightly. She'd mussed her hair and smeared her eyeliner, dabbing her fingers under her eyes to paint dark circles. "My name's Cassie Mortimer. This is James O'Donnell. He's a… a private investigator. I'm, uh… He's helping me search for my—" Cassie's words devolved into unintelligible sniffles.

O'Donnell's hand circled on her shoulder blade. "Her brother's been missing," he said softly to the orderly, as if Cassie wasn't there. "He's been in and out of psychiatric hospitals for the last few years. This is one of the hospitals he's been to recently."

The man nodded, compassion on his face. He was clearly not like his colleagues, which made O'Donnell wonder why he was socialising with them. Though he knew from experience, work was one thing and private life another.

"Your brother," the orderly said in deep thought, opening his tin.

He rested it within the lid, then placed it on his left forearm tucked against his ribs. "Is his name Nathan?"

Cassie's eyes light up. "You've seen him!"

The man shook his head, taking out a cigarette paper with a soft crinkle. "Not recently." Cassie's smile and her head lowered as he dropped a pinch of rich brown tobacco in the folded paper. "But he's been around, yeah." Holding the paper between finger and thumb, he closed the tin and pocketed it. "Popular bloke."

"Popular?" O'Donnell said.

"Yeah. With the other patients." The man rolled, then licked the paper sealing it shut, fixing a wrinkle in the side with a dab from his tongue and smoothing it out with his finger. "Sometimes someone comes in and they have a certain... gravitas."

O'Donnell raised his eyebrows at the man.

"You don't know my brother, Mr O'Donnell," Cassie said, voice soft, so unlike the woman he had been getting to know. "He is very charming and very persuasive."

"That's him," the man said, lighting the rollie. He proffered his hand, motioning it in the air before speaking, spreading the aromatic tobacco like incense. "Silver spoon in his mouth. And he would spoon feed the others with it."

"These others," O'Donnell said. "Any of them still around?"

"A few."

"Any way that we might be able to speak to them?"

"Might be I could arrange something."

O'Donnell smirked and reached for his wallet. "Like that, is it?"

The man's face wrinkled up, offended. "You might be used to that kind of thing in your line of work, but not everyone is on the take, Mr O'Donnell."

O'Donnell eyed the man. He was being genuine. "What about those guys with you before?" he said, closing his wallet and putting it away.

"Them? More than likely they would take your money."

"But not you?" O'Donnell was dubious. "Why?"

The man shrugged. "I like seeing the right thing done by people.

That's why I got into this job. Most people working in these places forget that. It becomes a job. And so many people here don't get real help. I try to help as many as I can in my own way, but I'm only one man."

"Very noble of you," O'Donnell said, still somewhat suspicious, but mostly curious.

"Not really." He dropped the end of the smoke and ground it out. "Tomorrow night. Here. At dusk."

"Thank you so much," Cassie said sniffling, her mouth forming a quick smile. "I don't know how to—"

The man pointed at Cassie sharply with his mid and fore-finger. "Not you. Just him. Or no deal."

Cassie blinked in confusion, Then stood straighter, her expression flattening. "Fine," she said, nodding.

The man looked her up and down, weighing her up rather than ogling her as his colleagues had. He gave a sharp nod then walked away.

"Hey," O'Donnell called out, the man turning to walk backwards. "What's your name?"

"Leigh," the man said, then swung around and hurried inside.

"I'm not really sure I trust him," O'Donnell said.

"You should." Cassie fixed her hair, her hands somehow enough to style it back into shape. Then she passed her hands over her eyes and her makeup was un-smeared and blemish free.

O'Donnell chuckled to himself as he watched her. He was afraid to ask how she was accomplishing the feat. "How do you know?" he asked instead.

"Because he doesn't trust me."

"And that's supposed to make me feel better?"

She smirked at him and took out a cigarette and started walking back to the Valiant. "What should we do until the meeting?" she said, voice low.

He grinned at her, shaking his head.

"What? Can you blame a girl?"

"Don't you think we should still go to the last hospital?"

Slowing, Cassie turned her gaze back to the smoking area. "I think we're in the right place with your new friend."

"*My* new friend?"

"Well, he certainly didn't like me."

"Why did you say his not trusting you was a good sign, Cassie?"

"I wasn't trying to hint that I'm a bad guy, James, if that's what you're asking. I simply meant he has good intuition."

"That almost sounds like the same thing."

Leading the way again, she turned to him with a smirk. "I told you, James. Some people are more sensitive to the supernatural."

"Supernatural? Is that what the Enlightened call themselves?"

"What we do is outside of the normal realms of people's under-standing. Outside science. What else would you call it?"

He conceded the point with a shrug. "So you think he's... what? A naturally Enlightened person? No... what did Nathan and... Awake. You think he's naturally been awoken?"

"Not awake. Maybe... sleepwalking."

"I think I'm getting more confused."

She let out a laugh. "If you're the only one awake in a room full of sleeping people, what happens when someone else wakes up?"

"You're... both awake."

"Exactly. You're aware of each other's waking state while the sleeping people aren't."

"And a sleepwalker... they might see you while they're up? Then forget you?"

"Something like that. They'll know subconsciously you're awake. They may even remember it when they wake up, or go back to sleep and dream about it, but they'll never truly know."

"Right. I think I get you. So basically... that man knows there's something different about you, but he's not quite sure what."

"Now you've got it. Plus, I think he has a better-than-average bull-shit detector."

"So what if, say, he was Gateway? Would you be able to tell, and vice versa?"

Her forehead wrinkled in a thoughtful frown. "I used to think so. But now I'm not so sure."

That was concerning, and he could tell it was worrying her. "Cassie." He caught her arm and stopped her. "Do I need to be careful tomorrow? With this man?"

She thought about it a moment. "I don't think so."

He dropped his hand and sighed. Reaching into his pocket, he pulled out his cigarettes. "Great."

"I'm sorry. I wish I could tell you with one hundred percent certainty. But things have been far more unpredictable."

Inhaling deeply, he let out a stream of smoke with another sigh. "But your gut instinct?"

"My instincts say you can trust him. That he won't harm you."

He tapped the end of the cigarette butt with his thumb, sucking in his lower lip as he thought. "Good enough for me," he said.

"What about your instincts?"

"Me?" He shrugged. "He was genuine enough. Concerned for the patients inside. His eyes, though..."

"What about them?"

"There was this kind of deep sadness or something. I thought they were like yours at first."

"What are my eyes like?"

"Fishing for compliments?" He smirked before frowning in thought. "Like you've experienced more than the average person. But his are different."

"How so?"

"Like... he's experienced more darkness than a single person should." He glanced around as he searched his memories. "Like soldiers who've been to war a long time and seen a lot of death."

Cassie's brows arched, her eyes searching his momentarily. "Maybe he *should* be enlightened if what you saw is true. It certainly sounds like he could use some unburdening."

"You didn't see that?"

Cassie shook her head slowly. "I told you, being Enlightened means we sometimes miss the smaller things."

O'Donnell found that hard to believe. There had such a weight expressed through Leigh's eyes, how could someone so insightful as Cassie have missed it?

"Too busy on solving the universe, huh?" he said.

With a hesitant nod, she started walking again. "So, what *do* we do until tomorrow?"

"I've been thinking about that."

"Have you now," Cassie said, giving him a wicked grin.

"Not *that*." She raised a brow. "Okay, maybe a little bit that. But later. No, I was thinking that I need to still track down the person who gave the bomb to Gunther."

"Why? He's dead."

"The man might be, but if Gateway is as much of a cult as we think, then the man's ideals and ideas aren't."

"You think the others will continue without him?"

"I was hoping you'd be able to answer that for me."

Cassie gave him a shrug. She was as much in the dark as O'Donnell, which given she was part of a group calling themselves enlightened was as funny as it was ironic. It stood to reason though. If Gunther had created a whole group like himself by tearing into their souls, their third eye, or whatever it was he was messing with, and they had followed him... killed for him...

"Why would they stop now?" O'Donnell asked out loud.

They were back at the Valiant. Eyes fixed on the empty space over the car, Cassie unlocked the car and opened her door.

"I think you're right," she said. She blinked, her long lashes batting, and turned her eyes to him. "But what can we do about it?" She climbed into the car and leaned over to unlock his door.

When he was in, he sat for a moment in thought, Cassie facing him and waiting. He turned to her suddenly, and she leaned forward.

"You hungry?" O'Donnell said.

The din of the shopping centre rose and fell as people came and went. As Cassie bit hungrily into her food, not being shy about making a mess, O'Donnell watched her, enjoying seeing her in such a normal act.

"What?" she said around a mouthful.

"Nothing. It's just… I dunno. It's refreshing to be eating with someone who enjoys their food."

She covered her mouth with her hand and laughed, working hard to swallow the food down without choking. "One thing that being Enlightened does not do is change old, already learnt muscle memory. Such as eating." She stopped short of biting in again. "And, if you keep staring at me, I'm going to start getting self-conscious."

"Sorry," he said, laughing.

"So you should be. Now, eat your souvlaki before it gets cold and the fat congeals."

"Yes, ma'am."

They ate in silence, O'Donnell doing his best not to stare at her like some teenage boy. Before he was halfway through, Cassie was done and wiping her lips and fingers roughly with several napkins and reapplying lipstick.

"I wouldn't have picked you for a souva type," she said, staring at herself in a compact mirror and finishing up.

He shrugged and swallowed. "Not sure why. It's one of the staples of the police diet."

"Is that how you found this place?"

He stopped mid-chew, then shook his head as he finished up and cleared his throat. "Ah, no, actually. I was out of the force a while by then. But I definitely developed the taste for fast food like this on the job."

Snapping the compact shut and putting it away, Cassie sat back in her seat and turned her attention to him. "Why did you leave?"

Shrugging, O'Donnell wrapped up the remainder of the souvlaki in its foiled paper bag and pushed it aside. He wiped his own hands and lips of grease and tzatziki, then placed the wadded-up napkin atop the food.

"Long story short?"

Cassie shrugged. "Whatever you're up for. It's not like we have anything better to do." She cocked a pencilled brow at him.

The corner of his mouth jerked up, then dropped as suddenly. "There was an incident. I'd been on the force a few years already."

"It sounds like it was something that had a profound impact on you."

"You could say that, yes."

Taking a deep breath, O'Donnell told Cassie about Jason. Their past together. His issues with drugs and going in and out of institutions. Then his final moments. How he'd feigned sickness and James had gone into the cell by himself with his weapon, a cardinal sin. How Jason had lunged for it and wrestled it from him.

"At first..." O'Donnell toyed with the napkin he had picked up at some point during the story. "I thought he was going to shoot me. That maybe he had some psychotic break. A million things raced through my head at the time. Not a single one of them, though, was that he was going to kill himself."

Cassie leaned into the table and reached for his hand. "I'm so sorry, James."

He shrugged, and glanced at her fingers on his, felt their warmth. "What can you do, huh?"

She shook her head. "Still, to go through something like that..." Her frown deepened. "And all of this, with Nathan and Gunther... it must be bringing up a lot of memories for you."

"I'd be lying if I said I hadn't thought about Jason a few times... or few dozen." He gave her a weak smile. "It must seem pretty silly to you."

"How do you mean?"

"Well, you must have the memories of how many people dying locked in your head. Not to mention your own... Your past self..." He waved a hand. "How do you refer to that anyway?"

She let out a small laugh. "It's funny that you ask. Most people don't stop to truly think about the implications of what being Enlightened means. The mechanics of it."

"How can't you?"

"Look around you, James. What do you see?"

Turning in his seat, he scanned the area with a slow sweep of his head.

"Families. Couples. Staff." O'Donnell shrugged. "People going about their daily routines." He thought deeper. That was what she meant, he thought as he turned back to her. "Going through the motions. Like a roller coaster ride, always on the same track, around and around."

"Most people don't think that way. I know I sure as hell didn't before Nathan came to me, offering to awaken me."

"But... isn't that irresponsible? Taking advantage of you?"

Cassie sat back, her lips parted and silent for a moment. "I suppose, if you look at it in that light... Yes?"

She suddenly appeared so young, every bit her physical age. A lost and confused young woman barely out of her teens. And O'Donnell had a pang of guilt.

If he was accusing Nathan of taking advantage of her, then what did that make O'Donnell? She may have lifetimes of knowledge, but how did that make him any better than Nathan or Gunther? To use his very own words to Cassie, knowledge did not equal wisdom.

He gently extracted his hand from her fingers. "Come on," he said, rising and taking his jacket from the back of the chair. "I need a smoke."

FOURTEEN

THE SKY on the horizon was burnished pink, gold and purple when O'Donnell arrived at the hospital early and parked as close to the meeting place as possible. It was a staff car park, but the little hatchback fit in with a group of others much like it.

Seeing nothing out of the ordinary, or of any real interest, he got out and walked to the unofficial staff smoking area and had a few himself. He kicked around the tell-tale signs of the smokers, disturbing the cigarette butts. There were as many of the rollie butts as there were a mix of pre-packaged brands. They weren't weathered enough to be that old. Could there be more than a few staff who rolled their own? It seemed unlikely. But the man smoking all those himself was equally doubtful.

It was an oddity, and something about it bothered him, but did it amount to anything? As he was contemplating it further, the man himself approached at a casual pace and lit up, acting nonchalant.

"You're quite the smoker," O'Donnell said.

Leigh glanced around him, then smirked. "More than you would know. But these aren't all from me."

"Oh? You been converting the masses inside?"

The man glanced at O'Donnell with an odd expression, as if he'd been caught by surprise. "Why on earth would you ask me that?"

O'Donnell shrugged, smiling innocently. "Didn't mean anything by it."

He knew he had. And so too did the man, Leigh. Though he didn't say anything. At least not for a few moments.

"I told you I do my best to help the people inside. Sometime that help comes from external places, when required."

Nodding, O'Donnell sized the man up. He was lithe and lanky. He appeared at first glance to be relaxed, but O'Donnell had seen men like that before. Exuding an air of ease, but always at the ready. Criminals had it when the police were around. Likewise the police themselves. But that wasn't it.

"Were you in the army?" O'Donnell asked, inspiration striking.

"Me?" Leigh said with a snort. "Why would you think that?"

"You seem the type. I was on the force, so I've met a few exsoldiers. They leave the reserves or do a tour then join up, wanting to do some good but not be away from their families. But the things that they see..." He shrugged a shoulder. "You kind of have the same feel about you."

"You're a perceptive man, Mr O'Donnell."

"James, please."

"Okay, James. Yes, you could say I've seen action," he said with some reserve. He eyed O'Donnell. "Still do."

O'Donnell chuckled. "Not sure what that means. I'm assuming your work." He pointed up at the building with his cigarette.

"Exactly. Like the Salvation Army, protecting those that can't protect themselves."

"Onward Christian soldier. Do you play in the brass band too?"

Leigh chuckled. "I've seen and done far too much to be either of those things."

"You're not religious?"

The man's face wrinkled in an amused frown. "Are you some kind of Jehovah's Witness as well as an investigator, James?"

"Just making conversation. I assume we're keeping up pretences.

Plus, I'm curious. The young woman I was here with yesterday, Nathan's sister... They both believe pretty heavily in reincarnation and weird shit like that. She kept going on about it."

"Ah," Leigh said with a knowing nod.

"Don't tell me you got the same sales pitch from the brother?"

"Not personally, but I heard Nathan talking to some of the other patients." Leigh frowned. "And them repeating it around."

"You don't sound too impressed with that."

"Would you be? Most of these people are down and out, easily influenced."

O'Donnell shrugged. "I figured it was some new age bullshit. But what would I know, I'm a simple boy from the country." O'Donnell gave his best small town grin.

"Uhuh. Somehow, James, I seriously doubt you're *just* a country boy." Leigh dropped the remains of his cigarette and ground it under his sneaker. "Come on. Way should be clear now."

Flicking his butt into the garden bed, O'Donnell followed Leigh, doing his best to act natural. A difficult task given that he was wary of Gateway infiltrating the hospitals. It had to be the only answer. If O'Donnell and the police could figure out that Nathan had been in and out of most of the psychiatric wards and hospitals around Melbourne, Gunther and his lot would have too. And then put up the necessary roadblocks and covered both their and Nathan's tracks.

Unlocking a door with a swipe card, Leigh held the door open and indicated in with his head. "This way," Leigh said, following after O'Donnell as he went in.

It would have been the perfect place for a trap. Darkened hallway, no one around. Leigh could have stabbed him in the back and there would be nothing O'Donnell could do about it. Instead, he led O'Donnell to a store room.

"Put those on," Leigh said, pointing at a locker.

O'Donnell opened it and saw an orderly's uniform like Leigh's. Older and worn around the edges, probably salvaged, but passable.

"Anyone asks," Leigh said as O'Donnell dressed, "you're my buddy, filling in for Rick at the last minute. No one will, but in case." Leigh looked O'Donnell over as he finished and, handing him a lanyard with some random pass hooked on it, nodded. "It'll do. Follow my lead, don't stare at any of the patients, and most of all... don't be an arsehole."

Leading him on his rounds, Leigh handed O'Donnell a tray of tiny paper cups with medication and a plastic water jug, the name of each patient written on the cup. Leigh carried a black zippered bag under his arm, talking pleasantly with patients and staff when they encountered them. Wherever he went, the man was well liked. If Leigh was Gateway, then he was hell of a good actor. But O'Donnell didn't get that vibe from him. He found himself, like the people they met, warming to the man.

As they entered a hallway, Leigh pulled to one side and stopped. He leaned in close. "These are the rooms of some of the most disturbed patients we have. Just stay behind me and stay quiet, okay?"

O'Donnell nodded, Leigh returning the nod before he continued to the first room. By that time, O'Donnell had already built a healthy respect for the man. But as they continued through the rooms, he saw Leigh for who he truly was. A compassionate and caring soul. When he said he was a soldier helping those that couldn't help themselves, he truly meant it. O'Donnell thought there was much more to it, however.

They then entered the third to last room.

O'Donnell stopped inside the doorway and watched Leigh approach the bed with caution. His posture didn't speak of fear, but rather a comforting gesture. As a person approached a timid animal might, afraid that they would scare it away. He'd seen his mother do it countless times with stray cats, injured animals.

A figure strapped to a cot in the corner, a man, jerked. His body tensed, but his eyes stayed fixed on something unseen by the either O'Donnell or Leigh.

Leigh spoke in a low, soothing voice as he opened the bag in his hands and took out a syringe and vial. After filling it, he very carefully injected the fluid into the patient's arm, veins and muscles bulking under the strain of his terror. O'Donnell presumed the medication to be an antipsychotic or sedative. The man's fists clenched tighter and shook. His eyes shimmered with tears at their edges, but he said nothing.

Running his tongue around his now dry mouth, O'Donnell lifted his gaze from the man, feeling like a voyeur, and he searched for something to hold his attention. The name card above the bed read "John Smith". They didn't even know this poor man's name.

Finishing administering the injection, Leigh gently held John Smith's hand, then rose from his side.

"What's his story?" O'Donnell asked in a low whisper as Leigh approached, his gaze not leaving the man's haunted eyes.

"Was transferred in the other day. Someone found the poor bastard wandering naked outside a town a couple of months ago, feet bleeding. No I.D. No idea who he is. He's just gone. Like someone emptied him out. Scooped his mind out like a soft-boiled egg."

"How does someone—"

Screams filled the hallway, breaking the relative silence of the ward.

"Stay here," Leigh said, and took off out of the room.

O'Donnell's eyes fell to the man in the cot again, the corners of his mouth turning down. He remembered the look of abject sadness on Jason's face before he pulled the trigger. As he welcomed death with open arms. Leigh said that this John Smith was empty, but he had the same look.

"What happened to you, John Smith?" O'Donnell said, shaking his head, chest griped with sadness. "What does that to a man? It must take some hell of a kind of darkness."

John Smith's breathing hitched and became ragged, picking up speed. With a gasp, his eyes flitted to O'Donnell's and locked on them, full of terror.

"The darkness!" John said in what sounded to O'Donnell's ears like an upper-class British accent. John Smith let out a sound like a cough, a laugh, and a sob, all at once. "The darkness eats you. It crawls inside and unmakes you before it re-knits, feeds and imitates. But it never lets go! No matter how much you pray and plead and beg! Let me go."

Blinking, the man's eyes focused on O'Donnell. "Let me go, I beg of you!"

John Smith's eyes were filled with a wish for mercy.

For death.

As O'Donnell watched, his sympathy for the man turned to shock as a black substance crept out from beneath his eyelids. Dark shadows played beneath his skin, his veins suddenly pumped with the same stuff. "Kill me," he whispered again, the dim light above reflecting in the blackened marbles of his eyes. "Before *it* takes me. Before it takes us all!"

Leigh shouldered his way past O'Donnell and fell on the bedside, shushing the man as he opened his bag of drugs. Turning to the man, he froze. "Jesus Christ." He shot O'Donnell a spiteful glare. "It's okay, John. It's okay, mate. I've got you." By the time Leigh had pulled the needle from his arm, the young man had already passed out. Standing slowly, he turned on O'Donnell. "What happened?"

"Nothing. I was talking to myself and he started babbling about darkness and—"

"What? What exactly did he say, James?"

O'Donnell shrugged. "Something about something eating him. Tearing. And then he… What the fuck was that, Leigh?"

Leigh's expression softened. "Darkness."

"Yeah, no shit! But—"

"Forget you ever saw it."

"But his eyes. And his skin. It was like… Something was *in* him."

"I said forget it, James."

Frown deepening, Leigh turned back to John Smith and went to take up his hand. A light from somewhere in his hands softly glowed as he examined the man, though O'Donnell had not seen him take a torch out. Then, patting the back of the man's hand, the light faded as he placed it on his chest and turned away with a deep, harrowed expression.

"He gonna be okay?" O'Donnell said. "Are you? I would have figured you'd get a lot of people talking like that."

"Eh?" Leigh turned to O'Donnell, tearing his eyes from the now silent man. "Nah. I'm all right. And yes, we get plenty that talk weird shit. Sometimes it strikes a nerve, know what I mean?"

"Strangely enough, I do, actually."

Leigh nodded. "Come on. The person you're after is next."

As Leigh led them out and through the hallway, the concerned expression didn't leave his face. Not until he lightly rapped on the door to the next room before opening it.

"Only me, Leigh," he said, a warm smile on his face.

Beyond the orderly, O'Donnell made out the feet of a figure laying on their side with their back to them, a light blanket draped over the slight form.

"Time for your meds," Leigh said.

The thin woman turned over, beaming sweetly at Leigh, the corners of her soft, rheumy eyes wrinkling.

O'Donnell crept back to the door, hand grabbing the frame tightly.

"Thank you, Leigh," the Crone said. "Who's your new friend?"

O'Donnell surged forward and pried his clenched jaw apart. "Fuck you!"

"Oi!" Leigh said sternly.

"Oh, my!" the Crone said, hand shaking as it rose to her chest, lip trembling. "I'm not sure I like this new nurse, Leigh."

"Do you know Glenda?" Leigh said to O'Donnell?

Letting out a bitter laugh, O'Donnell looked around Leigh at the woman. "Glenda? Really? You couldn't find a better name?"

Grabbing him roughly by the front of his uniform, Leigh pushed O'Donnell toward the door, several cups falling from the tray and water spilling from the spout of the covered plastic jug. "Back the hell out of here before I—"

"She attacked me with a knife, Leigh! Attacked my friend, a cop! Escaped from another facility, leaving a hole in the second storey brick wall somehow."

Leigh gave O'Donnell an incredulous stare, then shot a glance at the woman on the bed. "Glenda? You think she *punched* through a brick wall?"

"Oh my," the Crone said with a little laugh. "Don't I wish I could. I mean, sometimes I *dream* I can do such fantastic things, but..."

"I think... I think this was a bad idea," Leigh said, slowly pushing O'Donnell at the door.

"No, Leigh, I..." O'Donnell said, trying to fight the man. But the tray in his hands made it difficult. "You need to listen to me. She's dangerous, and—"

"What about my pills, Leigh?" Glenda said with a tone of fear, stopping the orderly in his tracks.

O'Donnell stopped pushing as Leigh's face tightened. Slowly, Leigh released his hold. He righted the cup labelled Glenda with one hand and pointed at O'Donnell with a threatening finger, then took the jug.

O'Donnell stood his ground and watched with anticipation as Leigh handed the woman the cup. She tipped the pills into her mouth before holding out her hand for Leigh to fill her cup, then drank in strained gulps. After taking a few breaths, she handed the paper cup back to Leigh, hand shaking.

"Who is this man, Leigh?" she said, voice so soft it was like two sheets of paper rubbing together.

"He's a private investigator, Glenda," Leigh said in a low tone. "He's searching for Nathan. You remember Nathan? His sister is looking for him."

"Sister?" the Crone said in surprise, her voice stronger. "But if it's about dear Nathan, of course I'll answer any questions. Is he missing?"

The woman sounded so genuine, even O'Donnell almost believed her. Her hair was brushed and tied back, her stained nightgown replaced with a hospital one. Her demeanour and expression both spoke of frailty. But it was definitely her.

Putting the tray in his hands on a side table slowly, he indicated for Leigh to come closer and leaned in. "What's she in for?"

"Glenda has violent bouts of dementia. This is her at her most lucid, so you caught her at a good time. Me on the other hand..." Leigh glared at him "You have any questions, ask 'em now. Before I change my mind and kick your arse out."

"Violent dementia?"

"She killed her husband. Stabbed him one time for each anniversary they'd had. They were married thirty-three years."

"Let me guess," O'Donnell said. "With a big butcher's knife."

Leigh didn't answer, but his eyes said it all. "I've still got two rooms to finish."

"Trust me," O'Donnell said. "You don't need to worry about me hurting her. Her hurting me on the other hand..."

Leigh sighed, then turned around. "Glenda, will you be okay if I leave you here with James? I need to check on Roberto and George."

O'Donnell scrutinised the old woman, unsure if he really wanted to be left alone with her. But what other choice did he have?

"Oh, I'm sure I'll be fine," Glenda said.

With an uncertain nod, Leigh opened the door. Then, as an afterthought, locked it open with the auto-closer above. Staring O'Donnell down, he left.

Turning back from the door, O'Donnell licked his lips, and settled in a chair beside it, far from the woman in the bed. Though he knew it would make no difference.

"So... Glenda, is it?"

"Nathan was such a nice boy, you know."

"So Cassie tells me." The woman didn't so much as flinch. "I heard he likes walks in the Dandenongs, too. In the forest."

Glenda frowned. "I wouldn't know about that. Not with my old knees." She smiled, her eyes taking on a faraway look. "My Leonard took me there when we were courting, you know."

"I'm sure he did," O'Donnell said with disinterest. "Was that be before or *after* you butchered him?"

"Oh, we used to go to the butchers together, too. I would cook us a nice roast. Or he would put on the barbecue and we'd have Rose and her Ian over. It was the best of times."

"Uhuh. What about Nathan? Where is he? Did you kill him after your magic tricks on me up the mountain? Or is he still out there, somewhere?"

"Rose and I would talk for hours, leaving Leonard and Ian drink and cook."

"What about Gunther? I bet you were pissed off when Nathan did him in, huh?"

"But then, Leonard changed. Or, I suppose, he had always been that way. It was the drink. The more he drank, the more it brought his true self out."

O'Donnell sighed. "I honestly can't tell if you're fucking with me or not anymore."

"And I couldn't tell anyone… Ever!"

O'Donnell frowned. The woman's voice had become increasingly distraught, but he hadn't noticed until now. She was close to tears.

"Was that when you snapped?" he said, leaning back and looking around the room with disinterest. "After all those years of abuse, your mind broke and you stabbed him thirty times?"

"Thirty-three."

O'Donnell's gaze shifted back to her.

Blinking rapidly, she turned to O'Donnell, eyes vacant as if she hadn't noticed him before. "Is it time for my meds again?"

She wasn't going to give him anything. He had no idea why he thought she would. She was either playing with him or was genuinely sick. Either way, this was not going to bring them any closer to Nathan or Gateway. O'Donnell closed his eyes and let his head fall back in frustration.

"I won't let you find him, James," the Crone said, whispering harshly.

O'Donnell's head snapped forward, alert.

The bed was empty.

Jumping to his feet, O'Donnell looked around the room, turning several slow circles. As he turned back to the bed, she was there, crawling to the footboard.

"What's wrong, James?" the old woman said, feigning concern. "Pussy got your tongue?" her voice came out as Cassie's.

"Stop it!" O'Donnell said, turning to the door.

With a snap, the auto-closer's arm broke, something metal skittering on the lino as the door slammed shut. He grabbed the handle, but already knew it was futile. The handle, like the door, was jammed tight. He pounded on the door with his fist, drawing in a deep breath to yell out for Leigh.

Bony fingers pinched his shoulders and flung him around and shoved him into the door with a thud. The Crone stared back at him in full force, her face etched in the familiar lines of her expression, her eyes now clear and fixed. Springing toward him, she pawed his face with a bony hand and forced his head to the side, her head darting forward and dry tongue slithering up his neck.

Pulling away sharply, O'Donnell threw himself at the adjacent wall and spun. When he regained his balance and looked up, ready to fight her off, she was gone again.

Breath ragged, he searched the room. Squatting with caution, he glanced under the empty bed. As he stood, her arms circled his body from behind and held tight, then flung him across the room onto the cot. Before his body came to a stop, the cot springs creaking, her weight pressed on him.

"Fuck me like you fuck Cassie, James," the Crone said into his ear in a parody of a sultry voice, then slathered O'Donnell's face with her tongue, now incredibly hot and wet.

No matter what O'Donnell did, he couldn't fight her off. His limbs were frozen, throat locked. And all he could feel was her tongue and lips on his face, tracing his jaw, then his lips as his gorge rose.

Then her mouth was at his ear, almost in it. "Gunther's alive!" she said, then inserted her tongue as she groped and fondled his paralysed body in a frenzy.

Rough hands took hold of O'Donnell and shook him and he found he was able to move. Forcing himself upright with a bellow, he raised his fists.

Leigh shook him again, staring into O'Donnell's eyes. "Where the fuck is Glenda, James? Where is she?"

O'Donnell looked all about him, shaking, face wet. But the Crone was gone. He tried to answer Leigh, but his voice wouldn't come at first. "I—" he finally managed to say, before he was interrupted.

"Thank you for your kind hospitality, Leigh."

They both jumped at the commanding voice from the doorway.

Leigh released O'Donnell and turned slowly. "Glenda? Did James do something to you?"

She laughed deeply. "If you want my advice, Protector," she said to Leigh, "tend to your young stranger, before the shades get to him and he turns. And forget all about Nathan. And me." She turned to O'Donnell. "The same goes for you, Mr O'Donnell."

The lights in the hall and the room strobed madly. When they settled, the Crone was gone.

Leigh rushed to the doorway, eyes wide in shock as he searched the hall. "What the fuck? Did she just... jump?"

O'Donnell let out a cry.

The Crone was on the ceiling directly above him, splayed face down, laughing madly. His body froze as she fell toward him, her wide mouth closing on his face. Then, before she touched him, she was gone again as the lights jumped on and off.

They two men glanced around the room, hunched over, and did not leave until they were both satisfied she was truly gone.

The night air was cool on O'Donnell's sweaty skin as he smoked. He hadn't bothered to change, his clothes shoved in a sack by Leigh so they could get outside as quickly as possible.

Leigh stood close by and shook his head again as he too smoked, hands quaking as he rolled another before the first was finished. "That was... something."

A nervous laugh escaped O'Donnell's lips and he had to calm his nerves before he could speak. "You can say that, yeah."

Leigh shook his head. "I have experienced crazy shit over the years, James, but that truly scared the ever-loving crap out of me."

O'Donnell nodded. "A few weeks ago I would have questioned how crazy shit could get. But now?"

They smoked their cigarettes in silence.

O'Donnell eyed Leigh. "Why don't you seem overly surprised at seeing an old woman vanish into thin air?"

"Because there's crazy shit… And then there's out of this world bat-shit-crazy."

"Like John Smith's darkness? The shades, as Glenda called them?"

Leigh gave him a small smile. "I'd better get back to it, hey."

"You going to be okay?"

"She's not after me, mate. You just watch your own arse, okay, and don't worry about mine."

"Yeah. And, if I have any follow up questions for you?"

Laughing, Leigh walked away. He lifted his hand up in a wave. "You know where to find me."

Nodding to himself, O'Donnell headed toward the carpark, his heel grinding as he turned back to ask another question.

But Leigh had vanished, like the Crone.

FIFTEEN

THE RINGING of the old phone woke O'Donnell with its urgent clamouring. The sound was no more or less different than usual, but to his sleep-deprived and tense mind, it was jarring.

Leaping from the sofa bed, he ran for the phone, bare feet slapping on the floor.

"Hello! Cassie?" He had spat the words from his lips before the bells of the phone had stopped echoing, holding his breath as he waited for the response.

"Are you okay?" Cassie said, her voice shifting from curiosity to concern in the space of those three small words.

"Yes!" He rubbed his face with his hand and tousled his hair. "Yeah," he said, coaxing his anxiety and voice down from the ledge it had climbed out on. "You?"

"I'm fine," she said with a hint of amusement. "I couldn't sleep thinking about what you might have found."

O'Donnell nodded repeatedly before realising she couldn't see. Or perhaps she could. He still had no idea what she and the other Enlightened could truly do. "Yeah. It was... Let's say interesting. I think we should meet and talk. Somewhere busy and crowded."

An hour and a half later, they were sitting in a cafe, eating breakfast and drinking coffee. After a brief greeting, a quick hug and kiss on the cheek from Cassie, they sat and waited, then ate in silence once their food came.

Halfway through her plate, Cassie dropped her knife and fork onto it with a clatter. People turned to stare, but she ignored them.

"I can't stand it," she said, wiping the corners of her mouth with a napkin. "What happened last night at the hospital? What aren't you telling me? Is Nathan…" Her eyes wrinkled. "Did something happen to him?"

Putting down his cutlery, he reached out his hand, and she took it.

"Sorry, I didn't mean to worry you." He shook his head. "I was shaken up. I couldn't sleep either, worried that she would come back."

Her narrowed eyes widened even as her brow furrowed. "The Crone? Why would you—" Slowly, the knot of her confused face undid itself. "She was there. At the hospital."

O'Donnell nodded. "Yeah. She was there all right. In a room, as a patient."

"What?"

"Glenda. Don't know if that's her real name, but I've got no reason to think otherwise. Leigh—the orderly we met—said she had been in for ages for killing her husband. Stabbed him thirty-three times."

"Jesus."

"Yeah. Violent bouts of dementia, he said. Bit of an understatement I reckon."

"You're sure it was her?"

O'Donnell stared at Cassie.

"Sorry," she said. "Stupid question."

"Apart from the fact that I will *never* forget that face, she went all… spooky."

Cassie laughed. "Is that what you call me behind my back? Spooky?" The smile on her lips faded. "Did she hurt you?"

"No. She scared the living shit out of me though. Both me and Leigh. Was disappearing and re-appearing. Threw me on the bed and dry humped me."

"He saw?"

"Oh yeah, he saw." Letting go of Cassie's hand, O'Donnell picked up his fork. He toyed with his food, then put it down again. "There's more," he said, eyes still down. He looked up and held Cassie's gaze. "She said Gunther's still alive."

Cassie jerked forward to lean on the edge of the table, the cups and plates clattering. "What?" She glanced around, ignoring a table of old women who were glaring at the two of them and muttering between themselves. "How is that even possible? You said you saw him—"

"I did!" He shook his head as he played the memories in his mind. "I *smelled* it." He leaned in and lowered his voice. "Cassie... I tripped and fell on his body when I got the hell out of there. But Robbie, the cops, their fucking dogs—none of them found so much as a drop of blood."

"She has to be lying."

"Why would she, though?"

Leaning back, Cassie crossed her arms and shook her head. "I have no idea. Crone, Glenda... whoever the hell she is, she has always had her own agenda. But more and more, her only agenda seems to be causing chaos."

O'Donnell pondered every appearance of the old woman and tried to piece it together, attempted to plot a logical end game. But none of it made sense. Unless...

"You said that the more experienced you are, the older as an Enlightened... awake... the closer to true enlightenment you get, right?"

"Yes. At least, that's what we've always been taught by Nathan. So?"

"So, how old is she?"

Cassie's eyes danced as the implication hit her and her face paled. "Fuckin' hell," she said, sounding very unlike her usual self. Or perhaps, more like her true self.

One of the old women rose and stormed to the counter and leaned in conspiratorially and pointed at them.

"Come on," O'Donnell said, pushing out his chair roughly. "I think we need to get out of here."

"I'm sure those old biddies—"

"No, Cassie. Not the café. Out of town!"

He threw open the door to the office, the bell letting out two dull clanks. Cassie followed him in as he ran about, grabbing up items of clothing. They had to go somewhere that neither the Enlightened or Gateway knew about. He had a few ideas, but they couldn't take off with nothing.

Clothes, money, whatever files he had, smokes… All the essentials.

"Cassie!" O'Donnell said, glancing up at her. He tossed her a bag and jerked his head to the safe. "Case files on my desk. Money and stuff in the safe."

"Got it," she said, and roughly shoved the manila folders into the bag, then crouched to pull the safe open.

The bell on the door clanked as it was hastily opened and closed.

Cassie turned to O'Donnell as he stood and held a finger to his lips. He walked to her side with deliberate steps, crossing the distance in silence.

"Jimmy!"

Frowning, O'Donnell rounded the screen. "Robbie?"

"Where the fuck is she?" Robbie pushed past him, swinging his head and eyes around like searchlights.

As O'Donnell followed close behind, she stood and casually sat on the corner of the desk. "Detective Thomas. How nice to see you again."

"Robbie, wait!" O'Donnell said even before his friend had turned on him, lips pressed tight.

"I fucking told you, mate. I *warned* you!"

"Robbie—"

Robbie held up a hand, silencing him. "Save it. I'm taking you and your little girlfriend here in for obstruction."

"Obstruction, Detective?" Cassie said, voice impassive.

"I know you two have been playing *Magnum PI* out at funny farms." Robbie shook his head at O'Donnell. "I told you to keep out of it, Jimmy. I fucking *ordered* you not to stick your nose in this Mortimer and Gateway shit."

O'Donnell hung his head. "You've been following us."

Robbie sneered. "Doesn't look good. First you send us on a merry fucking goose chase up in the forest. Then come back down straight to your girl."

No, it definitely did not look good. But O'Donnell also knew that if the only thing Robbie was holding on them was obstruction, he didn't have enough to prove his suspicions, false or not.

"Where are all your files on the case?" Robbie said, pawing through papers on the desk. Not finding anything, he bent down to the safe and pulled, grunting. Face reddening, he stood. "When did you get this fucking thing fixed?"

"I didn't. It's busted, like always."

"The fuck it is." Robbie bent down and tried the safe door, again with no luck. "Open this fucking thing!"

"I told you," O'Donnell said, quickly walking to it and dropping to a crouch. "It's—" He pulled the handle, but the door was stuck fast. Frowning, he pulled again, trying to turn the handle, but like the door, it wouldn't budge.

Cassie smirked.

"Fuck it!" Robbie snapped as he glanced at her. "I have enough on the both of you. We'll crack it open later."

Two paddy wagons waited for them outside, cops standing by them as his friend led them both out. Robbie was going all out. O'Donnell knew they would both be cuffed, taken in the separate cars. Divide and conquer and all that. Make a public spectacle.

As Cassie was led away by the uniforms, she turned and smiled at O'Donnell.

Unfortunately for Robbie and the other cops, O'Donnell knew the standard drill of questioning. Left for hours to sweat it out before anything happened let alone their being questioned. Someone "friendly" coming in and offering drinks so his bladder would fill. The wonky chair for the suspect, also cut lower than the interrogators', who would come in a pair, Robbie probably being one of them. In the past, he would have normally played the friend role, given his closeness to O'Donnell. But he was far too incensed now.

Unfortunately for O'Donnell, Robbie also knew he knew the process.

A tall, bald cop in uniform entered the room, his shirt bulging with a paunch like a he had a basketball under it. Sighing as he opened the door, he flicked his head at O'Donnell, then the hall. As O'Donnell rose, the cop grabbed his arm and led him out, playing his tongue around inside his lip like he was cleaning his teeth with great enthusiasm, mouth smacking endlessly. Stopping O'Donnell roughly at the end of the hall, he opened another door and motioned toward it, again with his head.

Frowning, O'Donnell entered. He knew the room. He'd never been in this one itself, but others of its kind. A small darkened observation room behind the mirror where interrogations took place. Standing in the middle of the room, he turned to the door, but it was already closing and being locked from the outside. The cop had probably been instructed to stand in front of it as well.

O'Donnell sat in one of several chairs and waited.

Not long after, the door to the interrogation room opened, echoing in a cheap speaker sitting on the desk. Cassie was led through and instructed to sit at the table by a young female officer, who gave her a friendly smile, and in a small voice asked if she wanted a tea, or coffee, or cold drink.

"Would a gin and tonic be out of the question?" Cassie said, giving the officer a wry grin.

The woman stood straighter and her expression shifted from friendly to hostile. Smirking, the cop left without another word.

"They really don't know what they're getting themselves into," Cassie said, shaking her head and rolling her eyes. She turned to the mirror, and as her curled lashes lifted, her eyes met O'Donnell's and she winked. "Do they?"

The door opened and Robbie walked in, another detective in tow. They promptly sat in the chairs opposite Cassie. There was another mirror behind her, and O'Donnell watched Robbie in it as he pulled a fresh cassette from his jacket pocket and unwrapped it, pulling the red plastic string and ensuring it crinkled loudly as he did. Robbie then pulled the cassette from the cover, peeled and stuck on a label, and wrote on it with great care before popping open the recorder on the table and sliding in the tape and pushing it into place.

Then he sat, hands folded, and grinned at Cassie, who mirrored him.

After an interminable stretch of silence, Robbie cleared his throat, set the tape to record with deliberate motions and the questions began.

Cassie was interrogated at length, Robbie and the other detective asking about Nathan. Gunther and Gateway. The murder. The Crone and the hole in the wall.

Then they threw Cassie as the other detective started talking about other missing people. Patients. Staff. People around the various hospitals.

Cassie's smile faltered. "I don't know anything about that."

"You expect us to believe that, Ms. Lawler?" the detective said. "We know you were tight with Nathan Mortimer. His girlfriend at one time, if not still."

"Believe what you want," Cassie said.

"And what about your partner in crime?" the detective said. "James O'Donnell. How did you sucker him into your little cult? Into helping you? Did you recruit him too? Like you did the people at the hospitals?"

Cassie leaned into the table. "James has nothing to do with any of this. We hired him to find Nathan, that's all."

Robbie snorted a laugh as he lit up a cigarette. "You know what, I believe you. You probably know this already, but Jimmy and I go way back. I know what he's like. Loyal. Sensitive. A good guy who tries to do the right thing." Robbie took a deep drag of the cigarette before expelling it in a jet of white. "And that's also what makes him such a dumb arsehole."

"Wow," Cassie said, sitting back and smirking. "I need to make some friends like you."

"Thing is, I've only known him to be that dumb when a girl is involved. He used to be in love with my missus. Did you know that?" Cassie frowned a fraction. "When we were kids, but I'm pretty sure he still has a thing for her."

Blood boiling, O'Donnell felt his head shake. "Fuck you, Robbie."

"So it all fits. Doesn't it, Cassie?" Cassie shrugged. "And all I can think is, you've got the poor bastard so pussy whipped he can't think straight."

Siting back, Cassie crossed her arms.

Chair screeching, Robbie stood. "You keep going," he said to the man beside him. He glanced at the mirror. "I'm just going for a coffee with my old mate Jimmy. See what he has to say."

As Robbie exited the interrogation room, the young female officer who had offered Cassie refreshments took his place. O'Donnell turned to the door, which opened moments later.

Striding in, expression blank, Robbie sat legs wide facing the two-way glass. He took a deep drag from his cigarette. Casting a sidelong glance at O'Donnell, Robbie leaned over and uncuffed him. "It's all right, mate. Don't despair." He slid over his pack of cigarettes and lighter on the fold up table in front of them. "I'm going to do you a huge favour. And I don't mean giving you a free fag."

Rubbing his wrists, O'Donnell took the packet and lit up, noting how empty it was. Robbie had been hitting them hard again.

"Come on, Cassie," the detective in the interrogation room said, leaning in, lowering his voice. He reached into his cheap suit inner picket and pulled out his own smokes and lit up, placing the pack on the table. "Give us something, or you'll be going down for a long time."

"In more ways than one," the female cop said, smirking and causing the detective to chuckle. "So unless you want to be flossing the crabs out of your teeth from Big Bertha's pubes…" She slid a notepad with a pen on it across the table. "Confess."

Cassie licked her lips, blinking rapidly and eyes darting. "Okay," Cassie said. "But leave James out of it, all right? He doesn't know anything."

"Whatever you say, Cassie," the detective said.

Cassie nodded. "First… You give me something, then I'll give you something."

"Depends what you want," the smirking female cop said, leaning back in her chair.

Cassie glanced straight at O'Donnell's through the glass, a corner of her mouth hitching. Lifting her hands to the table top, she gently placed the handcuffs that had been on her wrists with one link neatly atop the other.

The female cop sat up. "What the fuck! How did you—" She made to stand, but couldn't move from the seat, like she was glued to it.

The detective whipped his head to the woman then attempted to assist her. He jerked his body several times, but both chair and man were rooted to their spots. Mouth falling open, Robbie plucked the cigarette from his lips and stood, almost as if he was trying to prove to himself he could.

Cassie reached out her hand, holding it parallel to the table, almost touching it.

"What are you doing?" the detective said in panic.

"Nothing," Cassie said. "I just want a cigarette, that's all." Her fingers danced as she waved them at the cigarettes. The packet glided across the surface until it rested beneath Cassie's hand.

"The fuck is she doing?" Robbie said, staring intently.

O'Donnell didn't answer, himself transfixed on the scene.

The female cop tried to rise again, straining to peel herself free from her seat.

"It's okay, Officer…" Cassie glanced at the woman's name badge. "Visser." Cassie hummed to herself. *"Ben je Nederlands?"* The woman looked at her like she was crazy. "No? Oh well. Never mind."

"What the fuck did you do to us?" the woman said, eyes wide and muscles in her neck strained.

Cassie opened the flap of the cigarette packet with languid slowness, plucking one out. "Oh no, it's okay. Don't get up." Holding the cigarette between finger and thumb, her free fingers curled daintily, she moved it toward her lips. "I have my own light." Pressing the tip to her pursed lips, the cigarette flared up briefly.

"The fuck…" Robbie said. He turned to the door and grabbed the handle, but it wouldn't turn. "Open this fucking door, Cameron!" he yelled, and thumped the door with the flat of his hand.

The man on the door said something but it came through muffled, though O'Donnell was sure the man said it wasn't locked. Keys jangled and the pins in the lock scraped over and over as the man tried them all to no effect.

Cassie took out another cigarette and lit it with the first, now between her lips. Then, with a deep breath, she sucked the whole thing to ash in seconds. She reached out her free hand, and one of the coffee cups slid within reach. She dropped the now cold butt into its depths, then placed the second cigarette between her lips while motioning at the packet. A cigarette slid free and she pulled it out and lit it in the same manner. One by one, she smoked the entire packet, not once exhaling.

The cops had stopped fighting and were holding their breaths, the backs pressed tight into their seats. O'Donnell found himself sitting at the edge of his chair, leaning forward. He was barely conscious of Robbie doing the same from by the door, easing toward the mirror in expectation.

Grinning wide, Cassie's teeth flashed white as smoke drifted from between and around them. "Here's my confession," she said, smoke puffing in bursts.

Pushing forward, holding her head over the notepad, she opened her mouth wide. Her lips peeled back across her teeth. Smoke wafted through her hair. A hacking cough escaping the back of her throat, breasts and back heaving, her stomach lurched. A string of black tar fell to the pad, dripping and pattering to its surface to splash about, fine droplets leaping out to stain the table.

The cops were now shaking in their chairs, terrified. O'Donnell could imagine how they felt as his own heart hammered.

"The— The fuck is she doing, Jimmy?" Robbie said, voice strained.

Cassie sat up straight, black lines covering her lips, running down her chin, a long line of curving black saliva stretching down to the paper, settling on her skin and clothing. Her complexion was paler, almost that of a cadaver.

"What's wrong, officers?" she said. "You don't look so good." She flashed her stained teeth at them.

The interview room door suddenly burst open, Officer Cameron stumbling through it as it finally gave way.

O'Donnell and Robbie jumped in fright before turning back to the observation window.

Hands folded on the table, wrists handcuffed, a clean notepad sat in front of Cassie.

The detective and officer sprang from their chairs.

Robbie ran from the room and into the next, glancing about and eyeing the two-way glass, as if it had been a part of the conspiracy. He lunged at the table and snatched up the cigarette packet, tearing it apart with a growl as cigarettes and tobacco spilled from his shaking fingers.

"Is there a problem, Detective?" Cassie said.

Robbie's head snapped around to glare at her, then his nose wrinkled. "Why does it smell like piss in—" Robbie glanced at the officer and the detective.

Both had dark patches on their pants.

"Fucking Jesus! Get her out of here, Cameron!" Robbie barked at the man standing in the doorway.

The cop approached her cautiously.

"For fuck's sake!" Robbie stormed to Cassie and pulled her to her feet and led her out, giving the two urine stained cops a contemptuous glare.

The detective gulped, shook his head in shame, then picked up his coffee cup and took a swig. Coughing, he spat out coffee. His hand flew to his mouth and pulled out a cigarette butt, bright red lipstick on the filter.

SIXTEEN

Hours after the incident in the interrogation room, Robbie came to let O'Donnell out, Cassie in tow. He took them both to an interview room. O'Donnell knew the release interview was coming. What he did not expect was Robbie's superior in the room.

"I'm Superintendent Gerald Smyth," the seated man said as soon as they stepped into the room, not rising. He motioned at chairs across from him, Robbie sitting beside the Superintendent. "It appears that Detective Sergeant Thomas detained you both without sufficient evidence." The man's words were clipped and forced.

Something had happened. O'Donnell knew what sort of cop Robbie was. There was no way he would have brought them in with absolutely nothing. He turned to Robbie questioningly, but didn't dare say anything.

"Ms Lawler," Robbie said, not looking at Cassie or lifting his gaze from the table. "Mr O'Donnell. On behalf of Victorian Police, I would like to offer you my apologies. If you wish to pursue an official complaint—"

"That won't be necessary," Cassie said, giving the man a saccharine grin. "We both know how incredibly stressful this has been. For us as well. All I want is to find my friend, Nathan."

The Superintendent gave a rehearsed yet strained smiled. "Of course. And thank you for not wanting to take this any further. If you both wouldn't mind…" He pushed several pieces of paper over, then pulled a pen from his pocket and lay it down.

Disclaimer forms indemnifying the police and Robbie from any claims. They had already been filled out and just needed signing.

As he took the pen and signed, O'Donnell attempted to catch Robbie's eye, but he refused to meet his gaze.

In that moment, O'Donnell knew their friendship was over.

The police car took off without a single word having been said by either of the officers driving, or from either Cassie or O'Donnell. He led the way back into his office, locking the door behind them. It was well into the evening, and though he'd not eaten anything, O'Donnell went for a bottle of bourbon. drinking straight from it. He offered it to Cassie, but she declined with a shake of her head.

"I have no idea what you did in there," he said.

Cassie looked at him blankly. "What did you see?"

"I don't know. That's why I'm asking you."

"You didn't ask me anything, actually. You also didn't answer my question."

"It… was like it was happening, and also not happening at the same time. Like a live double negative."

"That's from what we did to you. At the club. Like I told you, we opened your mind. That's why it didn't seem as real to you as it did to them."

"Opened my mind for what though? I still don't get it. Get what you can all *do* exactly."

"The truth of the world. And the lies."

O'Donnell let out a snorting laugh. "I don't know what that means, Cassie! I mean… You made two grown people piss their pants. Two cops who experience all sorts of shit every day."

"You don't understand because you still don't believe. The Enlightened are real, James."

"I don't believe? What the hell does that mean?" He threw his hands up. "I've seen things I can't explain, and I'm still here helping you. Believing you."

"That's not what believing is."

His incredulous smile became a scowl. "You mean becoming a true believer, don't you?"

Her shoulders hitched in a shrug as she shook her head. "Why do you need to put a label on everything?"

"Because that's how I can sort everything out. Good. Bad. Real, not real."

"Even when your labels are wrong? Admit it. Part of you still thinks we're a cult, and you want me to confirm that for you."

O'Donnell threw up his arms. "What else am I supposed to do?" he said loudly. "I'm damn good at my job. Except when it comes to you, and the Enlightened, and everything else going on… I have no labels for that. No frame of reference. No experience."

"Because you're trying to work through this like it's a case!"

Letting his head fall, O'Donnell searched for the words to explain it to Cassie, but he couldn't find them. She was right. He had been running around hitting everything like it was a nail and he was the hammer. Cassie and the rest of them were something else entirely. Glue. And he had been smashing the tube and was now stuck in the mess.

Her hands gently clasped his. "Let go of what you think you know, James."

When he glanced up at her, deep into her soulful eyes, a wash of regret and pain welled up and overflowed, released in an unbidden torrent of tears.

"The last time I let go, I was careless. And a man—a *friend*—died because of it."

Cassie smiled, but it was free of her usual sarcasm and wit. It was genuine and caring, almost saintly. That was the only image he could conjure.

"If nothing else from what you have learned being in proximity to me, to the Enlightened, it should be that death is not the end. In whatever way, shape or form, we continue on. Whether we are aware of it or not."

O'Donnell let out a snort and sniffled, like he was a little kid again. Like he had grazed his knee and his mum was tending to it, his father not around to berate her for mollycoddling him. Is that what this was? Was she tending to his psychic wound?

Had he grazed his ego? Or his soul?

Her hand brushed his cheek and he nuzzle into her fingers, eyes closing. Feeling foolish, he pulled back, but her free hand was at his opposite cheek, trapping him in a tender prison.

"Shh," she said, her sweet breath playing across his lips, tickling his stubble. Her forehead and nose pressed lightly against his. "Keep your eyes closed."

He chuckled, his skin buzzing against hers with the vibration from his chest. "Why? Are we going to play hide and seek?"

Cassie's own laughter returned in the same manner. Her fingers tightened momentarily, the pad of a thumb brushing against his face. "If you like. Count to a hundred, and I guarantee, by the end of it... you will find *me*."

Unsure what she meant, he found himself nodding anyway. Then waiting, counting in his head. As he got to sixty-three and was about to ask what was meant to be happening, he gasped as he was enveloped in absolute darkness, a tingling cold washing over him.

He could remember, as a child, when he would lay awake in bed with his eyes closed. Sometimes, it would be so dark that he wouldn't know if he opened them or not. And he would force his eyes wide and stare in panic, unable to make out a single familiar detail. To ground himself, he would grip his blankets, make a noise... something to reassure himself that he was still at home. But then the panic would turn to something being wrong with his sight.

Now, he didn't even have a physical presence. He could not reach out and take a hold of anything. The panic was more intense as an adult, he found. Especially given recent events. He now knew there were things that could hide in the shadows. Things that he could barely explain let alone fight. If the Enlightened and Gateway existed, what more could be out there? That thing Gunther had shown him when the man's spirit attacked him in the car… What if it was not a mere imagined creature? What if it was something Gunther had seen? What if—

A soft sigh like a warm summer breeze blew through him. It was a blush of heat where he knew his face was… or should be.

"*Cassie?*"

His voice died as soon as the words were out, deadened by the darkness. He called her name again, with urgency.

Be calm, James, she said, her voice in his mind.

"What is this place?"

He felt her mental shrug. *No one really knows. Some say it's one of the astral planes. Some call it a void. Some think it's a place outside of time and space, what existed there before the big bang.*

"*What do you think?*"

The same sensation came again, an almost psychic shake of her head. *All I know is, it's a place of grounding,* she said pre-empting his question. *When I come here, I know how truly tiny I am. So then when I see what is to follow, I know how truly great I am also.*

Something tugged at his very being. It was like something had gripped his stomach in its ghostly hand and pulled. And with that, he was yanked briefly into another place of absolute white before being shoved into darkness once more. But it was not the same darkness as that void she had showed him. There was something inherently familiar with this new darkness. And it was not all consuming. Here and there were colours, shapes, and light.

"*We're… in space?*"

A sensation ran through his mind, like… a warm breeze tickling a wind chime. She was laughing.

Isn't it wonderful?

The dread within him was now completely washed away. It was truly awe inspiring. And, he now saw, they were moving. Soaring through the heavens ever faster. Light streaked, then coalesced, forming a tunnel. No, a ring. A ring of light ahead of them.

An image thrust itself into his mind, then another and another, superimposed over the ring of streaming light.

The gateway.

The question that had been forming in his mind went on without him as he came to a sudden stop.

He was back on Earth, though not where he expected. The surroundings were unfamiliar to him, but he understood in some primal way that he was still within the vision. Also, that as his physical body stood in his office with Cassie, and this place was somewhere at that same moment. Not too far away.

A young girl cried openly, hidden away in what appeared to be her bedroom. She couldn't have been older than six or seven. Stuffed toys lined her bed, other toys were strewn about the floor. In the same way he knew that this was happening in the present and that his body was relatively close, he could tell that there was no one else in the house with the girl.

She was alone. In more ways than one. Left at home with nothing but these toys as company.

"I know that feeling," O'Donnell said, letting out a sigh he knew wasn't real. Whatever he was, he wasn't breathing.

Sniffling a quick, wet breath through her nostrils, the girl whipped around and stared through O'Donnell. She peered into the corners, then rose and stepped lightly to crack her bedroom door open.

"Mum?" she said, her voice a squeak.

The house was silent.

Opening the door wide, she puffed up defiantly and stalked through the house.

You have a kinship to this girl? Cassie asked out of nowhere.

O'Donnell knew he should have been startled, he'd forgotten all about Cassie, but he had no breath or heartbeat. The momentary fright was simply that, a flash that lasted a thousand-thousandths of a second.

"Like I said, I know what that's like."

"Who the fuck's there!" the girl shouted.

O'Donnell couldn't help but grin. *"She's a fiery one."*

She's sensitive, Cassie said, intrigued. *Like you. You should try not to think so loudly.*

"I feel like a creepy stalker," he whispered. *"Can you take us out of here? Why did you bring me here anyway?"*

I didn't. You brought *me here, James.*

O'Donnell shook his head. He didn't know this girl. She was in no way familiar. And yet…

"You're right. I don't know why but I'm… drawn to her, or something."

Could it be her sadness? When he was around her age, he'd had that same loneliness after his father had left. Could still taste it's bitter tang in his mouth.

Following after the girl room, he glanced around the house. There were paintings and photography work covering most of the walls. On a small mantel, photos of a woman with the girl. Her mother. No sign of a man in any of them.

"She's like me."

You were sensitive when you were her age, too.

"How do you know?"

He felt her mental shrug and laugh.

"Right. Enlightened."

The girl re-entered the living room brandishing a large kitchen knife. She stood still in the middle of the room, listening intently. When she heard nothing more, her shoulders fell as her chest deflated with a sigh.

"Yeah, you better run, ghost!" the girl said, then swaggered back to her room, knife still in hand.

O'Donnell walked to the front door, and as he suspected, passed through it as if it was a projection on mist.

"Why would I come here?" he said, looking around, as if Cassie would appear. *"I thought I was meant to be seeing you."*

I said you would find me. And… I think you came here because you still have much resentment toward your father, and emotions from those times you have not resolved.

"So, I brought you here as... what? Therapy?"

Only you can answer that. As only you can find me.

Frustration growing within him, O'Donnell spun around, searching. *"I don't understand! I—"*

He reeled as his vision swam and his lungs filled with air as if he hadn't breathed in a very long time.

"Breathe. Breathe, James," Cassie said, catching and holding him up.

"Wh—" For a moment, he couldn't remember how to speak. The tightening and relaxing of his vocal cords, his diaphragm, his blood coursing through his veins... like a long-forgotten art.

"Try to relax. Ease back into the real world, one step at a time. Let your heart and lungs remember for you and do their work. Listen to their rhythm."

He did as instructed, and soon the fractured parts of his body fell into alignment, and that other place and state of being faded. A shade of a memory, like smells and sights from early childhood. One of those came back to him, assaulting him with unwanted senses. His father's shaving cream.

"What just happened?" he said, clutching his head to hide his battle with the fresh tears that welled behind his eyes.

"You wanted to know what it was we did. So I showed you."

Hands trembling, a sweat beaded on his skin. His body doubled over as he dry heaved.

"Here," Cassie said, caressing his face. "Stay here with me. *Be* here with me. Don't think about anything else but this moment. My touch."

The sickness waned. "Cassie, I—" The churning of his stomach returned with the words.

"Your problem, James O'Donnell," Cassie said, drawing him toward the bed, somehow working off his and her own clothing one handed, "is that you think too much."

Soon, he was on the bed with her, both of them naked, and all he could see, feel, taste and smell was her. All he could hear, was her, though she said nothing. Colours and sensations radiated from her...

From them. And they stretched on to eternity to join the gateway of light she had shown him on their journey.

O'Donnell ran his fingers through her dark hair, then down her face and neck over her shoulders and ribs then hips. "What did you do to me?"

"I believe they call it 'rocking your world'," Cassie said, smirking.

He let out a deep chuckle. "You know what? I think you did." He let his hand rest on her thigh, his thumb tracing circles on her skin. In a flash, his fingers clutched her leg. "Cassie, I saw it!" The ring of light flashed in his vision as it had in that spectral state. "The gateway."

Cassie nodded, her expression blank, gaze distant and removed.

"Cassie?" She hummed. "You can do so many fantastic things." She gave a small laugh. "Why can't you find Nathan?"

Her pale shoulder rose and fell. "My belief is that Nathan is the one that brought us into this. And as such, he knows how to shield himself from us also."

He nodded. "That makes sense, I guess. Is that why you really needed me, though?"

Her shoulders tensed momentarily before falling. "Why is it in moments such as this you are so perceptive?"

"Because I'm with you."

Pulling away and turning, Cassie sat on the edge of the sofa bed. "This was a mistake."

"Sleeping with me, or bringing me into this?"

Glancing over her shoulder, Cassie set her face to an unreadable and expressionless stare. "Both."

"Because I'm getting too close to the truth? Or too close to you?"

Her stare cracked, eyes and lips twitching. She turned from him again. "Both," she said, barely loud enough to hear.

"It had to be me, didn't it?" O'Donnell said, nodding to himself. He knew it was true before he spoke the words. "Nathan was always out recruiting. Looking for other 'sensitive' people. Like that girl."

"Stop, James." Cassie stood and pulled on her underwear, then picked up her bra.

"I wonder if that girl was on his list too." He shifted on the bed to catch her eye. "Is she, Cassie?"

"I don't know."

"Tell me the truth!"

"I don't know!" she yelled, turning on him. "I don't know, okay? I told you, I don't know anything anymore. Nathan's been running around behind my back. Behind *all* our backs. And now this old woman... the Crone... Glenda... And Gunther! Is he alive or not? I don't know!"

His eyes darted back and forth between hers, exploring her face. "You're scared. Scared because, just like before you joined Nathan, you don't know what your life is going to be."

Slipping her arms into the bra and pulling it into place, Cassie turned from him, clasping the garment as she spoke. "We found your name in Nathan's files. But the more I think about it, the more it seems it was *left* there for us to find."

O'Donnell jerked up straighter. Why would Nathan want the others to find his name? "That makes no sense."

Her hair parted as she leant to pick up her dress, showing a sliver of her face through the curtain. Her lips were pressed tight and her eyes narrowed.

"And that's what's bothering you the most. Because you can't make sense of what Nathan was doing either." But there was more to it. "And that he used you, too."

Slipping her shoes on, Cassie stood and zipped her dress. "That was truly amazing, James," she said. "But I think it's time we went our separate ways."

"Cassie, no," O'Donnell said, shifting to the edge of the sofa bed. "I—"

"It's okay, James. You've played your part." Reaching out, she took his face in her hand once more. His eyelids grew heavy, his neck suddenly too weak to hold his head up as it leaned into it her palm. "Nathan is our problem. And the Enlightened will find him without you. I won't let you risk your life any more than you have." Leaning in, she gave him the lightest of kisses as his body followed after his head, limbs weakening, and she lay him down. "Thank you, Mr O'Donnell." She turned and walked away with purpose.

"Cassie… wait." O'Donnell pulled at the leg still on the bed, but it would not move. Neither could he force his body to lift from the thin mattress. "Cassie."

Vision swimming, he watched as she strode out between the folding partition.

SEVENTEEN

WAKING CLOSE TO MIDDAY, O'Donnell had clutched his pounding head. As he sat up, he'd discovered it was not from anything Cassie had done to him, but as a result of sleeping awkwardly with his head at an odd angle.

That had been a week-and-a-half ago. In that time, Cassie had not once reached out to him. She'd said it was to protect him, but he thought in part she was protecting herself also. Protecting her heart.

His fist slammed on the desktop.

"Damn it, Cassie!"

He felt lost. Adrift in a world of danger and intrigue the likes he could only still guess at, and Cassie mired in its depths. How deep did that particular swamp run?

A secret war had been brewing under everyone's noses, and now he knew about it, there was nothing he could do. Though that wasn't strictly true. He could keep doing his job. He'd be damned if he would let Cassie and the others battle it out alone. And there was only one way he could do that now that she had shut him out.

Making his way through the building, O'Donnell was surprised at how busy how he found it. Around him, the patrons of the casino went about in a haze, oblivious to him and most others around them.

Poker machines appeared to be the draw at this hour of the early afternoon. Lines and rows of the things. He watched as an old woman with a large plastic cup in her hands went from machine to machine, dropping coins in each and pressing buttons, eyes glazed.

The woman turned to glare at O'Donnell, who found he was staring intently. He gave her a genial smile. With a possessive glint in her eyes, the woman turned back to her machines. Her hand fell on the next one as she huddled up to it and repeated her ritual.

That was it. It was a ritual. She returned to the first machine in line to begin her supplication to these, her new gods, anew.

Unwilling to witness any more or draw attention to himself, O'Donnell moved on.

A few rows away, he turned sharply as he spotted her, idly dropping a coin into a machine and stabbing at the buttons with disinterest.

"I hate these things," Mrs Inglewood said. "Just another drug pushed in through a different needle."

Sitting a few seats over from her, O'Donnell pretended to pay great interest to the screen, and pressed buttons. "Doesn't your husband own a few clubs that use these?"

"He does." She dropped another coin in, pressed buttons. A handful dropped out. "How is your investigation going, Mr O'Donnell? I haven't heard from you in a bit."

Reaching into his jacket, he pulled out an envelope and, without looking at her, reached over to place it on a machine between them. A casual observer might think they were doing something illicit. Depending on who that someone was, the consequences for the both of them could be dire.

Glancing up and down the aisle they occupied, Mrs Inglewood took the yellow envelope and lifted the flap. Taking out the photos, she flipped through them. "Good work, Mr O'Donnell. These will go a long way to helping me." She stopped at the last photo, frowning at the figure he'd circled in red. "Who's this?"

"His name's Gunther Franklin."

She shook her head. "Don't know him. He's not one of my

husband's usual… associates." Slipping the photos back into the envelope, she secreted them in her handbag. "Is there anything else?"

"I was going to ask you for a favour."

Mrs Inglewood laughed, smirking. "I'm not giving you any more money, Mr O'Donnell. I've paid you more than enough as it is."

"No. You were more than generous. That's not what I was going to ask. I need you to find out all you can about that man, Gunther."

Mrs Inglewood narrowed her eyes. "Why on Earth would you ask me to do something like that?" she said in a low voice, but loud enough that the anger in her tone came through strong. "Do you know what he would do to me if he found out?"

O'Donnell frowned. Did she mean Gunther? She's said he was a stranger to her, but everything about the man and Gateway said that could be a lie.

His expression smoothed out as he realised that was not who she was afraid of. "You read the papers, Mrs Inglewood? That's Australia's most wanted at the moment."

Her head turned sharply. "Those cult wankers?"

"You may have also heard about the shit they've been up to. Murder. Conspiracy. A bombing."

"Yeah. I heard. So what?"

"Well, one might suspect if a cult leader had paid a prominent Mob boss a visit, perhaps that was the source of said explosives."

That got her attention. She sat taller, a victorious smirk playing across her lips. "So, you did get me some more dirt on that bastard." Reaching into her bag, Mrs Inglewood pulled out the photo of Gunther. She tapped the corner of the thick paper against her free hand. "What makes you think I can find anything out about this fella?"

Smirking, O'Donnell stood from the tall, padded stool. "What's the expression, Mrs Inglewood? Don't bullshit a bullshitter?"

"I do this, then we'll be square, you got me? No more free favours."

"You're absolutely right. Because the way my ledger balances, I reckon I'll have some credit with you and your newly inherited business venture."

"I'll get back to you soon, Mr O'Donnell."

Turning from her, he said, "I thought you might."

He'd been naive when he'd thought she would only be using the evidence against her husband to escape. Inglewood was making a power play. Two birds with one stone: be free of the man who had been cheating on and possibly abusing her, and maintain her lifestyle by taking over.

O'Donnell took the recorder out of his pocket and pressed stop. He wouldn't underestimate her again. He'd stash his notes and the tape in case she ever decided to tie up loose ends.

As he stepped out of the dark casino into the light, he lifted his hand to shield his eyes. A figure stepped close to him.

"Mr O'Donnell," Leyla said, giving him a weak smile.

O'Donnell glanced around the crowds, searching for Gunther's psychotic grin. He grabbed the girl from Gateway by the upper arm and led her aside. "Leyla," he said, still scanning the crowd. "What are you doing here?" He forced his body to relax as people looked on with concerned interest.

"Can we talk?"

Picking at her curly fries and swirling the tall, bendy straw in her cola, Leyla told her story while O'Donnell listened, fifties music in the themed burger joint playing in the background.

"I was pregnant, like you asked when you came to Gateway House. I'm still not sure why Theresa—the woman you met at the roadhouse..."

"She's the one who murdered Judy? The waitress."

Leyla nodded. "She... She's the one that said my baby had to go. I think she was jealous. Of how close I was getting to Gunther.'"

"Jesus." O'Donnell pushed his own fries away, nausea stopping his appetite. "How did you end up with them, Leyla? You don't seem like the type. Or at least, not like Gateway."

She didn't answer. Her expression however, answered his question. She regarded him as an adult would a child when asked to explain some grand concept that was well beyond their grasp.

"I used to be a good Muslim girl, brought up in a semi-traditional Turkish house. My parents weren't too strict, but they weren't exactly open-minded either. I used to wear a headscarf, like my mother and grandmother and aunties and stuff."

O'Donnell's face wrinkled.

"It was my choice. They didn't force me."

"I didn't—"

Leyla waved a hand, her eyelids pressing tight as she shook her head. O'Donnell had never thought of himself as a racist. But maybe, like Leyla's family, he wasn't so open-minded, either.

When she opened her eyes, they shone with tears. "But then I met Kyle."

"The father?" O'Donnell said, prompting her after she had been quiet a while.

Blinking, she focused her eyes back on him, then nodded. "When my parents found out, they went ape-shit. I always thought they were sitting on the fence when it came to that sort of stuff. But…"

"They kicked you out?"

"No. But things got so bad I couldn't stay. Not and be myself. So I went to Kyle's." Her lip trembled as she pulled a napkin from a chrome holder polished to a high sheen, the mirrored surface distorting her features. She dabbed the tears that coursed down her cheeks. "But he didn't want me either," she said, voice cracking.

"I'm sorry, Leyla."

Leyla shot him a glance, as if she wasn't quite sure he was being genuine. "Thanks," she said, almost hesitant.

"I'm guessing that's when you met Gunther."

"No. I didn't meet Gunther for a while after that. Someone else took me to Gateway House. There I was, walking the street, pregnant and homeless. Lost. Then this van pulls up."

"A kombi?"

She nodded. "I was at Gateway a while before Gunther came to meet me. He didn't say he was the leader, but I could tell. The others all looked at him in that way. At first, I was a little freaked out. But he would just talk. He would want to rub my belly, talk to the baby, saying it was a miracle of life." She let out a soft laugh. "I thought he was some crazy artist. Then he invited me to meditate with them."

O'Donnell nodded. He could guess what came next. "Awakening."

She mirrored him, tucking her hair behind an ear. "It was the best feeling in the world, Mr O'Donnell. I was so alone. I hadn't only lost faith in my family and Kyle, but in humanity and God too. And when they awakened me…"

"I can see why you may have felt that way, Leyla. But Gunther—"

"He's evil, Mr O'Donnell."

He eyed Leyla for any sign of deceit. But he had no way of telling

"I know that now. Gunther isn't what he says he is."

Searching her face, he saw something in Leyla's big brown eyes. "You met him."

The smile she gave was as warm as it was large. "Nathan showed me the truth. Showed me that Gunther had been wrong. But it's not his fault."

"The man is a psycho, Leyla. Or at least he was." She frowned at that, but he kept going. "What did Gunther make you and Gateway do?"

Lowering her eyes, she worried at the napkin in her hands, twisting it up and pulling on its ends. "The worst part of it all is, he didn't force me. Didn't… trick me. But now that Nathan has helped me, I can… I—" Her already red, swollen eyes swelled with fresh tears.

The edge of the table bit into his palm as O'Donnell gripped it, his forearms trembling.

Nathan had reversed whatever damage had been done to her mind, her soul. And now that she was returned to herself, the memories of the things she had seen, and done…

"I am sick of these fucking pricks playing with people's lives."

Wiping the torrent from her cheeks, she reached out and placed a hand atop his. "It's not their faults. That's what Nathan wanted me to tell you before I leave. And that he's going to fox it."

As she made to stand, he knew it was probably stupid, but he thrust his hand forward and caught her hand, stopping her. She settled back into the booth.

Pulling his hand back, O'Donnell did his best to relax. "Where are you going to go, Leyla?"

She shook her head. "Somewhere better."

It was probably for the best. By the sounds of it, the poor girl had a lot of healing to do.

"Nathan also knows you've been looking into Gunther. The bombing and his connection to Killian Doyle."

Mr Inglewood. She knew something about the connection between Doyle and Gunther. He nodded, doing his best not to appear overexcited.

"Gunther worked his way to Killian by doing favours. It wasn't hard with all the stuff he. Knowing things what people like Killian need. Or want. After getting in, Gunther learned that Killian likes specific things. Like pregnant women." The shudder in her lip returned.

All he could do was watch and hand her napkins. Gunther had handed her off to Inglewood—Doyle—because he had wanted to satiate some sick desire. Gunther because he wanted something from the mobster, or probably a great many somethings. One of those being the explosive used in the mansion attack.

"I'm sorry," she said when her sobbing had died down. "All this stuff is coming back to me so strong after Nathan, and I can't stop them." She dabbed her nose and cheeks. "I don't know what's worse."

Pulling several fresh napkins, he handed them over. "You don't need to apologise, Leyla. Not to me. Not to anyone. What happened to you was terrible and not your fault."

"Maybe," she said. Her lips twitched before settling back to a passive expression, partway open.

She was still a kid. Was she even eighteen, O'Donnell wondered?

"I don't want you feeling sorry for me."

"I wasn't. Promise. I just don't understand how they— How can any of them call themselves enlightened with all of this pain and misery surrounding them."

The corners of her eyes and her forehead wrinkled. "I think... It's time for me to go."

O'Donnell let out a bitter laugh. "You know what? That's what Cassie said to me before she walked out on me. And I'm really starting to get tired of it, and everyone in both the Enlightened and Gateway assuming they know more than me."

"You're right, Mr O'Donnell. I've been on the inside of both of them now. Lost my baby to it all. It's weird, don't you think? After all this stuff about reincarnation and awakening, to be so sad over someone I never knew. Someone who was never born."

His lips tightened as he shook his head. "I don't have kids. Probably never will, so I can't even begin to imagine how you feel. But I don't think that's how it works."

Her head began to shake before it moved into a nod. "No. It really isn't. And no one ever tells you that." Lifting the napkins to her nose, she blew it and sniffled before dropping it into her unfinished bowl of curly fries.

"Thank you, Leyla. Thank you for coming to tell me all this even though..." He had no words. "Can... I at least walk you somewhere?"

She glanced around, then turned back and nodded. "A walk sounds nice."

Pulling out his wallet and placing few notes on the table, he ushered Leyla out. Exiting the restaurant through vintage double doors, he smirked to himself when it chimed pleasantly from above. He would have to get around to the bell on his own door, if he made it through all this.

Turning the corner, he took several steps down the path into the shade and leaned against the wall. Leyla followed close behind and stood side on, pressing her shoulder to the wall, arms wrapping around herself. O'Donnell held out his cigarettes for her.

"No. Thanks."

Lighting up, he pocketed the packet, then turned to face her, trying to decide what he might say to her. He settled for pushing off the diner wall and indicating the path and fell alongside her as they strolled.

"I know what you must be thinking," she said after a long silence. "How can someone who claims to be awake be so stupid?"

O'Donnell smirked, holding up his cigarette. "What's that saying about stones and glass houses?" He grinned as she let out a chuckle. "I don't think you're stupid. I do think you were taken advantage of, though. At least Gunther can't do the same to anyone else."

Leyla frowned at him. "Why do you keep talking like he's gone?"

His eyes narrowed. "Gunther's dead, Leyla."

"What? When?"

"Two weeks ago."

She shook her head, mouth open. "That's not possible."

Was she in denial? Did she still harbour some allegiance to that maniac? "It happened right in front of me. Nathan made him blow his own brains out."

He thought the revelation might give her some comfort. Instead, she became almost distraught.

"No. I saw Gunther this morning."

O'Donnell shook his head. Had the Crone been telling the truth? Had Gunther somehow faked his own death? Had it all been an elaborate hoax with her assistance? Or, as Cassie suspected, could Gunther be so powerful? And could that mean he had somehow cheated death itself?

"You're certain?" he asked.

"As certain as I'm talking to you. We were face to face."

Sucking on the cigarette, he pinched the butt and flicked it away, his arm springing out to lend it force. "Shit!" Pacing, he locked his fingers at the back of his neck. "Do you know where he is now?"

"No. He comes and goes like a ghost."

"Yeah. A ghost in a silver Merc." Again, more questions and not enough answers. "Do you know what his end game is, Leyla? Any idea at all?"

Her face wrinkled as she shook her head, her breath hastening. "I — I don't want—"

He hated to push her, but he couldn't let Gunther continue. Not with Cassie out there thinking he was dead. "Please. He's not going to stop, and we both know it."

"But he doesn't want to *ever* stop. Gunther wants to live forever," she said in answer to his baffled stare. "Him and Gateway."

"Just my luck to be going up real fucking loony tunes."

Her shoulders fell as she shook her head. "I wish I could help you more, Mr O'Donnell. But I think my time here is done."

He turned to her. "No, wait. Please, Leyla. If you help I know we can—"

"I'm afraid I can't help you any more, Mr O'Donnell." Leyla edged closer to the road.

"Leyla," O'Donnell said quietly, reaching out his hands with fingers wide. He shook his head, eyeing the busy city traffic. "Don't do this."

"I wish you the best of luck," she said, heels hanging over the edge of the gutter. Her teeth flashed. "Please, don't blame yourself."

Her body flowed back of its own accord, her feet not moving.

"No!"

O'Donnell flinched at the impact of the large delivery truck. The buckling of sheet metal panels. Something cracked and crunched, bone and glass he thought. He'd turned his head, unable to watch. He didn't think he could take a third person end their life in front of him. The sound and the image his mind conjured was worse.

Not knowing what else to do, he did what he had never thought possible. As people screamed and traffic came to a screeching halt, O'Donnell walked away.

He now knew what he had to do. He had to put a stop to this, once and for all.

EIGHTEEN

Sitting in the fifties diner, crying into a large caramel milkshake with his head in his hands, O'Donnell didn't know what to do. And, no matter how much he sucked on the straw, the milkshake never seemed to end.

"I don't know what to do," he said, voicing his thoughts, words strained through his deep lament.

Looking for assistance, he was struck with confusion. The diner was familiar, yet alien. Then it dawned on him. It was not the same diner he and Leyla had been in, but some conglomeration of it, the roadhouse near Gateway house, the fish and chip shop near the mansion, and the cafe he and Cassie had eaten at.

He was dreaming.

"Don't feel bad, Mr O'Donnell," a voice next to him said. Leyla was suddenly there next to him, smiling beatifically. "What goes around comes around."

He shook his head. "I could have saved you. *Should* have saved you."

"If wishes were horses..." she said, shrugging.

A horse cantered through the dream diner. He thought it was his father in the saddle, but for some reason he was also a mixture. Mainly of Burt Reynolds, David Hasselhoff and Tom Selleck.

"I used to be pretty good on a horse and handy with a lasso," he said absently.

"Then perhaps you know what to do with this?"

Something warm and wet pressed into his hand. He took the umbilical cord tied in a noose without second thought, the blood and amniotic fluid on it slicking his palm and fingers. The twisted rope of flesh slid through his hand as he gathered it in a loop over his left hand. Dark veins ran through the waxy, pale flesh, the blood pulsing through it throbbing in his fingers.

"Is there much more?" he said to Leyla.

She was on the floor, her feet pulled toward her and legs parted, the umbilical slithering from her as he pulled. "As much as you need," she said. "I'm here to serve."

Leyla lowered her eyes as her head bowed. Thick, dark blood pooled around her feet, large clots splashing into the fluid as he pulled. Unbuttoning her dress, she opened it to expose her engorged breasts and belly.

"Are you thirsty?" she said. Not waiting for an answer, she cupped a breast in each hand and squeezed.

Streams of almost clear liquid sprayed in every direction, covering O'Donnell's face. He laughed, as he did when he was a child, playing in the sprinkler in the summer heat. The clear spray turned to white. Then red.

Blood soaked O'Donnell's hair, spurted into his mouth, salty, hot and metallic on his tongue. Yet he kept on laughing.

Double doors to the kitchen crashed open, and he turned his head. Standing in front of an enormous oven with its door open was Judy, the dead waitress from the roadhouse. She shook her head as she basted something on a roasting tray. Something snaked from the pan in front of her.

He followed the charred length, its colour shifting to deep roast beef red, then a roast pork white. The line ran between Leyla's feet, then up into his hand.

He looked back to Judy, the doors flapping still. She was basting an infant on a roasting rack, its pudgy limbs curled up into the body.

O'Donnell dropped the looped coils and pressed his fingers to his temples. "I think I've had enough now," he said.

Leyla was gone.

He glanced around the diner. It was full with members of the Enlightened and Gateway. Across the restaurant, he spotted Cassie being served coffee from a glass carafe.

"Cassie?" he said, voice soft.

The waitress serving her turned. "Sorry love," the waitress shouted. "I'll be with you in a moment."

A shrill scream and a crash of utensils and crockery came from the kitchen. O'Donnell watched through the still flapping doors as Judy attempted to pick up the roasting tray with her bare hands, over and over. Her hands would burn, she would scream, then drop the tray. At each fall, the baby on the roasting tray slipped further and further off.

A knot tightened in his chest as he sat open-mouthed, head slowly shaking. "Someone needs to do something," he said, voice barely above a whisper. The waitress rushed past him and he threw out his hand, catching her by the apron. "You need to do something!" he said, pointing at the kitchen.

"Hold your horses, love! I'll be with you next, I said." The woman hurried away to continue serving patrons.

Turning back to the kitchen doors, O'Donnell's panic increased as a pale wraith-like figure stalked toward Judy. The Crone, a knife the size of a machete in her bony fingers. She lifted the massive blade high.

The doors to the kitchen crashed open. Gunther strode out, a cloche in hand. He placed it on a high, stainless steel bench, then rang a bell. "Order up!"

"What would you like, love?" the waitress said, grinning wide.

Looking up, he saw Cassie's face, but his dream mind did not make the connection, though his subconscious knew it was her. He glanced back to the empty seat where she'd been sitting.

"Don't let me eat his food!" O'Donnell said to the Cassie-waitress in panic.

"Our cook is one of the best in the business, sir," Cassie said.

Ding. "Order up, I said!" Gunther bellowed, growing impatient.

"Just a minute," Cassie said sweetly. She turned back to O'Donnell. "Your food is going to get cold. What seems to be the problem, sir?"

"He's not a good person. I won't eat his food!"

Cassie smiled. "I'm sure that—"

A shadow fell across O'Donnell. With a metallic gonging, Cassie fell to the floor. Gunther stood over her, the cloche in one hand, its edge coated in blood, and the dish it covered held high in the other.

"When I say order up, I mean, order up!" Gunther eyed the prone woman. He grinned as he placed the dish on the table in front of O'Donnell. "Bon appétit, James."

Swallowing hard, he trying to avert his gaze, but it was drawn unbidden to the plate. When he saw the raw human heart he relaxed. "I didn't order this."

"Compliments of the chef," Gunther said, his lips sliding wide. He turned to walk away, then motioned at the waitress on the floor. "Fresh from the source."

Cassie's blouse was torn open, like her bare chest beneath it, a ragged hole in her skin and ribs.

Turning to the heart, O'Donnell took up his knife and fork and cut it in half. As the two pieces slid apart, maggots spilled form it, writhing within the chambers of the organ and falling to the plate. "It's stuffed with fried rice," he said to the Cassie.

"It's Cook's specialty," she said, picking herself up.

O'Donnell hummed, uncertain, and positioned his fork. "Are you going to be okay?"

"I will be… if you give me a kiss."

"Okay," he said, smirking in excitement as he put his cutlery down.

Cassie fell on him, hands and weight pinning him to the chair. Her eyes and mouth ran with maggots as she leaned in to place her lips on his. The larvae poured from the hole in her chest, wriggling over her breasts and down her blouse, falling into his lap.

"Kiss me," she said, maggots tumbling from lips already mottled with gnaw marks from the. She lunged forward, mouth wide and planting it over his.

As his mouth filled with the crawling things, her tongue followed after them, exploring and sliding over his. He could feel the gouges missing from it, like her lips. His eyes widened as a figure crept up and pressed to Cassie's back, a butcher knife in hand.

The Crone smiled, then in perfect Vietnamese said, "Order up, Mr Bro'Donnell."

Taking a handful of Cassie's hair, the Crone slashed with the knife, swinging it like a sword. As the blade cleaved through Cassie's neck, a wave of blood and maggots spurted from her lips and into O'Donnell's mouth and down his throat.

O'Donnell pushed the corpse off and fell to floor, spitting the bloody crawling things out and jamming his fingers into the back of his mouth to purge.

The Crone cackled, holding Cassie's head high, then tossed it at O'Donnell—

—who leaped from the sofa bed as the phone rang.

Calling Cassie's name, panting and shaken, he lunged for the desk, grabbing the receiver and sending the phone toppling with a jingling clang.

"Cassie? I—"

A raspy laughter cut him off. "Don't worry, Jimmy," the Crone said, cackling. "She'll be next soon enough."

"What the hell do you want from me, you crazy bitch?"

He thrust the receiver from his ear as a loud stream of high-pitched beeps and chirps assaulted him, drilling into his head. Yelling in frustration, O'Donnell threw the receiver aside. As he clutched his head, the tone continued, then changed to an insistent chirping of the line disconnecting.

"Fax?" he said to himself, dropping his hands and frowning.

The nightmare came back to him in full force. The Crone had spoken Vietnamese. Called him Bro'Donnell.

"Benji!"

He tore through the office, knocking over the cheap divider with a clatter, the paper covering it rapping like a drum and tearing. He grabbed the front door handle and pulled hard. The door rattled but stayed in place. Fumbling and tearing at the lock and dead bolt, cursing and spitting as his laboured breath streamed air and saliva from his lips, he unlocked the door.

The damaged bell clanked behind him as his feet pounded the concrete, his legs burning from his sprint down the path. As he ran, he cursed again. Cursed his own stupidity for involving Benji. He'd brought Benji into this and into the line of danger. If anything happened to him, it was O'Donnell's fault.

He came to a stop in front of the restaurant. The sign on the door had been flipped to closed and hung haphazardly, the lights inside still glowing soft yellow. Wrong. It was all wrong. He knew for a fact they didn't close until later and did not leave the lights on when they did.

Expecting the door to resist, he pushed it anyway. It opened. The now familiar electronic chime on it rang. No one came to greet him. He also knew from experience that when they were all in the kitchen, they would not hear it. He glanced at the chromed bell on the counter, then into the dining area. No patrons. No staff.

The kitchen was the only other space. Whatever was happening, that was where he would find the answers.

Fear expanding to take his breath, he rounded the counter with cautious steps, grabbing the bell from it as he passed it. He had no weapon, but something heavy like that was likely to stun or distract long enough to make a difference. If the person he were going up against fought by standard physical means, that was. The flurry of debris that had assaulted him up the mountain came back to him. But he could not let that stop him now. Benji was in danger.

Parting the red beaded curtain, he glanced into the kitchen, which ran off to his left. The expanding fear solidified in his chest like lead.

Prone feet. Male. Another pair not too far away, female. As he approached, he saw the woman's face. One of the owners, Mrs Yao. Inspecting the man's shoes more closely, they weren't something Benji would wear. Mr Yao, then.

Fingers of terror tickled down his neck as he detected a wet, meaty sound, like someone playing with a bowl of stew. As he went around the body of Mrs Yao to the end of the metal bench in the middle of the kitchen, the back of a head came into view. Matted grey and white hair filled his vision, which quickly turned red with rage.

The Crone squatted over Benji's chest, her thumbs in his eye sockets, his face a red mask.

Screaming, O'Donnell aimed the bell at her head and hurled it with every ounce of his hatred. The thing missed by a hand's breadth. With the agility of someone a third her age, the Crone rolled behind the bench, her thumbs extracting from Benji's face with a sucking.

O'Donnell froze to the spot. All he could hear was his own heavy breathing and a gas burner off to one side. He had assumed Benji's face had been covered in blood. As he drew closer he recoiled. The skin had been minced by a blade. Hundreds of cuts hatched its surface, rendering Benji all but unrecognisable. Then he spotted the long, black handle of a cleaver splitting his sternum.

He cried out in surprise as a weight struck him in the back, sending him stumbling. Fingers like wet twigs raked at his face, the stench of blood filling his nostrils, her spindly legs locked around his waist. As he fought to dislodge the Crone, she punched him repeatedly him on the head and neck. Twirling and spinning, the continued blows disorienting, he fought to dislodge her, pin her to something or wind her until she fell. Reaching out, he screamed in agony as his hand fell on the cast iron ring surrounding the large wok burner.

Driven by the adrenaline from the pain, and in an effort to distance himself from its source, he pushed off and threw his weight, pivoting and thrusting his shoulder toward the floor. He was rewarded with a frustrated cry from the Crone as she went soaring over him, nails clawing his neck as she attempted to keep hold.

Like a feral cat, she rolled into a crouch facing him, Benji beside her. With a grimace and a snarl, she grabbed the cleaver and tore it free and was on her feet faster than was naturally possible.

And O'Donnell could see it all. In the moment her hand began to move, he saw knew what the Crone would do. And that he could stop her.

His vision sharpened. Items in his periphery, normally blurry, stood out in stark detail. The Crone's hand rose, cleaver gleaming. The nicks and scratched from use and sharpening sparkled, catching the fluorescent light and the blue gas jet of the stove.

O'Donnell's reached out and grabbed the handle of a steel wok. He swung his arm and struck the cleaver and the Crone's hand. The cleaver bounced off pots and pans to clatter to the bench top as the Crone let out a shrill cry, pulling her hand to her chest. Before she could cradle it, O'Donnell swung the wok backhand, turning it so the underside struck her full force in the cheek and jaw at an oblique angle and sent her falling back.

Dropping the wok to the floor with a clang, shoulders rising and falling with heavy breaths, he glanced down at the old woman. One hand holding herself up, the other laying limp on her stomach, she looked up at him, laughing. Blood splattered her lips and chin and more ran free from a nostril. Her bloody grin was now snaggled, a tooth or two chipped or missing. He couldn't tell from the blood. Dizzy from the exertion, O'Donnell fell against the bench.

"Well done, James," she said, the blood burbling on her already fattening lips. "You exceed my expectations at every turn. We'll make a—"

Her eyes went wide as the cleaver fell between them, O'Donnell roaring in anger and agony.

O'Donnell had felt its handle in his hand. He had been aware of it under his fingers on the bench. But not until he saw what he was doing—the blade rushing through the air, his knuckles white in the tight grip around the handle—did he realise his own intention.

The crone fell, head hanging back over Benji's leg. As sickened as he was from having taken a human life, from almost having split her head in two like a melon, he forced himself to not give in to the guilt and disgust.

He turned his gaze from the Crone to Benji. The sickening nausea was replaced with the anger that had welled in his chest when he had seen his friend dead, but it was now tempered with sorrow.

Stumbling from the kitchen, he made his way to the front desk. He sat on the stool that he had only ever seen Benji in, sometimes Mr Yao, and pulled his cigarettes from a pocket. As he thumbed open the packet, blood freckling his skin stood out on his fingers. Pulling a smoke out awkwardly with trembling fingers, he wiped the blood on his pants, then fished out the lighter and sparked it after several attempts, the flame dancing wildly as he brought it to the tip of the cigarette.

Taking a deep drag on the smoke and letting out a spluttering exhalation, O'Donnell licked his lips and swallowed hard. Picking up the phone receiver, he punched triple zero.

"You look like shit, Jimmy."

O'Donnell pulled another cigarette from his lips. He'd lost count but thought this was his sixth. "With all due respect, Robbie, go fuck yourself. My friend was brutally murdered and I had to kill a person, so forgive me if I don't put up with your bullshit."

Robbie stared at him a moment, then nodded. "Fair enough." He sat in the doorway of the ambulance beside O'Donnell. "Wanna tell me what happened?"

"I already gave the uniforms a statement. I'm sure you read it."

"I did. But I want to hear it from you."

"Why? So you can poke holes in my story?"

"Fucking Jesus, Jimmy. Why do you have to be such a difficult prick?" Pushing off from the ambulance, Robbie paced, then turned on him. His head fell side to side as if he was trying to crack his neck, then closed his eyes, shoulders falling. "Just because we had a falling out, doesn't mean I don't still care about you. Okay?"

O'Donnell lifted his gaze from the asphalt.

Robbie pulled out his own cigarettes. "And that's not some gay shit, okay? I don't want you to stick your tongue down my throat or lick my arse or anything weird." Robbie's lips cracked into a smirk. "So we're clear."

When O'Donnell didn't respond or smile back, Robbie lit up.

"I don't have anything to add to my statement," O'Donnell said.

Robbie shook his head. "Fine. Fucking be that way. But we'll be calling you in for a follow-up interview."

Taking a last drag, O'Donnell threw the cigarette down, its tip exploding into dancing embers on the dark asphalt. "Will that be all, Detective?"

"Yeah. That's fucking all. So fuck off out of my sight before I change my mind."

Placing his foot on the still smouldering cigarette, O'Donnell stood and crushed it, grinding it into the blacktop. Thrusting his hands into his pockets, head down, he walked away from Robbie.

NINETEEN

TRAFFIC PASSED and the clouds wheeled overhead. Someone with a dog ambled down the street, the animal glancing his way as he sat and stared blankly out the windscreen. O'Donnell didn't know what to say, but he knew he had to come.

He wasn't sure, but he thought the dog pissed on his wheel, its owner acting like nothing had happened. Only when he saw the pair of them in full in the driver side mirror did he open the door, the old rubber seals on the Falcon cracking as they peeled away from the car. He looked down in time to avoid the steaming pile the dog had left in his path.

Wouldn't that be the icing on the cake, he thought. Stinking of dog shit as he… What? Paid his respects? Gave his shallow condolences? What could the man who caused their son's death say to parents? I'm sorry that my actions, however directly or indirectly, caused Benji's murder?

No. There was nothing he could say. But inaction would be worse. It would be cowardly. Worse, it would dishonour Benji's memory.

The door creaked open a short time after he knocked. He had not had to inform families of deaths himself during his time on the force, but he had been present several times. People fell apart.

And he knew that this would not be that. They would have had that moment already. This would be more. Run much deeper. That was why he was here. They needed someone to blame. And O'Donnell would give them that so that maybe they could, in whatever small way, be able to move on.

But it broke his heart.

Benji's mother lifted her eyes to him. Recognition was a few moments coming, her eyes focused on something far away that only others grieving could glimpse. But as recognition returned, a shudder worked its way up her body, from her belly up through her chest, down her arms and up to her chin. Tears ran free from her red and rimed eyed, crusted with sleep and pain.

She tumbled from the doorway, fistfuls of tissue flying. Her voice broke as she yelled at him incoherently in Vietnamese.

He lifted his arms to protect his face, but apart from repeating the words I'm sorry, he did nothing. As numb as he believed he was from the internal pain, the repeated blows penetrated the emotional daze and began to bruise. But he held his ground until she relented. When he lowered his arms, he saw it was because Benji's father had pulled her away, muttering softly into her ear even as she continued her assault on the air.

O'Donnell could still hear her pained shrieks as the door closed on him. He waited until they quietened and the door opened again, closing softly behind Benji's father.

"What are you doing here, Mr O'Donnell?" he said, voice soft, broken and bereft of emotion, gaze fixed somewhere behind O'Donnell and toward the ground.

Opening his dry mouth, O'Donnell had to clear his throat before he could speak. "Mr Tran... I—" Something almost solid crawled up his gullet, muting him.

"Don't." Shaking his head, Benji's father lifted his wet eyes. "Do not tell me you are sorry, Mr O'Donnell. Sorry will not bring back my son. My only—" His lips started to tremble and he stopped, mouth open in anguish, face wrinkled up in torment. Curling his fingers into fists, digging his nails into his palms, Benji's father brought himself under control. "I think you should leave now, Mr O'Donnell. And never come back."

With that, the man turned to his door, opening it only as far as needed to slip into the darkness within. O'Donnell watched and listened as he heard the door lock and the deadbolt engage. Then the thud of weight against the wood, and muted sobs.

———

The sun was slinking deep into the horizon when he slipped his key into the lock of the office door. He pushed hard to sweep the mail aside, lashing at it with his feet, sending it flying and fluttering. Almost a week he'd been gone. A week of laying in his old room, feeling sorry for himself.

His mother was never one to shy away from the hardness of life. Whenever there was a funeral that needed attending, she'd taken him. Answered his questions frankly. In many respects, she was the hard one when it came to matters of life and the heart, where his father was the soft one, though he always played the big man. O'Donnell assumed, though, he played that softness to great effect when needed, though he'd rarely experienced it himself.

"What's the matter?" his mother had said sternly on the first night.

And so he'd told her, unburdening himself of what he could. Of what sounded rational and sane.

She'd given him a hug, told him he could stay and clear his head. "But you've got seven days," she added. "After that, it's time to pull yourself up by your boots and get back to it. You've got a job to finish. And your friend, by the sounds of him, wouldn't want you to mope about either. And neither does your mother."

Before the seven days was up, he'd packed up his room, kissed his mother on the head, told her to say hello to Vincent from him, and drove back to the office.

Now that he was back, all he could picture was Benji in the space, and the hole that had been torn with his absence.

When the phone rang, he let out a deep sigh, set his jaw, and ambled toward it. He dropped his hand on the receiver and held it down, like he could choke the sound. But it jangled on, the sound creeping through his bones. The plastic creaking as his grip tightened, he snatched it up to his ear, the spiralled cord bouncing.

"What do you want, Cassie?"

She was silent a moment, but he could hear her breathing. Could almost smell it through the line. Taste her perfume. He let his eyes fall closed as he remembered her sweet breath. But it now held a hint of corruption.

Of death.

"Where have you been, James? I've been so worried!" Her words spilled from her lips in rush. He could hear the emotion in them. But he doubted everything now.

"Well, you shouldn't have been. *I'm* fine." Benji's name crept to his lips, but he held his tongue. He would not use his memory in that way.

O'Donnell looked to the chair that Benji had occupied not that long ago. Full of life and memories.

The voice told me an angel would save me and that it wasn't my time. That I had things to do." He gave a small smile. *"Then you came along."*

His hand trembled as he squeezed the phone receiver. "Now, what do you want?"

"I— I'm sorry about your friend."

"Don't! Don't you say sorry to me, Cassie! Save your sorrow for Benji's parents."

"I—"

"No, Cassie! This is not about you. Or me. Or the stupid fucking Enlightened or Gateway! Or that fucking old crazy bitch that took his life! They lost their only son. Their son they not too long ago lost to drugs and a gang life. They barely pulled him back from the edge of death." He let out a bitter laugh. "And I came along and pushed him back. All the way over."

"I know this must be hard on you, James... but you can't blame yourself."

"Well, Cassie, I do. I blame myself. I blame Nathan, and Gunther and his deranged followers. You. Since you all came into my life, I've been surrounded by death and destruction. Witnessed innocent people getting caught in your crossfire."

Cassie didn't even know about Leyla. Her baby. Would it matter? Part of him still hoped it would. But a greater part doubted it, and he hated that.

He had to bring this all to a close somehow, but he couldn't do it alone. And now he was more alone than ever. Robbie hated him, thought O'Donnell a traitor and no doubt told the Tran's about his involvement in Benji's death. Could he truly trust Cassie?

He had to try.

"They won't even be able to see his face one last time, Cassie. And do you know why?"

"James, I—"

"Because he doesn't have one. She turned it into mincemeat." He thought he heard a gasp. "But I stopped her. Buried a cleaver in her face. *I* had to do that, Cassie. *Me.* Because if I didn't, she would have gone on hurting more people. While you and Gateway dance around each other, I'm out here *doing* something."

"Oh, James."

She sounded sad for him. But he didn't have time for pity. Didn't think she was truly capable of it any longer. Nathan had fixed Leyla. It had broken her irreparably, but at least she had died on her own terms and as herself.

"Just tell me that she's dead, Cassie. *Really* dead. Not like Gunther, doing whatever the fuck it is he did."

"I— I think so. We think that perhaps his death was an illusion. One so powerful it fooled even Nathan. The Crone was probably helping him. But if you killed her by your own hand…"

"Good. But we can't stop there, Cassie. It all has to end. You know that, right? Deep down? I know you and the rest of you feel like you're gods or some shit, high above us mere fucking mortals."

"We don't—" There was a sound of muffled, electronic static. Someone breathing into the receiver. "You're right." Cassie sounded tired, her voice not much louder than the sighing through the crackling line. "I know you're right. Others have said much the same. We've been trying to think—"

"No, Cassie! No more thinking. The time for that is over. You have to *act*. Don't be sorry. Do something."

"But what? What can we do?"

"You have to find Nathan."

"How, James?"

"Jesus! Don't ask me. You're the ones that have the psychic powers. Use it. I don't care if you need to pull a Ouija board out of your arses or use the fucking force. You use whatever you need to find Nathan and Gunther and put a stop to this shit before anyone else dies." He heard a croak of protest from her before silence. "It's either that or I stop this myself, Cassie. One way or another, I will bring the Enlightened and Gateway to an end. You have to see that the world isn't ready. *You* aren't ready."

She let out another sigh, but this one was different. And he knew that she was with him. Whatever that meant for her, for Nathan, for all of them… she was willing to put it all on the line.

"What do you need me to do?"

O'Donnell sat on the bench, legs jiggling, the manila envelope in his hands crinkling as he moved. He wasn't worried. Nothing would happen to him, not from this in any case. No. If someone was going to take him out, it was going to be Gateway. Probably Gunther himself. Not—

"Doyle," he said out loud.

She stopped metres from him, glaring even through the large sunglasses. Her tight lips shifted to a wry grin. "O'Donnell," she said, nodding as she continued to the bench. "We done with cloak and dagger are we?"

He shrugged. "I lost a close friend, had to split an old woman's skull in two. So yeah, you might say I've had enough bullshit to last a lifetime. Even multiple lifetimes."

The joke was lost on her.

Pouting her bottom lip in thought, she nodded. "My, you have been a busy boy, haven't you?" She let out a barely contained chuckle. "Are you telling me this to try and scare me, or you applying for a job?"

He let out a bitter snort of a laugh. "I have a job, thanks. I was just venting."

"Hmm. I see. Well I'm truly sorry for your loss. And if you change your mind—"

"I won't."

"Nevertheless, if you do… Well, you know the rest." She looked to the envelope, then back up at him. "Was he your age? This friend?"

"Younger."

Her mouth smacked with a single tut as she shook her head. "That for me?" She indicated his envelope with her head.

O'Donnell waved the envelop at her. "This is everything on your husband and my case. And I do mean everything. Notes, files, copies of photos and negatives… His appetite for very young, very pregnant girls. Every single scrap."

"And you're telling me this why?"

Turning to her, O'Donnell smirked. "Let's not be coy, Mrs Doyle. You're making a move on your husband. You've turned enough of his men by now I'm sure. He's gone and gotten into bed with cults. Soon, someone is going to make sure he has a nasty accident."

"And you don't want anything pointing back to you, is that it?"

"I'm not worried about that. I'm good at my job. I knew from the start I had to be careful. No. I'm more concerned about *unofficial* blowback, if you catch my drift."

"And you think this will guarantee that?" Her grin was as threatening as it was wide. "You should know better than that, Mr O'Donnell. In my line of business… sorry, my husband's line of business… the only guarantee is the pine box at the end."

"That's cute. Did you practice that on your way here? Or is it something you've had in your back pocket a while?"

Her grin fell. "I'd be careful if I were you, Mr O'Donnell. You don't want to make enemies in the wrong places."

O'Donnell hung his head, snorting a sigh from his nostrils. Leaning back, he nodded slowly, and put the envelope beside him, far from Doyle. "You're the one who should be careful, Mrs Doyle." He noted her body stiffening from the corner of his eye as he lit up a cigarette. "I noticed you've brought your own envelope."

Her hand tightened over the opening of her handbag, the yellow package within dog-eared.

"And from the way you were hugging your bag, it's something that has you very worried."

"You're very perceptive, aren't you?"

"So I keep being told. And that's why you hired me."

Nodding, she forced a smile onto her lips. "Fine. I'll guarantee your safety Mr O'Donnell. Now hand me the envelope and—"

He turned to her now. "You first."

Lips tightening, she yanked the envelope free and thrust it at him. She was more afraid of Gunther and Gateway than she was of anything else, possibly even her husband. If she succeeded in her plan to rid herself of him, she would be a formidable underworld figure with resources.

And she was terrified.

She talked him through it as he went through the files, what little there was.

"This Gunther character is slippery," she said. "Shadier than anyone I have ever come across. And it goes a lot deeper than pimping out up the duff girls." He hummed, and she turned to him with a deep frown. "I don't think you fully appreciate what that means coming from me."

"Believe me, I do. And I can guess the kinds of brick walls your people would have come up against."

She let out a laugh that was half crazed. It reminded O'Donnell of another deranged woman. "Forget brick, try metre thick titanium, mate."

"Well, then I'm impressed you got this. But what am I looking at exactly?"

She tapped the topmost page, a thin sheet of paper with perforated edges. A manifest or invoice of some sort. "Pharmaceuticals. High class drugs for high class clients. Top grade stuff, too. However your boy was doing it, Killian was lapping it up. Literally as well as figuratively."

Nodding, O'Donnell's jaw tightened at mention of her husband's name. It brought back Leyla's final moments. Her relaxed smile as she stepped onto the road. "Was there anything else he was supplying?"

"Information mostly. Other whores of particular tastes to people in high places. The slap and tickle kind. You know what men are like. Make a few loud moans and groans and they're ready to drop more than just their shorts."

O'Donnell nodded, more to cover his anger. Whores, she'd said. Leyla being one of them in Doyle's mind. "What I don't get is why. From everything I have heard about Gunther, he was well off. Had investments coming out his arse. All protected and always moving."

"You've got that right. Whoever his accountant is, I want to buy that man a drink or twelve. In the time since we last met, my accountant was only able to uncover a little. Peel back a few layers. And when I tell you my man's good, you'd better believe it. If my husband suspected I had a quarter of what I do..."

"So what was Gunther really after?"

She shook her head and looked as baffled as O'Donnell felt. "I have no bloody idea. He already had access to drugs, but if I were guessing, he wanted his girls—and boys—in the right places."

Frowning, O'Donnell went through the papers in his hand for the third time, trying to find the connections. Why would Gunther want his people in those places? The pharmaceuticals, that was obvious. Access.

As it dawned on him, he sat up. "Access."

"What?"

"Hospitals," O'Donnell said, and turned to the woman beside him. "These people, were there a lot of hospital board and administration?"

"Of course. Where else would he get all the prescription stuff."

"But I bet there were a lot more important people than that, right?"

She grinned knowingly. "I can neither confirm nor deny. I'm sure you understand."

He did. She would not deny herself such a lucrative revenue or information stream. But O'Donnell was more concerned about the information that had flowed in the other direction. And he only had one lead to follow.

"Can you at least tell me which hospitals?"

"I'm afraid not, Mr O'Donnell. Now, if you don't mind?"

Nodding, O'Donnell handed over his envelope. "This concludes our business."

"For now." She stood, and turned to him. "Like the Bon Jovi song says, never say goodbye."

Staying seated, O'Donnell gave her a thin-lipped smile. "Goodbye, Mrs Doyle."

"Lydia, please." Walking away, she glanced over her shoulder. "After all, I'll be a widow tomorrow." Winking, she turned back to the path.

TWENTY

THE SUN BEAT down on the concrete, baking it into a shimmery haze. Typical Melbourne weather—it could never make up its mind, cold one moment, hot the next. O'Donnell had his jacket over his arm as he took shelter in the shadows and smoked. The weather report said it would probably rain. The light, patchy clouds said otherwise, but it probably would. Then it would be hot again, and muggy.

"I didn't think I'd see you again," a voice said.

"Why's that?" O'Donnell said, turning to Leigh.

He shrugged and proceeded to roll himself a cigarette. O'Donnell got a strong whiff of the aromatic tobacco. "Well, why would you? Glenda's gone. There's nothing more I can tell you about Nathan Mortimer."

"What about Gunther? That name mean anything to you?"

"Should it?"

"You always this cagey, Leigh?"

"Comes with the territory, I'm afraid," he said, chuckling.

"Oh? You get a lot of people coming around asking about patients?"

"What's this about, James?"

He looked about to ensure they were alone. He trusted Leigh, and try as he might to convince himself otherwise, the feeling stuck.

"He's the leader of the Gateway Cult. I'm pretty sure he's been sneaking his people into hospitals like this one and stealing prescription meds. Selling them to the mob."

Leigh frowned. "You're kidding?"

"You heard of Killian Doyle?"

Snorting, Leigh lit up. "Who hasn't." Pocketing his tin of tobacco and papers, he turned to the building. "Damn. Makes sense, though, now that you say it. Stuff goes missing, but lately..."

"You seen him around by any chance?" He handed over the photo from the rooftop. He hadn't been completely honest with Lydia Doyle, but he had no reason to think she'd been with him either.

Taking the folded picture, Leigh studied it, then shook his head. "Sorry, James. Wish I could help."

"Yeah. Me too." O'Donnell stuffed the photo in his pocket. "Shit."

"If he's the boss though, why would he be hanging around here?"

"Glenda knew him."

"Knew?" Leigh's eyes twitching. "Gunther, or—"

"Glenda."

"How?"

"We... She killed my friend."

Leigh shook his head and took a drag from his cigarette. "Sorry. I wish I'd known what she was when I first met her."

"There's nothing you could have done."

His expression said otherwise. The kindness in his eyes that was ever present melted away, replaced by a hardness. A darkness. The sudden shift reminded O'Donnell of John Smith, the creeping darkness.

Leigh dropped his head, hooding his eyes. "There's quite a lot I can do, James. Believe me."

"I'll remember that if I'm ever in a jam."

Grinning, Leigh nodded, lifting his gaze, the darkness in his eyes, imagined or not, gone. "Please do. If you ever come across anything...

well, more out of this world than you've been dealing with, come find me."

"I'm almost too afraid to ask what shit you're mixed up in, Leigh."

"Me too, most of the time." Leigh's eyes held a faraway look as he nodded. He focused back on O'Donnell. "But you seem like you're more than capable."

"I don't know about that. Most days it feels like I'm stumbling through a paddock in pitch black night with a blindfold and a sack over my head."

Nodding emphatically, Leigh let out a loud laugh. "Yeah. That's exactly what it's like for me, too. Except, unlike you, I'm not alone."

"Now, that would be nice. Some help. We'll have to trade notes over a beer some time."

"I'd like that. I just wish I could do more to help you now."

"Maybe you still can. Can you think of anyone that might be into what I'm talking about? Notice anyone being dodgy?"

Scratching his head, then taking another puff, Leigh shook his head. "Not off the top of my head, mate. Feels like everyone around here is dodgy in one way or another most days, if you know what I mean?"

"Yeah. I'm afraid I do."

"But... now that I know what to keep an eye out for, I'll definitely let you know. I have your card."

"Thanks, Leigh. Appreciate it. And if there's ever anything I can do for you, or anyone in trouble... you know, whatever kind of trouble you can't help them with—" O'Donnell gave the man an enigmatic smile, which he returned. "Send 'em my way?"

"You can count on it, mate."

Nodding and shaking his jacket loose, O'Donnell pulled a wad of cards form a pocket and handed them over, then shook Leigh's hand. It was warm and firm, much like the man himself.

"Take it easy, James," Leigh said, still shaking and smiling. "Don't let the bastards keep you down."

"You too, Leigh." O'Donnell released the man's hand and turned.

He stopped and glanced back. "Oh… what happened to John Smith, by the way?"

Pouting, Leigh nodded, then shook his head and shrugged. "Bit touch and go, but I'm getting him help from the *right* people."

"Your people?"

A grin split Leigh's face. "That's right. My people."

"He going to be okay? Poor bloke looked like he could use a break."

"They're not sure, but I have a good feeling."

O'Donnell nodded. "That's good. At least someone is."

"Yeah, amen to that, brother. Maybe I'll bring him along, we can have a pint when he's on the mend. He keeps asking about you."

"Me?"

"Oh, you made quite an impression on him, you. He wouldn't shut up afterwards. Even got his name too. Fenton."

"Fenton, huh? Yeah, bring him along and we'll get that pint."

He couldn't say why, but as he left Leigh's side, O'Donnell had a sudden surge of positive warmth. He put it down to their conversation, the man himself almost exuding warmth. The sunny weather didn't hurt either. It did not last, though.

As he opened the door to the office, a single folded note on the worn concrete entrance caught his eye. Picking it up and unfolding it, a chill settled over him as he read the quick scrawl.

Your mate's funeral is this afternoon.

Thought you should know.

R.

Sighing, O'Donnell folded the note and slid it into his pocket as the phone rang. He eased the receiver from its cradle and held it up. "Cassie."

"How are you so sure it's always me?" she said, humour in her voice.

"I dunno. Maybe the same way you keep knowing to call whenever I walk in?"

Her throaty laugh was fresh, but it couldn't erase the bitterness of the note. "Did you have any luck at the hospital with your new friend?"

"Not particularly." There was a hissed sigh that came through as garbled mess. "He's going to keep an eye out, but I'm hoping this will all be over by then. What about you?"

"Same."

"Any ideas?" He was fast running out of them and couldn't help but think things were coming to a head. He wished he knew which way they would veer when they did.

"We do, actually."

"We? As in, all of you?"

"Yes. Meet us at the club tonight."

"Do I need to dress up? Because, I have to tell you, I'm not in the mood."

"Not today," she said, chuckling. "Come as you are."

"Okay." Closing his eyes, he squeezed them tight. "Cassie?" he said, eyes still closed. "Tell me we're going to win. Tell me it's all going to work out."

The line crackled and hummed. "It *is*, James. Trust me."

He nodded, wondering why he thought that last was a question.

"Tonight then," she said, the line clicking then becoming a rhythmic tone before descending into an urgent beeping before he hung it up.

A sea of black had descended on the cemetery, colours bobbing in and around it like corks the waves. Children too young to understand ran and hid among the tombstones in the periphery until some angry person or other told them off when they ventured too close to the grave.

O'Donnell laughed as the children played, oblivious to the gravity of things.

A little girl, she couldn't have been more than three, crept around the tomb stone he was spying on the funeral from, exploring far from her older kids. Her hair was short and close to her scalp, held in place at her temples with colourful clips, which matched flowers on her white dress. She peered up at him cautiously.

He waved at the girl.

A huge grin cracked her face, and she waved back before running away laughing as an older girl came after her, calling out in Vietnamese.

Turning his gaze to the sombre gathering, the sounds of sobbing and wailing filtered through and overtook the children as they got farther away.

O'Donnell lit up and watched until the coffin had been lowered, then as the crowd thinned, he fell back, giving the smaller group left behind space and no chance of spotting him. That was not why he was here. Then, when Mr and Mrs Tran had been led away, he waited a good while longer before approaching Benji's grave.

Regarding the rich, overturned earth, O'Donnell gave it a small smile. "Hey, Benji," he said. "I hope wherever you are you can hear me, and that you know how truly sorry I am. I didn't mean for..." He waved at the grave, then lifted his hand to his eyes as tears fell. Sniffing and clearing his throat, he fought back the deluge that threatened to break free. "If Cassie and the others are right, then maybe we'll meet each other again and have a drink. Until then..."

With a sharp sloshing, O'Donnell pulled a small glass bottle the size and shape of a hip flask from his pocket. He cracked the lid with a sharp twist and raised the bottle high. "See you next time 'round, brother."

He tipped a generous amount on the grave, the soil taking it in almost as quickly as O'Donnell as he lifted the bottle to his lips, guzzling enough to burn his throat and warm hugs. He didn't want it to affect his senses. He still had work to do.

Screwing on the lid and jamming the bottle into his pocket, O'Donnell turned from the grave and set off with purpose.

"It's time to finish this."

The sun had only begun its easing into the horizon as O'Donnell left the large cemetery so he took his time. He didn't have to try hard as peak traffic was in full swing. He melted into the seat and let the car carry him, ignoring the aggressive and frustrated drivers around him. There had been some sort of incident up the road and several lanes were blocked.

Spikes of red and blue light split the dusk air, painting the rooves of stationary cars. The traffic surged to one side as a siren from behind let out its banshee wails. In his rear-view mirror, the red paint of a fire truck flashed past as it blasted its horn, trapped in the grid-locked traffic.

Easing the old Falcon up onto a traffic island overgrown with long grasses and weeds, others in front of him cottoned on to the same idea and the truck eased its way through. It was some time until he caught up to it and grimaced at the wreck of the two vehicles. One a huge four wheel drive atop a sedan with its hood and cabin crumpled, too crushed to identify from his angle, the red and blue lights making it hard to even make out its colour.

His Falcon rolled along and he saw the untouched back end of the car. Silver paint. A three-pointed star.

"Shit!"

Hands flying, he forced the car around a slow-moving vehicle in front of him with a stamp of his foot on the accelerator and sheer will. He narrowly missed it and another car that was changing lanes. He glimpsed the cops in the mirrors waving their arms in anger, but none followed. They were too busy.

He only hoped that he would make it to the club in time.

Gunther knew. He knew that O'Donnell would go to Benji's funeral. Had the note he'd received even been from Robbie?

As he drew closer to the club, the now familiar sight of the red Valiant parked across from it welcomed him. His lips formed a smile as a dark-haired figure climbed out of it and crossed the road.

With a deafening boom and crash, everything became chaos.

O'Donnell's vision was obscured and his hearing overpowered with ringing. Heart in his throat, he instantly thought of bombs. The club. Then, with the sounds of broken glass falling and metal creaking, he realised what had happened.

Sitting up from where he was slumped sideways after the impact, O'Donnell looked himself over. The side of his head hurt where he had hit it on the driver's side window, but he was otherwise unharmed. At least as far as he could tell. Glancing at the rear mirror, he saw his car had not fared so well.

The semi-truck that had rammed the rear quarter of his car reversed and turned so it was now directly ahead of him, its high beams flashing on to blind him. His car had spun around, and he had no idea which way he was facing even before being blinded by its high beams.

The truck engine roared, O'Donnell's body quivering with its deep bass vibration.

Grabbing for the door handle with one hand and releasing his seatbelt with the other, O'Donnell shouldered the door. It moved, then came to a bone jarring halt. Either the truck had hit further in than he thought or the chassis was bent. Either way, he was not getting out that way any time soon.

Grunting his frustration, he shifted the car into reverse and stomped on the accelerator. Tyres screeching, the Falcon shot back, only to crash to a halt, O'Donnell bouncing off his seat, which catapulted him into steering wheel. The horn blared momentarily as his chest hit, but he had no time to recover.

The truck screamed toward him, the lights growing.

Eyes wide and locked on the looming juggernaut, O'Donnell pulled the door release and slammed his shoulder into it once, twice...

He spilled onto the road and rolled as the semi hit the Falcon like a brick wall on wheels. O'Donnell threw himself away, shielding his head. Debris flew around him, something hitting him in the back.

When he was sure he was safe, O'Donnell turned to the destruction.

The semi sat atop the cabin of the Falcon at an angle, several of its wheels still spinning. Both vehicles were metres from where he had come to a stop, and the rear of his destroyed car was embedded in another sedan.

Eyeing the truck's cabin, O'Donnell waited for a Gateway member or several to come rushing out. But there was none.

Head reeling and heart racing, he glanced around to get his bearings. He had been completely turned around. Groaning as he stood, he started into a run, only to find that he had been battered far more than he'd thought, breath gasping from his throat. His right knee and hip ached as he moved, as did his shoulder. He was forced to limp, but as he moved and adrenaline coursed through his veins, they loosened up. He knew it wouldn't last, but he only needed it now.

Strobing with his pulse, his vision was a speckled circle, like a grainy vignetted film, yet strangely sharp. Another effect of the adrenaline, he knew. He had to hold onto it for as long as he could.

He circled wide around the truck and stab of fear shot through him as the open driver's door came into view. Limping forward, his eyes were locked on the cabin of the semi. He found it empty, as he'd suspected. He hastened to his car and leaned to reach in through the broken window. The space was narrow, but enough to get the glove box open. Popping it, he felt around until he found what he wanted. Pocketing the pistol, he thrust his arm back in and ran his hand around to find the box of ammunition.

He put his back to the onlookers as he fished out six rounds and loaded the revolver, then, holding it close to his body, approached the truck. Wincing as he lifted himself up, he heaved himself inside. He would bet his life the truck was stolen. Also, given the pin-striping and stickers on the body, that it belonged to an old-school trucker.

In the sleeping cabin behind the seats, underneath blankets and a foam mattress, he found what he was searching for. Unzipping the old duffel, the corner of his mouth rose in grim satisfaction. He shook out a handful of rounds from the box of pistol ammo and shoved them into his pocket, then dropped the rest in the bag.

He slipped the revolver into his right pocket and zipped the duffel closed as he climbed out of the truck, taking the risk to leap down in his haste. He took the brunt of the force on his left leg but stumbled from the pain. He couldn't waste any more time. Slinging the bag behind him by a long strap, he broke into hobbling run, loose rounds jangling in his pocket.

He fell against the doorframe to the club and sucked in air as he caught his breath. Grabbing the handle, he yanked the door and pulled the revolver free and slid across the door to the far wall, pistol held high. Sighting down it, he jerked his head with it, checking every corner. But he already knew where he would find them.

Pistol drawn close to his chest, elbow jutting, he eased the door handle to the stairway until the latch released and snatched it back. The stairway was clear. Slipping through the small opening he'd made, he closed the door silently in the same manner, listening intently.

Nothing.

Revolver aimed at the landing above, he made his cautious way up, adjusting the angle of his arm with each step, wincing as his hip took his weight.

A third of the way, he found a rabbit's foot keychain. Cassie's key to her Valiant. Gun and eyes still on the landing, he scooped it up, jamming it into his back pocket before continuing.

As he neared the top and the open safety railing, he bent his knees to keep his head down. Grimacing as his knee complained, O'Donnell pressed his back to the wall, almost sitting on the stairs in a squat, his right foot higher than the left. He closed his eyes against the pain. Then shot up and around the railing, dropping to a kneel.

His free hand and eyes flew wide. Arm slowly lowering, he took in the scene.

Members of the Enlightened lay sprawled across the dance floor. Their eyes were wide in terror, their lips drawn in frozen screams.

They were all dead.

Hand falling to his side, he rushed from one body to the next, taking in their faces as he went. None of the bodies had a single wound. No blood. Not even a bruise.

A sobbing grunt made him spin, his hand up and eye sighting down the pistol. The sound had come from the bar.

Nearing it, jaw tense and arm iron straight, he eased sideways and shot his head over and around the counter. Quickly lowering the weapon, he ran around the bar to the figure slumped at the end.

The teenage girl from the hospital kicked her feet against the floor, whimpering in fear as he approached.

"Hey, hey… It's me. It's James O'Donnell," he said in a calm voice, hands out sideways, barrel of the pistol aimed at the bottles and his trigger finger across the guard. He didn't want to scare her, but he would not be putting the weapon away.

Lowering her arms from her shaking head, she opened her eyes and calmed as she saw him.

"Remember me?"

The girl nodded.

He mirrored her. "Are you okay?"

Her lips cracked open, saliva stringing between her teeth as her jaw moved, but she seemed incapable of speech.

"It's okay. Take your time. Do you want something? Water? A cola?"

"S— Smoke," she said.

Easing to sit, O'Donnell nodded and placed the pistol beside him. "You want me to light one for you?"

She nodded, lips trembling and fresh tears pouring from her eyes. He could only imagine for the moment what she had been through as he lit a cigarette for himself then another from the end of his own. Reaching out, careful not to touch her, he passed the cigarette.

Her trembling hand took the cigarette to her lips and she took several small puffs before one deep drag. When her shoulders eased, he sat against the bar, the pain in his hip momentarily lessening.

"You know," O'Donnell said, "I never did catch your name."

She sniffed and took another baby puff on the smoke. "Sarah."

"Nice name."

"Maybe," she said, shrugging. "Before all this, I would have said 'it sucks dog balls'." She cracked a grin, head swaying and eyes hooded. "All things being what they are though… Well…"

"Sarah, can you tell me what happened here?"

Chewing on the inside of her lip, she glanced at her shoes then nodded. "I don't know what happened, but it fucked me up in the head. I... I feel more and more like... *myself.*"

Like Leyla, he thought.

"Was Nathan here, Sarah? Did he fix you?"

Her gaze shot to the floor, eyes wide. "*He* did it."

"Gunther?"

She nodded, gnawing on her lip. "He did it to everyone, too. But different. I thought... I thought he was going to do the same to me. But then... Then he—" She choked up, jaw shuddering.

"Cassie?" he said, her name almost catching in his throat.

"He took her. The prick, he—" She shook with a sob.

"Okay, Sarah. It's okay now."

But it was far from okay. Why would Gunther be reverting the Enlightened to their old selves only to kill them? And why leave Sarah alive?

Her head shook, small jerky movements. She clutched it, wincing. "It feels like he juiced my fucking brain like an orange. And all he did was stare into my eyes."

"Is that what he did to others too?"

"Yeah. Everyone just... froze on the spot! And he just fucking walked up to us, one by one. And one by one we fell!"

Gunther had murdered the Enlightened single-handedly.

Eyes flitting as he thought, they stopped on the bar above. And widened. "Non-corporeal batteries," he said to himself.

"What?" Sarah said, on the verge of breaking down.

"Nothing. Sarah... I have to leave you, okay? I have to find Gunther and stop him. Do you understand?"

She shook her head. "He won't come back here now. He got what he fucking wanted. This is the safest place for me to be."

She had no idea what Gunther had done to her and the others. What he would do to Cassie and Nathan once he got his hands on him. Nathan had repaired Leyla, but that had ultimately broken her. Gunther on the other hand was draining them dry. And O'Donnell knew now why he'd left Sarah behind.

"You've been very brave, Sarah. Thank you. Just one more question. Do you know where Gunther took Cassie?"

Her eyes fluttered as they blinked in thought, then she gave her head a quick shake. "He said something about... going back to where it all started?"

"Thanks, Sarah. You know what? I think you might be more comfortable downstairs, what do you think about that?"

Her eyes wrinkled as she frowned, the fear being replaced by confusion. "Uhh... Yeah? Okay?"

Shielding her from the sight of the bodies, he led her downstairs. By the time they were halfway down, she had forgotten all about her dead colleagues. Had forgotten about Gunther, Cassie, even who O'Donnell was and was acting more and more like a teenager.

She shoved and slapped at O'Donnell as he helped her down the stairs. "Who... Who the fuck are you? Get your hands off me, you perve! Where... Where am I?"

He made a quick call to Robbie's station before he left her, doing his best to explain the cops and paramedics were coming and not to go upstairs, that there had been a gas leak and she needed medical attention.

He hoped she would stay in the club, but either way, she was out of this now and safer that way.

Slipping into the unlocked Valiant, O'Donnell slipped Cassie's key into the ignition and the car thundered to life.

TWENTY-ONE

CREEPING up the driveway to the mansion like a jungle cat, purring and moving steadily, the lights of the Valiant showed everything in golden starkness. The gate was open and waiting but O'Donnell didn't see a vehicle. He knew Gunther was there. And with him, Cassie. This was where it had all begun. For them all. From the Crone to Nathan to Gunther.

What he was not sure of was whether Gunther would have backup, and if he did what that would consist of. The things he'd witnessed the Crone do on the mountain... If the Gateway members could each do only a fraction of that, then he was in big trouble, weapons or not.

Cutting the engine, he slipped out and shut the door. The solid thud of its closing echoed in the early evening air, but there was no point in him trying to be sneaky. Gunther knew he would be coming. That was what the trap with the accident and the semi had been for. Why he'd left Sarah alive. It was all guiding him here. And as Cassie was to him, together she and O'Donnell were the bait to lure Nathan.

However Gunther had killed the members of the Enlightened, O'Donnell was sure Gunther had drained them all, like some kind of soul vampire. He had literally sucked the life out of them. And if he was right, Gunther was now one great big super-charged human weapon. If he finished the job with Cassie and Nathan...

O'Donnell's eyes roamed over the house, and when no one came, and items didn't fly at him, he pushed on. Revolver out, he made for the wide-open front entrance, its double doors painted gloss black. It was a clear invitation, but again, he didn't know if it was for him. He would find out soon enough.

A damp breeze from the hole in the charred hole in the floor met him as he delved deeper into the mansion. He gave it a casual glance before moving on. It wasn't long before he was provided with a direction, a sound drawing him deeper. An electronic ringing coming from the study.

Stepping into the room, he moved to the desk where a tall, black plastic mobile phone stood. The thing was the size of a large walkie-talkie, like those used by the military.

"So good of you to join us, Mr O'Donnell," Gunther said as he answered, his voice projecting the smug grin O'Donnell knew he wore. "Would you be so kind as to join us upstairs. And do bring the phone. They're rather expensive."

Without a word, phone pressed to his ear and pistol dangling by his side, he made his way to the staircase and ascended.

"Down the hall to the window, if you please."

As he neared the window, O'Donnell saw a small pocket binocular standing on the sill. He pocketed the pistol. They weren't here. But they were nearby.

"Straight ahead," Gunther said as O'Donnell picked up the binocular. "You can't miss us."

Over the back fence, through the torn husk of a building in the midst of demolition, Gunther and Cassie stood on the second floor of a partially constructed house. It sat at the end of a row of townhouses and looked to be the largest of what appeared to be six or eight. The binocular had been pre-focused for it.

"As you can see, James, we've been waiting for you."

Cassie stood close by, her body petrified but her eyes darting and quivering.

O'Donnell let out a grunt. "Still, doesn't explain why you're over there and not here. You're not afraid of me are you, Gunther?"

The man let out a reverberating chuckle. It was as if the air from his lungs reached all the way to the mansion. "Heavens no. I'm just setting out the pieces for the final game, as it were."

"You think this is a fucking game?"

"Oh yes. And I've definitely been playing the long game. As I'm sure you now well know. Inserting Gateway members in with Doyle and hospitals. Converting people when you needed. Spreading."

"Yeah. Your slimy tentacles are everywhere."

"And you. My, you have been a busy little beaver. But now it's time to stop, James. Time to stand still."

"If you expect me to stand here and watch you drain Cassie like you did the others, you—"

"Well… yes, frankly, I do."

The air around O'Donnell shimmered and contracted, wrapping him and solidifying. O'Donnell found his arms and legs unable to move, though his eyes, mouth and jaw were free from its effects.

"Let us go, you prick!"

"Come now, James. It's not as if you have any say in the matter now, is it? You're a spectator. But don't fret, my dear detective friend. You were a good sport… and good sport. Like the elusive fox, you'll live to tell the tale."

"How generous of you."

Gunther's lips split, then fell into a mock frown. "But—and there *always* has to be a but—if you cross my path again…"

Tutting, Gunther gave his head a slow shake, lowering the matching phone in his hand. His thumb stabbed at a button and the line cut. With it, so too the power over his body.

Fingers aching, jaw set firmly, O'Donnell mirrored the psychotic man. His first instinct was to fling the mobile through the glass in front of him. Instead, he swung the bag over his shoulder to his belly and opened it far enough to shove it within.

Gunther was waiting for Nathan. Once he'd done that, who knew what he would become. With most of the Enlightened and Nathan within him… O'Donnell shuddered to think what would happen in this new world of possible impossibles.

Something in the distance caught his eye. Lifting the binocular, he searched the construction site and focused on a figure strolling casually up the muddy path between the buildings.

"Nathan, *no*," O'Donnell muttered to himself.

Once Gunther had Nathan, it was all over. Cassie would be gone. And with no reason to stay in Melbourne, Gunther would disappear. He could go anywhere, do anything.

Angling the binocular up to the house at the end, he saw Gunther now standing at the edge of the second floor, arms wide and grinning, calling out to Nathan.

This was O'Donnell's chance. His only chance. Gunther was distracted. He had the prize in front of him, he wouldn't be watching his back.

He tore down the second-floor landing and took the steps almost blindly, gritting his teeth to the pain from his battered and bruised body, amazed that on his flight down he didn't fall and break his neck. He sprinted through the house, narrowly avoiding the hole in the floor as he pushed from the wall at the bottom landing and leaped down the last three steps, immediately regretting it as he landed.

The charred edges of the floor crumble and he tilted precariously, his limbs crying out from the toll. O'Donnell's shoes gripped at the last moment and he was moving again, racing outside and falling into the Valiant, jaw clenched at the deep ache in his hip as the engine roared to life. He hoped Gunther would either not hear the distinctive car or be too fixated on Nathan to recognise it.

Slamming the car into reverse, the tyres squealed on the smooth black concrete made to look like cobblestones curving around the mansion. He ignored the lump of the duffel and its contents pressing into his back as he threw his left hand onto the passenger seat headrest and swung his head around to navigate in reverse. Yanking the wheel, the driver's side mirror let out a sharp crack as it hit the edge of the opened gate and bent outward. He bounced wildly as the car dismounted from the drive, the front left wheel dropping from the gutter and metal grinding concrete.

The Valiant jumped forward as he stamped on the accelerator and willed it faster.

The car thundered passed the first street down, O'Donnell assessing it as too close to the housing construction to risk. At the second, almost passing it, he slammed on the brake and took the turn wide, thankful there was no oncoming traffic or cars parked close to the intersection. He'd forgotten to turn on the headlights, though even with the lights there was no way he would have avoided any obstacles at the speed he was travelling.

Flicking the lights on, he swerved through parked cars. His head almost hit the roof as he took a speed bump, then another and another. Passing the street the townhouses were on, he shot a look down the road.

The Valiant surged forward as he pressed harder on the pedal. The wheels complained with a shriek as he took the next turn, and he momentarily lost control as the rear wheels fishtailed. Visions of him running headlong into a parked car, power pole or some other obstacle filled his mind, and the resulting deaths of Nathan and Cassie when he finally got to them. But the car straightened out as he fought the steering and sailed between two cars parked on opposite sides of the road, narrowly missing one.

He flew over a speed bump, then slowed to a semi-crawl as he searched the properties for any sign of the townhouses. As his frustration mounted, the foliage cleared and he caught a glimpse of wooden studs painted like bones in the moonlight and thundered forward. Three houses down, he brought the Valiant to an unceremonious stop and rushed to switch it off, throwing open the door, snatching the key from the ignition and dragging the duffel after him.

As he ran into the drive of the house, he stashed the key into his jacket pocket. He thought about pulling the gun but curtailed his panic. He would need both his hands free.

Unlatching a gate, he slipped through and ducked low under a lit window. As he crept quickly along, the sounds of cutlery and low conversation or a television filtered through. With a quick glance around the corner, he spotted more windows, their curtains drawn.

Dashing for the back fence, he slung the bag over, using its handle as a hold to pull himself up and quickly scale the it by the wooden cross beams, ignoring the pain in his aching muscles and bones. About to drop to the other side, he made a hasty decision.

Throwing the bag ahead of him, O'Donnell leaped from the fence at the back of the townhouse.

They'd built as close to the fence line as possible, and as he arced through the night air, he feared he'd misjudged how far it was.

His chest hit the edge of the brick line and a muffled gasp escaped his clenched lips. His hands scrabbled at one of the pine studs, feet fighting for purchase on the dusty brickwork beneath. Slipping, he pulled with his hands and slowly made his way onto the second floor.

He lay a moment on his stomach as he caught his breath, a slash of pain across his chest telling him he would have a nasty bruise and grazes there to join the rest of his injuries. But the pain was forgotten as figures stood out through the forest of wooden frames.

Easing himself up as quietly as he could and fumbling for the duffle, O'Donnell pulled on the zip. Sliding his hand within, his fingers touched cold steel and he drew the weapon out. He stepped around and through the wooden frame, ducking low and turning sidelong, heading for the three figures, now in close proximity. He could make out Cassie to one side, and the other two within reach of each other.

O'Donnell stepped under a wooden beam, lifting the sawn-off shotgun he'd found in the semi to bear. "Gunther!"

The man dropped his hands from Nathan's head and turned, baring his teeth in a snarl. "No!"

In the same moment, Nathan shook his head, took in O'Donnell and Gunther, then turned and leaped from the building.

"NO!" Gunther screamed and turned on O'Donnell.

A burst of light lit up the area and Gunther's face as the shotgun exploded. His chest was peppered in black spots before blooming red.

With a dumb expression on his lips, Gunther stumbled backward, lifting his hand to his chest, blood burbling on his lips.

"Buh—" Gunther said, then gurgled before he fell from the edge.

Cassie let out a gasp. "N— Nathan?" She turned to him in confusion. "James?

He held his hand out, palm up, lowering the shotgun. "It's okay. Stay up here a minute, all right?"

She shook her head. "James? What's going—"

"Stay here, okay?" he said sharply as he bent low and scooped up the bag at his feet, slinging it over his shoulder with a grunt.

He ran for what would eventually be a staircase. A ladder was lashed to the beams in the opening and he quickly descended, dropping from four rungs up. Turning sharply, he popped the shotgun and shook the spent shells free. Reaching into the bag as he made his way through the lower floor, he pulled two fresh ones and slid them in. With a snap, he shut the weapon and held it two-handed at waist height.

He walked out of the empty front doorway to Gunther. He lay on his back in the mud, struggling to breathe, body jerking like he was trying to stand. Eyes blinking rapidly, he jerked his head toward O'Donnell and gave him an idiot grin, the blood smearing his teeth almost black in the dark.

"James. H-how did... you—"

"It's over, Gunther."

Choking on his own blood, the dying man let out a wet chuckle. "M-maybe f-for this body."

"You're broken, Gunther! Not just your body, but your mind. Don't you see that? You were a mistake. A fuck up that needs fixing."

Gunther began a wheezing, hacked cackle. "B-*broken*? You... you know nothing, James." He forced his hand up, flopping it onto his shredded chest to tap himself. "I know th-the *truth!*"

Looking down on Gunther's body, O'Donnell had a sudden image of Benji, lying on the floor of the restaurant kitchen, face hacked to pieces. Letting go of the barrel, he pointed the end of the shotgun at Gunther's face.

Gunther smiled back.

And in that moment, the image of Benji dead on the floor turned to one of Benji alive and smiling at O'Donnell.

Shoulders dropping, the muscles in his arms and hands went limp, and the shotgun was now aimed at the mud and dirt. Killing in Benji's name was no way to honour him. But when he turned to tell that to the man who had been the cause of his death, Gunther's eyes were vacant. Smile still on his lips, his now blank stare was fixed on O'Donnell and eternity.

"James," Cassie said, her fingers curling over his hand.

Turning to her, he didn't know whether to laugh or cry, and ended up doing something in between. He was still doing the same when the police finally arrived after the call he made from the mobile in his bag. But he had made another call before that.

Shaking his head and smoking, Robbie surveyed Gunther's body. "I still can't fucking believe it," he said. He glanced at O'Donnell and Cassie, sitting in the doorway of the townhouse, Cassie's arm around his shoulders. "*This* fucker did all *that*?"

Nodding, O'Donnell sniffed. His eyes were still puffy and nostrils still running. "He orchestrated it all. The bombing. The drugs and prostitution. The Gateway cult was a front for it all. A place where he could get willing followers to do his dirty work."

"I don't whether to hate the fucking prick or admire him for his genius. Because… shit, Jimmy! This is next level. James Bond villain level! I mean… did he have a white pussy, too?" Robbie gave his head another shake. "Fucking Jesus."

"He, uh… Also took out Killian Doyle, who he was working for."

Robbie turned his head sharply, then nodded as he inhaled deeply on his cigarette. "How'd you hear about that?"

"I'm telling you this in strictest confidence, okay?"

Stepping closer, Robbie nodded. "Yeah. Of course, mate." His eyes narrowed. "Client confidentiality?"

O'Donnell nodded. "Let's say, hypothetically, a certain abused wife of a certain man was a client of mine. Purely coincidental, by the way. And when I was gathering dirt on this certain man, I saw…" He waved a hand at the body only metres away.

Turning back at the body, Robbie's frown deepened. "Fuck me. *He* was working with Doyle, too?"

O'Donnell nodded. Of course, he knew Lydia Doyle had called up to make an 'anonymous' statement to Robbie about Gunther killing her husband. She had agreed all too willingly when O'Donnell had called her. It not only took the pressure and spotlight off her and what was now her business, but also Cassie and O'Donnell. A win-win, apart from the fact that he was the sole witness to it all. He would have to worry about Lydia Doyle later, if it came to it.

"Okay, so…" Robbie scratched his head, threw away his cigarette smoked to the butt, and pulled another. "What I don't get," he said around the cigarette, lighting it, "is what all this had to do with Nathan Mortimer."

O'Donnell's eyes shifted to Cassie. He'd told Cassie what he was going to say. She didn't like it, but she had reluctantly agreed.

"Gunther recruited people with weak minds," he said. "The homeless, drug addicts and lost, and psychiatric patients. That's where he found that old psychotic woman, Glenda. And that's where he found Nathan, too. The two of them actually were in the same hospital together."

"That old bitch and Mortimer?" Robbie said.

O'Donnell nodded. "But Nathan took it all to heart and created the Enlightened. Gunther didn't like that he was giving away his secrets."

"Right, right," Robbie said, shaking a finger in the air as he paced. "Someone who knew what he was up to would not be good. So that's why he was tracking him and started the feud between Gateway and the Enlightened." He turned to Cassie. "Did you know any of this?"

She cleared her throat, not looking up at Robbie. "No. When Nathan found me, I was homeless. He didn't tell me everything. Didn't tell anyone. When I joined the Enlightened, Nathan and Gunther were very close. Then they drifted apart. All he told us was that Gunther had lost his way. Then he disappeared."

Robbie eyed her but nodded as if he'd made his mind up. "Then you hired bugalugs PI here to find him. Talk about wrong place and wrong time, huh, mate?" Robbie said, giving him an awkward smile.

O'Donnell didn't respond. He was far too tired to try and puzzle out if Robbie was being genuine or not. And no matter how neat the story they'd fed him was, something fundamental had now broken between the two of them. Robbie might be back to talking to him and calling him mate without a sneer, but it was in name only.

"Yeah," O'Donnell said. "You could say that."

Chuckling, Robbie turned to examine the scene once more. He stepped to the body and paced around it. He came to a stop, and grinning, picked up an evidence bag. Standing, he smirked at O'Donnell and shook the sawn-off shotgun. "Bet you felt real bad arse using this little baby, huh?"

"Believe me, that was the last thing on my mind. But after the club…"

Robbie lowered the bag, a grimace etching deep lines on his unshaven face. "Yeah, that was some fucked up shit all right." He glanced at Cassie. "No offence."

Cassie shook her head but she said nothing. The edges of her eyes glistened.

"How's Sarah doing, by the way?" O'Donnell said.

"Fucked if I know, mate. She *seems* okay, but her memory is all fucked to hell. Doctors can't work out what she was given. They think he probably used some exotic, untraceable shit and she only got a small dose. They still have a lot of tests to run. Fucking beaker heads." He motioned at Gunther's body. "Okay, I think we're done here." He nodded to some uniformed officers, who began packing up and summoned the coroner. "You two go home. Get some rest. Just—"

"Don't worry," O'Donnell said, helping Cassie up. "We won't leave town."

They limped to the Valiant, which O'Donnell had moved around to the front of the townhouses.

"Your friend was quite pleased with the story you constructed." Cassie's words were clipped, her lips tight as she helped him along.

He shrugged, huddling closer to her. "They like it when things fit together nicely. We're lucky there were enough loose ends and evidence that we could wrap it up for them."

Her face tilted up sharply. "Lucky?"

He took a breath to apologise but couldn't bring himself to say the words. The mere thought sounded hollow.

She returned to studying their path. "At least we stopped Gunther. And got them some small justice. It's not over yet, but he got what he deserved."

"We still need to finish this for good, Cassie."

She nodded. "We'll find Nathan."

O'Donnell nodded, hoping to encourage her. But he had no idea how they were going to accomplish the task. Nathan had eluded them at every move, all but once when they had met in person.

Frowning, O'Donnell stopped. "On the mountain with Gunther and the Crone."

"What?"

"The only time I've seen Nathan," he said. "They were all together. Why?"

"You said yourself, it was an illusion." Shaking her head, she pulled him toward the car. "Does it matter? Let's think about this tomorrow."

He took several faltering steps, then stopped again. He shook his head. "No. This is... something. I don't know what, but if I've learned anything being around you and the Enlightened is to trust that itch at the back of my brain."

Her eyes narrowed. "Okay. What does it mean, James?"

"I... That's what I don't know!"

"Close your eyes. Concentrate on your breathing."

"Is that supposed to put me in a trance or something?"

"No. It's supposed to calm you the fuck down so you can think."

Cassie was right. He was getting worked up.

Taking a deep breath through his nose, he shuttered his eyes and slowly released the breath. As he repeated the motion, sounds faded into the background. He played everything that had happened from the start to several hours ago through his mind.

"*But we're not gone,*" Nathan said on the video to the doctor, pointing out a light bulb. "*We simply lose coherency to join with the aether. Then our soul is drawn back.*"

"What did you say?" Cassie said, bringing him back to the moment.

"I—" O'Donnell shook the strange sensation off. "I don't know."

"That's what Nathan used to say. About coherency and the aether. Where did you hear that?"

"On the tape. From the hospital."

Cassie looked up and down the long, muddy driveway. "Come on," she said, and headed for the Valiant.

"Do you know where to find him?" O'Donnell raced to keep up. "Do you know where he is?"

"No," she said. "We're going to bring him to us."

TWENTY-TWO

CLUTCHING HIS SIDE, O'Donnell rested as Cassie drove. He eased himself into a comfortable position and angled toward her. "How are we going to bring Nathan to us?"

Her eyes didn't leave the road. "By modifying the original plan."

The gathering at the club. How was she planning on finding Nathan now it was only the two of them?

"I know what you're thinking," she said.

"After all this, I don't doubt it." Nothing would surprise him now, especially her being able to read his mind.

She glanced his way. "I told you we'd make this work, James, and I aim to keep my word. We'll put an end to all of this. Make sure it never happens again. Once we have Nathan with us, he'll know what to do." She nodded repeatedly.

O'Donnell couldn't shake the feeling she was trying to convince herself. "What if Nathan doesn't want to stop?"

"Then we'll fucking convince him!"

"But how, Cassie? You didn't see the tape I did. You didn't see him up the mountain. And when he arrived at the house—"

She turned to him sharply, eyes wide and lips parted.

"You don't remember, do you?"

"Are you telling me that Nathan was right there? Right beside me?"

Doubt crept into O'Donnell's heart. "Cassie, that's why Gunther took you. He used you as bait to get Nathan there and was going to drain him like he did all of the Enlightened."

"It doesn't matter. That just proves I'm right!"

"Right about what?"

"I'll show you," she said with grim determination, and the car surged forward.

Using the car's door and frame, O'Donnell climbed out and glanced up the road. The truck, his car, and the other it had been sandwiched between were all gone, but the road still shone with fragments of glass and plastic. He stared up at the blackened second-floor windows.

"What are we doing here, Cassie?"

"Finishing it," she said, and powered toward the club.

By the time he had limped halfway across the road, she was already inside, the police tape she'd broken flapping in the breeze. He never thought he would see so much of the stuff in such a short time after leaving the police force, and even then, he doubted he would have—homicide detective had never been a goal.

"It's funny how things work out," Cassie said as he stepped onto the landing.

He grit his teeth, holding the rail tight. "What?"

She waved around at the small yellow markers still littering the dance floor. Moving to the bar, she pulled down an expensive bottle of whiskey and two tumblers and poured a generous amount in each.

"We going to talk about robots and batteries again?" O'Donnell said as he eased himself onto a stool in front of her, then placed the duffel from the truck on the next one over.

"No," she said, cracking a bitter smile. "Today's lesson is walkie talkies."

He gave the bag beside him a pat. "Afraid I've only got a mobile phone." She shrugged. "Is that the plan? We're going to call Nathan?"

"It is. That's what I think Gunther did, using the power of all the Enlightened within him, all the people that he awakened." She picked up the drink closest to her and lifted it.

O'Donnell drew his own glass closer. "But they're gone, Cassie. They died with Gunther, right."

She winked, then took a gulp from the whiskey.

Sighing, O'Donnell drank. When he lowered the tumbler, she was watching him.

"Like a walkie talkie or CB, the signal depends on the power of its transmitter. But none of it is much use unless you have a good antenna."

"Okay," O'Donnell said, still no closer to understanding what she was getting at. "And what was Gunther's antenna?"

"Not what. Who."

He sat up straighter. "You? You think that's why he took you and didn't kill you? How though? Why you and not anyone else? I mean, Gunther was the first. And why not the Crone?"

"Probably because of my connection with Nathan. I'm only guessing here, mind you. But it makes sense, doesn't it?"

He nodded. It made as much sense as everything else O'Donnell had seen and experienced, which was very little. But it all worked. He had no reason to doubt her. "Still," he said, brow creasing as he tried to work it in his mind. "Everyone's gone. How are you going to get enough power to send out your signal?"

"That's why we're here."

Turning to the dance floor, he took in the mess of evidence markers. Echoes of the bodies—the *people*—who had lain there. "You're going to hold some kind of seance, aren't you?"

She downed the rest of her glass. "I knew Nathan didn't just pick you because you're a pretty face."

"Will that even work?"

She shrugged as she came around the bar. "Not sure. It's something we toyed with in the early days. Communicating over distance, but... we kind of went off the idea."

"How come?"

"I... don't really remember." She ironed out her frown with a shake of her head. "Anyway, I seem to recall we had some small success. We also experimented with actual seances. Tried to draw in past instances of ourselves and possibly others."

"Others? Like how Gunther figured out how to absorb the Enlightened into himself?

"Yes. I think what he did to them was an extension of that."

"Okay. So... I, what? Sit at the bar and zip my lip while you—"

She shook her head. "No such luck, I'm afraid. I need a medium."

"You want me to go find you a black cat?"

"I mean you, James." She pointed at him and moved closer until the pad of her finger pressed against his chest.

"I feel more like than a medium these," he said, his insides flip-flopping despite his attempt at humour.

"You'll do fine. Like I said, Nathan chose you for a reason. You're sensitive, so you'll make a perfect medium."

"You're only saying that because you saw me cry."

Ignoring him, Cassie led him off the stool and into the middle of the yellow markers on the floor. "Don't be nervous. Stand here and let me do all the work."

"So, pretty much the defining basis of our relationship? I think I can do that."

She gave him a quick squeeze. "Don't be nervous. Just, close your eyes."

Chest thudding, he did as instructed. "Cassie?" She hummed in his ear. "When this is all done—"

"Let's get through this first. Then we'll talk about after, okay?"

He nodded. It wasn't a no. But it definitely wasn't a yes.

"Hold my hands. And relax."

"Easier said than done." Releasing a long breath from his pursed lips, cheeks billowing, he put out his hands and she took them.

The silence would have been deafening if not for the minuscule sounds that filled his ears. They increased in intensity by the second. The creak and crack of warming and cooling floorboards, pipes, traffic and life outside. The very coursing of blood in his veins.

"How long do you think—"

Cassie gave his hands a sharp squeeze.

O'Donnell's stomach lurched and nausea crashed in its wake as the world thrust up around him. That was the sensation that struck him. Not that he had fallen, but that the very planet, the very *Universe*, shifted around him while he was locked in time and space. And he felt utterly trapped by it.

Swaying, he opened his eyes.

It was much as when he had the vision with Cassie, but so much more surreal. Everything was off. It was the same, and yet slightly twisted, as if everything was off by a shade and a millimetre. The floor was too smooth, the walls too rough. And the yellow markers that had dotted the space were all missing. Along with Cassie.

"Cassie?" Even his own voice sounded odd to his ears. "Cassie, where are you?"

He searched for her, and as he did, he noticed unlit candles appear outside his vision, forming a circle around him, each a different shape and size and laying on its side.

"Cassie?" he said in a lower voice, glancing around him.

There was no answer.

Taking in the circle once more, one of the candles caught his eye. It was white and tall and, unlike all the others, standing. Its wick was also blackened where the others were clean. He moved to it, and as he did, an ember became visible in the charred length. Then it became a spark. As he took another step, the wick let out a puff as a flame leapt to life. Wax ran from the base of the flame, red as Cassie's lips and cascading over the edge and down the candle. By the time he stood over it, the candle was covered in that same shade of crimson.

Crouching low, he looked the candle over, its warmth seeping into him.

"Cassie."

It had to be her.

Taking the now red candle in both hands, it let out a sharp snap as he lifted it from the floor, breaking a seal of wax that had held it there. Turning to the next nearest fallen candle, an idea struck him. Cupping his hand around the flame, he moved to the fallen candle, the comforting warmth and light filling him, telling him without word that he was doing the right thing.

One by one, he lifted and lit the fallen candles, melting their bases with Cassie's candle before pressing them down so they would stand upright. And one by one, colour returned as he re-ignited the members of the Enlightened. She'd told him he was her medium for contacting the fallen members of the Enlightened and Nathan. Was this her interpretation of that, or his?

Lighting the last candle, he stood straighter and held the red candle close. He let his eyelids flutter closed and gave the candle a gentle squeeze. "Be careful."

Leaning down, he waved the base of Cassie's candle over the last flame, then pressed it to the boards where it had stood. Not knowing what else to do, he moved to the centre of the circle and waited, watching the flames dance and wave, his eyes always returning to the crimson. To Cassie.

The candles flared bright, sputtering and spitting wax. They burned so bright that O'Donnell had to shield his eyes. As they died down, their wax melted and ran, the flames travelling down the exposed wicks. Some ran clockwise, others in reverse, the colours weaving instead of mixing. O'Donnell's chest tightened as he recognised it for what it was.

"Gateway!"

The wicks fell to the wax and the lines of colour ignited, glowing brightly as if consuming the flames. He wanted to run, but his feet were glued to the boards as the gateway around him grew brighter. Stronger. The light so prevalent, it appeared to be lifting. And then it did move.

One end sprang up over his head so the ring of multicoloured light stood before him, blinding him as the colours bled into one another. Soon, the purest white filled his vision, so bright he had to press his eyes into the back of his arm.

A cool breeze played through his hair and chilled the sweat on the back of his neck and scalp.

"Hello, James."

Whipping the gun from his pocket, O'Donnell pointed it at the speaker's centre of mass as he'd been trained, the movement instinct now, part of his muscle memory. He looked himself over. Familiar blue material covered his body, the shirt the colour of a clear winter sky, his pants navy. His hand came to rest on his old service revolver at his side.

"The uniform suited you," Nathan said.

O'Donnell blinked. "You're a hard man to track down."

"That, James, is by design." Nathan glanced at the gun. "I was told you weren't a fan of firearms." O'Donnell shrugged. "Needs must, eh?"

"You've been hiding yourself pretty good, Nathan," O'Donnell said, ignoring question. He scanned their surroundings. The roof of a building somewhere. Maybe Melbourne. "I get that. But not why with everything going on. All the people dying. Your people."

"Oh, I haven't been hiding *myself*." Nathan gave him a wide, all too familiar grin. "I've been hiding Nathan, Detective."

"I don't—" A deep frown creased O'Donnell's forehead, his hand slowly lowering before jerking back to point at Nathan's chest. "Gunther."

Laughing, the man clapped. "Very clever, Detective," Gunther said though Nathan's voice. "You figured out what even Nathan himself couldn't. Even batty old Glenda didn't see it coming. Bravo."

Hand trembling, the muscles in O'Donnell's finger were like steel bands, unmoving even as he fought against them.

"Would you really pull the trigger on an unarmed man, James?"

"We both know you're anything but unarmed." Gunther shrugged. "How long?"

"Oh? Straight to the personal questions, is it? Didn't your daddy teach you it's not the size that counts?"

He shook the weapon. "How long have you been in Nathan's body?"

Pouting his bottom lip and shrugging, Gunther inspected his nails. "Your tape viewing at the hospital? A little while before that."

Unable to comprehend, all O'Donnell could do was shake his head.

"That... That doesn't make any sense. I saw you. *Both* of you. Up the mountain."

"Ah. A lovely piece of sleight of hand, don't you think? Allow me to explain. Only the one of us was truly there, I'm sure as you've already worked out. With our dearly departed Glenda's assistance, I was able to project an image of my old body. Unbeknownst to her of course, which as you might imagine was how our wires became crossed and she started that little tiff you witnessed. Apologies that you had to witness that. So ugly."

That was why there had been no body, and no trace of any murder. Gunther had never been there. He had been riding Nathan's all along.

"So... you've been a projection all this time? Then who did I—"

"Oh, you shot me. Or at least, my body. I can't be in two places at once, James. Or at least, I couldn't before." Gunther's grin shifted to a sneer. "And you... Oooh, James *bloody* O'Donnell! You almost ruined everything. Moments earlier, and you would have robbed me of eternal life. As it was, I was able to transfer into Nathan's— into *my* new body before you could do any real damage. Of course, my plan was to drain my old body dry, along with Glenda and dear sweet Cassie. Mmm, my I *will* so enjoy those delights before I do, however."

"Shut your mouth." O'Donnell's hand shook with more than his battle for control of it. The muscles in his neck bulged and heat flashed his forehead as the veins there throbbed.

"Oh yes, I forget. You've tasted those lips. Along with everyone else, I might add." Gunther let his—Nathan's—finger play across his lips

"I said shut the fuck up!"

"Or what, Detective?" Gunther craned his head forward. "You'll shoot?"

O'Donnell fought to move his finger, but it wouldn't obey. Tears pricked the corners of his eyes as he strained, the muscles in his arm tightening, his shoulder and elbow burning.

Stepping forward, Gunther pressed his chest to the barrel. "Pull the trigger, James."

"James!"

O'Donnell and Gunther turned in surprise to see Cassie standing at a corner of the building.

"Speak of the devil, and she arrives," Gunther said in a low, a predatory smirk pulling the corner of his mouth.

"Cassie, that's not—"

Gunther's fingertips pressed against O'Donnell's chest, spread wide. With a nudge, he sent O'Donnell flying back and tumbling across the gravel on the flat roof. The world tumbled in a flash of confusion and pain, which only increased as he came to a stop. He was battered, grazed and bruised, but not seriously injured.

Rolling to fall onto his forearms, O'Donnell struggled to push himself up and locate Cassie. As he did, he made to rise and stumbled, vision doubling and blurring as his head spun. "Cassie," he managed to mutter.

There was a sharp crack and someone cried out in pain.

"Cassie!" O'Donnell forced himself up and dragged his feet as he attempted to break into a jog, but he slowed as he took her in.

"Your terrorising is over, Gunther," she said, holding the man face down by his arm, twisted sharply behind his back.

"You stupid *bitch*!" Gunther screamed. "Do you have any idea the power I have accumulated? You think your pitiful memories will save you now?"

"All I know is, you're on the ground where I want you. And I have the power of all the Enlightened behind me."

Gunther let out a chuckle. "Ohhh, you stupid, stupid girl."

Cassie's face wrinkled in an angry frown. "What's so funny?"

"Why, simply this."

With a snap and crunch of ligaments and sinew, Gunther twisted and rolled, popping his arm out of its socket and other joints bending as if rubber. He twisted his body to hold up something, the long metallic tube with the wires embedded in metal caps at its ends glinting in the city lights.

"No!" O'Donnell yelled.

The revolver in his hand cracked again and again, the sharp pops echoing across the roof until the cylinder was empty and all that remained was wafting smoke.

Stumbling back, Cassie looked up at O'Donnell in shock. She had dropped Gunther's arm at the first shot, and frozen. "James?" she said, her lips now an entirely different shade of red.

"Ca— Cassie?"

Head slumping, she took another step back as blood pumped from the bullet holes and she fell to her knees.

O'Donnell sprinted across the roof, caught her as she collapsed. Dropping with her, he eased her body to the rough surface and lay her head on his lap. "No, no, no," he said, eyes wet. "Cassie, stay with me!"

"James... I— I'm sorry."

"It's not your fault," he said, jaw trembling.

"That really hurt, just so you know," Gunther said, rolling his shoulder, twisting his limbs back into shape.

His hands were empty, no sign of the pipe bomb he was sure he'd seen.

"Goodbye, Detective," Gunther said, walking away. "Perhaps we'll meet again in another life, eh?"

Gently placing Cassie's head on the gravel, teeth pressing tighter and tighter together, O'Donnell picked up his revolver. Eyes locked on Gunther's back, he popped the cylinder and reached into the ammunition pouch he knew would be there. With practiced ease, the spent casings dropped to the gravel with a ringing chime.

Turning, Gunther frowned, mouth opening as O'Donnell slipped the round into the cylinder, snapped it closed, and fired.

Gunther's grimace shifted to a smile. "Clever, detective... but not clever enough."

The revolver slipped from O'Donnell's grasp and fell to the roof as the muscles in his arm lost strength. Before the gun hit the stones, it disappeared.

"What the..." O'Donnell stumbled. His eyes swung from the spreading red patch on his chest to his revolver in Gunther's hands.

Gasping for air, choking on his own blood, O'Donnell fell to his knees, then onto his face. He couldn't feel the stinging of the gravel, the pain in his chest too great. He and Cassie would die on some strange roof, and Gunther would get away and continue his plan. Eternal life or not, he had won.

"No..." a voice close to him said. "No, James. We won't allow it."

"What?" Gunther said sharply.

But O'Donnell's eyes had already closed of their own accord. He fought to keep them open, but the closer his eyelids came to one another, the softer the pain became. Calm washing over him, O'Donnell's body relaxed. Even as someone rolled him over roughly, there was no pain, only peace. And high above the rooftop, in that dark space that Cassie had shown him in the vision, that he could see again now in his mind's eye, the Gateway.

"I see it now," O'Donnell said.

The colours called to him, spoke to him. They were not the harsh brightness he'd seen before. Or the chaos of the graffiti, or wires at Gateway House, or any of the others.

"I'm coming," he said, and felt his true self rise, the shimmering Gateway light cascading over him like the Aurora Borealis.

Something struck him in the chest with the force of a sledgehammer and he gasped as pain crashed back.

"This life is not yours to take!" Cassie said, her voice strange and booming through the air and into O'Donnell's body.

He screamed in agony as something was pushed out of his chest. Through the pain, he forced his head up. Light poured from her hands and the wounds in her body. The light of the gateway. And the pain was not something being forced out of him, but her glowing hand pulling out of his flesh. A small, dark misshapen blob went with it.

Eyes wide with more than mere pain, O'Donnell watched the bullet inched from his chest and the light from Cassie's hand streamed in around it, closing his flesh. As the light worked into him, it filled him with that same warmth that had enveloped him on the verge of death, but instead, it now reinvigorated him. Made him yearn for more life. This would not be his end, it said.

"You cretins!" Gunther hissed.

Throwing his head aside from the light in Cassie's hand, he saw Gunther imprisoned in a shaft of that same light.

"Do you think you can stop me? Nathan made us all and even he couldn't stop me!"

"No, he could not," Cassie said in that same unnatural voice. O'Donnell knew, without a doubt, that she was speaking as the Enlightened. Through her, they all had a voice once more and had healed her and O'Donnell. "But he will," the Enlightened said, lifting their hand to pour the light of the Gateway on Gunther.

Cassie leaned in. "Live well, James," she said in her own voice. Then stood.

In that moment, O'Donnell knew in his heart that he would never see her again.

"Cassie!" he said, attempting to sit. His chest burned as he moved, the numbing effect of the light now gone.

Cassie lifted her other hand to shoot another beam of Gateway light at Gunther. His body shook then tore in two, separating him from Nathan, leaving Gunther as a ghost of his former body. Nathan's body jerked and his eyes opened.

Gunther's eyes widened. "N— Nathan?"

Stepping out of the light, Nathan sighed. "I'm sorry. I failed you, Gunther. You had such high hopes and I let you down." He turned to Cassie. "I let all of you down."

"Oh, go fuck yourself!" Gunther screamed. "You were weak. You couldn't lead the group so I took the opportunity. Then, took you."

"You doped me with drugs to make me think I was insane, Gunther. Institutionalised me. Had your people shuffle me from place to place to place and stole my body when it suited you. Why? All so you could build an empire. Did you learn nothing from all those lives you touched and destroyed and hold within you?"

"Your thinking was too small. *Help* people? Look around you, Nathan. The world is sick! And it's getting sicker by the day. People selling and abusing their own children. Killing each other for nothing. Less than nothing! Letting their fellow brothers, majestic creatures of this planet die and suffer in starvation and ruin. So go *fuck* yourself, Nathan. You're no fucking messiah."

"You're absolutely right, Gunther. I am not a messiah." Nathan gave him a sad smile, eyes dropping. "But you are no devil, either. It's time to end this. The world is not ready."

Nathan held out his hand for Cassie.

"Stay back!" Gunther yelled as they stepped closer together. "Don't do this, Nathan, please. I swear, I'll— I'll change! I'll do whatever you want. I—"

Nathan held up his hand, silencing Gunther. His mouth moved in a silent plea, which became frustration then rage as Nathan and Cassie drew closer.

"Where are you going?" O'Donnell said, stopping them.

Nathan eased his head around, smiling. "Dear James. Thank you for taking care of Cassie and the others. I know none of this was not easy for you."

"You're killing yourself, aren't you?" O'Donnell said.

"I never existed. I killed the real Nathan Mortimer the moment the souls of others entered him. You saw the gateway. Did you understand it?"

O'Donnell found himself nodding. In that moment on the precipice of death, he had. Nathan, Gunther, the Enlightened and Gateway—all of them had been wrong. And it had taken Gunther killing Nathan, taking over his body, for him to see the truth and realise his error.

Seeing the truth in O'Donnell's eyes, Nathan smiled and nodded.

"Thank you, James," Cassie said, mirroring Nathan's serenity, her face and body unblemished. "We could not have done it without you. Don't mourn for Cassie Lawler or the others. Our lives are short on this Earth, but not without meaning. And by no means final."

"Sure. Except I... don't know exactly what I did," he said, bemused. "Thank you, Cassie. For... well, everything. Take care of yourselves."

Nathan and Cassie turned their beatific faces to Gunther, wrapped their arms and the light tightly around him. As the shimmering colours closed in, he threw his fists at the invisible walls. When Cassie and Nathan's hands broke through the shaft of multi-hued light to circle him, his voice returned.

"Nooo!"

The Gateway light exploded, throwing O'Donnell back, the light still burning his eyes until darkness took over.

TWENTY-THREE

GASPING FOR AIR, O'Donnell woke to alien smells and sounds, light assaulting his aching head.

"James! James, can you—"

Someone silenced the voice though many others took its place as darkness reclaimed him.

Groaning, he woke again. The smells were the same, but the blinding light that had seared his eyes was gone, though the sunlight streaming through the windows did little to help the throbbing in his skull. The rhythmic beeping had also gone. O'Donnell shifted and let out a wincing groan as his chest burned like he'd been branded by a white-hot iron.

"James?" a female voice called from somewhere to his right.

He attempted to turn, but the pain returned. "Cassie?" The name fell from his lips in rasped syllables.

"It's me. Mum."

With the creak of an old chair, she stood up and grasped something at his side, her knuckles whitening as her eyes reddened with fresh tears.

"Mum?" Blinking, he searched the room and did his best to remember what had happened. "Where's Cassie and Nathan?"

His mother shook her head and shushed him. "Try to calm down, love. You've been through a lot and you're... You're lucky to—" Her tears ran free as her shoulders jerked with each sob.

Reaching out, O'Donnell placed his hand over hers and gave a squeeze. "It's okay, Mum. I'm right here. Not going anywhere."

"You bloody better not!" she said through the sobbing. "If you do, I'll kill you my bloody self!"

He attempted a chuckle, but the movement made his chest feel like he'd been shot all over again.

"That was real, then," he said, eyeing the patch taped to his chest

"Careful, Mrs O," Robbie said from the doorway. "I may have to book you for attempted murder."

Sniffing and dabbing the corners of her eyes with her knuckles, she turned to Robbie. "You do and I'll get your mother to box your ears." Robbie let out a laugh. "I'll leave you two for a minute." Patting O'Donnell on the, hand, she walked around the bed, then stopped in front of Robbie. "But *only* a minute!"

"Cross my heart and hope to—"

His mother smacked Robbie on the upper arm as she left the room, closing the door behind her.

Stepping to the end of the bed, Robbie leaned on the tall foot-board. "Jesus, mate, you look like something the cat dragged in, ate, shat out, ate and shat again."

"What's that, Robbie?" O'Donnell lifted his hand, cupping it around his ear. "I'm not quite getting your message. The signal is weak. Let me extend my antenna." Letting his hand fall from his ear, he curled up all but his middle finger.

Robbie let out a guffaw. "Well, at least they didn't kill your sense of humour. Your body on the other hand." He let out a whistle before dropping his gaze and tilting his head and shaking it. "Tell you what,

Jimmy…" His fingers tapped on the top of the footboard. "We thought you were a goner a few times there."

"I died?"

"Died? Fucking Jesus, Jimmy, you were clinically dead at least *three* times that I know of."

He let his head fall back on the pillow and stared at the ceiling. "Huh. Shit."

"Shit? Really? Shit is all you've got to say to 'you died three times'?"

He attempted a shrug but stopped from the pain. "Still here, aren't I?"

"Yeah. By some miracle. The fucking luck on you, mate, I almost went and bought a lotto ticket. I was going to bring it back here and rub it on your bullet wound to see if it took."

"Bet Mum would have been real impressed with that." He smirked thinking of what his mother would have done.

"No fucking shit. She would have taken the bullet those fuckers shot you with and shoved it up my arse if we'd ever found it."

"You can't find your arse?" O'Donnell said. "Put your hands up to your neck, it's where your head should be."

Robbie's eyebrows shot up. "Fuck you, mate, and the horse you rode in on," he said, grinning. "Think you're king dick or something because you took a bullet to the chest. What drugs these nurses got you on?"

O'Donnell eased his head side to side, risking the dizziness and pain. "I'm just high on life, mate."

"Uhuh. Well I'm gonna find out and get me some. Maybe it'll make me as fucking funny as you think you are. Hey, I'll even go out on the Melbourne Comedy Festival."

"Yeah, you should do that. Bet Kell and the kids would think that was a riot."

Robbie frowned. "You sure you're okay? You seem… I dunno. Different."

"Yeah. I guess nearly dying does something to you." Robbie grunted. "Speaking of… Cassie and Nathan?"

Biting his lip, Robbie turned and began pacing. "Shit. I'm sorry,

Jimmy. I mean, I know you almost got shot in the heart, I don't want to be the one that breaks it too."

"They're dead, aren't they?"

Robbie's frown deepened. He tapped the footboard, inspecting his fingernails. "I'd tell you to sit down, but you're already on your arse. You know... Where you've been for the better part of two months."

"What?"

"I told you, mate. You were in a bad way. All that shit you went through, I wouldn't be surprised if you were a few cans short." Tapping the side of his head, Robbie gave O'Donnell a smirk that didn't reach his eyes. He cleared his throat. "Anyway. I don't know how you managed it, but you called triple zero from a mobile phone registered to a shell company owned by Gunther." Robbie threw up his hands. "Don't wanna know. Anyway, the ambos found you on the floor of that freak club, bleeding out."

"Let me guess... I was *not* wearing my old police uniform."

Robbie's lip curled. "What?"

"Nothing." O'Donnell, shifted in an attempt to sit. "Cassie and Nathan?"

It came to him in dreams. And went the same way. Flashes of events and things he's learned. Of the truth, which now proved to be elusive, no matter how hard he tried to cling to it. It was a watery mirage on a dusty outback highway that kept shimmying to the horizon, always out of reach. He would wake in the hospital bed searching for Cassie, or call out her name when picking up the phone on the bedside when his mother rang, expecting her voice on the other end. And then, when he could finally leave the hospital, in his old bed at his mother's home.

Months passed. Rehabilitation and physiotherapy rebuilt his movement, far better and faster than his therapist thought it would. A counsellor worked on his mind. But neither could heal the hole in his memory. Or his soul.

Finally, when he returned to his office, he sat in his chair with the knife wound, a large brown evidence bag with his clothing and items from the nigh he'd been shot on his lap, delivered by Robbie while he was still bed-ridden. He hadn't wanted to deal with it, but being back here now with all the memories, what he had left of them, it seemed appropriate.

Sighing, he unrolled the opening of the bag and upended its contents.

Something white hit the edge of his desk and fell to the floor. He threw the large brown paper bag aside, his chest twinging from the sudden movement. Pushing the chair back, he leaned down in search of the item. His hand stopped halfway to the floor.

Swallowing down the lump in his throat, he picked up a rabbit's foot keyring.

The key to Cassie's Valiant. He had no idea how it had ended up in his possession. She'd driven them to the club that night. Would it still be there, on the street outside the club?

Glancing at the mess on the desk, he shook the key in his hand, and made up his mind. He had to make some phone calls, but found it was infinitely easier now he was home and found that the phone, and his rent, had been paid up in advance. No one was able to tell him who had arranged it, however.

Once done, he drove out to the club. He smiled as he saw a covered car parked on the street. As he strode to it and pulled the dusty cloth back, the Valiant shone brilliant in the sun.

"Can I help you?"

O'Donnell turned to the man with the scraggly beard. His thin, muscly legs were bared from his work shorts, ending at thick socks in boots. He was a tradesman of some sort and had several coffees in hand from a nearby cafe.

"G'day," O'Donnell said, beaming at the man and reaching out his hand. The man held his coffees like a shield. "I'm here to pick up my car."

"Your car?" The man's eyes swept his body, brow furrowing.

"Yeah. I was in hospital a while and... I—" O'Donnell forced his expression to one of pain. He turned and pointed at the club, which appeared to be getting a makeover. Gone was the black paint job on the exterior, the windows scraped clean of it as well.

"Oh, *shit*! You're the guy that was—"

Nodding, O'Donnell placed his hand on his chest. "Sorry. I…"

Not knowing what to do, the man walked to his side, balanced one coffee atop the other and placed a hand on his shoulder. "It's okay, mate. Let it out."

Lowering his head, O'Donnell covered his face with a hand. He felt bad for deceiving the man, especially as he appeared to be quite genuine.

He lifted his head and rubbed at his nose and shook his head. "It's… I'm okay." He waved at the Valiant. "Did you do this?"

"Yeah. We've been doing the club up after… Anyway, I saw her rotting and had to do something. Beautiful car. Absolutely bloody gorgeous." His expression became sheepish. "The, uh, notes asking if you want to sell it are from me too."

"Thanks, but the car has a lot of sentimental value to me."

The man nodded, eyes wrinkling. "Pity. Anyway, you take care of yourself." He turned toward the club, eyes locked on the Valiant.

"Hang on," O'Donnell said, stopping him. "You want to drive her for a bit?"

Grinning from ear to ear, the worker—whose name was Trent O'Donnell had learned—climbed out of the Valiant, parking it on the quiet street. "Bloody hell!" he said. "That was a hell of a treat. Thanks, mate!" Trent reached his hand out to O'Donnell as he got out of his hatchback to shake it once more and hand him the key back.

"No, thank you, Trent. Least I could do after you looked after her. I really appreciate it."

"Any time. Believe me." A white van pulled up in the street and honked its horn. Trent turned and waved to his workmate, then slid his hand on the red paint of the Valiant. "Gorgeous," he said, then with a wave to O'Donnell made his way to the van.

Waving to Trent, O'Donnell turned to the house they'd parked in front of. Taking a deep breath, he made his way to the door, a thick folder of papers under one arm and the key to the Valiant in the other. The car key rattled against the door as he knocked, his hand frozen there as he stared at the rabbit foot.

"I'll get it!" someone yelled from within. Soon after, a middle-aged woman opened the door. "Yes?" she said tersely, then saw the papers in his hand. "I'm not buyin' anythin', mate," the woman said, and made to close the door.

"Mrs Lawler?" O'Donnell lifted his identification from his inside pocket. "My name's James O'Donnell. I'm a private investigator."

Her eyes narrowed, lips pinching. "Is this about my ex-husband's compo? Because I told those other fuckin' bastards, I don't know any—"

"No, Mrs Lawler. This is about Cassie and Nathan."

The sneer on the woman's face melted and her hand tightened on the edge of the door. Swallowing, the fingers of her free hand worked against each other. "Come in."

O'Donnell sat in the dark living room on an old sofa. It appeared to be as old as Cassie. He imagined photos of her as a child sitting on them when they were new. Birthdays. School pictures. Awkward teenage years.

He forced the lump in his throat down with the third cup of tea her mother had given him. It was already cold. He wished he had something far stronger to give him the strength to do this. Nothing could truly prepare him for it.

The front door flew open.

"Mum? What the fuck's goin' on?"

At the sound of her voice, so familiar yet so foreign, the pain in his chest returned. The one that had nothing to do with where the bullet had struck him.

Cassie stopped at the archway leading into living room and stared at O'Donnell. "Who the fuck are you?"

"Babe?" Nathan stepped in behind her and looped his arm around her waist protectively.

Tears in her red-rimmed eyes, Cassie's mother entered with a fresh pot of tea from the kitchen on a tray with fresh cups. "Cass. Nate. This is James. He's a bloody PI."

Cassie's shoulder jerked. "So?"

"He— He knows what happened to you's and..." The china on the tray rattled as Mrs Lawler's body shook, her sobs coming thick and fast.

O'Donnell rose and took the tray from her. Putting the tray down, he stepped outside, pulling the door behind him, and lit a cigarette. As much as it hurt him, they had been hurting far more.

He was on his third cigarette when Cassie emerged from the house. Her mascara had run, though her eyes were nowhere near as red as her mother's.

"I don't know if I should bloody hug you or punch you," she said.

He gave her a small smile as his throat locked up.

She hurried to him and pressed him in a quick, awkward hug. He held the cigarette in his hand far from her, and she glanced at it.

"Not good for the little one," he said, pointing at her belly, which was stuck out like a small ball beneath the singlet framed by her open hoodie.

Nodding, she dabbed tears and snot with her sleeve and stepped back. "So, you were the guy who was shot at the club they found us in, huh?"

He nodded. "Yeah. I was right in the thick of it all."

She shook her head. "Fuckin' hell! I mean, me and Nathan don't remember *shit* about it all. It's been crazy. Doin' our heads in. Now you turn up and fill in the blanks…" She shook her head again.

He inspected her face. The expressions were all wrong, the lines and features pulling in all the wrong directions. A memory faded back to him.

"I never existed. I killed the real Nathan Mortimer the moment the souls of others entered him. You saw the gateway. Did you understand it?"

In that moment, he remembered. Remembered what had been so wrong. The Enlightened. Gateway. They hadn't been drawing in their own past souls. The gateway was not a passage. And he remembered Benji.

In that moment near death, Benji had come to him. As had Jason. And the both had become Nathan. It was then the truth had come to him. All three of them were connected. Why Jason had chosen to end his life. Why Benji had seen his angel. And ultimately, why Nathan had chosen him. O'Donnell hadn't been Cassie's medium, but her antenna.

The souls the Enlightened and Gateway had tapped into each came from that ring of light, which was not truly a ring but a sphere. Surrounding the Earth. The souls of the dead returning to it, re-joining when a death occurred. And each time a new human was born, energy from that sea of life would surge into it, filling it with different colours.

The Crone, Nathan and Gunther had been forcing pieces of other souls into themselves, into others. And that force had broken them. Then Gunther had led the charge with his broken toy soldiers. If they had continued, they would have spread, fracturing and corrupting the purity of that ocean of life energy.

Nathan had learned the truth in those moments that Gunther had stolen his body. He had done what he could to repair the damage, but it had been too late. He was already a prisoner himself. He had started the healing process with Leyla. And when Gunther had drained the Enlightened, he had inadvertently done the same for Sarah, causing her memories to fall away like old cracked paint and revealing the real Sarah beneath.

As had Cassie and Nathan.

"Hey, you okay?" Cassie's hand was on O'Donnell's arm, holding him up.

Blinking the sensations away, O'Donnell swayed then stood straighter. "Yeah... Yeah, I'm fine. Just get dizzy spells sometimes."

"No fuckin' wonder!" she said. "You were shot and nearly died."

"I'll be okay. How about you, Cassie? You doing alright?"

"Well I am now that you turned up. I mean... all this shit with cults, drugs, fuckin' memory loss? It's all messin' with my little brain! But those papers?" She shook her head. "We've got more money than we know what to do with!"

"Well, hopefully you know what you'll be doing with some of it," he said, motioning to her belly.

A peaceful expression spread across her face as she placed a hands on the bump. "Who'd a thought it? Me, Cassie Lawler, up the fuckin' duff."

"You and Nathan seem to be getting along."

She nodded. "Yeah. It was fuckin' weird at first. We woke up next to each other on this roof, and it was like we knew each other, but didn't. You know what I mean?"

"Yeah. I think I do."

"Turns out we've both got you to thank for that too. You got us out of that crazy fuckin' life."

Leaning in, she kissed him on the cheek.

His eyes closed. The press of her lips, the smell and warmth of her skin was oh so familiar. He was conscious of the fact that she had moved away and his eyes were still closed.

He cleared his throat, winced and touched his chest. "No need to thank me," he said, feigning discomfort from his wound. "Live your life, be happy, and look out for each other and your baby. That's all the thanks I need."

She winced at his pain, making his deceit all the worse. "Well, I reckon we'll sort somethin' out for you too if we've got as much dosh as you say." She held up her hands. "No fuckin' arguin.'"

He nodded. "If you insist. Truth be told... I could use a new office. The old one has... too many painful memories."

"See," she said as she punched him lightly on the arm. "All's well that ends well, like my pop used to say."

O'Donnell grinned and nodded. She was not his Cassie, but he liked her all the same. "Oh," he said, pulling the rabbit foot from his pocket. "One last thing." He handed her the keyring.

Holding it between thumb and finger, Cassie eyed the keychain. "Uhh... Thanks?"

He pointed to the Valiant. "That's yours too."

Her eyes widened. "Holy fuckin' shit! Are you serious?"

"As serious as a bullet to the chest."

Her unpainted lips wrinkled at an unfamiliar slant. "Dude! So not funny!"

"Sorry. Guess it's a you-had-to-be-there kind of thing."

She shook her head, then frowned. "You know..." She eyed the keychain and the Valiant. "I'm gonna be a mum soon. Somehow I don't think that beast is economical."

O'Donnell let out a laugh. "With what you two have in the bank, economical shouldn't be an issue."

"Still... not exactly a family car, is it?"

"No. No I suppose it's not."

"What are you drivin'?" She let out a snort of laughter as he pointed at the hatch behind the Valiant. "Seriously? You're in that little plastic shitbox?"

His fingers pressed into his palms as he closed his eyes. Images flowed of her driving the Valiant on the highway, her dark hair waving in the wind.

He opened them as the real Cassie Lawler pried his hand open and pressed something into it.

"If you're gonna sell yourself as some hot-shit PI... you're gonna need a better ride." Opening his hand, his mouth fell open. "Swap you," she said, a mischievous smirk on her lips that he did know.

He swallowed hard, blinking at the rabbit's foot and key. "I— I don't think I can do that, Cassie."

"For fuck's sake, call me Cass. Please! I fuckin' hate Cassie. And you'll do this for me, because I asked you to. I need somethin' small. At least until we get everythin' sorted out."

His mouth opened and closed, the pain in his chest returning.

"Do this for me, James," she said. For a moment, she sounded so much like his Cassie.

"Okay," he said, giving her a smile he didn't feel. "Thank you... Cass."

"Don't thank me yet, dude," she said. "All those papers, we've still got a lot of fuckin' work to do, and I'm totally goin' to put you to work. Put you on, like... What's it fuckin' called? What they do on them PI shows?"

"A retainer?"

Snapping her fingers, she pointed at him. "That's the one. So, what do you say? Can we count on you to do all the runnin' around and thinkin' on all this shit? Coz we ain't got a fuckin' clue!"

The thought of being near her for extended periods after everything he'd lost made his stomach lurch.

"Not takin' no for an answer, so you know."

He put on another grin. "Whatever you say, boss."

Cass clapped her hands. "Smart man! That's why I hired you. Now, you take your new wheels home, have yourself a drink to celebrate, and we'll call you. Oh! Do you have a card?"

TWENTY-FOUR

DROPPING the key to the Valiant on his table and a heavier metal object beside it, O'Donnell lowered himself to the chair with a grunt. He glanced at the mostly empty bottle on it and the carton of cigarettes beside it. He pushed them aside and examined at the two items he'd put down.

He toyed with the rabbit foot and smirked despite the pain it brought him. He didn't know if he would have been happier having lost his memories as Cassie—*Cass* he reminded himself—and Nate had, but he knew he would not have wanted the choice to be made for him.

Standing, he picked up the new doorbell and went in search of a screwdriver. He didn't know how much longer he would be in this office, but there was something fulfilling about the thought of leaving behind a new bell for the next tenant.

As he rooted in a cardboard box of odds-and-ends, the familiar clunk of the front door opening and closing sounded. As he walked around the paper room divider, now held together with sticky tape, he found a well-dressed man inspecting the office with distaste. Outside behind the man, gleaming in the sunlight, sat a Rolls Royce.

"Mr O'Donnell?" the man said, hesitant.

"Yes. And you are?"

The man blinked at him. "My name is Robert Herald, Mr O'Donnell. I'm... in need of your expertise, as it were."

O'Donnell indicated the chair in front of his desk. "Please, Mr Herald."

Forcing a smile, which was more of a grimace, the man made his way to the desk, glancing at the chair like it might bite or infect him with something before settling onto its edge. His eyes flitted to the large metal bracket with its bell and the screwdriver in his hands.

"You seem a little worried, Mr Herald," he said, putting the items on the desk and sitting. "What is it you need an investigator for exactly?"

"It's a rather sensitive matter, Mr O'Donnell. You see, my employer's husband passed away over a year ago under... Let us say suspicious circumstances, and—"

"And you need someone to investigate it as she's the one under suspicion? I get these sorts of jobs sometimes. Investigate evidence for court cases, though it's not my—"

"You misunderstand me, Mr O'Donnell. My employer is well aware of how her husband died. And there is no court case against her."

"Okay," O'Donnell said, pausing in thought. "I don't do *those* sorts of cases, Mr Herald. So whoever informed you I did, was very much mistaken." The name Lydia Doyle was on his mind.

"Oh, I assure you, there is nothing untoward in the job. Well... not in the *conventional* sense, if you catch my drift." He gave O'Donnell another pinched smile.

"Yeah, I really don't think I do."

Herald shifted in his seat, brows shifting as his eyelids narrowed.

"How does she know what happened to her dead husband if she's not involved?"

"Because he told her, Mr O'Donnell."

O'Donnell gave the man a stunned stare, mouth open. "Excuse me?"

"The issue is not how he died, but rather that she can't get him to *stop* talking and visiting her. Do you see?"

Was the man saying what O'Donnell thought?

Herald sighed through his nostrils, his lips pinched. "She recently spent some time in a psychiatric institution because of these *visitations*. We really need them to cease."

Leaning back into his chair, O'Donnell looked the man over again. "You've seen him too."

The man's lips eased, but not by much. "I can assure you that my employer is in her right mind, if that is what you are asking. During her time at the facility the…" Herald's eyes fluttered closed, his hand doing much the same as he raised it.

"Visitations?" O'Donnell offered.

Herald nodded. "They continued. It was there that I chanced upon a Mr Leigh Porter on the hospital staff. He assured me that you were the man to speak to for such… *unusual* cases. He also assured me of your experience and absolute discretion. Is that not correct? Was I misled?"

Leigh.

O'Donnell gave his best salesman grin. "You've definitely come to the right place, Mr Herald. Now, why don't you tell me all about it while I make us some coffee?"

THE WARD SERIES

If you enjoyed The Enlightened then you may want to read the Ward Series ... which James O'Donnell and other characters share a universe with.

Stacey Trampler came home to find her boyfriend Paul and girlfriend Jasper missing. In their place, a strange man claiming to be a "Ward" and the creatures they protect Earth from ... the Umbra.

Then the Umbra evolved. The Wards were forced to evolve with them ... but with new enemies rising up, some from within, their mission will never be the same again.

Stacey does her best to stay out of trouble, but when that consists of kicking as much arse as she can to stop it, trouble kinda seems to keep hunting her down.

The Ward Series is intense dark fantasy full of action, sci-fi elements and a whole lot of sarcasm.

ALSO BY CEM BILICI

A THRILLING ALTERNATE HISTORY, STEAMPUNK ADVENTURE
FILLED WITH ACTION AND DIVERSE LOCATIONS AND
CHARACTERS.

The Ottoman Empire resurged when they unearthed the secrets of Greek Fire and steam technology, but Angelique Morreaux will be damned if she allows that to stop her from exacting her revenge!

Her scheme to hurt the Ottomans, however, did not include a British policeman being shackled to her as chaperone. Nor did Constable James Nathaniel Beechworth ever imagine when he swore service to King and country that he would one day find himself dragged across the world, escorting a criminal to the very enemy's heart: Istanbul.

If Angelique and Beechworth can somehow work together, and survive, perhaps they will uncover the truth of *The Mechanical Turk*!

ABOUT THE AUTHOR

Cem Bilici is an author of supernatural thrillers and fantasy adventures.

Born in Adelaide, South Australia and of Turkish heritage, Cem lives with 1 dog — Bucky the beaglier — and 0 cats (that will likely never change), and a couple of humans. Cem currently lives in Melbourne with said dog and humans — Australia, not Florida.

Cem is also an avid fan of horror films, video games, and heavy metal.

You can connect with Cem on various social media platforms. Or sign up to his newsletter at cembilici.com/signup to keep updated on new releases and specials and **receive an exclusive FREE ebook collection of short stories** set in the Ward Universe, *Wild Turkey and Fanta.*

goodreads.com/cembilici
bookbub.com/authors/cem-bilici
facebook.com/CemBiliciWriter
instagram.com/fullmetalwritechemist
twitter.com/CemBiliciWriter

www.ingramcontent.com/pod-product-compliance
Lightning Source LLC
Chambersburg PA
CBHW052019240626
47153CB00006B/1868